Advance Praise for *The Drum Within*

"Nothing makes me happier than the debut novel of a brilliant new writer, and I was wowed by Jim Scarantino's *The Drum Within*. An experienced prosecutor, Scarantino imbues his muscular legal thriller with authentic police procedure and legal detail, and drenches it with a canny insider's view of the way things really work in precinct houses and judges' chambers. Best of all, his main character Detective Denise Aragon ranks as one of the most fully-realized, strongest female characters I've read in crime fiction. Aragon powers her way through this twisty plot, racing after one of the most lethal and credible villains you'd ever want to meet, serial killer Cody Geronimo. *The Drum Within* is a superb novel, and this is a hearty welcome to an insanely talented newcomer, Jim Scarantino."

Lisa Scottoline, *New York Times* bestselling author

"*The Drum Within* is a gritty police procedural that will make you rethink everything you know about justice. A tour de force of good guys and bad guys. A masterpiece. I loved it."

Robert Dugoni, #1 Amazon and *New York Times* bestselling author of *My Sister's Grave*

THE
DRUM
WITHIN

JAMES R.
SCARANTINO

A DENISE
ARAGON NOVEL

MIDNIGHT INK
WOODBURY, MINNESOTA

FIRST EDITION
First Printing, 2016

Book format by Bob Gaul
Cover design by Lisa Novak
Cover art by iStockphoto.com/14256121/©RobertPlotz
Editing by Ed Day

Midnight Ink, an imprint of Llewellyn Worldwide Ltd.

This is a work of fiction. Names, characters, places, and incidents are either the product of the author's imagination or are used fictitiously, and any resemblance to actual persons, living or dead, business establishments, events, or locales is entirely coincidental.

Library of Congress Cataloging-in-Publication Data
Names: Scarantino, James, 1956–
Title: The drum within / James Scarantino.
Description: First edition. | Woodbury, Minnesota: Midnight Ink, 2016.
Identifiers: LCCN 2015041936 (print) | LCCN 2015047760 (ebook) | ISBN
   9780738747743 | ISBN 9780738748580
Subjects: LCSH: Women detectives—Fiction. | Women—Crimes
against—Fiction.
   | Serial murder investigation—Fiction. | Santa Fe (N.M.)—Fiction. |
   GSAFD: Mystery fiction.
Classification: LCC PS3619.C268 D78 2016 (print) | LCC PS3619.C268 (ebook) |
   DDC 813/.6—dc23
LC record available at http://lccn.loc.gov/2015041936

Midnight Ink
Llewellyn Worldwide Ltd.
2143 Wooddale Drive
Woodbury, MN 55125-2989
www.midnightinkbooks.com

Printed in the United States of America

To Kara.

ONE

"ONE OF THOSE NIGHTS," Detective Rick Lewis said.

"Cold enough." Detective Denise Aragon pulled a wool cap over her buzz cut. Spring around the corner on Santa Fe's Plaza, up here snow under the trees, headlights glinting off ice in the stream they crossed just downhill.

"I meant the moon. You could read a newspaper."

Or see dead eyes in the Volvo's trunk.

Aragon angled her flashlight at the young woman, her head on a spare tire, the rest of her zipped inside an orange and blue sleeping bag tapering from shoulders to feet.

Lewis forced latex gloves over his hands. He opened the passenger door, then the glove box.

"Maybe that's Cynthia Fremont," he said. "Vehicle registration with that name, from Asheville, North Carolina."

Aragon looked more closely at the young woman's face. Sunburned cheeks below goggles of pale skin around chalky eyes. Jet

1

black hair with a midnight-blue sheen. It had been dyed. Blond roots had continued to grow after her heart stopped beating.

She saw something she'd seen on homeless drunks who died face up on beds of folded cardboard. The girl's lips and nose had been shredded by birds.

But she still had her eyes. Birds had not touched them.

"She's been lying out in the open," Aragon said. "So why put her in here?"

The parking lot was at the very edge of the city limits. Some of the pavement under their feet was county jurisdiction. All of it was owned by the federal government, like the forested mountains rising to meet the bright disc of the full moon.

A sheriff's Suburban had preceded them up the winding road from the city. The bumper decal told them the officers inside were with Court Services. Two pickups with Game and Fish officers and a Subaru from Open Space had joined the caravan. Forest Service, Bureau of Land Management, even a white Ford Expedition from the Department of Homeland Security. Aragon was not going to let this crowd do anything but hold back reporters and camera crews.

Except no media was here. Just a mob from state and federal agencies tripping over each other in the silver light.

Another car arrived. Two women and a man stepped out, reflective letters on their windbreakers saying "FBI." They swung flashlights across the parking lot, leaving the Volvo to the detectives, nobody clearly in command yet.

She was ready to reach into the trunk. She pulled on two sets of blue latex gloves and leaned in. At the girl's hairline she noticed dark, blue skin. She pressed and the skin turned white, then blue again when she removed her finger.

Lewis moved behind her, his size blocking the moon. The beam of his flashlight joined hers.

"Her head was hanging down," he said. "Look how she's laid out. You're carrying her on your shoulder, you could roll her off, glad to lose the weight. But somebody laid her down carefully."

"Two people holding arms and feet."

"Used that tire like a pillow."

"Takes time for blood to pool under the skin like that. Face down, then they turned her over. How long you think she was carried?"

"What's with the sleeping bag? Not doing her any good."

They turned toward the whine of engines laboring up the hill, three Jeeps carrying U.S. Forest Service law enforcement officers.

"Great," she said. "A couple of housing inspectors and a crossing guard, we can get going for real."

Lewis's phone rang. He stepped away to take the call. Aragon felt along the bag. She had the sense the girl might be naked. At the bottom she was surprised to feel boots through the nylon and down.

"Walter Fager found his wife dead inside her store," Lewis said, back at her side, returning the phone to his pocket. "She was cut up bad."

"Somebody doesn't know how to use a knife."

"Say what?"

"Should have used it on Fager."

She wished the medical investigator would get here. She wanted to open the bag, see the rest of the girl, know how she died.

Lewis said, "I've answered hours of his questions. Now he can answer ours."

"Watch Fager take the case." Aragon, her mind in two places now, felt through the bag for the shape and weight of the boots on the girl's feet. "Defending whoever killed his wife. Show what a badass lawyer he is. Free advertising for life." The boots were heavy; stiff soles.

3

"Nobles wants us down there," Lewis said, "it being Fager's wife." Dewey Nobles was Deputy Chief for the Operations Division. It included the Crimestoppers tip line and Criminal Investigations, which owned Aragon and Lewis.

"What about Hotdog and Sauerkraut?" she asked. "They were at their desks, Omar talking about the kind of boat he wants, he had more OT."

"Fager's suing them. Black-and-blue gangbanger versus Omar Serrano and Conrad Fenstermacher. Risk Management doesn't want them anywhere near Fager."

"He's sued us." She caught a whiff of wood smoke under the odor of tissue decay. "Where we going?"

Lewis gave an address on the east side of downtown where Linda Fager ran a used bookstore and curio shop. Aragon knew it, one of many small shops that couldn't possibly make a profit under the weight of downtown rents. Fager probably propped it up with cash fees he didn't report for his law practice.

"Store's called Fager's Finds," she said. "Fager finds his wife. Fager finds her dead."

"What do you want to do here?"

"You know any of these people? I'm not trusting her to Smokey the Bear."

"Rivera with FBI. Tomas. Does reservation homicides."

The FBI trio was now at the front of the Volvo, camera flashes showing their profiles and the passenger door Lewis had opened. Rivera was easy to identify as the only male in the FBI team. He pointed out photos he wanted then dictated notes into a digital recorder. Aragon approached and interrupted without introducing herself.

"She was camping. She didn't die here."

4

Rivera turned and dropped his gaze to look down, everybody always taller than her. A cold breeze fluttered the black hair on his high forehead, making her think of someone else. She had to fight a memory taking her away from the moment, the job right here.

He chucked his chin at the mountain. Lights moved through trees. He already had people searching the mountainside.

"That's an expensive sleeping bag," Rivera said. "Big Agnes. Superlight, but rated to sub-zero. Not something for car camping. And she's wearing hiking boots."

Rivera was way ahead of her. He wasn't one of the Fucking Brainless Idiots dumped into New Mexico after screwing up somewhere else.

"Let's hope the laces are tied," he said. "Might give us something. Something small, like did she tie them herself. You with Lewis?"

She handed him a business card.

"Our boss thinks a lawyer's wife in a bookstore is more important than a pretty girl in a trunk. Keep us in the loop."

More FBI personnel had arrived at the edge of the parking lot and were marking off a perimeter with yellow tape.

Rivera provided his own card. "I'll need your report," he said, letting her know that this case was his.

"That's why you'll keep us in the loop," feeling a little better about this.

She walked to the back of the car for another look. She found the Big Agnes logo on the midsection of the sleeping bag. The letters had been arranged to make her see the outline of a camel or a Sphinx, maybe playing off the bag's mummy design. For the first time she noticed the empty box of Clif bars and crumpled packaging for a backpacking water filter. There was definitely a camp. It would be near water. A stream ran on one side of this parking lot, but she knew it wasn't there. The body had been carried from farther away. Carried for miles.

"I'll drive," Lewis said to get her moving.

"We have to go," she told the girl who might be Cynthia Fremont.

Lewis got the car warm. She peeled the wool cap off her skull. On the ride into Santa Fe she called Rivera. He should search the shores of a lake she knew up in the mountains.

TWO

It wasn't *his hand* beating the drum. The drum beat *in* his hand, pounding inside, his fist shoved deep in his pocket. The beating drowned out the football game playing above the bar and the women, shirttails knotted above flashy belt buckles, throwing down shots, shuddering, shrieking as the liquor hit the back of their throats. The rhythm wrapped in his fingers carried Cody Geronimo far away from the annoying people in this ridiculous tourist bar. He had work tonight. The drum would not beat forever.

"Ready for another?"

He looked up at a waitress balancing a tray of empties.

"Alone in your thoughts?" the young woman asked.

"Hardly alone."

He raised his beer mug. His hand shook a little, not nerves, not the excitement still with him. It was the beating of the drum running through his body. He hoped she didn't see it.

"Certainly, I'll take another." He uncrossed his legs, the silver tip of his cowboy boot catching light as it dropped to the floor.

She took his glass, recognition in her eyes. "I love your paintings. Finished for the night?"

"I haven't been painting."

"I'm a slob with a brush. Completely. Half goes on the wall, half on me. Forget ceilings. You only got a little bit on your hair."

"I said I haven't been painting."

"Sorry. I just thought."

She pointed at her temple before carrying his empty to the bar. He touched the spot she indicated on his own head and examined his fingertips.

Not paint. Blood.

He wiped it off under the table then patted his head to see if he had any more on him. He had tried to be neat. He was always neat in his work.

He rose and left before his beer arrived. He needed his studio while the drum still lived.

———

He had walked farther than he thought. Across the center of Santa Fe, through the tree-lined plaza, down a narrow alley to the tourist bar he'd never noticed before, on a street he couldn't recall. He never came here, t-shirt town, a world away from his gallery but less than two miles apart. He retraced his route as best he could, finding he hadn't been seeing anything outside his own head. Not street signs, nor familiar buildings and businesses, intersections he knew. What he'd been seeing: colors, far too many, overdone, truly a disaster; his hands at work, making sense of the chaos, his own heart beating, like an assistant in the room watching; finally the drum, taking it into his fist, seeing it pulse inside his fingers, actually seeing its vibrations ripple up his arms.

8

He'd been seeing sounds, seeing tastes, seeing textures, seeing heat and cold against his skin. Everything visual, one medium, one pure, ceaseless line.

Cars circled the plaza. Now he knew where he was. A white car with the hood painted black slowed and steered close to the curb. Bass notes thumped from trunk speakers. He saw them, black mallets flying from the vehicle's frame.

He stepped under the portal of the Palace of the Governors where, during the day, Indians sold jewelry off blankets. The two-tone car moved past, slowing again near a woman walking alone. She shifted her purse to the shoulder away from the street as something was yelled from the car. He saw the angry words: blacker than night, ravens with talons bared.

Music, laughter, the clinking of glasses drifted from a balcony above him, a sprinkle of reds, oranges, yellows descending in the night sky. More tourists. More ridiculous people. He didn't like this part of Santa Fe. He preferred Canyon Road, the winding rows of art galleries, his own near the top where the street narrowed. That was where he was headed once he reached his car, outside the bookstore where inspiration had struck.

Did he turn here, or was it the next block? No, a little farther yet.

He didn't remember closing the door to the bookstore or walking the first couple blocks. His head had cleared later, when he decided he needed a drink to calm himself, give his hands time to settle down.

This wasn't how he did his work. He had rules, guidelines, procedures. A proper workspace. The right tools for the right job. But the woman had looked at him when she handed him the book he wanted. More than looked. Opened herself. He saw straight into her, to the beating of the drum.

She had not fought much. When she turned away, a quick blow with the same heavy book she'd handed him had staggered her. Her neck fit neatly in his hands and he thought of clay on a potting wheel. He'd found a place to work in the little bathroom in the back. Cramped, but the sink was there at his elbow.

The boxcutter on the counter by the cash register did fine in place of the blades in the velvet purse in his studio. Her skin did what he wanted and he was pleased. He hadn't been into masks before. It could be a new genre to explore. The problem would be showing this line of work.

At least her mask would enjoy an audience. He wondered who would find her, how they would react. He hadn't thought of it at the time, but the staging itself became an integral part of the presentation. That's how the most genuine creative forces worked, without any conscious direction from the artist.

She should thank him, what he'd done for her. A Cody Geronimo original. No woman alive could say that.

Except for the spot of blood on his hair, he'd been meticulous. He used her plastic gloves from a box under the sink. He'd stripped to protect his clothes. Then he'd washed and dried himself with paper towels discarded outside the store. He stopped the sink and left the faucet running. Water was overflowing as he backed away, destroying his footprints, a tide smoothing the sand.

Yes, he had closed the front door on his way out. He hoped so.

He avoided the lights of the La Fonda Hotel and aimed for the darkness of a covered walkway. He paused at the lit window of a gallery offering Indian art. Unpainted frames held portraits of war chiefs shaded in greens and blues, their faces distorted as they morphed into wolves and bears. Eagles rose from their heads. Claws became eyebrows.

Not bad. But he'd seen it before. The godawful pink coyotes, the cowboys in yellow slickers, the repetitious pastels of New Mexico mountains, the Rio Grande Gorge always painted as a gash in dark earth. Only his work was unique, irreplaceable.

Another painting in the window stood out. A continuous single line on a plain background gave form to the face and torso of an Indian woman with exaggerated cheeks and thick upper arms. The simplicity was exquisite. Genius.

It was a mass-market poster of his own work.

That's how he could paint when his hands were steady. Tonight he worked in a more forgiving medium.

His Range Rover was almost around the corner. He would be alone in his studio, no human assistants, no tourists gawking through windows. He had a gallery opening tomorrow and much to do. He would be busy until dawn.

He was near the old, unfinished cathedral, still missing its spires more than a century after construction began. It should be dark here. It was dark when he'd stepped out of the bookstore. But now adobe walls danced in flashing red and blue lights.

THREE

ARAGON KNEW WHY THERE were no cameras for the girl in the trunk. The television stations with Santa Fe bureaus were setting up across the street from Fager's Finds. She wished she had more officers. She yelled for a young cop to put something over the business's front window so no one could see inside.

Lewis came out the front door behind her. He took a deep breath of the night's clean air.

"Santa Fe, the city different. That was different."

"I want to forget it," Aragon said. "Shit, that's never going to happen."

"Found this under her legs." He placed a key fob on Aragon's bright blue palm. They both wore plastic booties and two fresh pairs of rubber gloves. Crime scene supplies were going fast tonight.

"Fager's?"

"He drives a Mercedes. That's a Range Rover."

Aragon turned the key fob over and found the remote. "What are the chances?"

"That would be pure, stinkin' luck."

"You got a problem with luck?"

Aragon pressed the key's alarm. A car horn sounded down the block and they spun to the sound.

————

Geronimo was coming up along his Range Rover when the horn went off. He went rigid and slapped at empty pockets. Then he saw the cops, a white guy the size of a defensive end and the short Hispanic woman who looked bald.

The car horn blared. The Rover's lights pulsed. The cops took a step closer. Geronimo wrapped his hand around the treasure in his jacket pocket. He had lost his keys in the store. He didn't want to lose anything else important tonight.

————

The shadow darted into an alley.

Aragon leaned against a parking meter to strip off the plastic booties covering her cross trainers. Lewis was doing the same as he yelled for uniformed cops to secure the Range Rover.

Lewis could lift a man over his head and stuff anyone into a police cruiser. She was faster. It was her job to catch the shadows and hang on until he caught up.

She pushed off the parking meter and ran. The cool air caressed her head. No need for a wool cap down here. She almost had too many clothes. She'd be dropping her coat soon if pursuit went long. Above the roof line a State Police helicopter rose into view. Half a block behind her she heard Lewis radioing the chopper where to swing its searchlight.

She turned into a dark alley. She had lost sight of her target but not before seeing a ponytail flying behind him. Five-six to five-ten, medium build. Maybe a fringed leather jacket. The guy was running funny: knees pointed out, flapping his feet on the street, making her think of someone in a clown suit trying to move fast. She paused to speak that little bit of identifying information into her shoulder mike. Then she unholstered her Springfield Armory .40 and charged into the shadows.

———

Geronimo cursed his stiff cowboy boots. The steel tips wanted to trip him. The helicopter rose above the alley. He squeezed into a gap between two buildings and emerged into a neighborhood of bungalows and big trees. A thick hedge separated the closest house from the street. He checked the helicopter. It was rising, swinging its beam in ever wider arcs across neighboring streets. He had lost them.

He pushed his way into the hedge. Branches snapped behind, sealed him in. He pulled out his cell phone, hit number one. He got an answer on the third ring.

"Cody, goddammit. Call tomorrow. I have a life, you know."

"Marcy," he couldn't finish, too short of breath.

"So, I'm listening. What?"

———

Aragon knew this alley and the breezeway connecting to the next street. She had walked this beat when she first put on the uniform. This used to be D.I. Row—drunk Indian, but don't say that out loud. Back then you could locate the drinkers' havens by broken glass. Now it was the little plastic bottles of hand sanitizer distributed at homeless shelters, the people with big hearts ignorant about the alcohol they were giving away for free.

She stepped into the neighborhood of brick bungalows and big trees. Sweet-scented cedar smoke hung in the air. Branches were moving inside the tall hedge at the corner. The guy with the ponytail could be armed and aiming at her if she stood there in the open. She dropped to the ground to make herself small and was glad he hadn't caught her in the narrow breezeway.

Lewis's heavy breathing was now in her ear. "IR shows someone inside that foliage," he said on one knee, gulping oxygen. "He's not moving."

"Shh. I know. Let's spread out, come at it wide."

"Roger that," he said, sounding a little better. "I'll go right. Count of three."

She raised her hand to cut him off. A man was speaking inside the hedge. The talking stopped. Silence. Then the voice started again.

"Help."

"Cody, you only call, one, when you're in trouble, two, when you can't pay your bill. Which is it this time?"

Marcy Thornton took Geronimo's call at her mahogany desk, a dark brown fortress atop a Persian rug in the center of her law office. Beamed ceilings high above her. Paintings on the walls by the guy on the phone—fees from a case when he was out of cash. She pushed a thick legal file out of the way with her toes and leaned back into a wide red chair. Padding swallowed her tight naked body. Cody had interrupted a little party she was giving herself. Across the room she watched the two people on the sofa, where she had been before she jumped up to get the phone.

She twirled the stem of a wine glass and listened to a desperate man.

He was now giving her the full story, step by step, covering the past couple hours. Dinner and a photo op with the mayor about paintings donated to City Hall—paintings he couldn't sell in L.A. or New York. Later, drinks and tapas and something called *crudo* with people who had been collecting him for years, excited about the new path he was taking with his art. No other Native artist was going there: again, him, breaking new ground, standing apart, defining the genre. The prices he'd be able to ask.

"What is that?" Thornton asked. "*Crudo.*"

"Italian sushi."

She was bored with his windup, but if he wanted to run the meter talking food…

She studied the level in the wine bottle. He'd burn through a thousand dollars of her time before it was gone.

Thornton filled her glass and tuned him out when he started talking about the desserts after the raw fish, sketching portraits on the tablecloth, cognac and coffee. Then, finally getting to it, his voice excited, talking faster.

How later he went into the shop for a book on something called "found art." When this woman looked at him.

He stopped, as though he had now given his lawyer all she needed to know.

"Looked at you how?" Thornton asked. A woman looked at him. She was supposed to understand why that led to whatever had him calling, frantic, almost hyperventilating. When she had better things to do. And what the hell was found art? She wasn't going to ask and get him going in another direction, even if it was his money.

———

Across the office, Lily Montclaire sat up and leaned her breasts into the sofa's cool leather. She watched Thornton on the phone, the muscles in her legs taut as she stretched her feet across her desk, the kind of body Montclaire had twenty years ago. She checked her face in the mirror over the dressing table, the one Thornton used to get ready for court. She still had the looks that had earned her a living modeling lipstick and eyeglasses and clothes she never wanted to wear off the set. But the neck wouldn't do anymore. And she had little lines in the corners of her eyes and mouth that she could no longer hide. She could still do lingerie, the body was good. Maybe American Eagle or Penney's, but not a chance at Victoria's.

Who was she kidding? She hadn't been in front of a camera except for a driver's license since jelly shoes and skorts and everything was denim.

Her own modeling was petering out. No more calls, even for Walmart. Then the years of moving furniture onto sets for younger girls. Arranging cowhide chairs and Navajo rugs for a shoot in Santa Fe. Nights at a motel off the interstate, mariachis and shouting coming through the walls. Early in the morning, dragging rope and saddles from a van, the young models still asleep at the Hilton. Bringing in sandwiches and sparkling cider, running out for lint rollers. After-shoot drinks at the Staab House, finding herself alone. Not even the make-up hag interested. Except the hot little woman at the bar staring at her, Marcy Thornton coming over, forgetting her briefcase. Later cruising Santa Fe in a big English car with Montclaire holding a bottle of red wine between her legs. The top down, a full moon, just like tonight. Marcy's hand going for the bottle, slipping off, staying there.

After, lying on this same sofa, Marcy said her face could open doors. I need an investigator, she had said, drawing lazy circles around Montclaire's nipples. People will talk to you.

Grow old and dried up moving furniture for teenagers with eyes and lips painted black, one of the ghosts hanging off-camera, out of the lights, out of the action. Out of money. Or take a shot at being Marcy Thornton's private dick—the way Marcy put it, being cute and tough at the same time—and see what happens.

The investigating was mostly what Marcy had said, talking to people. Dressing from Chico's, almost going Annie Hall, to talk with white people. Sharper, crisper for Hispanics. In between, she served subpoenas, copied documents, backgrounded jurors, and fetched party supplies.

Warm skin brushed her arm. A young man with an unbuttoned shirt sat up on the sofa next to her. It had been a long day. They'd dropkicked the DA out of the courthouse. Five eyewitnesses, a co-conspirator who rolled on his *vato* brother, airtight ballistics, and they'd still walked their client. A special celebration, Marcy said. I deserve it. Go get us something fun, Lily.

She'd found this one at the mall, wearing a white hoodie, by himself. She couldn't understand why.

Marcy mouthed "Cody." Montclaire rolled her eyes. She sank her teeth into the boy's ear and pulled him down and out of sight.

———

Geronimo said, hushed, Thornton could barely hear, "I think the cops found me. I think they're listening."

All the wine she'd been drinking didn't matter now. She saw it and told Geronimo, "Tell me in detail how you killed her. Don't leave anything out. Speak up and speak clearly."

"They'll hear me. I'm in in this bush and they're out there. I see one of them."

18

"I want them to hear. Everything. Now do it."

And Geronimo told her. Then they turned to business.

The man's voice inside the hedge was indignant. "I've got cash. My show's almost sold out. You don't have to hold my work as collateral again."

Aragon was taping it on her belt recorder, unclipped and held at the edge of the dark green hedge. After wandering all over the place, talking about food and hanging with people from L.A., he had now given them a full confession, what set him off, what he did to Linda Fager, ugly stuff, really brutal, but he talked like he was in front of an art class, explaining technique, composition, staging. Proud of himself. How the cops had chased him, but he wasn't worried. He'd lost them.

Now he was negotiating.

He spoke a woman's name and Aragon knew who was on the other end of the conversation.

"Marcy," the man's voice pleaded. "What do I do?"

Aragon had heard enough. She didn't want this guy getting any bright ideas from a lawyer she hated even more than Walter Fager. She wanted him now, while he was scared and vulnerable.

She met eyes with Lewis. He had his gun out and nodded. Aragon parted the leaves and exposed a man she recognized.

She had seen 60 Minutes with Anderson Cooper tagging along through his studio and stables, the barn that held his car collection, to the tumbledown hogan on the Navajo reservation, his home as a boy, open now to the sky with the roof fallen in. At the end, his story told, Geronimo faced the orange glow of a New Mexico sunset, the lights of Santa Fe twinkling below the veranda where he threw his famous parties.

"To all my ancestors, I thank you from the depths of my humble, unworthy soul."

Fade to black as he pressed a fist against his heart and squeezed eyes shut.

Aragon remembered saying out loud, "Oh, give me a fucking break."

The Native American Picasso, the *60 Minutes* producers had dubbed him. A genius with brush and canvas. But he was stupid to hide in a hedge while his voice broadcast every detail of his crime up and down the street.

"Excuse me for interrupting, sir." Aragon leaned in with a smile. Then her face went hard as she dangled the key fob Lewis had found under the body. "Drop something?"

———

Sitting on a curb with Geronimo between them, wrists zip-tied behind his back, Aragon radioed again to ask where was the car to transport their prisoner to the detention center. She'd been taking calls on her cell while they waited, talking about other things not for the ears of the police-scanner fan club. Already the department was scrambling to manage news of the celebrity arrest in the murder of the wife of the city's top criminal defense lawyer. They would get no sleep. They'd be in conferences with deputy chiefs and PR flacks until dawn, working out the department's line, getting grilled about anything that could blow up on them, writing and rewriting their reports with prosecutors and captains flyspecking every word. They'd be the lead story tomorrow on the TV news and grab headlines in the Albuquerque and Santa Fe papers. This would go national in twenty-four hours.

Lewis leaned forward to catch Aragon's eye. "One of those nights. Didn't I call it?"

"I hope Rivera's as good as you say," she said, thinking of the girl in the trunk they had to leave behind.

"We can get back to that. This one's done except for paperwork. We solve the crime and catch the killer, half an hour from call to cuffs. New SFPD record. Taking longer for a car to get here."

"You mumble something?" Aragon asked Geronimo.

He said, "I lost a toe." He lifted a foot. The silver tip had fallen off his right boot. "These are Tres Outlaws. From El Paso. Not another pair like them anywhere. They cost more than you earn in a year."

"Shoot," Lewis said. "I got Western Wearhouse State Fair specials. Forty bucks. Look just as good and don't break."

"Where you're going," Aragon said, "you get a new pair of plastic slippers, free, every year for the rest of your life. They come all the way from China, how about that?"

Geronimo said, "Keep your slippers. I'm going home. I have work to do."

"Yeah?"

"Yes. Marcy says so."

FOUR

"COUNSELOR, I CAN'T IMAGINE what you're going through."

Walter Fager rubbed his eyes and nodded back at the clerk clutching an armful of files against her chest. He had almost dozed off on the bench in the hallway of the Steve Herrera Judicial Complex. The police kept him until dawn. He had shaved badly. He hadn't eaten. But he forced himself into a crisp white shirt and his standard pin-striped suit.

He wanted to see the man who had killed his wife.

The clerk hovered, then continued down the hallway with her files. Fager rose and crossed to the courtroom doors. They had been locked when he arrived. They were still locked. The electronic bulletin board said the case of State of New Mexico versus Cody Geronimo was set for a 10:00 a.m. bail hearing. It was now almost eleven.

Fager moved to the alcove leading to the chambers of the Honorable Judith A. Diaz. He pressed the black intercom button.

"Yes? How can I help you?" a woman's voice crackled through the wire mesh speaker.

"I'm here for the Geronimo bail hearing. Has it been postponed?"

"Judge Diaz is hearing that matter in chambers."

"I would like to attend."

"She wanted only lawyers."

"Twenty forty-seven."

"Excuse me?"

"My State Bar number. This is Walter Fager."

He stepped back and faced the camera.

"Oh, hi, Mr. Fager." Pause. "I'll check with Judge Diaz."

The speaker went dead. Fager closed his eyes. He saw Linda from the back, over a kitchen sink washing tomatoes from her garden. In the sun, under a broad hat, reaching for a rose from the bushes she cherished. In her store, shelving books.

He could not see her face.

Last night she had not met him at their restaurant. He had gone to her store, found the front door open, darkness inside. A crack of light toward the back, the small bathroom lit from within by the bulb over the sink. Water running. The rug soaked. Linda's cat hissed at him before fleeing into the shadows. A foot blocked the bathroom door. Linda's shoe. Her green pants, her orange linen shirt, the silver necklace he had bought her on the plaza. A staple gun and boxcutter on the sink. On the wall, God, waist high, still dripping …

"Mr. Fager?"

He blinked at the intercom.

"The hearing's over. I'm sorry about your wife."

The door opened as the intercom clicked off. Out came Marcy Thornton in a black silk suit carrying a thin attaché case. She had been on friendly terms with Linda. When Thornton was a first-year associate in his office, it had been almost mother-daughter. He had seen her name on the electronic bulletin board. Now she was representing the man who had stapled Linda's face to a bathroom wall.

"Walter."

"Marcy."

She hesitated. Then her narrow shoulders squared and she moved off, high heels clacking on the marble floor.

The door opened again and Assistant District Attorney Joseph Mascarenas stepped out. He was squat and obese, in a rumpled suit with scuffed shoes too small for his body. Fager had to move aside so he could get to the hallway.

"Joe, what's with holding a bail hearing in chambers? Was Cody Geronimo back there?"

"Never brought him up." Mascarenas smoothed his soiled tie. "We dismissed pending indictment."

"The fuck?" Fager rubbed red eyes. "You don't dismiss murder cases."

"Pending indictment. All the time."

"In stupid DWIs. Stupid shopliftings." Fager's hands balled into fists. He caught himself and forced his fingers open. "Not murder, Joe."

Mascarenas dropped his voice and tilted his head at the intercom. "Hold it 'til we're outside."

———

Fager towered over Mascarenas as the prosecutor rested on a precast planter in front of the courthouse. It was a familiar staging for them. Fager on his feet, pacing, filling out his tailored suit with a body still trim and fit from his Army days. Mascarenas, a lump of flesh on concrete, listening to his smarter, more energetic, more prosperous adversary.

Mascarenas noticed something different. Fager used to be all right angles. He still had the square jaw of the Special Forces lieutenant. But today the ninety degrees at his shoulders came from padding. Fager was stooped, sagging.

"We've done how many cases together, Joe?"

"Maybe two hundred. Stand 'em up, knock 'em down."

"I've never seen you release a murderer just to pull back and reload. What the hell?"

Mascarenas shielded his eyes from the sun.

"Hey, amigo. Two hundred times you screwed me in holes I don't have. With you, Walt, nothing's straight. But now you want *me* to be straight with *you*?"

"I can't stand it. I need to know what's going on."

"Don't like the view from outside the huddle? Big difference, counsel of record," Mascarenas jerked a thumb at civilians lined up to pass through security, "or one of them."

"I wanted to see Geronimo up close."

"Only thing you missed was Thornton showing leg. Nice leg. Judge Diaz thought so, too."

"Marcy always plays Judy Diaz like that."

"No studs in that clubhouse. All tongue and groove construction."

Fager came to a stop in front of the prosecutor. "Joe, I should have been in there. Fuck what you think about Marcy Thornton."

Mascarenas shrugged. "You got no standing, Walt. If we get into this with Thornton, you'll learn fast you don't count."

"*If* you get into this?" Fager shouted the question.

The sun's heat beaded sweat on Mascarenas's plump face. He wiped a yellowed handkerchief across his forehead and took his time folding it back into his pocket.

When he was ready, Mascarenas said, "I liked Linda. She can't be blamed for you."

"I guess that counts as sympathy. Now answer my question. What do you mean *if* you get into this with Thornton?"

Mascarenas sighed.

"Thornton's screaming profiling. We've already heard from tribal presidents she rousted out of bed. Another Pueblo Revolt if we prosecute America's favorite Indian artist. Throw in that Aragon eavesdropped on Geronimo consulting his attorney. Thornton lit a lawyer-client privilege bomb under Diaz and blew her through the ceiling."

"Sanitize the investigation. Seal Aragon off. Reassign the file and start over. The profiling stuff is routine posturing."

Mascarenas hauled himself to his feet but avoided meeting Fager's stare.

"No one left to vaccinate. Aragon was so proud of herself she played her tape at roll call. Brass from State Police was in the room. They're out, too. In steps Dewey Nobles."

"Not Dewey No-Balls. Please don't tell me he's messing with Linda's case."

"You never complained when one of your guys needed a weak link on our side. Dewey pulled the case from Aragon and made the call to dismiss. I can't prosecute a case the police won't own. Diaz ordered us to give Thornton the recording and everything seized from Geronimo."

Fager threw his head to the sky and swore. Mascarenas picked up his cracked briefcase.

"Sucks, don't it, Walt? This conversation we're having right now, I have them every day with people who learn the guy who hurt someone they love counts more than they do. Every time I charge someone, I give them power and rights their victims will never know. All it takes is that word, *defendant*, and a shitbag becomes a player with a pile of chips on his side of the table."

"Marcy doesn't have any moves she didn't get from me."

"You're not in the game, Walt. You're in the stands watching the teams on the field." Mascarenas pulled a crumpled business card from his pocket. "Give Aragon a call. She gets yanked from a dead girl in a trunk because your wife's case gets special attention. Then she's told to sit in a corner and shut up. Call her right now, while she's still loco about Geronimo walking." He mimicked a sing-song Mexican accent. "Eeeee. Tell her cousin Jose sent you."

"What can she tell me you won't tell me yourself? I'm getting a bad feeling here."

"You always had the good instincts."

"Joe."

"Call Aragon. But don't use the accent. Seriously."

FIVE

"Job opening: Santa Fe Police Department Deputy Chief of Operations. Must be paper-trained and spineless. Testicles strongly discouraged. SFPD is an equal opportunity employer. Any idiot can get the job."

Lewis put down the sheet of printer paper he had found taped to the fridge in the break room. He gave Aragon a long look across the tiny office they shared.

She raised her eyes to meet his. "What?"

He had three other examples of the "Help Wanted" ad, taken from the water cooler, the soda machine, and the glass door leading to Administration.

"We have real work to do," he said. "Reports about two dead women and a famous artist who thinks he's getting away with killing one of them. Instead I'm cleaning up after you, to save us the time we'd lose hauled in front of Dewey."

Lewis shook his head and dug into pancakes left over from breakfast with his wife and girls. He tried never to go twenty-four hours without seeing his family. He had rushed home after Nobles

28

yanked the Fager case from them. When he returned he found Aragon in the parking lot staring through the windshield of her personal car. He tapped on her window, mouthed *hot food*, and led the way to their office.

Just when she was calming down over breakfast, they learned Geronimo had been released. The news came from a smirking Omar Serrano and Conrad Fenstermacher, the detectives who would have been in their position if Nobles had not wanted the more senior team of Aragon and Lewis to handle the Linda Fager killing.

They kicked it back and forth over reheated pancakes. Why was Nobles surrendering so easily on a solid arrest in such a brutal crime? They did paperwork, returned calls, checked court schedules. Then went at it again.

Aragon started. "Because some judge has a wild hair, we forget what happened in the back of that store?"

"When we took the kids to Disneyland, the hotel had his paintings everywhere. That Marriott had over a thousand rooms. Two Cody Geronimos over the bed. Two by every elevator. I swear I was seeing the same picture over and over except for little things I noticed."

"The great detective. And art critic. Made for Santa Fe."

"Chubby Indian women," Lewis said, "maybe one holding a basket. By the elevators they hold blankets. The one to the right of our bed, the woman looks up. The left, she looks down. Wow. Heavy. Like, really deep."

"You're saying it's because of who Geronimo is, why Dewey's laying down?"

"Can't be scalping the city's most famous Indian with an election coming. The Mayor needs casino money. Or maybe there's something bent with Nobles. He threw in the towel over an hour before court began, before Judge Diaz said anything about a problem with the tape. Thornton didn't file a written motion. So how did he know what was coming?"

"And Geronimo sitting there, hands zipped behind his back, telling us he was going home because he had work to do?" Aragon unfolded the day's *New Mexican* and passed it to Lewis, opened to the arts section. "Guy rips a woman apart. Goes to jail. Gets out. Doesn't break stride."

"Secret Canyon Gallery," Lewis read. "New works by Cody Geronimo, America's premier Native artist. Fourteen daring multimedia masterpieces celebrating his metamorphosis from painter to sculptor. Experience Cody's passion, genius, and spirituality in three mystical dimensions."

"Now he's a *Native* artist," Aragon said. "Shit, I'm the Native. I was Santa Fe before pink coyotes and opera parties and movie stars claiming *they* discovered this town. Before the best place for carne adovada and sopapillas became a French restaurant with a pre-op tranny handing out menus on fucking parchment."

"Okay." Lewis had heard some of this before, especially about the fabled New Mexican café lost to hipper cuisine. Aragon had ratcheted it up today. Maybe he should tell her she'd gone too far and had better watch it, you couldn't talk like that around SFPD and not get burned eventually. Somebody besides a partner who looked out for you would take it to Nobles.

Maybe she resented him, too—Richland Ellison Lewis, now just Rick, so it came across friendlier when he gave his name in court. A white guy who moved here from Pennsylvania because he'd read in *Outside Magazine* that Santa Fe was a great place to live, better than the rowhome above the remains of a Bethlehem Steel Plant. Maybe she resented him just a little, though he felt their partnership was solid.

"I bet his show'll be packed tonight," Lewis said, wondering if Aragon was done. He made a note of the gallery's address. "All this publicity."

She wasn't done. "The great *Native* artist busted for murder. The art snobs will wet their pants, stain their designer clothes."

"Okay," Lewis said again.

In the larger work area outside their cubbyhole, Serrano and Fenstermacher deposited donut boxes by the coffee pot.

Lewis said, "They never buy."

"Showing how happy they are to duck the Geronimo case. Everybody in this division would have done the same as us, caught the same shit."

Serrano entered their doorway and held an opened box out to Aragon. Fenstermacher looked in over his shoulder.

"Not a good night for Butch and Sundance." Serrano had a fake grin plastered across his face. "Cheer up with a cherry cruller. Or maybe you want something with a hole?"

"Watch it, Hotdog," Lewis said, jumping ahead of Aragon. "Five Ten."

"Five Ten" was the section of the Santa Fe Police Department's regs requiring officers to report to the Professional Standards Unit any hazing or harassment based on race, ethnicity, age, religion, tribal membership, gender, sexual preference, or marital status. It was the department's equivalent of mandatory child-abuse reporting—exactly what he was going to remind Aragon of about a few minutes ago.

Serrano got defensive, stammered that Lewis was Cassidy in the partnership, not Aragon. He was talking about an Old West outlaw. A real hombre. A legend. And, hey, as he started backing away to escape Lewis's glare, making Fenstermacher backpedal with him, who wouldn't want to be compared to Robert Redford?

"Butch was Paul Newman, dumbass," she said.

She'd been getting it from Serrano ever since she declined a weekend of alcohol and few clothes on his boat at Elephant Butte. She'd seen female cops compelled to testify about affairs with fellow officers as a way of impeaching their testimony. In the trial of an Albuquerque cop charged with murdering his wife, the defense showed the jury a chart that could have been an organized crime network. It mapped out who was screwing who within that department. The female officers testifying against the accused cop were bitter spurned lovers, the male investigators were jealous competitors. A murderer walked.

She'd find her men outside the SFPD, thank you very much.

Besides, a guy like Serrano probably needed to believe she was a lesbian. She didn't care. But she did get tired of him proving what an idiot he was.

"Five Ten yourself, Denise," Serrano said, and she regretted saying anything. "Gender hostility. Profiling men as stupid."

Lewis said, "Omar, she's not saying you're not stupid because you're a man. You're just stupid."

"Smarter than you think," Serrano fired back as he took his donuts to the next office. "I'm not the one who blew a murder case strutting my stuff at roll call."

"Let me out of here," Aragon said as she answered a ringing phone. "Aragon. Criminal Investigations." She covered the mouthpiece. "Walter Fager." Into the phone she said, "You know Juanita's on Airport Road? Yeah, next to Latinos Unidos. Three-thirty."

"Walter Fager's calling you direct?" Lewis asked as she dialed another number.

"You were flipping pancakes. Joe Mascarenas and I brainstormed. How do we keep Linda Fager's case on life support while Dewey's pulling the plug? I'll explain in the car. I think you'll like it."

32

She held up a finger and spoke into the phone.

"Mister menudo man. Can you do Li'l Jane's at three?"

Lewis spoke before she hung up.

"Who's menudo man?"

"That part," Aragon slid an accordion file from the file cabinet against the wall, turned and looked into her partner's eyes, "maybe you won't like so much."

SIX

Lokos.

Black spray paint connected points of light in a plywood back-board, rim bent and no net. The points of light were bullet holes.

"We're supposed to guess Westside or Southside," said Lewis.

"Even a Glock 17 doesn't hold enough to spell it out," Aragon replied. "Westside spells Locos with the 'k' to save ammo and let you know it's them."

They unwrapped Lotaburgers and popped lids off their coffees. One thing about working without sleep, you learned fast after the rookie mistake of loading up on sugar and caffeine. Crash and burn two hours later, sometimes in the middle of testifying, your brain shutting down with the answer locked in your head. Then you went stupid, became the numb cop the defense lawyer wanted jurors to see.

Aragon and Lewis went for protein. Her favorite protein delivery vehicle was the Lotaburger double patty from the Blake's chain. She'd been eating those burgers with green chile, cheese, onions, tomato, pickle, and lettuce since she was five years old. Now she had Lewis eating them, too, when she was buying.

They had parked on a small street among old cars with bumpers held on by rope and Chevy Silverados with Mexican flags and Raider decals in rear windows.

"Second time you brought me here," Lewis said. "First time was that IAD ruckus. It's not IAD anymore. We're supposed to call it Professional Standards."

Around the basketball court a chain-link fence kept nothing in or out except plastic bags carried on the wind.

"I come here to remember why I do this job," Aragon said.

Lewis followed her gaze across the patch of urban decay hidden in the midst of hip Santa Fe, just blocks from a brewpub and bistros and a bakery producing artisanal bread nobody on this street could afford.

"Why Miller Park?" he asked.

"The neighborhood changed the name. It's Killer Park even if Rec and Parks can't find that on their official directory."

She chucked her chin at single-story stucco houses across the lot.

"My family had the third house from the left. There used to be grass and rose bushes along the fences. My father helped build that basketball court with material left over from a paving job. I decided to become a cop right there under the backboard. I was thirteen years old."

Three years working together and this was the first Aragon had talked about herself. The only family he knew about was a brother who lived in the mountains east of town and rumors of another somewhere on the West coast. He let her open up at her own pace. He dug into his burger and washed it down with watery coffee.

"Westside was moving in," she said after a while. "They put a bounty on Mann Street bangers."

"Never ran across anybody throwing Mann Street signs."

35

"Extinct, hunted out like native elk. The Aragons had nothing to do with gangs. My father lectured my brothers, checked their skin for tats, searched their bedroom for knives and money they shouldn't have. He didn't worry about me. Just don't date a gang boy and you were okay. Except Westside Lokos decided the way to draw out Mann Street was to rape their sisters. They thought my brothers were hiding to avoid a fight. They didn't know my father sent them to Roswell, to the New Mexico Military Institute, when he caught them riding with some wannabes."

Lewis stopped eating. His partner was showing more than the scar you could see under her buzz cut. Cables tensed in her neck. Small hands, but strong ones, gripped the steering wheel. Her nails were unpolished, cut short so she wouldn't draw an excessive violence beef by accidentally raking someone's face.

"They broke a bottle over my head. Dragged me out of my yard. Making a point, four o'clock in the afternoon. This place was theirs now. Miguel came running from that house on the corner with the trailer in the yard."

"Miguel?" Lewis put his half-finished burger on the bag folded across his lap.

"Miguel Martinez. He was beautiful. He sang. He boxed. He could take a ball up the middle against any high school in the state. Only sixteen and nobody could stop him. I thought of him last night, by the car with the dead girl when Rivera turned around. He reminded me of Miguel, the way the wind moved his hair like Miguel's when he ran."

"You don't have to say any more, Denise."

"Miguel came from one of the families where every night the father sat his children down and asked what they had learned in school. No dinner 'til they told him something new. He vaulted that fence right over there and slammed into the boys holding me down. He missed the

36

one with the thirty-eight. He shot Miguel in the spine. Then they passed the gun around, each putting a bullet into him. The cops who came later convinced me that was what I wanted to do with my life."

"They impressed you."

"Complete fuck-ups. Every one of the shooters got off. I was never going to let that happen again."

Lewis noticed she called them "shooters," ignoring what they had done to her.

"You didn't fuck up, Denise. Geronimo was a solid arrest. Fucking up would have been *not* recording him telling it to Thornton."

"A very bad guy walked out of jail today. But my cousin Joey and I have a crazy idea on how to stop that from being the end of the story. You and I and everyone else who heard that tape may be benched. We lost everything we seized in the arrest. Dewey's scared. Thornton's gloating. Looks grim."

"I hate it."

"And Marcy Thornton is standing in our way no matter which way we go at this."

"Joe Mascarenas is a good guy. But he's no match for Thornton."

"He's a bulldog wearing a choke collar, who's had his teeth filed down, fighting Rottweilers that chewed through their leash."

"So what's the answer?"

"Our own Rottweiler."

Lewis now understood the phone call that brought them here. "Fager."

"Joe knows how he ticks. Says he and Fager are like a married couple that fights every day."

"What's the part you said I'm not going to like?"

"Sam Goff."

"You're right. I don't like it. I didn't like Goff when he was a cop. Why should I like working with him now?"

Aragon's phone rang and they broke off the conversation. It was FBI Special Agent Tomas Rivera.

"The girl in the trunk was Cynthia Fremont," she relayed, then put the call on speaker so Lewis could hear Rivera directly.

Aragon had nailed it with her suggestion to search the lake. Rivera's team found a tent on the shoreline four and a half miles from the parking lot. The murder scene had also been found, a rock ledge a hundred feet above the lake at the head of a rough scree slope. A ranger had climbed up to find out what had attracted a cloud of ravens. Blood collected in cracks was feeding birds and a million ants.

"Was she naked inside the sleeping bag?" Aragon asked Rivera.

"Except for boots. And exsanguinated. Slashed wrists, deep gashes on her thighs. A cut across her belly, not deep like the cuts that killed her."

"What about the boots?"

"Laced up and tied. We're working on it to see if she did it or possibly someone else."

Rivera said he was damn glad she got the call for SFPD and wanted her at a meeting tomorrow morning to discuss what they had learned so far.

She was saying if you want me you want Rick Lewis, too, when Rivera asked, "How did you get the lake right?"

"My family camped there, when there were fish in that lake."

"Camping's prohibited in that area."

"So's homicide."

"Why'd you guess she was killed so far from the car?"

"*We* didn't guess." She caught Lewis' eye, signaling him to jump in. "The lividity told us."

"Confused lividity," Lewis said. "The blood didn't pool in one place."

"*We*," Aragon said, "deduced she had been face down long enough for blood to pool near her hairline. She didn't bleed out completely."

"Exsanguinate," Lewis said.

Aragon said, "I think that hands gripping her arms acted like tourniquets and kept some blood in her. A guess to run by a pathologist. What you're telling us about the wounds, they're not the kind that would drain her without a lot of help from gravity. There should have been lividity in her back, especially buttocks."

Lewis nodded agreement and she asked Rivera, "You find that?"

"Negative."

She went on. "And maybe they carried her face down so she wouldn't be looking at them while they got her off the mountain."

"Where did you guys take forensic training?" Rivera's voice asked over the speaker, like a third person in the car with them. "You're spot on."

Aragon said, "You're the only cop I know who uses a four-syllable word for 'bled out' and now it's 'spot on' a minute later."

"The cops you know, what do they say?"

"Great fucking job."

"Okay," Rivera said, "great fucking job. Where'd you learn forensics?"

"Rick," Aragon asked, "what's that fancy school we attend every day at taxpayers' expense?"

"The Santa Fe Academy for the Advancement of Police Science and All-Around Street Smarts."

"What about that call you took last night?" Rivera now had a different tone in his voice, no longer FBI talking to small-town cops. "A case like that, sensational murder, celebrity suspect, all the racial stuff, it can eat you alive. I hope you can spare us some of your time."

Lewis mouthed, *He doesn't know,* then said, "I think we can fit you in."

Aragon said, "We haven't forgotten Cynthia Fremont. Glad you haven't forgotten us."

"I need your report," Rivera said and ended the call.

Lewis had finished eating, was wiping his mouth with the delicate little napkins Blake's had been using since the Sixties.

"Hey," Aragon said, her voice gentle. "Before, at the office, I was going on about that Native stuff. I didn't mean anything. Just pissed about No-Balls. And that thing about the kind of people passing out menus."

"The pre-op tranny."

"I got nothing against anybody, whichever way they go."

"You were just describing the restaurant the way it is today, remembering when it had belonged to a different Santa Fe. I heard your words, but I knew you were talking about something else."

"You did?"

"Comes from being married and raising kids. Sometimes, words don't mean anything and you have to wait for the talking to end to figure it out in the silence that follows."

"You need me to shut up to know what I mean?"

"What I heard you saying is sometimes you don't recognize this city you've lived in all your life. It angers you, and scares you just a little since you can't do anything about it. The pre-op tranny passing out menus on fucking parchment, your words, that was about you being overwhelmed with all the change and things not the way they were when the world was familiar and you thought you understood it."

"You heard all that?"

"And you really do miss that old place with the great Mexican food."

"You don't know how much. Places like that never come back."

They were quiet for a moment, then Aragon spoke. "You good with this? The Fager thing?"

"I'm worried about Goff." Lewis turned away while he thought it over. When he came back to her he said, "We've got work before we meet Fager. You weren't the only one with wheels turning last night. I made calls between flipping pancakes for the kids."

"Yeah?" Aragon said with a mouthful of burger and fixings.

"Reached out to Matt Kennicott at OMI. I didn't want Linda Fager forgotten in a drawer. He's putting her on the table at noon."

Aragon checked her watch.

"Fifteen minutes. Shit."

She heaved her unfinished burger out the window, threw the car into drive, and floored the gas. Lewis capped his hand over his cup before coffee jumped into his lap.

SEVEN

"Really, Mr. Fager. We have what we need," said the voice on the phone, some assistant pathologist in the Office of Medical Investigator.

He did not explain why he was sparing Fager the ritual society demanded from next of kin, no matter the condition of their loved one's remains. But Fager understood why they didn't need him at the morgue. He had already identified Linda's body three times.

First, his 911 call. He said, "I found my wife murdered in her store." He gave his name, her name, the address, and a description of her condition. The 911 operator made him repeat the last part.

Maybe because there was no face, it had been easier to handle. Just another body. He had seen lots of bodies. He did not hold them in his mind. None had been wearing Linda's clothes, though, or her shoes and the jewelry he had bought her.

The second time he identified Linda was for the officers who arrived at the bookstore. Third time was for detectives Aragon and Lewis. They had questions and put him in a patrol car. There he sat until he learned Linda's murderer had been apprehended. Until then, he believed they considered him their lead suspect.

He tried again to call up memories of Linda's face. He concentrated on their honeymoon in Mexico. On the inside of his eyelids he saw tanned legs, red toenails, hands holding a drink with an umbrella. But when he ordered his mind to show her face, his memory clicked off like it had been unplugged to keep from blowing a fuse.

On the sidewalk, after calling 911, he had reached out to his only friend. Leon Bronkowski doubled as Fager's investigator. They had been together since the Balkan War, when Bronk carried the squad's M-249, a powerful guy back then who could pull field artillery into position without dropping his pack. Fager reached him in Pinedale, Wyoming, four days into a vacation, his Harley on the sidewalk outside his motel door. He was eating pizza in bed and watching black-and-white Westerns on the little TV that came with the forty-dollar room. Since the call, Bronkowski had been riding all night. He last checked in from Denver. He would hit Santa Fe this afternoon.

Fager had been facing a morning of arraignments and afternoon hearings in three courtrooms. His secretary phoned judges and rearranged his calendar. As for Linda's shop, there was nothing to do. He would sell the building and inventory—after he found a cleaning service willing to step in. Without thinking what else she would see in the building, his secretary had offered to corner Linda's terrified store cat and take it home. They would do it together when the police were finished. He'd ask them to put out food and water until then. They'd find the bin of dry food under the front counter.

His decks were clear to hunt Cody Geronimo. Mascarenas may have folded. The cops may have botched another case. Marcy Thornton may be standing on a mountain of technical Fourth Amendment issues and evidentiary privilege.

But a case never finished the way it started.

For every action there is an opposite and equal reaction. That's a law of physics. What went on in courthouses was theater and negotiation, a work of storytelling, no scientifically predictable forces determining what The Law should be. The rules were man-made, enforced by man, ignored by man. Broken by man.

In theory, a fair fight legitimized whatever result an imperfect court system produced.

But prosecutors were often baby lawyers who couldn't sense a freight train coming if they were tied to the tracks. That cop on the stand with a high school education, or maybe a piece of paper from the community college, she'd been on duty thirty-six hours before confronting a trial lawyer primed for that exact moment. Prosecutors had fifty cases to the defense lawyer's one. The District Attorney's office couldn't neutralize every scripted expert rolled out to bolster the narrative the defense lawyer wanted told. The crime lab was understaffed and underfunded. That judge on the bench depended on lawyers with the spare change to fund campaigns. Assistant DAs could barely cover car payments.

Forget fair fights. The law was what you made of it. So make as much as you can.

In his home office Fager had a framed pencil-drawing Bronk did after their close call in Bosnia: A stork with the outline of a frog lodged in its gullet. Hands reaching out of the stork's beak and wrapping around its throat. The stork's eyes crossed and bulged in alarm. Bronk had scrawled *Never give up* at the bottom.

Fager's phone rang. It was his secretary, Roberta Weldon, distraught, calling again to ask about his welfare, but now also wanting to know if she should make funeral arrangements.

"No, Robbie," Fager said, using a level voice to reassure her. "I don't know when OMI will release Linda's body."

He told her to go home. He knew how much she had liked Linda. She gobbled up romance novels Linda sold for fifty cents off a rack on the sidewalk outside the store. Linda's store cat had been her gift.

Fager spent the next two hours researching Geronimo and printing out everything he could find, regardless of source or relevance. A search of tax records turned up a house near the Santa Fe Opera. He found galleries on Canyon Road in Santa Fe, and Old Town in Albuquerque, and a warehouse in Espanola. All the properties were heavily mortgaged and subject to judgment liens. Marcy Thornton held the mortgages.

Geronimo's Wikipedia and gallery website bio said he was born in Alamo, the remote Navajo reservation in west central New Mexico. But a story in the *Magdalena Mountain Mail* said he had been born in that village, thirty miles south of the rez, the son of a Basque rancher. An obituary in the defunct *Catron County News* quoted a hand on the Adobe Acres Ranch, another hundred miles south, saying that Geronimo had been born there, to Mexican parents working the national forest round up. The ranch bordered the abandoned Warm Springs Apache reservation, where the warrior Geronimo had once spent the winter. The paper later retracted the story, with an apology to settle a suit filed by Thornton. Some money was paid. Fager found the reports not in an online edition of the newspaper—there was none—but a blog written by a ranch wife from that empty part of the state.

Geronimo was forty-two years old by one account. Fifty in another. Never married. Attended Albuquerque's Southwest Indian Polytechnic Institute. The earliest record of the artist had him in Madrid, a former coal-mining town south of Santa Fe on the Turquoise Trail. He turned a crumbling mercantile into a fashionable gallery. His success drew other artists fleeing Santa Fe's rents and rapacious gallery owners. He went the other direction. He moved into a compound on pricey Canyon Road and branded himself the Native American Picasso.

Fager noted that over the years Geronimo had gone from being Indian, to Native American, to simply Native. Geronimo never specified whether he was Apache, Navajo, or something else. Fager presumed Geronimo had claimed a tribal affiliation when he sought admission to SIPI, but his school records were not publicly available.

In Google images he found photos of Geronimo with celebrities and politicians. The former governor had used a Geronimo watercolor, a cartoonish vista of a New Mexico landscape, as background in his campaign logo.

Despite the millions flowing in, more millions flowed out. Geronimo had been through bankruptcy twice. Fager found a photo of Geronimo's mansion near the Opera. He threw lavish parties, jetted off to Europe and Asia to hawk his wares, rented an apartment in San Francisco, and once owned a 100,000-acre ranch of checkerboarded public and private land in the wilds of New Mexico.

A telephone call interrupted his reading.

"I'm still doing okay, Robbie. Yes, I'm fine alone. Go home, please."

Fager checked his watch. Half an hour until his meeting with detective Aragon. He organized what he had printed off the Internet and headed for the door.

EIGHT

ARAGON AND LEWIS WATCHED through the restaurant's front window as Fager parked his black Mercedes next to their tan Crown Vic. Sam Goff was at the table with them eating a bowl of menudo and scanning the preliminary report on Linda Fager's autopsy. The rest of Juanita's was empty, except a janitor cleaning up between the lunch and dinner traffic, and waitresses at a table rolling napkins around silverware.

Fager bent low to enter the door and waited while his eyes adjusted to the dim light. He saw them and came across the room. Nobody stood or reached to shake his hand. He hesitated opposite Goff.

"I'm not sure I want this conversation if he's part of it."

"Sit down," Goff said, red sauce coloring his teeth and lips. "My career's finished, but don't give yourself all the credit."

"We know what you pulled on Sam," Aragon said. Fager's cross-examination had been the last time Goff ever testified as arresting officer. He was forced into early retirement a week later. Goff hated Fager. Fager despised Goff. But her plan required them both. "You want this conversation, and we want you in it."

"Best menudo in town," Goff said, and returned to reading.

Fager pulled out a chair across from Aragon and sat, rigid, ready to get up anytime.

"You want something? A cup of coffee?" Aragon asked. "I'm sure you didn't get any sleep."

Fager nodded. "Thanks, black." Lewis went to the kitchen.

"We're here for your wife," Aragon said. "Understand up front that none of us likes what you do."

On the way to his mouth, Goff's spoon dripped broth on the pages of the autopsy report. "You deserve what you're feeling right now," he said.

"Sam, cut it out," Aragon snapped, then turned back to Fager. "I don't think anyone deserves what you're going through."

Lewis returned with coffee for Fager and sat next to Aragon.

"Detective, if you called me here for a lecture on ethics," Fager pointed at Goff, "you've got the wrong person delivering today's lesson."

Goff threw down his spoon. It bounced off the table onto his lap.

"Setting me up to argue I planted a gun on Luis Gallardo ... "

"It wasn't my client's gun."

Goff leaned forward, hands shaking.

"You want to talk about the man who stapled your wife's face to a wall, we got a conversation. You want to justify your bullshit, I'm gonna finish my meal like you're not here."

Fager pushed back his chair and half rose. "This is a mistake."

"He worked the first Cody Geronimo murder," Aragon said.

Fager didn't move. "Linda wasn't his first?"

"Tasha Gonzalez wasn't his first," Goff said, looking straight at the lawyer.

"So tell me exactly why I'm here with this asshole," Fager said to Aragon, then settled into his chair. "Who's Tasha Gonzalez?"

"We know you can take cases apart," Aragon began. "You want the man who killed your wife, you're going to have to put one together. Sam will be your contact. He hasn't heard the tape, so he's not tainted."

"Except in other ways," Goff said as a Mexican woman placed a dish by his bowl of menudo. He picked up a fried pork skin and plopped it in his mouth. "Awesome chicharrones," he said, licking his lips. "Amazing stuff, skin. It's actually an organ, the body's largest. It sweats. Gets goose bumps. Tickles. Makes footballs, lampshades if you're a Nazi. And if you're Cody Geronimo, it makes lovely wall hangings."

Aragon's eyes told Goff to shut up.

She said to Fager, "We want you to put Leon Bronkowski on this."

"I'm already on Geronimo," Fager said. "Why do I need you?"

Goff produced an accordion file from under the table and pushed it across to Fager.

"You didn't get that from me," Aragon said. "Maybe I don't even know what's in there."

Lewis cleared his throat and spoke for the first time.

"On this, Mr. Fager, you're a citizen. Thornton would always have more information on your wife's murder than you would ever see. That just changed."

The detectives stood to leave.

"Don't call me again," Aragon said. "Go through Sam."

They left. Fager thumbed through the file.

"I trust everything's here."

"It's not," Goff said, fried pork skin crunching in his teeth.

"Something's missing from the file?"

"Nope," Goff said, and slid the preliminary autopsy results across the table. "From your wife."

————
49

Fager took the files home and set up a place to work on the dining room table. For some reason he pulled down the shades in the middle of the day. He put aside the preliminary autopsy report, spotted red with Goff's menudo, and dug into the rest of what the police had assembled in less than twenty-four hours.

The first officers on scene reported his statements, what they found in the bathroom, and their efforts to secure the property. Detectives Aragon and Lewis later found a credit-card receipt giving the time Geronimo purchased a used book, a hardback, entitled *Transformation: Mastering the Mystery of Found Art*, by Paolo Merced. He had paid eighteen dollars and eighty-four cents. The file contained a copy of the receipt and a forensics report that the original held latents from Linda and Geronimo. The book was purchased one hundred and thirty-four minutes before Fager's 911 call.

The inventory of seized property was short. A cell phone, a belt with turquoise stones set in silver. Coins. A wallet with credit cards and four hundred sixty-seven dollars in cash. Indian totems, a small bear made from coral and a snake in onyx. A baggie containing very small bones, likely avian, and pieces of a tiny snail shell.

Fager was studying diagrams of the scene when he heard a motorcycle throttling down in the driveway.

"Hell you doing?" Leon Bronkowski, dressed in leathers, face red from wind, filled the doorway. "Your mission is grieving. Leave this to the cops."

"It's a mess, Bronk. We could do a better job ... "

Bronkowski swept the taller man in his arms and lifted him from his chair.

"You cry yet?"

Fager avoided his eyes.

"I should make you cry." Bronkowski crushed Fager until he groaned. Photographs by a coffee cup caught his eye. "Jesus," he said and released his friend.

"I haven't opened the photos of Linda. That's Tasha Gonzalez. Geronimo killed her, too."

Bronkowski peeled off a leather vest and unsnapped his chaps. "What are you doing with this stuff? You should be thinking on your years with Linda, unlocking those iron bands you got round your heart. How did you get these files?"

Instead of answering, Fager shook out a folded section of the newspaper. Below the front-page story about Linda's murder and Geronimo's arrest was a sidebar announcing a new show at Geronimo's Secret Canyon Gallery.

"He rips Linda apart and gets front-page advertising."

Bronkowski's eyes locked on a Beretta on the breakfront. Fager had carried the nine millimeter through Bosnia and managed to keep it after leaving the service.

"That for you or Cody Geronimo?"

"What? Oh," Fager looked over his shoulder at the pistol. "Don't know why I got that out. Get up to speed on these files. Gonzalez as well as Linda. Then we'll talk about how to proceed."

"How about we proceed to shoot the piece of shit?"

Fager pushed forward a stack of papers and turned to his laptop.

Bronkowski looked at the files scattered over the dining table, legal pads filled with Fager's scrawl, crime scene photos, diagrams, photocopied pages bristling with Post-It notes, three empty coffee cups. He looked again at the Beretta and kept his eyes there as Fager tapped keys.

NINE

Marcy Thornton and Associates, P.C. occupied all six thousand square feet of a Prairie-style mansion on Paseo de Peralta, across from the state capitol and next to some low, cinder-block buildings Fager had connected to form his office complex. In the conference room, reporters occupied chairs arranged in a semicircle on an enormous Persian rug. In the middle, Thornton sat at a writing desk. She worked on a brief while camera crews set up.

She had learned media skills as a young associate for Walter Fager. She bought the much grander building next to his complex when she rang a bell on her first case after going solo. They shared a parking lot, where her red Aston Martin often pointed at his black Mercedes.

Thornton's secretary said everybody was ready.

"I'll be quick." Thornton put down her pen, pushed back from the desk and stood, smoothing her black silk pants. "I have an appointment across town." They didn't need to know the appointment was with her stylist. "First, my heart goes out to my colleague, Walter Fager, upon the loss of his lovely wife. Linda was a bright light in this dark world, and I hope the authorities will quickly apprehend her killer."

Her eyes and voice darkened.

"That said, there is no excuse for the way Santa Fe police treated my client. Cody Geronimo is a respected member of our community. Clearly he was profiled. Instead of conducting a careful, patient investigation, they grabbed the closest Indian at hand. Snap judgment driven by prejudice and bigotry has permitted the real killer to remain on our streets."

She took a drink of water to give reporters a second to write that down. She was almost done.

"We could fire off a tort claim notice for his unlawful arrest. But there has been enough grief over this incident. Mr. Geronimo wishes to state that he prays the police henceforth focus their resources on making Santa Fe a safer place for all citizens, regardless of their racial or ethnic background. That is all."

Thornton waved off questions with the excuse that she was running late. As she escaped through a side door, her secretary distributed copies of her statement so no reporter could misquote her. If they caught her on her way to her car she would repeat her canned lines. In handling reporters, Fager had once instructed, "Screw them and their questions. Their job is to print what you want future jurors to read."

Thornton stopped by her office to collect her purse. Montclaire was on the leather sofa painting her nails. Today it was blue.

"I wanted to see you before I took off," Thornton said. "Cody left some of his toys out."

Aragon and Lewis returned to the office. They caught up on overtime requests. A stack of interdepartmental memos told them the seminars they were required to attend by the end of the quarter and the chief's decision to leave unfilled the position of captain for Criminal Investigations, putting Dewey Nobles in charge by default. They'd pulled an old case two days ago, a stabbing at the South Capitol complex. The file covered Lewis's desk. Three years together and this was the only case they hadn't closed.

He tried to dig into it, but his mind was on Linda Fager's murder. He couldn't remember a more solid arrest. They knew the killer, knew how he did it. But there was now little practical difference between Geronimo and the assailant behind their only open file. Both were beyond their reach, free to do whatever they wanted, including shed more blood.

Aragon wasn't concentrating on paperwork any more than he was.

"Because Dewey No-Balls," she said.

"You're talking to yourself."

"You should hear what I'm keeping inside. What's for dinner tonight?" she asked as Lewis drew on his notepad.

"You want to join us?" Lewis asked.

"I get a kick hearing a big dude like you planning meals for his kids and wife."

"Mac and cheese, three cheeses: parm, cheddar, and jack. Green beans and salad."

"No dessert?"

"That's the salad."

"You're a hard-ass, Lewis."

"Really, we'd love to have you over. It's not good, always eating dinner alone, when you're not eating it here."

"Next you'll tell me to get a cat."

"I already did."

Aragon smiled and said, "Geronimo had beer on his breath." She slipped her Springfield into a holster behind her hip and dropped her shirt to cover the gun. "I want to know where he went for a cold one after cutting up Linda Fager."

Lewis turned his notepad. Aragon saw a timeline of the Linda Fager murder.

"And I thought you were focused on a mid-level bureaucrat getting a blade in the kidney."

"We know Geronimo strangled her," Lewis said. "We've got a fractured hyoid and petechiae. But no bruising from fingers squeezing the neck, no thumb marks on her throat. Talking to Thornton, he didn't say exactly how he did it, just that he choked her. I would guess he used his arm in a chokehold, another reason they haven't raised latents." He touched the back of his head. "Contusion here. First he clubbed her. She went down, he was at her throat from behind."

"Weapon?"

"Didn't break the skin. How about a heavy book? Maybe the one he bought. He pays, she gets back to work. Wham."

"He hit her hard enough, she'd go down."

"Small woman in her fifties, thin arms."

"Not a mark on Geronimo. She didn't put up a fight."

"Once she's down," he said, trying to see it, "Geronimo had to prepare for what came next. He told Thornton he hadn't gone in with anything on his mind but buying a book. Linda Fager looked at him. Whatever that did to him, he went off. Killed her then dragged her to the bathroom. I would guess she had the boxcutter where she received packages. He didn't bring a staple gun with him. Probably found that in the store, too. Walter Fager says she had one, but couldn't identify it positively as hers."

"He should have been covered in blood. He stripped down to keep his clothes clean. But that wouldn't take long," she said.

"And after, took a bath at the sink, head to toe. Poured water over Linda Fager to take care of prints and trace evidence. Let the water overflow to cover the floor. Then somehow he dried himself." Lewis paused. "Pretty sloppy, you think of it."

"Except the boxcutter and staple gun clean and drying on a paper towel. Like he was caring for his tools. Maybe he used paper towels on himself, but we didn't find them in the store. He might have taken his trash with him when he went for his after-work beer. If we were still on the case, officially, we'd delay garbage pickup, search every trash can between the store and wherever he had his beer. I need a copy of this." She tapped her index finger on the timeline.

"We'd be knocking on doors up and down the street. We'd be searching his Range Rover, his house, poring over his clothes and those fancy boots and everything in his pockets. We'd get that book he bought, see if Linda Fager's hair or blood is on it."

"We'd be doing it right."

"Keep my half-assed timeline. Fill in the blanks. Tomorrow's chest and triceps." They worked out three times a week at Brazos's weight room on the south side of town, not far from Killer Park. "We can talk about Tasha Gonzalez then." Lewis lightly kicked the heavy document box on the floor by his chair. "I'll read up tonight."

"When do you plan on sleeping?"

"I'll sleep when I'm dead."

"Catch you tomorrow, Super Dad."

———

Aragon faced Fager's Finds. The plate-glass window had been covered with newspaper, the last order she gave before No-Balls yanked her off the case. An additional padlock had been installed and the key delivered to Fager. Not even Lewis knew she had kept a copy on her key ring, and the extra to the original deadbolt she discovered inside, under the cash register.

She lifted the crime-scene tape and went straight to the doorway to the little bathroom in back. The carpet was still damp. On a hunch, she opened the rear door. A garbage can sat in the alley fifteen yards away. She untucked her shirt and used its loose end to lift the lid. Inside she found a basketball-size clump of wet paper towels stained pink. Lewis's theory about Geronimo stripping then bathing at the sink made sense. She slipped on the last pair of latex gloves she had and carried the can inside. Using one of the store's garbage can liners, she bagged everything in the can. The lid went into a separate bag. She sealed the empty can in liners taped around the outside.

The pool of blood that had made young cops swoon had dried into a thick syrup, coating the linoleum and the edge of the toilet seat. The wall looked like it had been slapped with a mop dipped in red paint. Perforations in the drywall marked where eight heavy staples had been pried loose.

A cat had stepped in the blood and left paw prints heading into a far corner of the store. A defense lawyer could have fun with that. There was nothing she could do about it.

Aragon went to the counter at the front of the store. She stood behind the cash register, imagining what had passed between Linda Fager and Geronimo. She walked through it, noting how long each step might have taken, adding in time to wash and take out the trash.

She stepped outside onto the sidewalk, locked the door, and settled the crime-scene tape back into place. The evidence bags went in her car's trunk, the empty can in the back seat. In the evening's last light she studied Lewis's timeline. Now to find the bar where Geronimo had been drinking after he killed Linda Fager. She turned left and headed toward the watering holes south of the plaza.

———

Lily Montclaire had just steered her car into the alley when she saw Aragon taking the garbage can into the back door of Fager's Finds. The Mexican dwarf. The bald Mexican dwarf. Those hips were something. Powerful all across her thighs and pelvis. You could break a finger in there, lose a hand snapped off at the wrist.

Arms bent, turned wrists up as she walked, the way a guy proud of his biceps carried himself. Aragon's eyes were something, too. Cutting off her hair had done a lot to make them stand out. They were the kind of eyes you could make a living from doing ads for Luxottica or Maybelline. It would be a short career. These Mexican women lost their looks young. Not long past thirty they turned into the fried bread they ate with too many combo plates.

Maybe not Aragon. The senior partner on a homicide team, at least five years patrol before that, she had to be older than thirty. Ten more years the way she kept herself, hitting the weights to build those shoulders and arms, she'd be a human bulldozer. Paint her yellow, Caterpillar could use her.

Montclaire phoned Thornton to report that some of Cody's mess had been cleaned up by the wrong person.

"She's still working the case," Thornton said. "I'll get on that. You find the bar."

Montclaire shoved her cell into her jeans. Geronimo didn't remember where he had his beer. His head had been somewhere else, on "the drum within," more of his flaky bullshit. He remembered turning right when he came out of the store. He wandered until he heard country music. Inside, women with bare midriffs. Tecate girl posters. Guys yelling at a big-screen TV. A table where he left fingerprints in Linda Fager's blood.

Montclaire skipped the first bar she came to. Attractive men in tight pants and turtlenecks hung by the door smoking cigarettes. The next bar, inside a hotel, was decorated with Chihuly glass, woodcuts and orchids, and some guy with white hair playing flamenco guitar in a corner—nothing close to the dive Geronimo described.

Next a piano lounge. A block farther something called an *enoteca*, where only wine was served. Then she found the place.

She ordered a gin and tonic and picked a booth that allowed her to survey the room. On the back of a menu she sketched the tables and chairs, marked the location of the bar, the television, and front door, and added the men's room to help Cody get his bearings. The schematic went into her back pocket. Geronimo could point out where he had been seated without having to come here again.

She waved for another drink and turned her attention to the people. Women with big hair and tight jeans. Tourists with shopping bags on tables next to tall drinks and nachos. Two men tilting back longnecks at the bar looked promising. Strong shoulders, large hands, not too much extra weight above their belts. Good butts on both, some sweet man tail just twenty paces away. When her G&T arrived, Montclaire told the waitress to give them a round of what they were drinking.

Cody had interrupted last night's fun. It was make-up time.

TEN

BRONKOWSKI LISTENED TO THE copy machine in Fager's home office burning off pages of what Fager said was "a Geronimo prep sheet and legal research for the worthless DA." Fager had moved down the hall and given him the dining room table for a work space. He left behind the unopened brown envelope containing the medical investigator's preliminary autopsy on Linda. He noticed another envelope Fager had not yet opened. It was marked *Linda Fager*, with the date, case number, and police photographer's name.

He could not bring himself to view photos of the mutilated woman who had served him many happy dinners at this very same table. He packed the files into a banker's box and strapped it to the back of his Harley. He dropped in on Fager before he left.

"I'm going to do the DA's motions and briefs for them," Fager said without taking his eyes from his computer screen. "Be here at seven. We'll size up Mr. Cody Geronimo."

Bronkowski rolled his shoulders, stiff from holding the Harley's handlebars for fifteen hours straight. "Sure you want to do that?"

Fager hit "print" for the hundredth time today.

"There's a string of cases out of the Tenth Circuit. Federal law, but persuasive. Mascarenas missed them. Probably never looked. With this he'll have a head start on a motion to reconsider Diaz's ruling."

Bronkowski patted his friend on the shoulder and headed home to shower and force himself to read about the murder of his best friend's wife.

Bronkowski parked his bike in the Tuff Shed behind his home. He decided to get to work with a thousand miles of road dust caked on his face and arms. He knew he would need a shower anyway after what he was about to read.

He started with the Tasha Gonzalez file and read enough to get an understanding of the case. Then he took a deep breath and opened the crime scene photos from Linda's store, with her still there, the photographer's bright lights showing everything.

An hour later he had finished with the homicide detectives' reports, reviewed the transcripts of radio traffic, the inventory of items seized from Geronimo, the DA's memos to Deputy Chief Dewey Nobles on legal problems raised by Aragon's conduct, and the preliminary autopsy. Bronkowski rose from his chair, cracked open the door to his backyard, and threw up on a rosebush Linda had planted for him when he bought the place.

He forced some fruit juice down his throat, then showered and dressed in what he thought was appropriate for a Santa Fe gallery opening: jeans, Doc Martens, and a leather vest over a pressed white shirt, the only article of clothing he had altered from his usual attire. He rode his bike to Fager's and found him outside, pinstripe suit and dark blue tie, watering Linda's garden. The landscaping would soon die. Fager was not a man to keep anything alive except clients on death row and the low simmer of anger always inside him.

Fager turned to him, his eyes vacant.

"You've got the thousand-yard stare, buddy," Bronkowski said. "Ya need to connect?"

"I'm okay. I don't need anything." Water pooled at the base of the rosebushes as he forgot about the hose in his hand.

"Suit yourself. It wouldn't hurt to shoot the shit at the VA center. I let it out on Tuesdays. We'll pull up a chair for you."

Fager looked past him. Spray from his garden hose drifted toward Bronkowski and he stepped out of the way.

"You take it out on DAs and cops. Other than when you were with Linda, the only time you smile is coming back to counsel's table after ripping the prosecution's star witness."

"I don't need to sit in a circle of fucked-up vets and hear their shit."

"And I don't think kicking ass in a courtroom is gonna be enough to ever make this right for you."

Fager turned off the faucet and dropped the hose.

"We'll take my car. You can tell me about Tasha Gonzalez."

"Walt, buddy. I gotta ask. You carrying?"

"No. I can't trust myself when we get close to him."

Bronkowski still checked the way Fager's suit hung on him.

In the Mercedes, rolling down out of the hills, a view across the Rio Grande basin to lights coming on in Los Alamos, Fager asked, "Geronimo's first. Who was she?"

"Tasha Gonzalez, age forty-nine, single, modeled for Geronimo."

"Little old for a model."

"Not for his paintings. All middle-aged Indian women, chunky, no teenybopper bulemics. They found her bones clogging an irrigation ditch near Belen."

"Geronimo lives here in town."

"So did Gonzalez."

Fager drove onto Paseo de Peralta, looped around the capitol and courthouses, past office buildings for state workers and the tourist center of Santa Fe, and headed for the old residential area fanning the center of town.

"Say Goff is right," Fager said at the next light. "That Geronimo killed Tasha Gonzalez. What was he doing with a dead woman in Belen more than ninety miles from home? What did he do to her?"

"Scratches on the skull and jawbone suggest her face had been cut away." Bronkowski paused, wanting Fager to see the connection to Linda but not wanting to say it. When he got no response he said, "But animals could have done that."

"Have you read Linda's autopsy? Goff hinted something was missing from her remains. I couldn't get started. I didn't want to learn the contents of her stomach, or the weight of her brain."

Bronkowski changed the subject to ask what he thought of Aragon and Lewis.

"I'm glad they're on the case," Fager said, "and not losers who'll screw up and make it easy for the defense. But they better keep a tight leash on Goff. I understand why they brought him in. Goff could get the job done when he was a detective. Just *how* was the problem."

Fager turned onto Acequia Madre, the city changing back to something hundreds of years old. These houses were built before this was part of the United States. They may be mud and straw but sold for millions, with expensive cars parked behind artsy grillwork gates. Ancient cottonwoods canopied narrow streets hemmed by adobe walls.

A man walking his dog got out of the way so Fager's Mercedes could squeeze by.

The approach to Geronimo's gallery was blocked. Teepees and hogans had been erected in the street, with horses tethered nearby and sheep confined to a pen on a floor of dirt trucked in for the occasion.

Fager parked on another street leading into Canyon Road and they walked the rest.

"He's a one-man theme park," Bronkowski said as drums and Indian singing cut the night's stillness.

A drum circle was going between the tents and hogans. Seven men—most hugely fat, one lean and tough, all in faded denim with blankets around their shoulders—sat round a drum the size of a hot tub. With bones and sticks they beat out a complex, persistent rhythm, their high-pitched, wailing voices rising and falling to the drum's booming bass.

A crowd in western clothing and heavy silver jewelry, even the men wearing bracelets and pendants, watched from inside the gate to the grounds of Geronimo's gallery. Beautiful young Native American men and women distributed glasses of champagne. A Rolls-Royce was permitted to pass the barricades to discharge a woman who had won an Oscar when the awards show was still broadcast in black and white. Her male companion was forty years younger. A tall Navajo man with long braids and wearing a tux ran to open their door.

Over the doorway hung the skull and antlers of a large elk, bleached white from the sun.

"This place looks familiar," Bronkowski said.

"One of our first cases. The Navajo laundromat."

"Yeah. This was where Leroy Yazzie laundered coke money through his rug store."

"Most of these places would be t-shirt and tattoo shops without cash coming in the back." Fager scowled at a fifteen-foot pink bear rearing on hind legs in the garden of the gallery next door. "Who buys this crap?"

They slipped through the crowd in the wake of the movie star and made their way to the door. A young Indian woman sat behind an antique table signing in guests.

"Welcome to Secret Canyon Gallery. Would you sign our register so we can alert you to Cody's latest work and upcoming shows?"

Fager pretended to be distracted by a fountain spouting water between a pair of wings where a bird's head should have been. Bronkowski signed in as Lee Tomski, a fieldwork alias. He left the street address blank but wrote Malibu as his home.

"I'm moving to Santa Fe. I'm liking a place 'bout half a mile from here, higher up the mountain."

"Your friend." The young woman nodded at Fager. "Would he like to be on our mailing list?"

"No friend there. That's my lawyer."

"The brochure for Cody's new works." She lifted two booklets off the stack in front of her.

"Good, you give prices," Bronkowski said as he flipped pages. "I'm thinking of one wing in Cody Geronimo, another in more traditional Santa Fe artists. My O'Keefe goes in the great room, no offense to Mr. Geronimo."

"You're considering a number of purchases?"

"I've got a lotta bare walls."

Bronkowski returned one of the folios to the stack.

"I don't want my lawyer seeing this. One Cody Geronimo in his office, I'll remember his meter doesn't stop for piss breaks."

Some signal had passed from the young woman to an older Indian man, tuxedo jacket over black jeans, who glided over. He leaned down to read the guest register then nodded at the folio in Bronkowski's hand.

He said, "The fourteen new works are explained in addition to Cody's paintings on display. If I may answer any questions ... "

"I need something in the den." Bronkowski waved the folio. "Did our boy go through a brown period, something that would match a leather couch?"

The tuxedoed Indian man put a fist to his mouth and coughed.

"Cody's work is extensive. I am sure you will find a number of pieces suitable to your taste. What is it you do in Malibu?"

"Spend money, mostly." Bronkowski tapped Fager on the shoulder. "Counselor, whaddya say we stick our noses in the air and poke around?"

Bronkowski headed deeper into the crowd. Fager followed and asked, "How many of these people are here because they think the great artist might also enjoy killing women?"

"Like you said, who buys this crap? People who need their heads filled with the idea they're in on something special. They want to think they see things other people can't. They're enlightened, shit, more highly evolved. Add some blood, a touch of evil: the inner circle's a very special place for only very special people."

"Run a con like this on poor people, you go to jail."

Bronkowski grabbed a flute of champagne. He headed for a spot between an abstract structure of animal skin, rocks, and feathers, and paintings of women drawn with a single, continuous brushstroke.

"Three hundred grand each. Statues, I guess you call them. They're weird, but listen to the oohs and aahs." Bronkowski drained his glass and flipped through the folio. "Some of the paintings are actually kind of neat, that one line doing it all. What do red dots mean?"

"Bronk, we're not here for entertainment."

"Walt, you work where a judge can make someone talk. I'm the one goes into the real world where nobody talks 'less they want to. We won't learn anything if they think we're only here for free booze. I need to get into this."

"Dots mean the piece is sold."

Bronkowski traded his empty glass for a full one from the tray of a passing waiter.

"That him?" Bronkowski aimed his chin at a man in a circle of people.

Geronimo also wore the uniform of tuxedo jacket over jeans, but he had added a blue bandana around his head and leather strings encasing his ponytail. A long feather dangled from his right ear.

Bronkowski and Fager moved closer.

"It speaks to me," said a woman wearing ten pounds of turquoise and silver. "Something deep. Raw. A hidden force."

"Yes, very good." Geronimo pursed his lips as he contemplated the woman's words. "A hidden force. You sense its presence."

The woman smacked the back of her hand on the arm of the man next to her, a bandy legged guy with no butt and a gut over his buckle. He was grimacing at a price list.

"How about that," the woman said. "I felt the same thing Cody did. The very same thing. This baby has to come home with us."

The man checked the price list and eyed the statue.

"Pardon me for saying. It looks like what blows up against my pump jacks."

"Why Grady Fallon," the woman said.

Geronimo reached back and stroked his ponytail. A light flared in his dark eyes. It passed. He brought the ponytail around across his shoulder, heavy with all the leather wrapped into it. With a patient smile he said, "Some of the greatest artists of the genre don't hesitate to call their work trash. The scholarly term is *object trouvé*. Found objects. Pablo Picasso, Marcel Duchamp, Man Ray—"

The woman cut in. "Grady." An elbow to the man's ribs. "Picasso!"

"—are among the masters who have shown the world that everyday objects we cast aside as trash are capable of transformation into profound art. I am the only Native working in the genre."

Bronkowski felt Fager stiffen. The thousand-yard stare returned.

"Dang," the oil man named Grady Fallon said, and scratched his head. "Guess that settles it. But Ginger, darling, we're not putting this in the bedroom. I'd be sleeping with one eye open."

The Indian salesman materialized from the crowd and led the lucky couple to a table for a check to be written. Another assistant affixed a red dot to the base of the statue.

Bronkowski stepped up to Geronimo. He pointed into the folio of artworks.

"Is this 'Inner Being' or 'Spirit Wing'?"

"'Spirit Wing.' May I?" Geronimo eased the folio from his hand and turned to the right page.

Bronkowski said, "These things are kind of spooky."

"You're feeling their spirit. Each is unique. Unlike a painting, you will never see a reproduction. Impossible. They are truly one of a kind."

"Explains the price tag."

"I leave economics to others. I choose the creative realm."

Bronkowski checked on Fager. He had moved against a wall. His hands were balled into fists. He felt the tension in Fager's body across the room.

"You're from Malibu?"

Geronimo's salesman must have briefed the artist on one of the night's promising marks.

"Until I find the right place in Santa Fe. You put these together here?"

Geronimo delivered a condescending smile.

"I 'put them together,' as you say, in a very special place, one with its own heartbeat. This gallery has too many old voices," he waved at walls of paintings, "competing with new voices I want to hear."

"I get it. Secret Canyon Gallery. Your secret getaway."

"We all need some place separate from our public lives, especially those of us who know so little privacy."

Bronkowski checked again on Fager. The spot where he had been pressed against a wall was now occupied by a woman in a jean dress and a red hat sipping wine through a straw.

"So, my Malibu friend, do any of these pieces speak to you? Perhaps I may translate."

Bronkowski wanted to strangle him with that blue bandana. Grab that ponytail and swing his head against a wall. He searched for something to keep the man talking and his own emotions under control.

"This one," Bronkowski gestured toward the closest statue, a concoction of grasses, willow reeds, tumbleweed, baling wire, and things he could not identify. "'Spirit Wing.' I don't see a wing."

Geronimo seemed pleased with the inquiry. He stroked his chin and admired his own work.

"You're limiting yourself. You seek what you recognize. But a spirit wing, what is that? The title doesn't describe a thing. It acknowledges a presence."

"A presence."

"The fourteen statues together, unified, concentrate their sympathetic energy, like drops of water combining to form a pool. Together, they are transformed. And transforming."

"Together, that's," Bronkowski paused to do the math. "Four point two mil."

Geronimo shrugged. "This is my most serious work."

Bronkowski couldn't keep it going. He would drive his fist through Geronimo's face in another second.

"Thanks for the talk. I gotta find my friend. He's a mess when he's not suing somebody."

Geronimo didn't let him go without again shaking his hand.

Outside, the beautiful woman at the sign-in table looked strangely at Bronkowski when he poured a glass of wine over the hand that had briefly held Geronimo's. He caught her staring.

"The alcohol fights infection," he said. "So I don't have to cut it off."

Bronkowski found Fager in the Mercedes, behind the wheel, ramrod straight, staring through the windshield at nothing. He wondered how long Fager had been out here, alone. He slipped into the passenger seat and joined him looking through the windshield.

"That was hard," he said.

Fager started the car and eased to the corner near Geronimo's gallery. The crowd had grown. A jazz vocalist and ensemble had replaced the drum circle. Geronimo embraced a woman in a flamboyant printed dress while people applauded something.

"Why are they smiling?" Fager asked, but it didn't sound like a real question.

"I'm with you, you want to handle this the other way," Bronkowski said so quietly he wasn't sure Fager heard him. "The way I said before."

Fager drove slowly, working his way around the blocked-off street, then farther up Canyon Road. Brown adobe walls narrowed

then pulled back where the road dead-ended at the Audubon Center at the edge of the forest. Fager turned the car around in the parking lot and finally spoke.

"If I were to kill Geronimo, I'd do to him what he did to Linda. Nothing less. I'd want him to know what was coming. Let him see the boxcutter up close. You could hold him down. We'd drive staples into his face before I peeled it off, not do him the favor of killing him first."

Bronkowski had been with Fager in Bosnia. Back then it had been a K-bar in Fager's hand, the blade against the cheek of a Serbian militiaman the Muslims had left alive because he might know radio codes.

"And the minute Geronimo turned up missing," Fager went on, "they would be after us. Being criminals would dishonor Linda. No, I want Geronimo to see his world destroyed. Then spend his life in a cage with animals who eat him alive, spit him out, and start over every day, chewing on something new. What did you learn talking to that monster?"

"He's making a fortune selling crap."

"So why the bankruptcies? Why does Marcy hold mortgages on everything he owns?"

Fager retraced his route back into town. They crossed a two-lane bridge over the trickle of the Santa Fe River and approached the district around the plaza. Stars sparkled in an indigo sky. Santa Fe was beautiful at this hour, but Bronkowski couldn't see any of it. He saw the perfect teeth in Geronimo's mouth, an honest-to-god twinkle in his eye, the silver tip on his boot—just the left boot, what was up with that? The grotesque statues, the glitzy crowd, tittering, sharing the thrill of being next to the guy who killed Linda.

The man's smooth fingers in his hand.

"Something else," Bronkowski said. "It may sound like bigoted bullshit, but every Indian at the VA center, even guys who were Green

Berets and Special Forces, they give you the dead fish. Their hand just lies in yours like it's asleep. Geronimo shook my hand for real."

"He has to live in the white man's world."

"Indian vets do, too. They're tough guys. But they don't crush your hand."

"So Geronimo's a fake Indian?"

The pink castle of the Scottish Rite Temple, a little Moorish and King Arthur at the same time, slid by as Fager headed north to his house in the hills. The building, taking up almost a whole city block, was up for sale, for millions. The city's next boutique hotel, they could keep the color.

Bronkowski said, "If you're not buying what he's selling, the Indian act, the art trip, you see a guy dripping bullshit."

"I represented a Basque once. A sheep rancher. Shot his neighbor, a Southern Ute, rustling ewes with a horse trailer. The Basque was dark and swarthy, as they used to say. He looked like an Indian, face wrinkled by sun and wind, the big black eyes, black hair. The Ute, he had blue eyes. Geronimo's bio says he came from country where there's Basques, the ranchers, and seasonal help."

"No Basque galleries on Canyon Road. Better to be Indian, if art's your gig."

"Now give me the hard stuff, Bronk. You read the preliminary autopsy? You didn't answer me before."

Bronkowski took a breath and decided not to soften it.

"He dug out the little bones inside Linda's ear. The inventory of stuff seized from him listed a baggie with small bones, probably from birds, the cops thought. And pieces of a snail shell. I thought it was stuff he used in his art. Like the cops I didn't put it together right away. I researched those little ear bones. One looks like a tiny snail."

"Judy Diaz ordered everything returned." Fager's voice flat, showing no pain or anger. "I'll e-mail Mascarenas a motion to order Geronimo to place that baggie in court custody, if it hasn't already been destroyed. I could go civil. Judge Santiago would give me an ex parte order before Diaz was any wiser. I want you to get with Goff. I'm sure Aragon banked a copy of the tape with him. We need it. If Geronimo's recorded saying the bones came from Linda, that establishes my standing for a replevin action."

"Replevin? You going numb on me, buddy?"

"It's a question of derivative taint for the prosecution, but a property interest of the estate in a civil action."

"Damn it, Walt. Listen to yourself. You're analyzing pieces of Linda like loose change hacks take from a guy's pocket when he's booked in. This is gonna kill you from the inside out if you don't cut loose what's really going on in there." Bronkowski throttled down. "I'm worried, real worried, 'cause I don't think that's something you can do."

An uneasy silence filled the car. Fager stared straight ahead as he drove. Bronkowski rolled down the window to let cold air wash his face.

Fager said, "Call Goff tonight."

ELEVEN

THE NEW MEXICO LAW Enforcement Academy requires female candidates to meet half the physical strength requirements for men. Aragon hated that. As if the critters coming at you were going to weigh half as much, or try half as hard to kill you. Fifteen pushups in sixty seconds is what the state wanted of women. On her first test as a cadet she was at fifty-one when the instructor ordered her to stop.

Next time, before class started, when she couldn't be accused of disrupting the lesson plan, she dropped and did an even hundred.

The apprehension test had been her favorite. Candidates started from a standing position wearing a ten-pound belt to simulate a fully equipped gun holster. At the whistle they dashed thirty feet, jumped across a four-foot barrier, ran twelve-point-five feet, hurdled a three-foot-high and four-foot-wide barrier. Then pushed a police car thirty feet to where a victim extraction took place, the victim being a one-hundred-ninety-pound dummy strapped inside the car. The candidate had to release the dummy from its seatbelt and drag it twenty feet across the finish line. All in forty-two seconds or less.

Fun.

Aragon showed off by carrying the dummy on her back and finishing five steps ahead of the first man.

At Brazos Gym, an old-school weight room, no juice bar or Body Flow classes, York barbells without any plastic or rubber, this was upper body day, with triceps thrown in. Aragon and Lewis drove from home to SFPD's main office, switched into their assigned car and arrived in time for a 6:00 a.m. start. The place was already busy and smelling of sweat. After moving through separate routines they convened at the weight bench. Aragon was up to benching one-hundred-eighty pounds in three sets of fifteen reps. She did the last set with hands inches apart, using the strength in her wrists and forearms to hold the bar steady. Lewis spotted, but knew she wouldn't need him.

Then came her turn to spot for Lewis. He went heavy and forgot about high reps. She helped him put three hundred and fifty pounds on a bar weighing forty-five pounds. These lifts would be his personal best.

Lewis had just enough air in his chest to get the bar back onto the rack.

"I'm fried. Let's do our real job."

They showered in their respective locker rooms. Aragon was out first and checked text messages. Her brother Javier wanted her to join his family on a mule ride in the mountains. He was always trying to get her out of Santa Fe. Rivera wanted them early to brainstorm on Cynthia Fremont, off the record, away from the ears of competing agencies. She appreciated the show of respect.

"Lotaburger?" she asked Lewis when he joined her.

"What, to cancel out the last hour?"

Lewis drove them to Whole Foods. Aragon waited in the car and read his notes on Tasha Gonzalez. He returned with smoked salmon bagels, fruit salad, and French Roast coffee. Aragon tucked his notes under her leg. She pulled the plastic tub with the fruit salad from her bag and turned it around in the sunlight slanting through the windshield.

"I like fruit better after an animal's turned it into red meat and gotten rid of the parts it can't use."

"You think a taco salad is actually a salad."

"I get salad every day. The onion, lettuce, and tomato on my Lotaburger. Green chile for vitamin C. Makes a complete meal."

"You're one of those people who puts Lotaburger in restaurant reviews on Urban Spoon."

"Four stars. You can get fruit if you want. A slice of lemon in the iced tea."

They unfolded the wrappers around their bagels.

"Jesus," Aragon said with her first bite. "Who eats fish for breakfast?"

She threw the sandwich out the window and dug a MaxMuscle protein bar from her gym bag. She snapped off half in one bite and chased it with coffee. She gobbled the rest and dug under sweaty socks for a second. Maybe she still had some of her brother's elk jerky in there, too.

"Top of the first page you wrote 'Ladron,'" Aragon said, bringing his notes on Tasha Gonzales from under her thigh.

Lewis stretched it out, rolled the "*r*," gave it his best Spanish accent. "*Lah-drrroanuh*. Ladron Peak. Off by itself on the way to Socorro. It means robber."

"Senorita Aragon knows what *ladron* means. Tasha Gonzalez wasn't found anywhere near there."

"It's where Geronimo once had a big ranch. Before bankruptcy. Tasha Gonzalez was found between here and there."

Aragon dragged a flat palm across her buzz cut, stopped with her finger pointing up, getting what Lewis left unsaid. "You're thinking he killed her on the ranch and dumped her on his way back to Santa Fe?"

"Not thinking anything. Just gathering data."

"I still want to find that bar where Geronimo went after killing Linda Fager. I hit three places last night. Three strikes. Lots of bars within a mile of that bookstore. I'll try another three tonight in the opposite direction. If we had an open file, with us leading the investigation, and ten other detectives assisting, we'd have it by now."

They weren't far from the FBI offices. Lewis drove east on St. Francis almost to the interstate, then turned into one of the business parks ringing Santa Fe. The FBI occupied a territorial-style building appearing more like a Spanish colonial hacienda than federal office complex. It even had gabled windows and a corrugated tin roof.

In his text Rivera said to come to the basement. This would be the first interagency meeting since Cynthia Fremont was discovered in the trunk two nights ago. They found a large, cold room with a conference table and file cabinets still on hand trucks. A nylon tent had been set up at the far end, along with a compact gas stove, aluminum pots, plastic water bottles, and a collapsible stool near the unzipped door. The Cynthia Fremont camp, dismantled, transported, reconstructed. Spread on a conference table Aragon saw something that flew from many Santa Fe homes, a string of pastel prayer flags.

One wall was covered with photographs of the camp as it had appeared next to the lake. Other photos showed Fremont in the trunk and the Volvo from different angles. A map of the Santa Fe National Forest had been tacked to the wall. Red string connected pins on the map.

String tied to a pin very close to the campsite location ran to photos of a rocky ledge high above the lake. Four poles had been erected around a flat rock. The prayer flags on the table had flown between those poles. Close-ups showed dried blood caught in cracks and depressions in the rock.

Rivera entered the war room carrying a pot of coffee and a stack of Styrofoam cups. His black hair and high forehead made Aragon think again of Miguel. When he smiled she saw a boy who never had the chance to grow into a handsome man.

Rivera said, "You got the lake right. Saved us days of searching. Maybe you'll nail something else."

Lewis and Aragon helped themselves to coffee.

"What did you find inside the sleeping bag?" Aragon asked.

Rivera tapped a stack of photos. They showed a young woman's pale, naked body, with lacerations down the top of each thigh. A deep cut into the right quadriceps. The wavering line of a superficial laceration crossed her abdomen. Close-ups of her wrists showed lengthwise incisions following the direction of blood vessels exposed in the wound tracts.

"Do you have a tox screen yet?" Lewis asked.

Rivera answered without consulting anything. "THC, alcohol, and extremely high levels of acetaminophen and acetylsalicylate. Almost enough to knock her out."

"The second one," Lewis followed up. "Acetyl..."

"Aspirin. Also semen in anus and vagina, deposited within twelve hours of death."

"They could have dumped her up in the mountains," Lewis said. "There wouldn't be much left after a few weeks. But they carried her miles to the car, with their autograph inside her. Is that careless, or arrogant?"

Aragon turned back to the photos. Small wounds were scattered randomly around the body.

"Birds," she said. "She was laying out naked."

"The ravens that told us where to find the murder site," Rivera said.

"Her lips were gone, but she had her eyes. I wonder if she wore glasses."

"We found a pair of Oakleys on the rocks where she died. The kind that wrap around the sides."

Aragon now understood the goggles of pale skin above Fremont's sunburned cheeks.

Lewis had moved over to the campsite reenactment. Inside the tent was an inflatable backpacking mattress, and a lot of space.

"This is a four-man tent, at least."

Aragon remembered the empty packaging for a water filter she had seen in the trunk. She did not see a water filter in the equipment laid out next to the tent.

Rivera asked, "Any thoughts on the sleeping bag, in the trunk with her inside?"

Lewis said, "Maybe they carried her in the bag in case someone came along. A body lying by the trail, that's hard to explain. With the bag they could put her down quickly, lean back, taking a break. Or maybe it was just easier to carry her that way, arms and legs tucked inside."

"We're checking cars parked overnight. The ranger snaps photos of license plates before he heads home."

"They moved her at night. Coming out of the woods carrying a dead girl, inside a sleeping bag or not, picnickers would notice something like that."

"They didn't want animals eating any more of her," Aragon said, still thinking about the ravens who had gotten a start on Fremont's corpse. "The trunk was like a bear locker you find at campgrounds. Animal-proof. Any other place in the mountains, she'd be food."

"So they changed the plan after letting the birds have at her?" Rivera asked. "They went to a lot of trouble to preserve evidence for us to find."

"The sunglasses," Aragon said, "Did the killers not want to see her eyes? People who do this to women want to see the fear, see the light go out."

Lewis said, "Cody Geronimo on Linda Fager: 'She looked at me.'"

"Your celebrity killer," Rivera said.

"Not officially ours anymore." Aragon saw Rivera's confusion. "We'll explain later. Back to those boots. Did they strip her, put on the boots, before forcing her to climb the mountain? They sliced her up but worried about her feet? I'm not seeing something."

Rivera said, "The lab's on that, who tied the laces."

"You really have shoelace experts?" Lewis asked.

"Really, yes."

"I think you were right," Aragon told her partner, "about how she was laid out in the trunk, with the tire for a pillow. Somebody cared about her. In a bizarre way. But they cared."

Rivera nodded. "Agreed, as a working hypothesis."

There he was again, tossing off another word she didn't hear Santa Fe cops use.

"A theory good enough for now," Aragon said. "Any food in the tent?"

"Empty bags for freeze-dried provisions you can buy at REI," Rivera answered. "Cans that held corn and beans. Empty Clif Bar wrappers."

"How many, the wrappers?"

Rivera checked a sheet of paper.

"Three."

"There was an empty Clif bars box in the trunk." She couldn't remember how many in a box. A lot more than three. "They went back into the wilderness. They took a water filter and the rest of the food. And their own gear. It's just Fremont got left behind."

A pair of backpackers could be emerging right now, tomorrow, any time, out of the woods fifty miles from where they left Fremont. Walking into Santa Fe down one of the drainages, or moving east toward Pecos or Las Vegas. They could hike north into Colorado. There was no way to seal off several hundred thousand acres of wild country.

They were interrupted by more than a dozen men and women in uniforms of state and federal agencies. Chairs were brought in. Rivera convened the meeting. He made brief introductions, announced the FBI would take lead. The murder scene and the body's resting place were on federal land. Nobody objected, especially when Rivera described the resources he could bring to bear. He didn't even have to mention shoelace experts.

Rivera turned to an agent named Barone who launched into forensics. Cause of death: blood loss, inducing circulatory collapse and cardiac arrest. Weapon: extremely sharp, large, thick blade. "A hunting knife, maybe," he said. "Something heavy but without a serrated edge."

Barone held up an enlarged photograph of Fremont's midsection.

"We believe it started with a superficial incision, left to right across her abdomen." He held up another photo, Fremont's right thigh. "Here the cutting began in earnest. This wound track shows repeated slashing, expanding the cavity, butchering muscle. There is only a single slash on the left leg."

Rivera spoke. "At some point she might have passed out. That possibly explains why there's no evidence of a struggle. The lacerations on the thighs are fairly straight. They were antemortem."

"She was restrained," Barone said, "after sedation with sizable doses of painkillers and alcohol. There's bruising on her collarbone consistent with strong hands gripping her very tightly. The wrists." He raised another photo. "The incision targeted the radial artery. Excuse me, arteries. They succeeded on both wrists. Death came slowly."

81

"I've got questions."

The room turned to Aragon. Barone nodded for her to speak.

"One, was there other evidence of scarring on Fremont's arms? Two, how cold was it up there? Three, do we have the knife?"

Barone said, "No other scarring. We haven't found a knife. And the temps for the previous week swung wildly. Almost single digits at night, up to sixty during the day. Warmer in the sun. I presume you're wondering how that impacts determining time of death?"

Aragon caught motion from the corner of her eye. Two women in robes had entered the back of the room. One was robed in black, the other in orange. Their hair was cut as close to the scalp as Aragon's.

Aragon turned back to Barone. "More like how long it took her to die." She nodded toward Lewis. "We've seen I don't know how many suicide attempts where a slashed wrist clots up or the artery collapses before blood loss goes fatal. Cold weather slows blood flow, muscles constrict. Less chance a slashed wrist means death."

Barone studied her, then answered. "Death by cutting the radial artery is rare, but not impossible. Here we have both arteries sliced lengthwise. Somebody knew what they were doing. That made closure significantly more unlikely and, in fact, resulted in eventual death. As for ambient temperature, yes, we don't have a Roman in a hot tub—"

Rivera cut him off.

"Let me introduce Roshi Larson from the Koyasan Buddhist Temple. I promised not to take much of her time."

The woman in the black robe looked familiar. Aragon had done a few cases involving Santa Fe's Buddhist community. When word hit the street they did not report property crimes, Buddhist temples and meditation centers drew burglars like metal filings to a magnet. SFPD at least persuaded a temple representative to identify items recovered from a stolen property operation at the Flea Market, though the Buddhists refused return of anything that had been theirs. Aragon wondered if she had met the woman in the black robe back then.

"Roshi Larson has graciously agreed to interpret the prayer flags found above the lake," Rivera said.

The woman approached the table where the flags had been laid out. She examined them then faced Rivera.

"This is not Tibetan. I doubt it's Asian at all."

Aragon recognized the voice but couldn't place it.

Rivera's face showed disappointment. "I'm sorry to take your time for no reason."

"Nothing is without meaning. You have now learned these are unusual prayer flags."

Rivera thanked her and nodded for Barone to resume. Aragon noticed the Roshi's assistant staring at photographs on the wall. Roshi Larson joined her and also stared. She had worn a pleasant expression to that point. Something dark crossed her face and she ushered her assistant out of the room.

Aragon listened to Barone as she rose to inspect the photos that had held the women's attention. She slipped out after the Buddhists and caught up to them in the parking lot.

Aragon was surprised to see the Roshi unlocking a white Audi roadster with red leather seats and chrome wheels. She'd been expecting something more along the lines of a VW bus, or a wagon so old it said Datsun.

Something about the way sunlight played on her face tickled Aragon's memory.

"Buff?"

The Roshi turned. Her eyes met Aragon's and widened.

"Jeep?"

Aragon grinned. "Nobody's called me that in years."

"Last time I heard Buff was eighth grade."

The old friends clasped hands and leaned back to study each other. Their eyes traveled to their heads and they broke out in laughter.

"You had beautiful black hair," said Roshi Buff.

"I don't want anybody grabbing it in a fight."

"We sure have traveled different paths since De Vargas Middle School. Miguel's death started me on Buddhism. Well, my parents sending me away from here did it. But I've never forgotten him, and how you were hurt."

"Thanks for remembering."

"You took another path, straight at the pain. You always were brave. Like taking your brother's Jeep four-wheeling in the mountains. That was a truly great day. How old were we?"

"Twelve. I needed your help with the shifter."

"How's Javier?"

"Won't come into Santa Fe. He sticks to the woods. He still has that Jeep."

"He has established his own monastery."

"I wouldn't call a double-wide with two gun lockers and dead animals on the walls a monastery. He'll get a kick out of what you said. Listen, Buff. I mean Roshi. I want to catch up, but I need to ask something else."

"Buff's fine."

"I saw you and your friend staring at photographs back there. They seemed to upset you. Can you tell me what you saw?"

The Roshi's calm, joyful smile disappeared. "Who was buried there?"

Was buried? The photographs did not show an excavated grave.

"Why do you put it that way?

"The deceased ascends from there. It was the site of a celestial burial. Everything matched what I've seen in Tibet except for the writing on the prayer flags. Someone has taken a ceremony of the most profound generosity and turned it into a ritual of evil."

"Tell me."

Fifteen minutes later Aragon brought Roshi Larson into the meeting room.

"Something you need to hear," Aragon told Rivera, then turned to the Buddhist priestess to explain about birds as undertakers.

TWELVE

Lewis talked as they climbed stairs to their office. Aragon went first, taking them two at a time, holding up for him at the landings.

"Celestial burial, the deceased giving their body to feed life in the sky. New Agey," he said. "Very Santa Fe."

"Worms go in, worms go out. Same difference. Nothing groovy about it, you don't make up fairy tales about what's really going on."

"Tibetans with butcher knives—I guess you'd call them morticians—chop up the body and toss pieces to condors and vultures? Come on. That's different."

They reached their floor, pushed through fire doors and entered the hall to their office.

"Showing up in bird shit," she said. "What a way to go."

"Detective Aragon, you need some solid sensitivity training, get your mind right, this hostility towards other cultures. Bird shit to you. Enlightenment to someone else."

Her comeback, telling him to suck a crystal and take a flying leap at a power vortex, never made it to words.

Joe Donnelly from Professional Standards was rifling a drawer in her desk. He had handled the investigation that almost drove her off the force ten years ago. He had dug deeper into her life than her bullet had traveled into the Lokos enforcer whose lawyer filed the complaint. When Donnelly was short on evidence, he tried to provoke her into making mistakes so he could riff off them and loop back into the excessive force charge. Only at the very end, when he had exhausted every false trail and run out of low-rent tricks did Donnelly morph from black-hooded persecutor to impartial judge.

Aragon wondered which Donnelly had showed up today.

"Glad to see you've started your investigation of Dewey Nobles' interference in the Geronimo case," she said. "You won't find what you need in that drawer."

Donnelly closed the drawer with his foot. He used the phone on her desk, dialed, spoke. "They're here."

Aragon had an idea who he had just called. But she had Donnelly's ear until that person arrived.

"We have a brutally murdered woman, the killer observed fleeing the scene, two officers overhearing him detail his crime. He left evidence under the body, and in his pocket he had tiny bones from the victim's head. And Dewey let him go."

"You don't know what those bones were," Donnelly said. "Could have been chicken bones."

Aragon pried a pencil from her desk organizer and rolled it across the blotter at him.

"Draw the incus."

"What, like Machu Picchu?"

"In-cus. That stumps you, I'll settle for stapes and malleus. Or the cochlea. Hint: a snail."

"What's she talking about Lewis?"

Lewis said, "We all thought they were bird bones. Until OMI found them missing. Then we put it together. Geronimo had bones from Linda Fager's inner ear."

Aragon pointed a finger at Donnelly. "What can we do to assist your investigation of gross misconduct that turned loose a killer who'll probably kill again?"

"Knock it off," Donnelly said. "Judge Diaz delivered a formal complaint to the Mayor. Shit rolls downhill. Nobles is on his way to suspend you while we feed the judge a tranquilizer. You didn't help yourself last night."

"What?" She took her chair to move Donnelly away from her desk.

"You checked in evidence after you had been taken off the Geronimo case."

"It was biological material that would degrade. You wanted it hauled to the dump?"

"Showing off, playing the tape for everyone to hear, was a really stupid move," Donnelly said, looking down at her in her chair. "Celebrating before you cross the finish line is never a good idea. Any dumbass who watches TV knows two sacred rules of criminal procedure cops can never, ever break: Miranda and attorney-client privilege."

"I don't watch TV."

"Well, now you can start. You'll have plenty of free time." Dewey Nobles stood in the doorway. Aragon smelled his aftershave across the room. Christ. Clove and cinnamon shit. Salt and pepper hair, thick with gel. Skin tightened from his last bad investment in plastic surgery made him look like he was squinting into the sun. He stepped forward, the only guy in the building who wore wingtips, and dropped two envelopes on her desk. "Lieutenant Donnelly will contact you about a formal interview. Starting now, you're both suspended. Be glad it's with pay."

Lewis swept the envelopes into his hand. "We're not saying anything until formal notification of the Professional Standards charge and we have union representation."

"Sounds like something you heard watching TV," Nobles said.

"I only watch *SpongeBob SquarePants*. You remind me of Plankton."

Nobles squinted harder at Lewis. "Well, you can now enjoy cartoons all day. I thought a family had made you just a little smarter. But only hours after I took you off the case, you're leaning on OMI to prioritize the Fager autopsy." He turned to Donnelly. "We need to maintain good relations with Judge Diaz. I expect your best with these two."

"Good relations for what?" Aragon said. "Why kiss ass if it won't get us someone like Geronimo?"

"Denise," Donnelly said. "The suspension's with pay. Don't push it."

He had only used her first name when he came around to her side at the end of his first investigation. It made her wonder again which Donnelly was in her office this morning.

"Detective Aragon," Nobles said, lifting his chin, "Cody Geronimo is on the street not because of what my job requires of me. All you know is frontal assault. Scorched earth, nothing left standing when you're in action. That style of police work does not produce desirable results in Santa Fe, New Mexico."

Nobles left. Aragon wished he had taken his aftershave with him.

"Stay away from Geronimo." Donnelly looked back and forth between the detectives.

"It's not us you should be investigating," Aragon said, not letting it go.

"Denise." Donnelly opened his hands and tamped down air. "Just pack up and get out of here." He lingered in the door to point his finger at her before he left.

Lewis hunched his shoulders and let them drop. He reached for the phone.

"I better let my wife know."

Aragon eyed her partner. The Glock 19 high on his hip in a black leather holster, a sap inside his belt. The bulge of the five-shot revolver on his ankle. The shirt stretched across his powerful back.

"Yo, Lewis. *SpongeBob?*"

––––––––––

Lewis called his wife, Sandy, with the news. She told him he'd be getting a text of the shopping he could do with his suddenly free time. Aragon had not said a word since Donnelly left.

"How about joining us for dinner?" Lewis offered to get her talking. "You can relax. Get your mind off the job."

"Cartoons and plates on our laps?"

"We eat at the table."

"Glad we moved the Geronimo files to the car," she said as she inspected her desk to see if Donnelly had taken anything. Then she read the notice of suspension. "I'm going to make the Honorable Judy A. Diaz a project. She goes on my to-do list."

"Now as long as your arm."

Lewis's cell chirped. His wife's text. He texted back to inquire if the soy milk should be nonfat and unflavored and where was he supposed to find something called Ezekiel bread. He and his wife went back and forth finalizing the shopping list as he watched Aragon unlocking the big drawer in her steel desk. She removed the black plastic case for her pistol and a stack of ammo boxes. She got busy loading extra magazines.

"I take it you won't be joining us?" Lewis asked between negotiations with his wife.

Aragon didn't answer until she had five loaded magazines on her blotter.

"Thanks for the offer. But talking sponges don't do it for me."

THIRTEEN

THE GUN FELT RIGHT. She loved the sound of jacketed lead pinging off the target twenty-five yards down range. She loved even more each tear in the photo of Dewey Nobles taped over the steel disc held steady in her sights.

Jimmy Arenas stood behind her with a spotting scope, grunting as each shot rang against the target. He ran the Law Enforcement Academy's shooting range, partial retirement from his career as firearms instructor. She had wanted the end of the firing line, preferably three stations from the next person. He always put her dead center. He stuck to his routine again today, with one exception. When she told him about the suspension he slipped Nobles' photo out of its frame on the wall for former members of the Academy's staff and taped it to a steel disc.

Arenas checked his watch and called cease-fire. The line quieted. He announced they were free to check targets. Aragon kept her place. Arenas would have let her know if she had missed.

She ejected the empty clip and laid out the five magazines she'd loaded at the office.

On her left a young cop wearing an Albuquerque Police Department uniform rested a Glock on his table. To her right, a guy bigger than Lewis from the State Police tactical unit opened a box of .45s. Farther down the line she saw AR-15s and a shotgun mixed in with semi-auto side arms. She saw only one revolver, a Ruger Blackhawk, in the hands of a man whose active duty was decades in the past.

"The range is hot and live. You are cleared to fire."

The metallic chime of bullets striking her steel disc rang above the staccato of pistol shots and the boom of the shotgun. She squeezed off the remaining cartridges in the Springfield's magazine without a miss. Each hit came with the exclamation point of metal striking metal. She ejected the spent clip combat style, letting it fall to the ground and slammed another home. Next to her the young APD cop fired as fast as his finger could jerk the trigger. His gun bounced with the front sight rarely reacquiring the target set at a mere ten yards. The State Police SWAT officer fired patiently, sighting down the four-inch barrel of his Colt, trying to maintain the tight group that admitted sunlight through the center of his target. Down the line, the shotgun exploded.

She slapped in another clip and fired off double taps.

Starting into her last clip she noticed that the range had gone silent. She worried she'd missed the cease-fire order. She looked left and right. The line was empty except for the two guys on either side. They were watching her. Keeping her weapon pointed down range, she turned her head. The rest of the men had gathered a few yards behind her.

"You got nine more in that clip," Arenas said.

She showed the kid from Albuquerque how fast the Springfield could fire without bouncing around. The metallic target never stopped reverberating. When she was done she removed her ear protection and faced her audience. Arenas was smiling and spinning an empty picture frame on his index finger.

"Dang," someone said. "Ninety-six shots without a miss."

"Ninety-seven," Arenas said. "She started with one in the pipe."

"How's she do it?"

Arenas glassed Aragon's target. The Dewey Nobles photograph had disintegrated.

"Motivation."

———————

She drove to her efficiency apartment on the city's west side and brought dirty clothes downstairs to the laundry in the basement. Her .40 holstered on her hip, she separated colors and whites, watching a Holly Holm fight on her phone. Holm went almost a full five rounds at the Route 66 Casino before a TKO gave her the win over a bloodied Juliana Werner. Somewhere in the fight Holm's left ulna snapped in two. Aragon had watched the video a dozen times, trying to see where Holm protected the arm. At the end she's pummeling Werner with both hands. The ref raises her right glove in victory. A second later there's Holm, pumping her left fist in the air.

While her clothes dried, she cleaned her weapon and defrosted some of the green-chile stew Javier's wife, Serena, had sent home with her last time she visited their home in the mountains. The stew lit her up, but then she felt empty and ragged. The calm from blasting Dewey's face was a fraud. She needed to be working her cases.

Aragon drove to Fager's Finds and parked in the back alley. She imagined Geronimo opening the door to dump the paper towels he had used to wipe off Linda Fager's blood. He had stood here, naked in the moonlight. She could still feel the Springfield alive and fierce in her hand, spitting fire a couple hours ago at the range. She sighted with her finger and cocked her thumb.

She drove around the front and parked, retracing her steps upon arriving at the scene. She couldn't see where she had gone wrong. They had done it by the book. Even the rookie cops had toed the line and held puke in their cheeks until they rushed outside. She grilled herself about the chase and remained convinced she had sufficient reason to pursue Geronimo from the second the key fob found under Linda Fager's body triggered the Range Rover's alarm.

She mentally rewound the recording of him speaking from inside the hedge. His voice could be plainly heard on the sidewalk. Up until he said the name "Marcy," she had no clue about the identity of the person on the other end of the call. Even then, it was only a first name and the DA could argue insufficient notice that he was consulting his attorney. She supposed she could research how many Marcys lived in the Santa Fe area to reinforce the argument.

She remembered something Mascarenas frequently muttered after getting slammed by one of Santa Fe's judges. An ounce of the judge is worth a pound of the law, he'd say. In this case, the good guys had the law on their side. They had a ton of evidence. But Thornton had every ounce of Judge Diaz.

Her stomach ached. Breakfast and lunch were gone, vaporized by anger and stress. She felt as thin as cellophane. She drove out to the Cerrillos strip and swung into a Blake's for a Lotaburger and fries. With the paper bag warm on her lap, she drove to Killer Park. She needed a place to work through an idea that had come to her at the range, when her mind was calm.

She was surprised to find Lewis in his Chrysler minivan eating an apple and reading a file. She drove past and turned around to park. He waved for her to come to him.

"Your phone is off. I knew I could find you here," he said when she slipped into the passenger seat.

"I thought you would be deep into your honey-do list."

He jerked a thumb at shopping bags in the back.

"I'm standing in check-out at Costco, screaming kids, old people not starting to write their check until all their bags are filled, you know? Instead of worrying whether I've got the right soy milk, all I could think about was Tasha Gonzalez."

She unwrapped her burger.

"I've been thinking about her, too."

"Damn, that smells good."

"Have some fries. They won't kill you."

Lewis alternated bites of apple with fries as Aragon tore chunks from her burger.

Lewis said, "Senior officer first."

"So Thornton has a lock on the judge," she said with a mouthful of beef. "We've got Fager flying wing. I think he'll keep things stirred up. If we can get another agency to take up Tasha Gonzalez, focus on Cody Geronimo, we've found a route around Thornton's roadblocks."

"Tasha was found outside Belen. Valencia County Sheriff's jurisdiction. Not Keystone Cops, but not the Untouchables, either."

"Imagine the Feds jumping in. I'm liking what I see in Rivera."

"He's liking what he sees in you."

She blinked. That caught her off guard. "We find a federal connection," she said, regaining her train of thought. "Maybe a hook to federal land like with Cynthia Fremont."

"That place out by Ladron Peak. The one asset Geronimo has tried to keep whenever his finances tanked. It's mostly leased federal land with scattered private inholdings."

"Super Dad strikes again." She gave Lewis's shoulder a friendly punch. "Show me."

She wiped greasy fingers on her thighs and took up the map on the console.

"Private inholdings are colored orange. The rest is public," Lewis said. "I think these parcels go with the ranch." He pointed out orange rectangles. "No roads. You'd need a four-wheel drive."

"Like a Range Rover."

They peered more closely at the map.

"I just figured out what I'm doing with my suspension," Aragon said. "I was going to check every bar in Santa Fe until I found where Geronimo drank beer after killing Linda Fager." A smile spread across her face. "Instead, I'm going hunting."

"The season's not open yet. Or it just closed."

"Always open season on varmints. No bag limit, no restrictions. Any kind of ammo, any weapon is legal."

"Do I want to know what you're talking about? Don't answer."

FOURTEEN

WHAT'S HE GOING TO be like without Linda?

Fager heard his secretary outside his door talking to the only other employee of Walter Fager and Associates, P.C. His associate lawyer, Kate Morrow, and Roberta Weldon thinking he didn't hear everything that went on in his law office.

Weldon: Linda made him human.

Morrow: A work in progress, never to be completed.

Weldon: Now I have to go in and give him a message about Linda's body. And something else he's going to hate.

Morrow: Tell him to go home. He doesn't need to sign motions for postponement. We know his scrawl.

Weldon: I don't think he's eaten in two days. Since Linda, he's living on coffee and hatred.

Morrow: What else is new?

Since Linda.

Since Linda, he'd been glued to a computer screen, using up printer cartridges. He finished the one in the printer in his home office as light through the curtains told him it was morning. Dumped everything in an empty box for printer paper, e-mailed research to himself, and came down to his law office, the first one there in the morning, hours before anyone else, turning on lights to make coffee, not bothering to turn up the heat before he got back to work and closed his door on the rest of building, still dark and cold.

He heard a knock, then the creak of hinges, a footstep on the old plank floor.

"OMI called," Roberta Weldon said to his back. "They're ready to release Linda for burial."

"Call that Italian place, Berar-something."

"Berardinelli."

"I want a cremation. As soon as they can. A small service in their chapel. Nothing elaborate. We can play some of her music."

He focused on his computer screen. He was reading an interview in *San Francisco Arts Monthly*, Geronimo on how his use of found objects reflects the story of the American Indian. How the way he obtained supplies isn't scavenging, but a twenty-first-century version of hunting-gathering. Some of his work used what others discarded or overlooked. Or he accepted what nature had to offer, from polished stones in a stream bed to dried cactus—so many textures and forms that he could never exhaust the resource. His more serious work engaged the hunting side of traditional Native cultures, harvesting what he needed to add vital spirit and individual voice, the way a shaman would hunt eagles for feathers. But it was too hard to get eagle feathers these days. You had to be a tribe working within limits set by the federal government. To infuse his work with similar power he had to be creative, resourceful, "tapping into the ancient knowledge that helped my people survive in the harsh Southwest desert. I express their struggle and spirituality in art that speaks to us in this modern world, in a contemporary idiom."

"There's something else," Roberta said.

Fager had forgotten she was in the room.

"What else?" Impatience in his voice. He needed to read this. He turned to face her, get it over with.

She held an obsolete appointment book from a time when the office ran on paper.

"Cody Geronimo called here."

He came out of his chair, his legs stiff from sitting so long.

"When?"

"February 4, 2004. He called for an appointment. I sent him through to Marcy. She handled intake then."

"This office has never represented Cody Geronimo. That date again?"

She repeated the date of Geronimo's call, her face telling him it meant something more.

"Marcy left the firm that month," he said, understanding the expression on her face. "Went out on her own. And she's never looked back."

Through his window he could see the mansion Thornton used as her law office. The high-gloss hood of her red Aston-Martin threw sunlight into his eyes.

————

Marcy Thornton hurled the New Mexico Criminal Code against the wall.

"The autopsy's completed? I wanted this slow-walked, forgotten. I wanted Linda Fager to be that hamburger in the bottom of a freezer nobody remembers."

"I thought you liked her," Lily Montclaire said. "Weren't you friends?"

"I have a client. What else do you need to know?"

Montclaire picked up the heavy legal tome and replaced it on Thornton's desk.

"It was Aragon and her partner. They got someone in OMI to move Linda Fager to the top of the list."

Thornton fell back in the oversized chair behind her mahogany desk. Montclaire kicked off her pumps and stretched out on the leather sofa.

"When's Cody returning from New York?" Montclaire asked as her eyes fell on a sock under the coffee table. The boy she had picked up at the mall for Thornton's office party had been given a wad of cash and hustled out when Geronimo called in a panic. Blue eyes, narrow hips, smooth, almost hairless legs. She wondered if he shaved or was just that young. She could see the starburst tattoo around his navel but his name escaped her.

"He's with some filthy rich collector," Thornton said. "Said he'd be gone a couple days."

"Can we reach him by fax? I want to send him that drawing of the bar."

"Why didn't you photograph it, send it to his phone? A fax? You're wasting time."

Montclaire wanted to tell Thornton a photo wouldn't have done the job, you couldn't get the whole bar in one shot, all the tables, the doors. She had done it right her way. But she said, "Give me his e-mail. I'll scan it and send an attachment."

Thornton exhaled. "And Fager's in motion. Cody said he was at his gallery for the opening of his new show."

Montclaire wasn't interested in Fager or Cody's new works. At that moment, her mind drifted across town, back to the two men she had taken to a room at the Eldorado to make up for the interrupted party with the hairless boy from the mall. Instead of a slow night for them watching a game in a bar, a woman who had once been in *Cosmo* had taken them to a fancy hotel. The *Cosmo* job had been a photo to go with a short article about getting ready for summer. She was riding a classic fat tire bike along a beach, flowers and shells in the basket on the handle bars, a sheer beach robe over a bikini. Barefoot, toenails painted ten different colors. It had been hard as hell to pedal in the sand.

"Fager was there with a big slob pretending to be a dude from Malibu," Thornton was saying, pulling Montclaire out of her thoughts. "Wanted paintings to hang over his couch. Leather vest, about three hundred pounds, biker's boots. Uncomfortable in a starched shirt. Something-ski, Cody said. Something Polish. We know who that is."

Montclaire sat up, interested, her mind back on the job.

Thornton said, "Get Cody to identify the table at the bar where he was sitting before Bronkowski finds it. Or Aragon." She reached for the criminal code. "After I finish this brief, I'll work on getting Walter off our tail. You watch, he's going to pull some patented Fager street-fighting move. But we're killer drones, high in the sky where he can't see us, where he won't even look, waiting for a clear shot to put him down."

"Sometimes I worry about you."

"You love it. Speaking of which, you free tonight?"

"Depends." She was thinking of trolling the mall to find the boy with the starburst tattoo, kicking herself for not getting his number, not writing down his name.

"Judge Diaz wants me at eight."

"Kind of late."

Thornton let a smile spread across her face. "At her house. Bench-bar relations working group. Tonight's agenda: whatever the Chief Judge wants."

Montclaire bit her lip and thought it over. Judy Diaz was older than Marcy, doing something else before law school. Not the kind of woman she would lock on when other choices were available. But Diaz had a good figure under that robe.

She'd done judges, of a different sort. It was how she got her start modeling, throwing something at the men and women whose ribbons determined whether she would be wearing bras and panties in a warm studio, or outside, freezing on a winter shoot while the photographer flipped out because his cocoa was gloppy. But it was *hot,* while the girls were told to chew ice so you couldn't see their breath in the air.

She let Thornton know she was interested. "Will this be one of those forbidden ex parte conferences?" she asked, a playful tone in her voice.

"Party, yes." Thornton winked. "X, you bet. We'll be conferring about trying something new. Our Judge Judy likes what she knows. But she's open to creative interpretations of existing precedent."

FIFTEEN

Bronkowski saw Lewis's name on the sign-out sheet at the clerk's desk when he asked for the Geronimo bankruptcy files. Lewis was a good cop. He had handled Fager's cross-examination in the Gallardo trial a couple years back because he did his homework. Lewis was doing his homework on Cody Geronimo.

Bronkowski signed for files Lewis had just returned and took a seat at a table among paralegals he recognized from the big firms in town. Bankruptcy law was the world of the insane to him. He never understood how debts of hard money could vaporize like morning mist hit by the sun. He opened the stiff folders and found the creditor claims and asset lists. A two-hour review of that basic information told a story he could understand.

Fager was right. A lot of money going into Geronimo's businesses was disappearing. Geronimo had lost second homes to creditors, and held onto his principal residence only by giving Thornton a first mortgage. Several investment properties were obvious tax shelters. He relinquished them without a fight. The files showed

Geronimo struggling to retain ranch land in Valencia County. Eventually he accepted the surrender of the property to a white knight corporation with a string of letters for a name: SCR, LLC.

Bronkowski used his iPad to access data at the Public Regulation Commission. He did not recognize any of the corporation's directors. The designated agent for service of process was a woman unfamiliar to him, though he thought he knew all the shops that provided this service in Santa Fe. But the address stood out. It was next to Fager's law office. Thornton's office was the only other building on that block.

Two possibilities spoke to him from the court files. Thornton was shielding Geronimo's assets, putting herself between him and his creditors, playing straw man for a fee. Or she was cleaning him out.

He made a note to get a map of the ranch land and check tax and utility records. He returned the file to the clerk and went outside to his Harley parked at a meter under elm trees surrounding the old courthouse.

Fager had given him a long list of assignments, and he had come up with as many inquiries on his own. Two items moved to the top of his list. He sensed the Tasha Gonzalez case might hold secrets worth exploring. And he wanted to determine what Geronimo did between leaving Linda's store and being run down by detectives Aragon and Lewis. Since the cops didn't know either, it was an area of possible leads not tainted by Aragon's breach of attorney-client privilege.

He called Goff and set a breakfast meeting for tomorrow. He wasn't looking forward to that. You could never trust Goff's work as a cop. They were supposed to trust him now?

At least Goff's file held an address for Tasha Gonzalez's family. Their last known address was a mobile-home park near the abandoned race track south of town. He swung by his house and switched to the Camry he used for fieldwork.

Enchanted Acres Estates sat on a barren mesa exposed to a steady wind. The ruins of the old race track were visible to the north. Cars and trucks moved in the distance along Interstate 25. This was a commuter satellite for hotel maids, gardeners, busboys, and burger flippers, deserted in the middle of the work day.

A woman in a red tank top answered the door matching the address for the Gonzalez family. A child clung to her leg as she leaned out. Bronkowski smelled boiling beans. A television blared Spanish voices. She spoke very little English. She repeated "*no conosco*" and "*lo siento, no se*." He understood enough to gather she had never heard of the Gonzalez family. She had been at this address for a year and didn't know who had lived in the tin can before her. She closed the door and left him on the stoop.

He tried four more single-wides before anyone answered. The thin Hispanic man who opened the door at the fifth reeked of beer and cigarettes and clothes that needed washing. On the hand holding the doorknob, age spots covered faded tattoos. Stained pant legs were worn thin over his bony thighs. The frayed cap on his head said, "The Chosin Few."

"Were you there? Chosin Reservoir," Bronkowski said.

"First Marines. You remember? No, you're not old enough."

"I know what you guys did. I was Army, the Balkans." He left it at that. He had his war stories. But nothing like what this man faced on that frozen Korean lake. "I'm looking for the family of Tasha Gonzalez."

"Come in. I hear better out of the wind."

The living room was a battered sofa with a television on a milk crate, aluminum foil wrapped around a rabbit-ear antenna. Bronkowski was glad to see it was off so they could talk. But he wondered what the old man had been doing before the knock at the door. No newspaper, magazines, or books he could see. No sign of other activity.

Maybe he had been napping. Maybe he had been thinking about Korea.

His name was Narciso Roybal. "Take a seat," he said.

Cigarette ashes spilled out of saucers on the floor. Empty fast-food bags covered a card table. Bronkowski saw nowhere to sit except next to the old man on sofa cushions leaking chunks of foam. He decided to ask his questions standing.

Yes, he had known the Gonzalez family, Roybal said. He remembered Tasha; she had been pretty but was getting fat. Then she disappeared. One night, two white vehicles, "those fancy Cadillac Suburbans," came for the family. Their place went up for sale the next day. That was ten years ago.

The old man's left hand lay lifeless in his lap, though the middle finger twitched as he spoke. He lit a cigarette and said, "Escalades, that's what they were. Not Suburbans. I had a Chevy once. I don't drive no more. Can't hardly see you except you're so big."

"What's wrong with your hand?"

"The damn thing don't work, that's what's wrong. But God gave me two. So I can't complain."

"Is anyone caring for you?"

"That boy down the street brings me something now and then. I think he's keeping most of my money for himself. Says gas is really expensive. Drives all the way into town for take-out. I told him bring me Dinty Moore or Campbell's. Not Taco Bell again, please. But I don't know."

Bronkowski nodded at a black dial telephone on the counter. "That work?"

"Better than my hand. My daughter calls from California. She's a teacher. Three kids. Smart enough to dump her no-good husband. Smart enough to get out of this place."

Bronkowski wrote the number for the VA outreach team on one of the fast food bags.

"They'll come to your home to help, if you want. The guy in charge was a jarhead like you. The next war after yours."

The old man took the piece of paper bag in his only good hand while the cigarette burned between his lips. It was hard to believe this frail, withered human being had been with the Marines when the Chinese poured out of the hills. He had seen some things.

"Thank you," Bronkowski said and let himself out.

He made one more stop before checking in with Fager. He swung by the assessor's office to see tax records for the mobile home where the Gonzalez family had lived. The annual bill was being sent to Thornton's law office. He needed to call Fager, share the ideas coming into his head.

———

"Maybe Marcy's cleaning out Geronimo by blackmailing him, stashing the Gonzalez family somewhere, reminding Geronimo every time she wants something, like an Aston-Martin or a big house above Santa Fe."

"Get in here," Fager said over the phone to Bronkowski, still at the Assessor's Office, but outside now where he could talk.

"You want me to bring food to the house? Burritos from Tomasita's? When's the last time you ate anything?"

"I'm at the office," Fager said and hung up.

Bronkowski drove across town and parked in the lot, next to Fager's Mercedes. He climbed the steps and entered the waiting area. Empty chairs, no prospective clients hoping to see a lawyer. He stopped to give Roberta Weldon a hug and heard about Fager telling her to make arrangements for Linda's funeral, like ordering up exhibits for trial or telling her to get out subpoenas. What will he be like without Linda? He didn't have an answer for her.

He stuck his head into Kate Morrow's office. She was on the telephone begging a prosecutor for more time to provide the defense's discovery. She blinked, her eyes tiny beads behind thick glasses, and waved. Bronkowski continued down the hall to Fager's office. He heard typing before he got there.

Fager was dressed in the same suit he had worn to the opening at Geronimo's gallery. Roberta had not been able to keep up with the empty coffee cups topping the room's furniture. Pages overflowed his printer tray.

"Robbie told me about the funeral. Anything I can do?" Bronkowski took the chair in front of Fager's desk.

"Barela's is handling everything," Fager said without turning around. He pounded out a paragraph then added, "I want it simple."

"Berardinelli."

"What?"

"Jesus. Don't you remember who's doing your wife's funeral? What the fuck is wrong with you?"

Fager stopped attacking his keyboard and spun in his chair.

"So I mixed up the name of the funeral director." He had not shaved. Coffee dribbles stained his shirt. "When Cody Geronimo is wearing an orange jumpsuit I'll slow down to mourn. Now, what's this about Marcy blackmailing him?"

He wanted to lift Fager again, really crush him to make him cry, shed just one tear.

"Bronk?"

He told Fager about the ranch, Geronimo's house, the Gonzalez family being driven out of town in style, and Thornton picking up the taxes on their place. "Marcy got rich too fast for the kinds of cases we've seen her handling in court. All of Geronimo's assets coming her way, it's got me thinking she's doing more than lawyering."

Fager sat back and crossed his arms over his chest. "She's had some big settlements, women raped by prison guards."

"Think of what your clients tell you. Not only what they did, but where the gun's buried, where the money's hidden, where they slipped up, and you'd better know before you learn it at trial. I've seen them come in with documents that would send them to prison if they couldn't trust you to keep them locked in your safe. Somebody else, Marcy, might see an opportunity instead of an obligation."

"There's easier ways than blackmail to steal from a client," Fager said. "But I agree to some extent. Marcy's been milking this guy since she stole him away from this office."

"Explain that."

"Roberta found the phone message from Geronimo when he was shopping for a lawyer. Probably the Tasha Gonzalez matter. Marcy sized him up and went solo with a career client in her purse. If she had processed the intake straight and called me in, I probably would have been representing him."

"And Linda would be alive. He wouldn't have killed his own lawyer's wife."

Fager stood up to stretch, move his neck, roll his shoulders.

"Concentrate on the Gonzalez family," he said. "Let's find out where they went and how they've been living. Marcy got them out of Dodge for a reason. She might be paying them to stay away."

"Should I keep running down Geronimo's assets? You could sue him, take everything he has. The Gonzalez's might get homesick when the money stops coming. Other families might come forward. The way he handled Linda, he's got experience."

Fager shook his head.

"Going civil, collecting would take a decade. He'd run to bankruptcy again when we'd cornered him. But see if you can find any pattern connecting Geronimo's financial transactions, like unloading real estate or mortgaging property, with women disappearing from Santa Fe or turning up dead. Those would be times he might have needed lots of cash if he was buying silence."

"SFPD won't give me their missing and unsolved lists."

"Goff can get it through Aragon."

Fager turned backed to his computer. Bronkowski wondered what he was writing so intently. Fager cursed and deleted his screen. Bronkowski left him alone and went to start a skip trace on the Gonzalez family.

As he was unlocking the door to his Camry, Thornton and Montclaire passed on their way to Thornton's Aston.

"Of all the people you could work for," he said. "And on Linda's case. Why?"

Thornton pushed sunglasses off her face.

"I don't remember Walter turning down *any* case, as long as it paid. I'm in the same business, Bronco."

"Reasonable doubt for a reasonable fee."

"Not this lawyer. My fees are never reasonable."

———

Thornton and Montclaire slid onto the Aston's leather seats while Bronkowski squeezed into his Toyota. They watched him struggle to pull the shoulder strap across his chest, unable to turn in the space between the seat and steering wheel.

"There's your competition, Lily. He may look like a lunkhead, but he gets the job done."

"He has terrible posture."

"He'll do anything for Walter, and he really liked Linda. You could see it when he was around her. Other people in the room, she'd be the one he always talked to. Dinner at her house, he'd be helping with dishes, getting up from the table to bring out food, pour wine, until she had to tell him to sit down. We need to know what he's doing. It will tell us what Walter's doing."

"They had something going, Bronkowski and Linda?"

"For her it was like petting a guy's dog to show you liked him. Her guy was Walter."

Montclaire snapped her fingers and said, "Andrew. That's his name."

"Who?" Thornton pressed the ignition and the Aston responded with a low rumble. She backed out fast, just as Bronkowski was pulling from his space. He had to brake to avoid hitting her.

"That hot guy you shooed away when Cody called. Just when it was getting fun. That kid would have gone all night."

"So glad your mind's on work," Thornton said. "I bet Bronkowski thinks about nothing but work."

"He looks like that, there is nothing else."

SIXTEEN

JOE MASCARENAS WAS WORKING late, assembling jury instructions on his own because the DA had pulled money out of the paralegal budget. He told Aragon he would meet her at the coffee shop across from the Rail Runner station.

She arrived first and watched her cousin labor as he carried his obese body on its small feet. His face was flushed when he stepped in the door. She had his usual waiting, a twenty-ounce French Roast with whipped cream.

"Did you walk the whole way?" The DA's office was half a mile down the street.

"Trying to lose some pounds. I take the stairs. Park a block from the office. Carry my files instead of rolling them into court."

The loose flesh under his chin quivered. It would be a long time before his program showed results.

"I'm always sweaty." They took seats by a window. "How are you handling Judy Diaz's vendetta?"

"What's with her? This is about more than me taping Geronimo talking to his lawyer."

"We see stuff like this whenever Thornton's defending. This is the worst I've seen."

"Why didn't you strike her?" Under New Mexico criminal procedure, each side gets one chance to disqualify a judge for no reason at all. The DA's failure to use its peremptory challenge had been bothering Aragon.

"Diaz has been wising up. If it's a Thornton client, she's making discretionary rulings immediately. That closes the door to our challenge and she's along for the rest of the ride. We could appeal, fight her up the line. But she's Chief Judge. She'd involve other judges she got elected and make us pay." He slurped the whipped cream from the top of his coffee and wiped his mouth with the back of his hand. "I've made a friend in Diaz's office. This person saw what happened on the Fager case and came to us. She'll let me know next time there's a whiff of Thornton's perfume in chambers."

"Explain the connection there."

Aragon sipped at her own coffee. Mascarenas took a long drink before answering. She could see him wrestling with something. He spoke with a foamy mustache.

"They've been at it since law school. Their study group met in Judy's bedroom."

"You know this?" Aragon leaned forward and used a napkin to wipe her cousin's face. "Take it to Judicial Standards. A judge banging a lawyer appearing before her. That's gotta break some rule."

"It does, but try proving it. We take a shot like that against Diaz and don't put her down, it's the DA and every at-will employee in our shop who's out next election. That's why you're getting a paid vacation. Diaz wants a sacrifice to appease the angry girlfriend god. You're the paschal lamb."

"What bullshit. The union will back them down. Rick is getting us representation."

"The union needs Diaz more than they need you or any rank-and-file. Who do you think appoints the mediator when collective bargaining stalls? Who's been granted power to give union officers administrative leave to run the union? Two little clauses in the contract say it's the Chief Judge of the First Judicial District. Enjoy your time off and come back ready for the next battle. Fager's gearing up, something will break loose. I got three motions from him today, a research memo, and a case-strategy outline. He has some good ideas. Diaz and Thornton can't bar the doors forever."

Aragon looked through the window at the Rail Runner. It was painted red and orange, with a road runner down its side. Doors opened to commuters heading home. Aragon recognized two police officers boarding for the run south to Albuquerque and Rio Rancho, where cops could afford houses.

"I gotta get back." Mascarenas pushed himself to his feet, groaning a little as he straightened his back.

"You're welcome to join Rick and me in the gym. We could help you put a routine together. Hard as you work, the nights you're at your desk after a full day in court, you need to take care of yourself, cuz."

"I'm doing what I can." He smoothed his tie over his stomach. She could see little threads at the bottom where the silk was fraying. "One hour with you, I'll be so sore I'll give up completely."

She watched him waddle out the door and take the steps one at a time. At the bottom he caught his breath then faced his body north and put his legs into motion. He walked half a block then stopped for air. She felt sorry for him and proud at the same time.

Aragon called her brother to borrow his hunting truck. He promised to have it at his place in Pecos, ready to go, with beer iced in a cooler. He was always riding her about not taking time off. Anything to get her away from the job—and out of Santa Fe—he was there for his little sister.

She took I-25 east into the mountains, below the slopes where Cynthia Fremont bled to death by a hidden lake. She exited at Glorieta and wound her way along dirt roads to her brother's place in the pines. Javier lived in a manufactured house with two wings constructed of repo'd single-wides he'd added for the kids. A hundred yards from the main house sat two more manufactured homes where Lobo Loco Outfitters boarded hunters before Javier and Serena led them into the Pecos Wilderness after trophy elk. His wife was his match in finding the big bulls.

The company's mules resided in barns below the main house. Javier was inside the pipe coral dragging a wire brush through the coat of a tan jack. He wore a shirt from the Saints and Sinners bar in Espanola, once a biker's hangout, now a package store on a highway where cops disrupted heroin deals. Javier had washed out of two state agencies but found a living doing what he loved, roaming the mountains and shooting things. Outfitting had paid for a hundred acres in the pines and was building his children's college funds.

Add a few prison tats and Javier could fit in with the Saints and Sinners crowd, except his drugs of choice stopped at beer and hot peppers. Woolly black beard, long hair as wild as a tumbleweed, big arms like Lewis. Denise always wondered where he got his genes. She'd stopped growing in eighth grade. Javier could wrestle the mule he was grooming.

Serena waved from the porch on the house, her hand slicing smoke from a barbecue grill.

"Detective Aragon." Javier dropped the wire brush in a bucket of water and climbed out of the corral. He lifted her into the air. His fingers found her ribs.

"You're assaulting a police officer."

White teeth gleamed against his dark black beard. She thrashed, but it was pointless.

He swung around and sat her on the corral's top post.

"I hosed it down good," he said and tossed the keys to his F-350, four-wheel drive, Super Duty XLT Supercab, with Ruger mud flaps and an I-beam and winch replacing the original front bumper. "You don't want to sleep in what I've been hauling. We can put the shell on before you go."

"I'll sleep in the cab if it rains. An entire family could live in there."

"You wanted a spotting scope and my camera with the telephoto. In the console. You want my Mini-14? Thirty-round clip. Any coyotes within two hundred yards are fucked."

"It's not exactly coyotes I'm after."

"You want my Weatherby?"

Serena called from the porch. "I hope you're staying for dinner."

"What's cooking?" Aragon yelled back. "Smells incredible."

"Cat," Javier said.

Aragon wasn't sure she heard him right.

"A lion won't be sniffing my mules anymore."

"What the hell." She could brag about it to other cops. None of them had brothers who butchered a mountain lion for dinner. "I have to ask. Does it taste like chicken?"

"Not even close," Javier said, and lifted her off the fence to carry her to the house.

Over beers before dinner, Aragon mentioned how her old friend Buff, now Roshi Larson, said Javier's place in the woods was his monastery. Serena started calling him "Monk." He reminded her monks took vows of chastity and silence. How would she like that?

"Deal. Five kids and a husband with opinions about everything," Serena said and passed a bowl of chips. "After the dishes, I'll shave your head, make you a hooded robe."

Driving Javier's truck back to town, Aragon decided never to mention this dinner around cops. Mountain lion was surprisingly damn good eating, especially the way Serena did it with red chile, onions, oregano, and cumin. On the side, frijoles and papas under melted jack and more of the red. Homemade tortillas. Flan at the end with coffee. That was a meal to beat Lotaburgers.

But if Omar Serrano heard about it:

Yo, Butch. Which way you like your pussy—excuse me—your cat, best of all?

She'd have to break his nose to shut him up.

SEVENTEEN

ONE HUNDRED NINETY-SEVEN NAMES of officers killed in the line of duty are etched in the charcoal-colored Wall of Honor at the Law Enforcement Academy. The wall says "No Greater Love Hath Man," but four of the names belong to women.

Bernalillo County Deputy Sheriff Angelica Garcia crashed her patrol car rushing to a bar fight where a gun was pulled.

Navajo tribal police officer Esther Todecheene died speeding to answer a fellow officer's call for assistance.

Victoria Louise Chavez of the Farmington Police Department was conducting a routine check when a man who had been avoiding a competency hearing emerged from a house that was supposed to be empty. He fired four shotgun shells into her head at close range.

Sierra County Deputy Sheriff Kelly Fay Clark was transporting a prisoner from Truth or Consequences to the Western New Mexico Correctional Facility in Grants, a distance of two hundred and two miles. With only seven miles to go, the prisoner reached from the back seat through a gap in the Plexiglas barrier and grabbed her gun. He shot her twice in the head. The car veered across the interstate into a semi. The prisoner car-jacked a Presbyterian minister who stopped at the accident scene to help. He was caught making a call at a gas station with officer Clark's gun still in his hand and cuffs on his wrist.

The list of officers killed in the line of duty goes back to when New Mexico was a territory and Billy the Kid shot lawmen in Lincoln County. The list grew every year, and there was plenty of blank space for new names.

As a cadet, Aragon spent hours reading names on the memorial in the garden at the Academy. She knew the stories of the female officers by heart. They must have confronted a lot worse than Omar Serrano, especially in the rural departments where female officers still were rare.

Only a handful of men like Serrano remained in the SFPD. The women who had gone before her would have welcomed those odds. So why was she spinning a dialogue in her head from one asshole cop she hadn't talked to for days? Make it two asshole cops. No way to overlook the Deputy Chief who cared more about "preserving a valued relationship" with a bent judge than protecting and serving. And maybe Fenstermacher, Serrano's partner, quietly going along with Omar's crap. And Joe Donnelly, after her again for no reason except she tried damn hard and cared so much about what really mattered.

Okay, so things hadn't really changed.

Lewis wanted her to report Serrano. She only wanted to do her job. Why let Serrano know it even bothered her?

Twenty miles of driving and she convinced herself Serrano wasn't worth thinking about.

Mascarenas called her as she neared the Old Pecos Trail exit.

"My new friend wants us to know Judge Diaz is meeting with counsel on the Geronimo case tonight."

Aragon steered Javier's truck onto the exit ramp.

"Must be important, opening the courthouse this late."

"Not a meeting in chambers. At Diaz's house, and the prosecution's not invited."

Aragon knew where Diaz lived. She had once responded to a burglary in an east-side neighborhood. The Chief Judge came from her house across the street to complain about a patrol car blocking her driveway. Diaz's place was in the Acequia Madre neighborhood, not far from Geronimo's gallery. Old Pecos Trail was the fastest route.

"You still at work?" she asked.

"The defense is pushing nonstandard instructions. I have to research other jurisdictions. I should be out of here by midnight."

"Get some rest, Joe."

She headed into the maze of narrow streets built by Spanish conquistadors. The neighborhood association had fought installation of street lights on grounds they would make it harder to see the stars. Aragon had to get out to peer at a street sign in the dark. She didn't realize she was coming upon Diaz's place until her headlights picked out Thornton's Aston, a car she had seen outside the courthouse, the kind of car you didn't forget.

Aragon squeezed into a turnout that served as a space for garbage cans on collection day. She killed the engine and lights and removed Javier's camera from the console. He used it for wildlife shots for gunshow brochures and the website that Serena had built for their outfitting business. She was tanning the hide of the mountain lion they had eaten for dinner. Serena could repair ATVs, run hounds on a cold trail, negotiate leases for hunting rights on sprawling ranches, and still manage five kids.

Rick Lewis, Super Dad. Serena Aragon, Super Mom. She was in the company of giants.

After half an hour of staring at Diaz's front door, Aragon opened the Tasha Gonzalez file. She needed to catch up to Lewis. She'd moved their files from the trunk of her car, now at Javier's place, to the pickup's back seat. In the glove compartment she found a Maglite. When she turned it on the pages glowed red. Javier had covered the lens with tinted plastic so he could use the light without ruining his night vision.

Lewis's handwritten notes were clipped inside the folder. She would add her own notes to the free-flowing stream of thoughts, impressions, and theories. They had discovered they obtained fresh insights into a case if they jotted down where they were at each step along the trail to catching a killer, even if the thoughts made no sense and never proved more than random speculation. The scratch sheet would not go into the official file. They never wanted to give the defense a road map to alternate explanations they had considered and rejected before settling on the defendant.

Right now, she had nothing to contribute. Her only information had come from Goff and what Lewis had shared in passing. He had already filled two pages of notes, raising questions likely answered deeper in the file, perhaps putting his finger on something the prior investigation had missed. His handwriting was as careful as his thought process. She saw his mind probing the case from different approaches. He drew arrows connecting two questions: "How did she get in the irrigation ditch?" and "Roads from the west?"

Every investigator who had touched the file had asked the first question. Lewis raised the second because he had located Geronimo's ranch, twenty-five miles west of where Gonzalez's remains had clogged an irrigation gate. Aragon unfolded the map in the file and examined it in dim red light. The location where she was found had been circled. A tiny blue line across alfalfa fields indicated an irrigation ditch paralleling the Rio Grande. Aragon didn't see any route to the site from the west.

Either Tasha had floated downstream or somehow her killer had found another way to the water.

Tasha's larger bones, the skull, femur, hips, and shoulder blades, were recovered from the ditch. Smaller bones had been found in the field. Much of her skeleton was missing. Hair matched by DNA was found snagged at the base of a barbed wire fence two hundred yards from the irrigation gate. In his notes Lewis speculated that maybe an animal had dragged her scalp from the rest of the body.

OMI identified her through records from the emergency room at Christus St. Vincent Hospital. Several years before her death, Tasha had bought a round-trip ticket to take advantage of cheap dental work in Juarez. She came home with an infection that nearly killed her. X-rays taken in the ER matched the upper palate of the skull in the irrigation ditch.

A forensic anthropologist Goff brought into the case noted that strands of her hair were caked with a white substance. Testing revealed it to be sodium chloride with traces of calcium, arsenic, and magnesium. The investigators had been encouraged by the arsenic as a possible means of death. But a consulting geologist said arsenic was a common element in the New Mexico water table. The geologist concluded that salt, the sodium-chloride base, had been deposited on the hair by naturally occurring water containing the other elements.

Farmers frequently complained about high levels of salt in irrigation water. Deposits could be seen on the ditch banks, like the ring in a bath tub. Lewis's notes pondered whether Tasha's hair had soaked up the salt while she decomposed in the irrigation ditch.

Aragon added a new question to the scratch sheets: "Flooding schedule?"

Goff had come to Santa Fe to escape the humidity of St. Louis. He probably didn't know how alfalfa farmers flooded their fields when the Middle Rio Grande Conservancy District released precious water from Cochiti dam. It would have been impossible to drive across those fields while they were under water.

Out of the corner of her eye she saw the door to Diaz's house open. She killed the light. When she reached for the camera she knocked it into the foot well. By the time she came up, the Aston was backing out of the driveway. The silhouette of the driver—long neck, too much hair for the lawyer's bob—ruled out Thornton.

She debated leaving. She concluded that Thornton was still inside the house. Whoever was driving had gone out on an errand and would return.

Aragon turned back to the file. Tasha had modeled for Cody Geronimo. But "model" was not the job description Aragon would have attached to the woman in the photographs. She was soft edges everywhere. The corners of her mouth indicated neither a smile nor frown. Her cheeks were heavy but not jowly, neck and shoulders thick but not muscular. Overall her looks were too indefinite to be either pretty or unattractive.

Aragon wondered what Geronimo had seen that he wanted to incorporate into his art. The file did not reveal how much he paid. Tasha had ignored taxes. In Goff's single brief interview, Geronimo said he paid cash but could not recall the amount.

Tasha's only other employment was with a home-cleaning service called Mujeres Bravas that kept very sketchy records. That's how Geronimo met her. Mujeres Bravas had cleaned his gallery after a party.

She had shared a trailer south of town with her brother Estevan and his family. The brother dropped her off at a park where she was picked up for the modeling sessions. He had never met Geronimo, nor had he seen the vehicle that came for Tasha.

She had not returned from one of those sessions. Her brother waited a week to report her missing. Geronimo told Goff she was not at the park when he went to meet her. He had not tried to track her down since she did not have a telephone or know where she lived.

Then Thornton stepped in and Geronimo stopped talking.

A pair of headlights appeared at the end of the lane. Aragon recognized the shape of the British car. She took up the camera and unrolled the window to avoid glare.

The Aston pulled into Diaz's drive. Now two heads were silhouetted inside. The headlights went out. Thornton's investigator—a real looker, what was her name?—left the driver's door, went around to the passenger side, and pulled out a thin young woman. Something was wrong with her arms. The light came on over the house's front door and lit the driveway.

Her hands were cuffed behind her back. Montclaire—that was it—led her toward the front door.

Aragon dropped the camera and reached for her pistol. Heedless of the dome light, she got out and moved quickly to the corner of the wall at the entrance to the long drive. She needed an angle so the young woman would not be in the line of fire. She put the front sight on Montclaire's back and calculated how she might react when ordered to halt.

The front door opened. Judge Diaz stepped out holding a wine glass. The fabric of her judicial robe shimmered in the light from inside the house. With her free hand she pulled at the zipper. The robe fell open. She was naked underneath.

"May it please the court," Montclaire shouted.

"I'll be the judge of that," Diaz shouted back and the three of them, including the girl in cuffs, broke down in laughter. Montclaire prodded the young woman into the house. Judge Diaz followed and closed the door behind her.

EIGHTEEN

By THE TIME SHE reached her apartment Aragon was done beating herself up. A photograph of the young woman in handcuffs, walking up the driveway, Montclaire at her back with a handgun, Judge Diaz exposing herself in the porch light—she needed it all, in one view, just the way she had seen it. But she would have needed to zoom in on the cuffs so they would be recognizable. Same for the gun in Montclaire's hand, hard to see in the dark. Diaz opening her robe would have been good for passing around the office, but on its own proved nothing.

At least she had confirmed Mascarenas's suspicions about why the Geronimo case was chucked out the back door of the Santa Fe County courthouse. The Honorable Judith A. Diaz was rising fast up her to-do list.

She climbed the stairs to her efficiency apartment in a garden complex occupied by city workers and retirees. She was as far from the tourist district as she could get and stay within city limits. Inside, milk crates of files and law-enforcement manuals strained a hollow core door laid across cinder blocks. Her sofa was still pulled out into a bed, unmade, photographs and loose pages of unfinished reports scattered on the sheets.

She brought a sleeping bag and inflatable pad up from her locked storage space in the basement. The cross-trainers she wore during the day were replaced by hiking boots. One of the oranges in her fridge had not grown mold. It went into a shopping bag with peanuts and energy bars. She filled plastic jugs with tap water and crammed extra clothes into a day pack. With her gear behind her inside the truck's cab, she headed south on I-25.

Ninety miles to Ladron Peak and Geronimo's ranch.

Traffic was light and moved fast. She joined the stream but cut back a mile from La Bajada hill where state police maintained a speed trap. Ten miles later she caught herself breaking a hundred, the pickup's V-8 letting her know it could go as fast as she wanted.

Congestion slowed her at the Sandia Pueblo Casino on Albuquerque's northern edge. Rio Rancho sprawled to the western horizon. Tall office buildings missing from Santa Fe's skyline pushed against the highway here. City lights wiped out stars. Not until she passed the exit for the airport on the other side of city, where empty desert reclaimed the landscape, did she feel she was back in New Mexico.

She pulled off at the Los Lunas exit to grab a late snack. Next to the railroad tracks she found one of the oldest Blake's she had ever seen, everything about it frozen in the Sixties. She bought a large coffee and two Lotaburgers. The coffee would get her through the rest of the drive. The second burger would be tomorrow's breakfast.

Back on the road, she could now see Ladron Peak rising against the Milky Way. New Mexico's other tall peaks were part of larger mountain ranges. Ladron stood alone. She drove south of Belen, close to where Tasha Gonzalez had festered in an irrigation ditch, and took the Bernardo exit. Years ago a bar in the middle of nowhere had justified this interchange. After the Legislature outlawed drive-up liquor, the alcohol license had been sold and the building turned over to tumbleweeds hugging its walls.

A dismal RV park had sprung up since she last passed this way. Smack against the interstate right-of-way, fifth wheels and motor homes shook as heavy semis thundered by. No trees, no shade, no grass. Nothing but hookups for water and liquid waste, and a hand-painted sign saying, "Cash only. No credit. Kids and dogs free but don't let them run loose."

Despite that rule, a pack of dogs chased the truck until it crossed a rusting bridge over the Rio Puerco, a muddy thread between tamarisk trees crowding its banks. The pavement ended and a dirt road forced tires into ruts dried hard as concrete.

Yellow clay reflected headlights, but darkness yawned at the top of every hill. She sensed vast emptiness surrounding her. From nowhere the reflective green and white of a street sign appeared in her headlights. It said, "Menaul Boulevard," a busy thoroughfare in Albuquerque, and she wondered how it got here.

Several bumpy miles past the street sign she turned off onto a rough two-track running toward the mountain. She engaged the four-wheel drive and plowed through soft sand and loose rock. Soon she was in a canyon barely wider than the truck. A half mile later she found a level spot to park and called it a night.

She used Javier's red lens flashlight to set up camp. In the bed of the truck she rolled out the inflatable pad, then the sleeping bag. She made a pillow of extra clothes. She hesitated before crawling inside the bag, thinking of Cynthia Fremont. She wondered how Rivera was coming along, able to run his own investigation and do the job the way it needed to be done, no idiot like Dewey Nobles getting in the way. She thought of Buff, now Roshi Larson. She was glad she had followed her outside the meeting in Rivera's office. She'd provided the break about celestial burial, and pinpointed the campsite by the lake, without an army of FBI experts.

They needed to do something together, reach back to happy times. She wanted to know where Buff had been all these years, what brought her back to Santa Fe. Instead of abusing Javier's old Jeep, they could tool around Santa Fe in Buff's convertible. A Buddhist beemer. Pull up next to bangers on Cerrillos and blast them with Tibetan chants, or whatever Roshis had on their stereo.

Maybe Spice Girls. Buff had loved "Wannabe." It would drive the bangers nuts.

She kept the rifle and handgun within reach, but not so close that she might roll over them. She snapped off the flashlight. No man-made light reached her in the slot between sandstone cliffs. The night air had grown cold. The sky shimmered. That crazy bright moon Lewis had noted the night they found Fremont still lit the land. She could make out cracks in the cliffs above her. She could see the teeth in the zipper running down the side of her sleeping bag, and read the label sewn into the canvas. Javier had given her a Walmart special, heavy as a child, lined with flannel, nothing like the expensive goose down in Fremont's high-end Big Agnes bag.

Something swooshed overhead. Too cold for bats. It was an owl, now hooting from an alligator juniper whose cracked skin shone in the silvery light.

She loved New Mexico. She would never live anywhere else. But goddamn, why did it have to be so fucked up?

Aragon forced her mind to empty to make room for sleep. She had four hours until first light.

A familiar dream returned near dawn. The weight of the sleeping bag brought it on. She was pinned on the concrete. Her pants had been pulled to her knees, her underwear ripped away. She saw Miguel vaulting the fence of his front yard, charging to her rescue. He ran so fast the breeze he created pushed back hair from his high, brown forehead. He was so beautiful she no longer felt the hands between her legs, the foot on the back of her neck, the rough concrete under her cheek.

Miguel charged into the boys holding her down and sent them flying. He reached to lift her to her feet, to hold her tight, protect her. Behind him another boy, one Miguel missed, pulled an ugly revolver from his waistband.

Now came the part that made it easy to sleep and wake up happy.

A pistol appears in her hand, a larger, more deadly weapon than the gangster's gun. The barrel spouts flame. It becomes a machine gun. The gangster's chest explodes. There are more of them now, rising from the concrete, from behind trees, attacking from lowriders pulled to the curb. Her gun never runs out of bullets. She fires again and again as Miguel's arms wrap around her from behind, his lips on her neck, the soft breath of the life she saved caressing her hair.

NINETEEN

2:10 A.M. SANDY LEWIS entered the garage in her red flannel nightshirt and fuzzy slippers, carrying a bowl of chocolate ice cream topped with peanuts. Rick Lewis was in their Dodge Caravan working on his laptop. An extension cord snaked across the floor to an outlet by the chest freezer. Inside the van files and photographs covered seats, floor, and windows. A yellow sheet of paper with blocks of handwriting dangled from the rearview mirror.

He asked his wife, "Why are you up?"

She handed the ice cream through the driver's side window. "You never came to bed."

"I'll sleep when I'm dead."

"I don't like it when you say that."

"You know what I mean."

"It's not funny. Or clever."

They had a rule against his working inside the house. Close-ups in stark light showing how a woman's head had been opened to remove the bones from her inner ear. Their daughters didn't need to know this much about daddy's job.

She knew he was worried about the suspension. They had discussed it after the kids were in bed. They needed his salary, but could get by if he was fired. She had a good job as Public Information Officer for the Game and Fish department. She talked to reporters about license fees and ranchers wanting elk permits, and the effects of drought on snow geese. He made half her take-home pay dealing with the horrors in those photos taped to the windshield.

She came around the other side to get in. She didn't look at what she moved from the passenger seat. She kept her eyes on him.

"Denise is down south, around Ladron Peak, trying to find a piece of private property where a murder may have been committed." He never disclosed the names of people he was investigating until they were arrested. "I tried Google Earth but got lost. There's too much open country and too few landmarks to know what you're seeing."

"Could have saved you time. We've got a bighorn program there."

"I don't follow." He dug into the ice cream.

"We filmed that area in low-level flights. You can find a puddle of water on those films."

"Who do I talk to about seeing them?"

"The PIO. But she won't entertain your inspection of public records request unless you come to bed now."

He tried. The clock read 3:30 a.m., but he just stared at the dark ceiling. Sandy rolled onto her side and rested her head on his shoulder.

"Think about something besides work."

"I'm sorry."

"We can still get a couple hours if you settle down."

"I'm keeping you awake. But I meant sorry for being so stupid."

"*What* are you talking about?" She sat up and turned on the light to see his face. He continued to stare at the ceiling.

"A smart guy, thinking of his family, he wouldn't mind kissing a little ass. He'd watch somebody like Dewey Nobles instead of Denise Aragon to see how it's done. They hate her, you know. We had this guy, cranked up clunk, yelling out a window, shooting at trees, blowing out windshields. Denise went in the back of the house, came up behind him while he was calling us pig fuckers and knocked him out with a frying pan off his stove."

"They hate her for that?"

"She was supposed to be in Dewey's meeting, listening to the big plan, memorizing lines Dewey drew on an aerial of the house he called 'vectors of opportunity.' Next thing we're outside, Denise in that window shouting come get the guy. Dewey standing there with his pointer, a complete idiot, nobody hearing him anymore. A smart guy would have asked for a different partner right then, learned to say 'vectors of opportunity' when Dewey's around."

"She's one of those."

"She scares the hell out of them."

"How did she know she could take that guy so easily?"

"I told her."

Sandy played with a button on his pajamas, trying to get him to look at her. "What are you leaving out?"

"I found the door unlocked, the clunk facing away. I told Denise on our way to Dewey's meeting." He had more to say. Sandy waited. "I couldn't have gone in there, on my own call. Denise made things happen while the rest of us were stuck in cement."

"You've been on fire since you two teamed up."

"I need to kiss a little more ass, is all I'm saying."

"Detective Lewis, you are so full of crap tonight, you know?"

She lifted her top over her head. Now he was looking at her. She stood on the mattress and hooked her thumbs in the waistband of her underwear.

"If you need to kiss ass, we can fix that right now."

Later, lying naked on sheets falling to the floor, she ran her fingers through his hair. "You're my hero." She kissed him slowly, patiently now that their bodies glowed instead of burned. "That's how I see you every day walking out the door. You're a warrior fighting against a world gone mad. I don't want somebody different coming home. You hear what I'm saying?"

"I do. Yes."

"Great. Now can we get some sleep?"

TWENTY

GOFF LOOKED UP FROM his bowl of menudo, grinning under a wet, red mustache.

"Big, dumb *Po*-lack walks into a Mexican restaurant, says to the girl, give me a nice, fat kielbasa. Girl says back, *meester*, you got this wrong. You give me a nice, fat kielbasa and I give *you* ... "

"Cut the crap," Bronkowski said. "What do you have for me?"

"Nothing tops the Polish joke in your mirror." Goff chased his food with a long drink of coffee. "Christ. You're wrapped as tight as Fager. Have a seat. Get some breakfast. This place is great."

Bronkowski pulled out a chair across the table. A young woman with fake eyebrows painted two inches higher than natural arrived with a coffee pot and a glass of ice water. He ordered eggs, sunny-side up, Christmas-style—green and red chile. She didn't speak English. "Huevos rancheros," he said and let it go.

"That guessing game you played with Fager, when you were here with Aragon and Lewis, about something missing from his wife's remains, you enjoy that?" Bronkowski set his eyes on Goff's face.

135

"Fager didn't flinch. Learns bones were cut from inside her head, trophies for Geronimo, he picks up his coffee and keeps reading." Goff met Bronkowski's stare. "Just another case for him. Cold-blooded bastard."

Bronkowski tried the coffee then pushed it away. Dishwater laced with cinnamon.

"Let's make this quick." Bronkowski removed the little notebook from his jacket pocket and clicked a pen. "You first."

"What did you think of Geronimo?" Goff scooped diced raw onions into his menudo, followed by a tablespoon of oregano. "Fager in one of his memos to Mascarenas let us know about your visit to his big gallery opening. You shook his hand, had a nice talk. You talked to him longer than I did on the Tasha Gonzalez case. Using art bullshit to get close. Not bad."

"How far back did you dig into his background?"

"Enough to doubt Geronimo is his real name."

"None of that's in the file."

"We were getting a river of PC shit for casting suspicion on the Native American Picasso or Michelangelo or whatever he is. The chief assigned his community relations director to our team, sitting there correcting our language, editing our reports, bugging us to unpack our feelings and assumptions toward *the other*. I still don't know what the fuck that meant. We had to go to a white privilege workshop. I learned I was no longer Jewish but Anglo, and a bigoted turdball deserving a lifetime of guilt 'cause I don't have ancestors massacred at Wounded Knee."

"You *are* a bigoted turdball."

"Now you're the one with the jokes."

"Geronimo," Bronkowski said.

"Right." Goff pushed his bowl away and leaned forward. "It's not a Navajo name, but he claims he was born on the Alamo Rez. That's Navajo, the Alamo Band they're called—sounds like a music group from Texas. It's a damn poor, sorry place, worse than the big rez around Shiprock. These people are out on their own, hundreds of miles from any other Navajos, in even harder country. I found nothing to back his claim about being Indian except stories that always came back to him."

"He built himself a legend?"

"It's not an Apache name, either. The Mexicans gave it to one man only. Yet our guy doesn't blow that horn, that he's a direct descendant of a real Indian war chief every school kid's heard about. For someone so good at self-promotion—his true game, you know—he'd use that. You seeing this?"

"I been thinking 'Cody Geronimo' is too good. Like a movie star picking something that rings. Charles Bronson. He was Charles Dennis Buchinsky."

"You'd know. America's only Polack action hero."

"Tom Cruise's real name is Thomas Mapother. The Fourth."

"You sit around reading *People* magazine? Fager must not have enough for you to do."

Bronkowski let it go, coming from a guy who spends his days collecting retirement, Goff's mind was stuck in the past when he had something to get him out of the house every day. "So what is Cody Geronimo's real name?"

"I never found a birth certificate. Records on the rez are a mess. Not every squaw who pushes out a papoose does the paperwork. Maybe that explains it. But still."

"Still, you are a bigoted turdball."

Bronkowski's order arrived. The waitress with eyebrows high on her forehead delivered a plate of eggs exactly the way he ordered it. He thought she didn't understand.

"What else you keep out of the file?" Bronkowski asked as he broke egg yolk with a tortilla.

Goff flipped a brown envelope across the table. "Only Aragon knows about this." Bronkowski wiped his fingers and opened the flap. Inside were approximately twenty photographs. They showed an artist's studio and rooms in a large house crammed with Navajo rugs and traditional Native American artwork.

"He didn't do Tasha Gonzalez in his studio," Goff said. "Windows everywhere to let in light. Tourists can watch the great genius at work. He's got apprentices and students coming and going all the time. The last five shots are his house, just to give you the flavor. I doubt he wanted blood on those rugs. Even the bathrooms are full of pretty things. He did her somewhere else."

"I didn't see search warrants in the file." Breaking and entering to sniff around was exactly what he expected of Goff.

"I never got resources to find where else he might have done his killing. Thornton brought the roof down on me. I was cleaning out my desk in a week."

"Shit." Bronkowski dabbed his napkin at a spot of chile splashed on his leather vest. "Walt and I thought we ended your career. We were kind of proud of that."

The waitress dropped off their checks. Bronkowski put his hand over both of them.

"We appreciate your assistance on this, despite the history between us."

"Let go of that." Goff slipped the checks from under Bronkowski's palm, found his. "I'd have to puke up anything Walter Fager paid for. Shit, I'm breaking kosher just eating at the same table with you two."

"Menudo's kosher?"

"Funnier by the minute, Bronkowski. Today I learn you're a comedian. Still, two things I can't figure about you."

"Just two?"

"What the hell are you doing with Fager? He hurts people. That half-assed Bandidos look you got going, I know that's not you."

"Dang." Bronkowski tugged at his vest. "I was going for Hells Angels."

"He doesn't just defend scum of the earth." Goff wiped his mouth on the back of his hand. "That case where a drunk slammed into a family on Christmas Eve, killing the wife and three kids. Fager turned an expired prescription for narcolepsy pills into a line dad killed his family nodding off at the wheel. That father never got off the stand. He killed himself the next day because he couldn't live with the seed Fager planted in his heart."

"We did that case by the book. Just like the one that took you down."

"I bet you can't remember the name of that drunk, or the family he wiped out." Goff pointed his spoon across the table at Bronkowski. "Another day, another dollar for you and Fager."

"Get that out of my face. You got ten seconds. What's the other thing?"

"I've seen that antique belly gun in your belt. Why don't you carry a semi-auto like everybody else in the twenty-first century?"

"Now you're getting personal. This interest in another man's gun, people gonna start talking."

"You gotta crack a joke to duck the question."

"Something I haven't figured about you."

"Oh, your turn now." Goff put down his spoon, like he was freeing his hands to fight.

Bronkowski saw them, no longer eating or talking. Staring at each other, the smaller brown people at other tables sensing something between the big men, shifting in their chairs to turn away.

Bronkowski broke the silence. "Why didn't you get Geronimo the first time?"

"I told you, Indians drove me off."

"Sure, like the old movies. Indians smelled white men before they saw them. A dirty cop does have a certain air about him."

"You just stopped being funny."

"I can't help thinking. Had the case gone to a cop who did the job straight up, a beautiful woman I cared about would be alive and I wouldn't be sitting here trading spitballs with you."

"Second thought, you buy." Goff flipped his check at Bronkowski.

"I've got a meeting across town with your favorite lawyer." Bronkowski dropped money on the table. "The family's name was Shelby. Daniel, the father. Shirley his wife. Dawn, age twelve, Susan, eight, and Billy just five years old. Susan was into gymnastics. Dawn liked horses. Shirley sang in her church choir. It's our client's name, the one who killed them, that's who I can't remember."

TWENTY-ONE

Right where Geronimo stood? The exact spot, Fager insisted. It was the strangest instruction he had received in almost twenty years as Fager's investigator.

So here he was, where Geronimo had stood, inside the tall hedge. Fager would arrive soon and give him his cue.

As he waited, his mind ran back to Goff's questions. Why did he stick with Fager? Why carry a Dick Tracy gun anybody would leave at home in a bedside drawer? The answer to the second question answered both.

Bosnia 1994, he and Fager were half of a Special Forces unit that did not officially exist. But the artillery fire they were directing against Serbian militia was very real.

Fager had been right about the field cannons and the Muslims they were supposed to be helping. The cannons, leftovers from some other war, had trouble with high explosive shells. The antique guns could not be trusted. Neither could the Muslims. Many of these men had come from Libya, Egypt, Syria, learned killing in Afghanistan. Fager believed

Bosnia was only a flashpoint in some bigger war they were fighting. "We'll see them again," Fager would say, "closer to home."

As the Special Forces team was watching a NATO strike in a valley below their outpost, the Muslims attacked. Pat Johnson and Murph Talbott took the first bullets. Bronkowski never got off a shot. His M-249 jammed. He used it as a club before gun barrels forced him onto his belly and boots broke his ribs.

Fager disappeared.

They concealed Bronkowski in goat carts under bales of hay. Other days it was piles of garbage. Once it was dead bodies. He knew they were moving south. He started hearing "Libya" mixed in among words that sounded Arabic, nothing like the peasants' Albanian.

At a camp in deep woods Bronkowski heard grunts and gasps, then Fager was standing there, wiping a knife on his pants. It took a week to reach the coast. They sat on the beach until they were picked up by Italians poaching in fishing grounds abandoned during the fighting.

The Army corrected their incident reports. They had never been in Bosnia. Johnson and Talbott had been lost in a training accident in Africa, their bodies never recovered. Bronkowski's injuries came from barracks roughhousing after a night of drinking.

Bronkowski went to Walter Reed. Fager went AWOL.

Bronkowski traced him to Truth or Consequences, New Mexico, to a 1920s motor hotel with moldy hot-springs pools. Fager was drunk in steaming green water. Bronkowski pulled him out then lost him the next morning.

Two years later he received an invitation to Fager's wedding with Linda.

There's your answers, Goff. I will never again bet my life on a spring inside a gun. And I will never forget what I owe Walter Fager.

He heard the distinctive clanking of Fager's diesel Mercedes. Through the leaves he saw the front quarter panel of the black car. Doors opened and closed and he heard Fager's voice. He thought this all a little crazy. But Fager knew his business. Ever since Bosnia, he had never doubted him.

Mascarenas was with Fager. They moved in and out of sight as they retraced Geronimo's steps. They peered into the narrow gap between buildings that had allowed him to escape the searchlight of the police helicopter. They crossed the street to where Bronkowski now hid in that hedge.

"You've won weaker motions," Fager said, apparently continuing a discussion begun earlier. "Why are you gun-shy now?"

Mascarenas was perspiring through his suit jacket despite the cool air. Fager slowed his steps so the heavy man did not fall behind.

"Everybody understands attorney-client privilege, like the need for a search warrant." Mascarenas pulled up and took a deep breath. "Reporters think it's a sacred right, so the stories will come out like press releases from Thornton's office. The Bar Association will weigh in, the Trial Lawyers. Faculty at the law school. Already the Pueblos and tribes are beating the drums. Justice for Geronimo. Wait for the bumper stickers. Damn thing has a ring. Not the campaign theme my boss wants."

"Geronimo went in there." Fager pointed to the hedge concealing Bronkowski. "The DA avoids an embarrassing loss by not even prosecuting, is that it?"

"Her version of the Hippocratic oath. First do no harm—to herself. She doesn't need Marcy Thornton high-fiving Geronimo outside the courthouse a week before early voting starts."

"I've nothing to lose. My wife's gone. I'm not running for office."

Mascarenas shot Fager a look saying he was out of patience.

"What did you bring me here for?"

"A proposition."

Inside the hedge, Bronkowski recognized his cue.

"That damn detective Aragon," he said, louder than a normal speaking voice. "Listening in on a world-famous artist and pillar of the community consulting his highly respected and greatly feared attorney. Fucking cops. If you can't trust 'em to follow the rules, who can you trust? I'm asking."

The corner of Fager's mouth turned up, then he killed the smile. They had not decided on a script. Bronkowski was improvising.

"The cops are idiots," Bronkowski continued. Mascarenas's eyes swung to the hedge. "The DAs are idiots, especially that slob Joe Mascarenas. He couldn't convict a combo plate of being two tacos, a tamale, and an enchilada. He couldn't convince a jury that breathing in and out was good for their health. When it comes to Joe Mascarenas, ADA doesn't mean Assistant District Attorney, it means 'Another Dumb Ass.' Shit, Joe Mascarenas couldn't ... "

The branches of the hedge shook as Bronkowski pushed his way into the open.

"Oh, it's you," he said, brushing leaves off his shoulders. "Hi, Joe."

Mascarenas wheeled to Fager, anger turning his face a deeper shade of red.

"Kinda game you playing, Walt?"

"Joe, how far are we standing from that hedge? *Comprende, amigo?*"

"*No, no comprendo. Comprendo nada, pendejo.* What is this?"

"An unnecessarily offensive demonstration of why Geronimo had no expectation of privacy in his conversation with Thornton. Anyone walking by could have heard him. It's like he was walking down the street yapping on his cell for the world to hear."

Mascarenas pointed at the dense leaf cover behind Bronkowski.

"He was hiding. Hiding implies seeking privacy."

"Next flaw in Marcy's argument. Whose hedge, Joe? That's a private residence behind there, and the owner ... " Fager looked to Bronkowski.

"Margaret Kimball."

"Doesn't like murderers ducking into her landscaping to call their lawyer. He was trespassing. Joe, this is a motion I know I can win."

Mascarenas flinched at the last sentence. "It's not yours to win, or lose."

"Which brings us to my proposition. Appoint me special prosecutor. That insulates your boss. If I lose, which I won't, the media lynches me. I could give a shit. In my line of work, popularity has never been a measure of success."

Mascarenas's fat shook under his clothes.

"You're jumping sides now that you're hurting? You're going to show the full-time good guys how it's done? And after your noble moment in the sun, you go back to raking in on one case for a sleazebag client more than I make in a year? You'll probably bump your rates. And the free advertising from playing hero for a day. Fuck you."

"Because a cop screwed up, and the DA is a coward, I'm supposed to calmly watch Linda's murderer get back to being America's favorite Indian artist?"

"That's how it works for lesser people than Walter Fager. I didn't mention your little conflict of interest, the victim being your wife. I'm not going to even think this through with you."

"Joe." Fager opened his hands. "I'm sincere about this. I want to lend my skill, my experience ... "

"His ace investigator," Bronkowski said and got a sharp look from Fager.

"I want to lend all my talents to seeing justice done in this case."

Mascarenas stuck a finger in Fager's chest, the first time he had ever touched him through all their years of close combat, standing shoulder to shoulder competing for the last word with a confused judge, or face to face, almost spitting, hurling plea negotiations back and forth like insults.

"'Lend' being the key word. Followed by 'in this case.'" Mascarenas emphasized the last words with three jabs in Fager's ribs. "Not where a woman you don't care about gets raped. Not where a drunk wipes out a family coming home from church. *In this case*, you take injustice personally. All other cases, you'll take a check, but cash is better."

Mascarenas brushed past Fager and headed down the street, faster than they had ever seen him move.

Bronkowski said, "That went well."

TWENTY-TWO

"Who kicked me in the head?"

Marcy Thornton rested a cheek on a stack of *New Mexico Supreme Court Reports* piled on her massive mahogany desk, an open bottle of Tylenol near her bent elbow.

"Gran Patron Platinum," Montclaire said. "Half a bottle makes an impression." She lifted a foot onto the coffee table and applied gold polish to her nails. "Repeat after me. 'The defendant waives formal reading of the indictment and enters a plea of not guilty on all counts.' You can do that in your sleep."

Thornton groaned. "How can you be so perky? I saw you throwing down Stoli shots like tap water."

"Old modeling trick. Tell the photographer you'll bring the booze, gets him excited, maybe it's more than him holding your contract, maybe you actually like him. Bring two bottles, his eyes pop out, *hey, she's ready to party*. But the Stoli bottle is water for you. You're always jumping up to refill his glass with the real stuff. Push him off you when he passes out. Or a chief judge who's had too much. You get home for a good night's sleep. You'll be hydrated without those dry scales by the corner of your eyes in the morning."

Thornton rubbed her temples. "Who was that girl? She was worth this hangover."

Montclaire thought for a minute and gave up.

"You and Judy were in a hurry. She was all I could find on short notice. I put your gun back under the seat. Judy got a kick out of that, a girl in handcuffs, me flashing a shiny gun. Something different for Her Honor."

"Three new clients waiting in orange jumpsuits. I'll be back before noon. What are you up to?"

"Cody returned my drawing of the layout in the bar. I scanned it and sent it to his e-mail. He marked it up and faxed it back. Some people still do use fax machines."

"Now we know where he was sitting. Here." Thornton pulled out a desk drawer. She handed over an envelope. "Buy that table. That's ten grand. Use it all if you have to. Whatever you think. Whatever you decide."

"What would that idiot do without us?"

"Have a lot more money but live in a six-by-eight room with a little window way up high." Thornton dropped a legal pad in an attaché case, snapped it shut, and winked at Montclaire. "I like this attitude I'm seeing. You're getting it, girl."

Montclaire wondered where the wink thing was coming from. Second time this week. Made her think of a photographer, greasy hair and a smell, winking when he told her how sexy he was going to make her look. *Inch up your skirt, darling. Scoot that little bottom closer to the edge of the stool. A bit more. Now hook your heels on the rung, no the one higher. Higher, I said. Oh, yes, this is going to be good.* Her, three weeks to her fourteenth birthday, scared when he locked the door, everybody else suddenly gone, the studio so dark behind lights inside silver umbrellas. *Why am I alone with this man?*

Montclaire dropped the envelope with the money in her purse, a classic Lancaster she had picked out on a shoot in Paris when she was seventeen. She left while Thornton sat at the dressing table in her office and worked on her eyes.

Her BMW 3 Series wouldn't work for the job. She dropped her car at a U-Haul on St. Francis and drove a rental van to The Howling Coyote. She parked at the curb, in front of a beer truck.

She liked this assignment, liked this day from the minute she saw Marcy hung over, rubbing her temples and asking why she was so perky. Last night, finding the girl for the judge. Today, charged with doing whatever necessary to take care of evidence that could take down a famous man. Her call. No photographer telling her to show something she wasn't feeling. No modeling scouts wanting more than they said at the start of the interview, and having to give it to get the job.

Marcy said, "Whatever you think. Whatever you decide."

She was feeling some of what she felt taking two men at a time to a hotel room she paid for, telling them how it was going to be if they wanted what she had to give. Watching what she could do to them by nothing more than popping a button. Being the first one off the bed when it was over, drinking a glass of water, standing over them.

Whatever I think. Whatever I decide.

Inside the bar she unfolded Geronimo's fax. He had circled the table where he sat after murdering Linda Fager. Where the idiot had wiped blood from his fingers. She approached a young woman mopping the floor.

"I'd like to see the manager."

"He'll be out in a minute. If it's about work, I can get you an application."

"It's something else. I'll wait."

She located the table Geronimo had marked on her drawing. She sat there until a man stepped through the swinging doors to the kitchen. A belly pushed against his patterned golf shirt. He wore a gold chain around his neck and a cigarette behind his ear. His spiky haircut, thick with product, had taken a lot of time to get right.

"We open at eleven," he said.

"I want to buy this table."

"Lady, we sell beer and burgers."

"One thousand dollars."

The table was nicked and yellowed, leveled with a matchbook.

"What's this about?" He came closer.

"My husband proposed to me here." She patted the table. "I want to surprise him for our anniversary."

"I can't sell you the table."

"Two thousand. Cash."

"Honest, I don't have the authority."

"Ten grand. Tell your boss a drunk busted one of the legs. Buy a replacement for a couple hundred bucks, keep the rest. How long does it take you to make that kind of money?"

"This must be a very special table."

"You have no idea."

He checked the room. The young woman who had been mopping was partially blocked by the bar, kneeling down to scrape gum off the floor.

"Twelve grand, it's yours," he said.

Montclaire stacked a bundle of cash on the table.

"Ten grand disappears in five seconds. One one-thousand, two one-thousand."

"Okay."

He grabbed the money, needing both hands to hold it all.

"You don't have a husband." He nodded at her hands. The only ring she wore was on her pinkie.

"Smart boy. I want the table because it has my initials."

"Don't see any."

"Underneath." She dragged her fingers slowly along table's edge. "I carved my initials every time I gave a blow job under there. I could add another set right now."

"Just like that, you'll go down on me."

"I'm surprised you didn't add it to the price. I only said no more money."

He checked again for the girl cleaning the floor. She was now out of sight, completely behind the bar, only the sound of a scraper against floor tiles. He looked Montclaire over, down her legs to the gold nails in her open-toed shoes, then back to her face.

"My office."

"One condition."

"You don't swallow. What do I care?"

"I bite off your dick when you come."

He backed away, the money in fists pressed against his chest. "Lady, you are one sick bitch."

"Why that's the sweetest thing anyone has said to me today. I don't know how it can possibly get better."

———

The guys working the beer truck were happy to load the table into her rental van. As Montclaire was closing the doors, the young woman who had been cleaning floors came outside to empty a bucket of water in the gutter.

"That was sweet, what you pulled on Randy," she said to Montclaire. "His name's Randy? No."

"Yeah. Why'd you do that, jerk his chain when you reached a deal?"

"Because I could?"

"You're asking me?"

"I saw you behind the bar. I hoped you were listening. Randy's a bit of a prick, isn't he?"

"Let me say this, you weren't the first woman he told to come back to his office. You knew that."

"Something about him just pissed me off. And you on your hands and knees. Long ago I used to model."

"I can see that."

"Who do you think did the real work so a man with a belly could have it easy?"

"Well, you read Randy right and you made my day. But you wasted your money."

"How's that?" She admired the tattoos on the girl's shoulders, gnarled vines curling around dozens of small skulls.

"This is about that Indian artist in here the night the bookstore lady was killed."

"Is it?"

"I waited on him. That was where he was sitting out on the floor, where you sat down. He had his legs crossed, a boot on his knee. Those boots were something, I swear, real silver tips. But that wasn't the table. You bought a dud."

She forgot the girl's tattoos.

"I rearranged tables yesterday to seat a party of four. Your boy with the ponytail and fancy boots was at a two-top."

"Shit."

The girl fired a cigarette. "I thought you might say that," she said in a cloud of smoke.

Montclaire drove to the courthouse and found Thornton waiting with her last client to be called up for arraignment. She caught her at the back of the courtroom.

"Problem?" Thornton asked.

"You could say the table's been turned on us."

Thornton raised her eyebrows and followed Montclaire downstairs to the concrete planter in the center of a treeless concrete plaza.

Montclaire said, "Her name's Laura Pasco. She has no idea what's so important about that table. But if we're willing to shell out ten thou for the wrong table, she's thinking, why not twenty for the right one?"

"How do we know she's got the right table?"

"She says it's at her place for repairs. Her boyfriend's a cabinet-maker and fixes furniture for businesses around town. She saw Cody wipe his hand under the table. He was acting odd so she remembered it. We could shine one of those lights, the kind that shows blood, before we pay."

"She sees twenty, she might demand more. I would. I've got fifty grand for expenses from Cody. Pull it all out."

"How much should I pay?"

"We have simple instructions from our client. He's got only one ass to keep out of jail. There's always more money if we need it. And get some cheapo prepaid cells. You can't be running me down to talk and I don't want to do it over our regular phones."

Montclaire snapped her fingers.

"Andrea," she said.

"Huh?"

"That girl from last night. Just came to me."

"The way your mind works."

TWENTY-THREE

ARAGON WOKE AN HOUR before dawn. Sitting on the tailgate of Javier's truck she ate a cold Lotaburger then stowed her sleeping bag and pad in the cab. As she was about to pull on her boots, Cynthia Fremont jumped into her mind. She tied her boots off her feet, then again with the boots on.

Rivera said the FBI had an expert who could tell them if Fremont had tied her own bootlaces. Aragon saw a defense lawyer having the expert remove his own shoes and tie the laces, pass them hand to hand among jurors. Sitting there maybe with holes in his socks, wiggling his toes, until the lawyer told him to put his shoes on, lace up, stand on a table so the jurors could see. The jurors would try it at night. They'd see what she was seeing right now: you couldn't tell the difference. What did Dr. Shoelaces know anyway?

But she saw something else. She could never find a pair of boots that fit right. Always her heels wanted to slip and slide, guaranteeing blisters galore by day's end. Javier had shown her a way to snug her heel by cinching the laces before they threaded through the top eyelets.

She wanted to see a photograph of Fremont's boots before they were taken off her feet. She'd call Rivera when she was back in Santa Fe.

She programmed a waypoint on Javier's GPS to record the location of her campsite. She might not know where she was going, but she had better know how to get back. This country was folded up like crumpled newspaper. She could pass within a hundred feet of the truck and miss it if she was in the wrong drainage.

She carried a daypack with protein bars, a jar of peanuts, the one unspoiled orange from her refrigerator, and a liter of water. She wore her .40 caliber and the Mini-14 slung over her shoulder. In these vast spaces, the only weapon that made sense was a rifle. But she wasn't going to leave her sidearm behind in the pickup truck.

It took three hours of climbing in and out of arroyos and crawling under barbed wire strung a century ago to find the first private inholding on the Bureau of Land Management map. It was a sandy field with a windmill and earthen stock tank. The windmill was too rusted to turn. The tank was dry. There was no sign anyone had been here in years.

She climbed a ridge and used the rifle's scope to scout the country ahead. Movement behind a clump of brittle grass drew her attention. With the cross-hairs on the hindquarters of a coyote, she judged the distance at a quarter mile. Javier could make this shot, maybe even without the scope. She would need a tripod, a favorable wind, and a ton of luck. But with a pistol, she could outshoot him at everything from stationary firing to combat shooting. He had given up trying to beat her.

She lowered the rifle and moved downhill. Leafless cottonwoods two canyons away suggested water. She cross-referenced the BLM map and found the symbol for a spring inside the outlines of private land.

The trees were farther away than she had guessed. When she arrived she found the ruins of a corral and packed earth that showed no tire tracks. The spring had dried up. Though it had been cold in the morning, the sun was now blazing. She squinted at the jagged spires of Ladron Peak and longed for a little relief from the sun. She cursed herself for forgetting sunglasses.

Sunglasses. Cynthia Fremont's face in the beam of her flashlight, pale goggles of white skin in a red face.

Naked, drugged, sliced open, but wearing sunglasses to protect her eyes from the sun's blinding glare.

It wasn't about the killers not wanting to see her eyes. They didn't want her staring into the sun. Just as Fremont had been laid out carefully in the trunk, some degree of compassion for the young woman fit into a broader picture of merciless pain and agony.

She gobbled a protein bar, chugged water, and set out for the next square of land on the map. Across a mesa, down a rocky slope into an arroyo, back up a steep ridge to a stretch of rolling land dotted by cactus and clumps of juniper. A turkey buzzard floated overhead. Farther above, a plane crossed the blue sky. Higher still, sunlight flashed off something in the low atmosphere. It could be a satellite. The elevation here approached two miles above sea level. The air was thin, the sky perfectly clear, zero humidity.

"You idiot."

She had been so angry at the suspension she had not been thinking clearly. Instead she had charged off to do a Lewis and Clark to find where Geronimo may have done his killing, one mesa, one canyon, one gully at a time. There would never be a substitute for legwork. They would always have to eyeball the ground up close. At least the sweep of her search could have been narrowed by using satellite imagery.

She tried to reach Lewis but the mountain blocked the signal from the cell towers along the interstate corridor.

She explored empty land for the rest of the day, finding nothing useful, but wasting not a minute. As her feet covered the miles, her mind worked through every piece of information they had on Geronimo. She walked step by step through the Tasha Gonzalez investigation looking for what may have been missed. Instead of dusty hills and cholla cactus, she saw Thornton and Judge Diaz taken down in twenty different scenarios, all imaginary, but as detailed as any case file that had been worked by a corruption task force.

The sun was moving toward its bed below the western skyline. She checked the GPS. She would have to move quickly to get back to her truck before dark.

She swallowed the last of her water just as she reached the canyon where she had parked. Another set of tire tracks headed in and had not come out. She slipped the Mini-14 off her shoulder and hid it behind a boulder. With her pistol in hand she moved forward, hugging the canyon wall, sprinting between cover. Up ahead she saw the rear bumper of a pickup blocking hers. Inside the cab a man wearing a large cowboy hat sat at the wheel, a bolt action rifle in the rack behind his head. She moved to the driver's side. The window was down.

She heard snoring.

"Wake up."

An elderly Hispanic man under the sweat-stained hat lifted an eyebrow.

"You're on my land," he said in a voice as dry as the landscape.

She relaxed and lowered her gun.

"I didn't mean to trespass. I'll pull out of here immediately."

"I saw your lights on the road last night, then they disappeared. I was worried for you. I don't mind you being on my land. I just wanted to know you're okay."

Aragon holstered her pistol. The old man had not reacted to the sight of a weapon in her hand.

"What are you doing here?" he asked.

Aragon showed her badge and identified herself.

"Is this about the sign?"

She remembered her headlights picking out a street sign in the middle of the desert on her drive in last night.

The old man said, "My boy brings a sign from Albuquerque when he visits. They stay up until the county blades the road."

"This is about something more serious than stolen street signs." Without giving him the background, she said she was inspecting all the parcels that went with the Secret Canyon Ranch. "I want to see if there are any buildings on those lands."

"You're on the wrong side of the mountain." He pointed with a brown hand missing the index finger. "Up the river there's a big house with electricity. Pretty nice place. Some Indian goes in there sometimes." He turned his head to her truck. "Is this your camp?"

"All the comforts."

"I don't see a campfire. How did you eat?"

She told him about her cold burger for breakfast.

"My wife's making tamales for dinner. Tomorrow, I show you the way to that house."

———————

His name was Fermin Bustamante. He backed out of the canyon, then took a dirt road leading into empty country. Aragon followed in his dust and didn't see the ranch until she slowed at a cattle guard marked with coyote hides and another Albuquerque street sign, this one saying "Lomas Boulevard."

The ranch had once been a busy cattle operation with loading facilities and hay barns. But the pens were empty. Tumbleweeds clogged the squeeze chute. Dogs of all sizes and colors rushed from the shade by the house to greet Bustamante's truck, then broke away to surround her as she drove into the yard. He whistled and they came back to him. She grabbed Javier's six-pack from the cooler behind the seat and followed Bustamante to the mud-colored ranch house under a rusted tin roof.

They entered through a hand-made wooden door and two-foot thick adobe walls. Cooking smells triggered memories of her grandmother. Bustamante went deeper into the house and returned with a little woman, dark and weathered with white hair loose about her shoulders. A stained apron was tied around her waist.

Fermin introduced his wife, Flor. She took the beers and returned to the kitchen. Fermin stoked a Franklin stove while Aragon admired family photographs on the mantel. She would ask about what appeared to be nine children during dinner.

Pillows covered with dog hair surrounded a cowhide chair. Next to the chair was a small table with a telephone atop magazines about cattle and horses.

"May I use your phone?"

"Help yourself," Fermin replied as he shoved a split log into the firebox.

She dialed Lewis's number. He was glad to hear from her, said Donnelly from Professional Standards wanted an interview. Lewis was holding him off with the excuse that the police union's attorney was in Washington and would not return for a week. He passed along a message from Rivera. The Forest Service had sent horseback teams into the wilderness searching for Fremont's killers. So far, they had encountered only day hikers and a Boy Scout troop that had illegally dug a latrine trench too close to a waterway.

Aragon reported on her day. He cut her off when she brought up Google Earth and said he had already wasted hours until his wife suggested something better. He had spent the afternoon viewing footage of aerial surveys conducted by the Game and Fish department. He had found a building on one of Geronimo's parcels. It was an old but well-kept ranch headquarters to which had been added a new wing with a metal roof. The Game and Fish Cessna had flown low enough that the camera picked up outlines of the septic field. A bleached elk head hung over the front door, just like the one above the entrance to Geronimo's Santa Fe gallery. A broad, shallow stream lined with tamarisk and reeds flowed within a hundred feet of the house.

"It's called the Rio Salado."

A charge of electricity rippled across her back. A river named Salt. Salt in Tasha Gonzalez's hair. Aragon was bone tired, but doubted she would sleep tonight.

TWENTY-FOUR

Bronkowski worked on filling the gap in time between the register receipt for Geronimo's book purchase at Fager's Finds and the moment he fled detectives Aragon and Lewis. In files Goff supplied, he found Aragon's observation that Geronimo had the sour smell of beer on his breath. He knew all of Santa Fe's bars and thought the classy Staab House, a Victorian mansion turned into a bar and restaurant, would be Geronimo's first pick in the neighborhood of Fager's Finds. But his inquiries there of the evening manager and her service staff found no one who remembered seeing the artist on the night of the murder.

He walked to the next upscale watering hole on his list and struck out again. He was wondering if he would have to expand his search to restaurants when he heard country music drifting down the alley that led to the Howling Coyote Saloon. He decided to give it a shot. Peanut shells crunched under his heels as he made his way to the bar and asked for the manager. The bartender pointed him to a hallway leading to a small office, where he found a man in a patterned golf shirt, hair full of gel, punching numbers into an adding machine.

"Excuse me," Bronkowski said, his bulk blocking the entryway. "I'm a friend of the family of a woman murdered a few days ago." He showed a photo of Cody Geronimo. "I'm wondering if you remember this guy being here."

"You're not with that bitch?"

"Which bitch would that be?"

"The one looks like a woman in pantyhose commercials when I was a kid. That one has a mouth on her."

"She was asking about this same man?"

The manager was about to say something then turned his attention back to his adding machine.

"I got work to do. Ask for Laura. She couldn't stop talking about serving the guy. She's the short brunette with a gallon of ink on her neck."

He saw her distributing bottles of beer around a table of middle-aged men and women wearing shirts about rafting the Rio Grande Gorge. He caught up to her as she counted loose change from her apron. When he showed her Geronimo's photo he caught the recognition in her eyes, followed by a forced flat expression.

"He had a beer. Ordered another, but left before I got the order in." She swept coins into her palm, jiggled them a little, shoved them in her apron.

She was in her early twenties, dressed in a tank top. The hair on one side of her head had been cut short to reveal tattoos of vines curling around her ear. She avoided his eyes.

"Tony," she shouted past him to the bartender. "Tap another Fat Tire. Those last were *flat* tires."

"Did he say anything?"

"Look." She smoothed her apron. "I'm busy here. He had a beer. Ordered another but left. That's all."

"Where was he sitting?"

"He was at the bar."

"Why were you serving him? You wait tables."

"Two Negronis and a G and T," she yelled louder than necessary. "Pronto!"

"Linda Fager was a wonderful woman."

The waitress finally faced him. "Who?"

"Linda Fager. The woman murdered that night. She loved cats and roses. She loved books. Her husband loved her more than he can say in words."

"Yeah, well. I'm sorry what happened to her." Her feet shifted to carry her back to the floor. He was losing her.

"Nice ink," he said to keep her talking. He nodded at her tattoos. "That blue and green woven together. Almost glows."

She turned her head so he could see her neck more clearly. He had missed the small skeletons entangled in the vines curling from clavicle to ear.

"I like it freaky."

"Those tats make you look hard."

"Thanks."

"Harder than you really are."

"I've got customers waiting."

"Just one more second. Since you're into freaky." He reached inside his jacket, "Here's something like nothing you've ever seen."

He held the photo in front of her face so she could not miss a detail.

"He had pieces of her with him while he enjoyed the cold one you brought him," he said to a young woman growing pale. "That really freaky skin art stapled to the wall." He tapped the photo. "There above her body. That's her face."

She took a step back but couldn't peel her eyes from the photograph.

"That wasn't paint in his hair," she said so quietly he barely heard her. "He said he hadn't been painting." She looked away, then back at the photograph. "Damn. I can't do it now. Thanks a lot."

"Do what? Is there some place we can talk?"

She blinked her eyes and took a breath.

"I need a cigarette. Wait here."

She served her customers then led him out the front door, a few steps from the entrance. She fired up, dragged hard, kept repeating the same limited set of facts she had given him inside. She lit a second cigarette off the first and picked at a nail. Her eyes kept drifting to the photo, turned so she could see it.

"Laura, what do you mean that wasn't paint in his hair? Tell me about that."

"Shit. Alright." She told him: About the dark, wet stuff in his hair and Geronimo's hand inside his jacket like he had something alive in there. And yesterday a woman willing to pay crazy money for a beat-up bar table.

Down the street Montclaire, pressed into a doorway, wearing a cowboy hat and glasses, watched Laura Pasco blowing her shot at fifty grand. She had been hanging out in the bar to keep an eye on the waitress and had planned to follow her home after work. She wanted to see this workshop where Pasco said her boyfriend was working on the table before they talked money again. Now she had to worry Bronkowski might get the table before her.

She watched him showing a photograph to Pasco, saw her go pale and dig cigarettes out of her apron. Montclaire slipped out the side entrance and stood in a doorway as they talked on the street in front of the Howling Coyote.

The conversation ended. Pasco crushed a cigarette under her heel and went inside the bar. Bronkowski walked off down the street. She decided to follow him. She could return later to catch Pasco heading home.

As soon as Bronkowski was out of sight, Montclaire ran after him. She pulled up at the corner and saw him halfway down the block. Empty streets made it hard to tail him without being seen.

When he neared the Capitol she realized he was heading to Fager's office. She took a shortcut through the Capitol's grounds and arrived ahead of him. She slipped into her car and watched him approach. Instead of that cheap Camry she had seen him driving earlier, he mounted his Harley, kicked it to life, and roared onto Paseo de Peralta. She pulled out after him. The fact he took his bike suggested he was not going for the table right now.

He took major roads out of downtown then turned onto quiet residential streets winding past houses on big lots with automatic gates at the end of driveways. He stopped at one gate to speak into a box. A second later the gate slid back and he rode in.

Montclaire knew this place. It belonged to a man who did computerized investigative work. Thornton used his services. He was not in the furniture-moving business. Cody's table was safe for another night.

Montclaire drove back to the Howling Coyote and changed from the cowboy hat and glasses to a straight black wig and turtleneck. She took a seat in the bar away from Pasco's tables and ordered a Diet Coke. She had two hours until closing.

Bronkowski rolled up the gravel drive to the rambling adobe home where John Pitcairn ran his investigative services business. Pitcairn had called to report he already had results on the Gonzalez family trace. He worked nights. Midnight was a fine time to meet.

Pitcairn met him at the door. He was dressed in a bowtie and short-sleeved, button-down shirt with a pocket protector holding pens and pencils, and a phone and calculator in cases on his belt. Bronkowski always wanted to tell Pitcairn it was okay to stop dressing for the job at Los Alamos lab he had left long ago. Classical music played as Pitcairn led him to a living room converted to his central workspace. An office chair was surrounded by three connected desks with large monitors. File cabinets ran along the walls, behind a white greaseboard full of arrows and columns of names and numbers. A mobile sculpture with the wingspan of a small plane hung from the high ceiling, spinning above Pitcairn as he handed Bronkowski a manila folder.

"Coffee while you read?"

Bronkowski waved him off. Pitcairn was in the middle of his work day, Bronkowski was looking forward to bed.

"I'll have more tomorrow," Pitcairn said as he worked an elaborate brass Italian espresso machine squeezed between scrapped motherboards and vinyl binders. "I found activity ten years ago, the day after you said they disappeared from Santa Fe. A credit card issued to Estevan Gonzalez was used at locations along I-25 as far north as Cheyenne, then several times in Pinedale, Wyoming. The twenty-thousand and change balance on that card was paid off in one bite and all use ceased. Years of silence. No financial activity at all until Estevan started buying property recently."

"Where?"

"Jackson Hole." Pitcairn dropped a sugar cube into a demitasse and waited for the espresso machine to stop hissing and shaking. "A gutter-cleaning and yard-care company. Then a tire store. This year he bought a cute little cottage in Teton Village. There's a view in the folder."

Bronkowski paged through the report until he found the photograph. He whistled at the multi-story stone mansion against the backdrop of the Teton Range.

"It has a sixteen-seat movie theater," Pitcairn said.

The Gonzalez family, minus Tasha, had come a long way from the single-wide on Santa Fe's dusty south side.

"What does the guy do for this kind of money?"

"Nothing I can see. He was dormant, then his Spring arrived. Time to blossom."

"Thanks, John. It's a great start."

"I'll eyeball tax records tomorrow. Lovely thing about those police files you gave me. They've got DOBs, Social Security, INS and passport numbers, everything a fellow needs for a very good time."

Outside, before getting on his bike, Bronkowski called Fager, knowing he'd be up, pounding at his computer, drinking cold coffee.

"That waitress was a nervous wreck just telling me she brought Geronimo a beer at the bar. She waits tables. That's when I knew she was holding back. I'm going to be at her house tomorrow morning, get her out of bed before Montclaire shows up with her bag of money."

"Marcy's cleaning up after her sloppy client," Fager said. "Taking a breather to grab a beer was a mistake. That blood in his hair was Linda's and I'm betting he left some on that table. Tell that woman I'll beat any offer from Montclaire."

"My night's done. Why don't you shut it down? Mascarenas is not going to read any of those briefs you're spitting out."

"I'm going to petition to empanel a grand jury to investigate Linda's murder. Press conference tomorrow. I'm hiring temporary staff to collect signatures, those enviros who go door-to-door on everything from whales to wolves. They're in between rants right now, hungry for something to piss them off. We need two-thousand two-hundred and forty-one signatures to meet the statute's threshold. The DA will have to act. This will force a special prosecutor. That's going to be me."

"Who's this on our team?"

"And I'm filing that replevin action. To force Geronimo to turn over those bones he took from Linda. He'll have to answer. I'll get his deposition. Marcy will instruct her client to assert the Fifth. Fireworks ensue. That little civil suit will generate publicity for the petition drive. The media can't slam me for chasing his money. I'm just trying to put *all* of my wife to rest, see justice done. That will be the story line. Sympathetic, something new for me."

"Walt, get some sleep."

Whales and wolves. For the first time he wondered if Fager knew what the hell he was doing.

TWENTY-FIVE

FERMIN BUSTAMANTE TOLD ARAGON how to find the dirt road to Geronimo's ranch. But she wanted to get in without leaving tire tracks alerting Geronimo that he had had a visitor. Even worse, Geronimo might come up behind her while she was in there. She could run, but Javier's pickup would be trapped, traced back to him, then her.

The rancher led Aragon to a dry arroyo the Ford could handle in four-wheel drive. The swath of sand and gravel ended two miles later at a sheer wall of rock. She left the truck and clambered through cactus and busted granite to look down on a shallow stream sliding between black basalt cliffs. Even at a distance she could make out salt encrusted on the banks. The Rio Salado. A salmon-colored house with a large wing under a new metal roof had been built next to the stream.

In a road passing under a closed gate, only old tire tracks filling with sand. No smoke rising from the chimney. No light from inside. Curtains pulled across all the windows.

She climbed over barbed wire and approached the building. A bleached elk skull and antlers hung over a front door of weathered oak with two deadbolts above an antique latch. She pulled on thin leather gloves from the bottom of her pack and tried it, then the door to the modern wing at the back of the house. It also had twin deadbolts. Both doors were locked.

Lewis could pick locks. She never had the patience. A rock took care of the lowest window. She snapped out glass shards and pushed herself up and in.

She landed on a cold concrete floor. When her eyes adjusted, she made out shelves against walls, a work bench, specimen cabinets like those in a natural history museum and a metal table centered in the room. The table was from another age.

It was coated in porcelain and mounted on a steel base. An indented channel led to a hole under which sat a galvanized tub. Unlike its modern counterparts, it lacked wheels and a hook-up for water. This was an embalming table. An antique, a collector's item, but it looked ready to use.

Aragon pulled out her phone to take photographs but held back. She did not want any permanent record, even on her private phone, of her illegal entry. She checked to see if she could call out. On this side of the mountain nothing should obstruct the signal from the cell towers along the interstate. She'd be leaving a record of her call on those towers, but it would show only that she may have been traveling the interstate when her call was made. She dialed Lewis and he answered immediately.

Aragon heard excitement in his voice.

"When you get to Geronimo's ranch house ... "

"I'm in."

Silence. She knew he was weighing what she had just told him, his partner admitting to breaking and entering, him on the edge of being complicit.

"When you leave," he said, "head up the canyon, upstream about a quarter to a third of a mile. I found something on the aerial survey. Flyovers taken in the late afternoon caught shadows in at least a dozen depressions. They're not random. They're set out in rows. Like graves. I don't know what else it could be."

She felt that lovely electrical current rippling across her back.

"You're not going to believe what I'm looking at." She described the embalming table, the specimen cabinets, the room's layout. On the shelves, bits of bone, twisted metal, feathers, dried cactus husks, smooth river stones, a chipped brick, rusted coils of wire, a railroad stake, swatches of animal hide, wasp nests. The items in Geronimo's odd collection ran into the hundreds.

"*Object trouvé*," Lewis said. "Found art. Objects from everyday life considered junk turned into creative works by, I'm quoting here, the spirit, imagination, and talent of the artist. I've been reading the book Geronimo bought from Linda Fager. You're seeing his art supplies."

"You found time to read a book?"

"Skimmed it during my daughter's soccer practice."

Geronimo had taken the small bones in Linda Fager's inner ear. Aragon wondered if any of these bones were human. Not all of Tasha Gonzalez's bones had been recovered. They might be here.

"I'm going to check the main house, then I'm going up the canyon." Lewis didn't respond. She had lost the weak signal.

She made another sweep around the room. A storyteller figurine in the corner of the top shelf seemed out of place among the busted, faded, decaying junk everywhere else in the room. Storyteller dolls were favorites of Indian art collectors. The basic design was a rotund woman, not unlike the women in Geronimo's drawings, dressed in leggings, a blanket around her shoulders, with tiny children sprouting from hips and thighs.

Maybe it was Geronimo's muse, inspiring his work, watching over his creative activity.

She turned her attention to the specimen cabinets and studied the bones. She and Lewis had already made the mistake of misidentifying the small bones seized from Geronimo as avian. She considered taking some of these bones to the medical inspector. But what she learned could never be used as the basis for a search warrant or an arrest. She needed to return here, legally.

She saw Japanese paper, silk scarves, flattened chicken wire, glues, brushes, tacks, string. Other drawers held sketch books. She found bird feathers, shells, and more polished stones. In a bottom drawer she found rulers, stencils, pencils, pens, and markers. Surgical knives in a velvet pouch, rolled up and tied around the middle. And a remote control.

She stared at four fine, precise blades. The electrical current across her back turned into a chilling cold. She put the knives carefully back into the exact spot where she had found them.

The remote control puzzled her. The room did not have a television or stereo. She had seen no antenna or satellite dish.

That would be pure luck, Lewis had said right before she played with what turned out to be the key fob to Geronimo's Range Rover. She pressed the remote's power button. Nothing happened. No lottery hit this time. She was about to replace the remote when she noticed a faint glow in the mouth of the storyteller figurine.

A step ladder, tiptoes, and a full extension of her arms brought the figurine down to eye level.

The figurine concealed a security camera. And it was running.

On her belly she looked under everything in the room. She double-checked the shelves and drawers. She entered the main house through a connecting door and opened cupboards, peered under furniture, tapped walls, felt on top of closet shelves. She found no device that could be receiving a signal from the camera.

She leaned out the broken window for a better phone signal than the thick adobe walls allowed.

"I could be fucked," she said when Lewis answered, then calmed down and asked him to research what she was holding. She described it in detail. Embossed lettering said it was manufactured by an outfit called SleuthCon. She read the model number and waited while he found it on the Internet.

"It's inside the camera. An SD card, just like in a digital camera. Motion-activated. Runs off a lithium battery. Any bets what's on there besides you poking around?"

"We'll see." She put the entire camera in her day pack. "I'm going up the canyon after I make sure he doesn't have other cameras watching me."

She searched the house and workroom once more. With her pen knife she removed electrical face plates, inspected the wall clock in the kitchen, shook tissue boxes, poked fingers into the dry soil of potted plants. She found no other camera. She hoped she was right.

In her search she noticed that the house needed dusting. Dead insects lined window sills. Cobwebs hung in corners. But the workroom with the embalming table was immaculate. Geronimo was a neatnik where it was important to him. He had washed the boxcutter and staple gun he used on Linda Fager and placed them neatly on a folded paper towel to dry. Photos Goff had taken inside his Santa Fe studio also showed an immaculate work space.

She found only one thing of interest in the main house. The bedroom held an ancient green steel bed that looked incredibly uncomfortable. It appeared to be the same vintage as the embalming table. The rest of the house was furnished with worn upholstered or rough wood furniture. The dresser in the bedroom contained nothing more than spare clothes. The refrigerator ran on propane and held champagne and bottled water. Food was stored in plastic bins as protection against mice. Stacks of magazines about the art business were scattered on the coffee table in the living room. If she had missed anything, it would take a more intensive search than she could make today.

Aragon went out the window she had used to enter and dropped down to the streambed. A white line ran unevenly along the banks. She wet a fingertip, touched white crust, and tasted salt. She scooped up a handful and sealed it in a plastic bag. She wanted the chemical composition of this salt deposit matched against the salt in Tasha Gonzalez's hair. Trace elements might work the same way as a DNA signature.

She passed under a three-strand, barbed-wire fence hung with a sign notifying her she was entering a Bureau of Land Management Wilderness Study Area. She followed the stream until she saw it churning ahead between black cliffs. There at the foot of the cliffs was a smoothed rectangle of sand, free of rocks and brush.

Lewis was right. Repetitive depressions of equal size and shape were arranged in straight, neat rows.

Last night, between talking about his children and the fading of the ranching industry, Fermin Bustamante had thrown in history lessons about Ladron Peak. In addition to being a hideout for robbers who attacked Spanish wagons on the Camino Real from Mexico, it was the site of battles between Apaches and Buffalo Soldiers of the U.S. Cavalry. A large engagement had been fought on the Rio Salado. Many men fell on both sides.

She doubted these were Apache graves. Indians either carried away their dead or the soldiers left them to rot if they were not burned. They could be the graves of Buffalo Soldiers, buried anonymously, in precise military order.

Or someone who was precise and orderly in the work most important to him.

She could be looking at the graves of women Geronimo did not dump into a drainage ditch or butcher in the bathroom of a used bookstore. Women who had been on the embalming table less than half a mile away, in the same room with the surgical knives. Under the camera in the mouth of the storyteller.

The figurine had stories to tell, and they weren't Navajo creation myths.

Aragon plotted her location on the GPS unit then inspected the open area. She counted fourteen distinct depressions. She shoved a stick into the soil of one to see if it was a shallow grave. She struck nothing.

This time she took photographs on her phone. This was public land. She had every right to be here without a warrant. She took a wider shot, then scaled the nearest black cliff to get a higher perspective that would show the entire plot.

From here she could see the rooftop of Geronimo's compound and vague tire tracks, eroded by weather, between the house and graveyard. She followed the tracks back to Geronimo's property and found where the barbed wire was only loosely connected with hooks so it could be folded back to allow a motor vehicle through.

It was time to hike over the mountain and back to her truck before she lost daylight. She turned around and faced whoever was buried in the sandy clearing.

"I'm sorry, I've got to go now."

TWENTY-SIX

ARAGON DROVE FROM GERONIMO'S ranch listening to the country stations programmed into Javier's radio. At Albuquerque she left the interstate and headed to a Radio Shack she knew by the university. A young woman in a wrinkled white shirt and thin black tie greeted her. The plastic tag pinned to her breast pocket said her name was Donna. Aragon showed her the surveillance camera she had taken from Geronimo's ranch.

"I found this in my bathroom after I kicked my boyfriend out."

Donna said, "Men are such bastards."

"I need to see what's on it so I can tell the police. Or maybe not, depending. I wouldn't want them seeing, well, you know."

"Here." Donna took the camera and slipped out a plastic chip the size of a postage stamp and nearly as thin. "You just push this into an SD reader and plug that into a USB port."

Aragon's computer was in her apartment in Santa Fe. She wanted to know right now what the camera had recorded.

"He took my laptop. And my credit cards."

"Bastard." Donna motioned Aragon to a counter near the register. "I won't look," she said, and slipped the SD card into the side of a new Lenovo. "Just go to 'computer' and open the F file."

"That simple?"

"Simpler than boyfriends."

Aragon followed her instructions. She saw three files. The first showed Geronimo entering the workroom carrying a narrow silver box. He walked across the room and opened the drawer where Aragon had found the remote control and surgical knives. He pointed the remote at the camera and the screen went dead. The next time the screen lit up it showed Geronimo pointing the remote again at the camera, replacing it in the drawer and leaving the room. The screen went dark after a few minutes of inactivity in the empty workroom.

The most recent file showed breaking glass skidding across the floor, Aragon squeezing through a broken window, moving around the room, and finally her face growing large as she looked directly into the camera lens. The images continued to roll until the flap of her day pack blocked the light.

She called out to Donna, saying she wanted to buy another card, and hide the camera in a different spot in her apartment, catch her boyfriend breaking in, catch his face when he can't find the camera where he hid it. Donna let her have the card for free.

She got back on the road. For the rest of the drive to Santa Fe she talked with Lewis, who said he was working at home tonight. Aragon wanted them to think through why Tasha Gonzalez was not buried near Geronimo's ranch in the graveyard, if that's what it was, but was dumped miles away in an irrigation ditch. They didn't have an answer but concluded that Rivera and the FBI were the key to their next moves. The charge on her cell died before they settled on how to make the approach.

She wanted food and a shower but drove into old Santa Fe onto the narrow winding streets off Canyon Road. Again she had trouble finding a place to park Javier's big truck. She found space in a church's lot four blocks from Geronimo's gallery. Music poured down the street from somewhere nearer the mountains. Geronimo's section of Canyon Road was dark and quiet.

She walked past his gallery to determine if he used external surveillance cameras. Her scare earlier today was still with her. Unlike the camera hidden in his ranch house, there should be no reason to disguise an outside camera. You wanted people with the wrong ideas to know they were being watched. She saw nothing to make her pause.

A stout adobe wall along the side of the gallery separated Geronimo's property from the business next door. The wall was decorated with flower pots, metal frogs, and blackbirds, as well as a grab bag of terra cotta figurines. Between coyotes rearing back to howl, ceremonial Indian dancers, parrots, bears, and turtles, Aragon saw at least three storyteller figures. She took one with her as she moved into the deeper shadows between the buildings.

She positioned the storyteller at a window into Geronimo's gallery, then settled the camera inside and aimed it through the glass. From the moss and cobwebs on the junk along the wall she doubted the camera would be discovered. If Geronimo found it, let him enjoy the thought he was being watched with the very camera he had set up inside his ranch ninety miles away.

She returned to the truck and drove to Lewis's house, knowing he was at work in his home office, the Dodge Caravan parked inside his garage.

———

"What's this?" Aragon asked about the small photographs taped on the inside of the minivan's windshield.

"I pulled the reports on missing women from Santa Fe County going back twenty years," Lewis said. "That's them."

She had never worked missing persons. She only met women like this when they turned up dead.

"Something's been bugging me," she said. "We heard Geronimo saying he was set off by Linda Fager looking at him. But he didn't take her eyes. He took the little bones from deep in her ear."

"Maybe he couldn't use the eyes. They don't keep. Bones he could clean, shellac, hang onto forever. We've got to get back in his ranch, learn if those bones you saw are human."

"Rivera," she said, steering them to what they needed to discuss. "This can't come from us. How does he take it upstairs that he's launching a multiple homicide investigation on what a suspended Santa Fe cop saw while trespassing on the private property of America's premier Indian artist?"

"*Native artist*. Remember. He's evolved."

"But what if Rivera goes upstairs with photographs that the bereaved husband of a murder victim took of graves, and turns over maps and GPS coordinates showing the location on federal land? This bereaved husband takes photos of the embalming table inside Geronimo's house and the knives in the drawer and hands them to the FBI. Rivera can ask his boss, what's a guy like Geronimo, arrested for killing one woman in Santa Fe, digging around inside her head, what's he doing with surgical knives, an embalming table, and graves a shout away?"

"I get the picture. "

"Will it stand up? You're the reader. Read anything on this?"

"A little. Because Fager's not law enforcement, there's no Fourth Amendment violation, no suppression of evidence remedy. Geronimo can sue Fager all he wants, wipe him out. But we get to use the info handed to us on Fager's dirty spoon. It's actually called the silver-spoon doctrine, this exception to illegal searches."

"And if it goes bad, it's on him, he pays the price. He'd probably be disbarred. Walter Fager serves the cause of justice, one way or another." She bounced a fist off her thigh. "I'm feeling it. It's coming together."

"Yeah."

They sat in silence, eyes on the faces of the missing women, thinking how close they might be to some answers.

Lewis broke the silence. "Rivera called. He's interested."

Aragon smacked his shoulder. "You've known all this time he's interested in Geronimo."

"In you. They've confirmed the celestial burial angle you brought them on Fremont. They've got another expert working the case, a Buddhist expert from the Smithsonian. FBI can't use a local who had tea with the Dalai Lama. They need a white guy with a Harvard degree. And they expect a translation on the prayer flags soon."

"What does any of that have to do with me?"

"He had a question about you." Lewis didn't finish, but raised his eyebrows and waited for her to notice.

"What? Oh, I see. He asked if I was a lesbian."

"Wrong. He did ask about your hair and why. He never asked if you like men or women."

"The hair was his way of asking."

"Really, it *was* about your hair. I told him why you cut it short, so it can't be grabbed in a fight."

"And he said, what, a catfight?"

"No. He said, 'makes sense.' Hey, he's a nice guy. Federal pay-check. Handsome. Smart. For you they have to be smart."

"So I should call him?"

"I saw you look at him. Other people might be talking, but you have your eyes on him."

"He reminds me of someone. That's all." Aragon dialed Rivera's number on her cell.

"Ask him out. When was the last time you … " Lewis stopped when he heard Rivera's voice coming through her phone.

She said, the phone by her mouth, "Listen, a question for you. Yeah, this is me. Those knife wounds on the Fremont girl, on her thighs. They run towards her waist, right? I know its Saturday. One working day 'til Monday. The Eldorado's bar. Tomorrow at eight? Bring photos of Fremont's boots. Yes, on her feet."

She hung up.

"Which direction was she cut?" Lewis asked. "What kind of pick up line is that?"

"One that worked."

"Hey, I think you're an interesting person. I'd like to hear about your job. What say we grab a drink? Or, I saw you looking at me across the room. Let's try it a lot closer. That's how normal people hook up."

"Normal people don't think about dead girls in sleeping bags and pieces of nice ladies stapled to walls. Normal people couldn't sleep with that on their mind."

Aragon flattened a palm over photographs taped inside the windshield.

"Fourteen of these women are buried by that salty river. Let's find out who they are."

TWENTY-SEVEN

THE SCREAM OF A ladder truck woke Bronkowski hours before he wanted to get up. He smelled smoke in the air when he went for the newspaper. Waiting for Mr. Coffee and his morning fix he watched the news out of Albuquerque. Another crack mother left her baby alone with her stash. A pit bull mauled a jogger. Johnny Depp dropped a couple thou at the Man's Hat Shop downtown. The store's owner, standing outside on the sidewalk so you could see the sign, said, "I thought he was another homeless fella come in to stay warm. Then someone said, that's Tonto. He's got the long hair, you know. I never sold so many hats to one guy."

"Mighty big doings down in Duke City," Bronkowski said.

An alert flashed across the bottom of the screen. A fire in Santa Fe was threatening a development on the hill above West Alameda. Cameras showed fire brigades dousing trees in the Santa Fe River Park to prevent flames from jumping to the east side.

He came alert without the caffeine. Laura Pasco lived on the hill above West Alameda.

From his car he called Goff to see if he could get details about the fire through his contacts at the police and fire departments. Goff did not answer. He left a message.

The streets approaching Pasco's address were blocked by pumper trucks and police barricades. He parked behind a fire-rescue van and approached a uniformed officer handling people trying to reach their homes.

"I have to find someone. She lives in there. I need to know she's alright."

"San Isidro Catholic Church on Agua Fria," the officer said. "Evacuees are there."

He found Pasco at a tent behind the church's bell tower, a blanket around her shoulders, steam rising from a Styrofoam cup in her hand. Her feet and legs were bare.

She saw him and said something to a bearded man with workingman hands. He stepped toward Bronkowski, the big hands in front, jaw forward. He was dressed in a t-shirt and jeans, also nothing on his feet. Bronkowski let the man come to him.

"Go away," the bearded man said.

"I wanted to see if she was okay."

"She's got nothing to say to you. Don't bother her again."

"Was her house in the fire?"

"Our house. What we're wearing is all we've got left."

"I'm sorry, but I need to ask. The table Laura told me about?"

"Didn't you hear me? Get your fat ass out of here. The fire started in my workshop, where that damn table was. I cut the power at night so there's no chance of an electrical spark, all the solvents and paints I had back there. That building exploded, got us running for our lives down the street. No way that was an accident. I'm wondering if you didn't start it. You or that bitch who got to Laura first. Now nobody gets the fucking thing."

———————

"You had fun," Marcy Thornton said and Montclaire had to agree, the two of them talking on the cheap cells Marcy had told her to buy. Burners, the clients called them. You could learn some things from them, stupid as they were, not needing to hire Marcy if they had any real brains.

"I thought of Diego Gavilan, how he bought the gasoline, the cans, the safety flares in a Walmart, not thinking it put everything in his hands on the store's security video."

"And left the gas cans with his prints in his car at the end of the driveway," Thornton said. "First place the fire inspectors looked. They hadn't pulled Diego's girlfriend out of the ashes before he was arrested."

Montclaire sat in her robe on the flagstone patio of her home watching the fire spread in the valley below. A cup of hot chocolate warmed her against the morning chill. A fist of orange flame shot into the sky above a bank of black smoke. A barbecue propane tank had exploded.

Laura Pasco. Stupid girl, talking to Bronkowski.

Marcy had told her, whatever you think. Whatever you decide.

"Run it by me so I know if we have anything to worry about," Thornton said.

"Pasco drives an orange Mazda. It was like a match burning in the night, flashing beneath the street lights." Montclaire was more excited telling it than trailing Pasco from the bar because now she knew what was coming. "She was easy to follow. She turned into the driveway of a little house over there off West Alameda. To the side, under trees was a garage with its door open. I saw paint cans, benches, vises, tools on a pegboard, things like that. From the street I could smell it, like nail-polish remover mixed with lemon oil. A guy with long black hair and a beard was bending over a wood table, on its back, screwing on a leg. It was a two-person table. Pasco called it a two-top."

Another fireball shot into the sky. Another propane tank. More sirens. A black cloud of smoke—asphalt shingles burning—rolled over the city.

"Like a match burning in the night," Thornton said. "That orange car under the lights gave you the idea."

"We pay, she gets a hook in us. How do we explain paying fifty grand for a lousy bar table?"

"Never going to happen now."

"I was going to use gas cans, but then I'd be on video somewhere buying them. I bought the biggest thermos bottles I could find." Montclaire's chocolate was growing cold. She moved inside to the microwave. "I went to the truck stop by the casino in Pojoaque. I got the gas all the way on the other side of town, at the station where St. Francis goes under I-25. I was filling my car and bent down to fill the thermoses. Nobody around. The cameras were inside the station, on the other side of my car."

"How'd you get the gas out of the Thermoses? I don't like that. You could splash yourself."

Montclaire squeezed the cell between her shoulder and ear and put her cup in the microwave, set it for a minute and watched the cup rotate on the glass plate. "I bought an aluminum bucket at the Walmart down on Cerrillos. I drove back to Pasco's house, the lights were out. I walked around the block, nobody awake, no dogs started barking. I stayed in the shadows to the side of the garage. The garage door was down, but the regular one on the side had a dog door. The fumes were really strong, so I knew it wouldn't take much. I emptied the Thermoses into the pail, tipped it through the door, set the fire and ran. I threw the Thermoses into different dumpsters five miles apart, the pail into a recycling bin behind Whole Foods. Oh, and I was wearing gloves. Forgot that part."

"Please tell me you didn't use flares. They don't burn completely. That was another thing Diego did wrong. The fire inspectors checked purchases for flares all over the county for a week before. Dumbshit used his debit card."

"Matches burn completely. I lit a book and flipped it through the doggie door. The sky was orange before I was back to my car."

Thornton said, "My smart, tough girl. You paid cash?"

"You just said I was smart. We didn't spend much of Cody's fifty grand. A few bucks."

"We don't give change."

Through the phone Montclaire heard a faucet running and the sound of a medicine cabinet closing. Marcy was talking to her from her bathroom at home. Outside her own house she heard sirens. She went to the door to watch fire trucks racing into Santa Fe from the direction of Espanola.

She had been up all night and should be tired. But she was just hungry. Really hungry. The microwave beeped, she took out her warmed chocolate. A hair dryer came on at Marcy's end. She wondered how long Marcy expected her to wait.

The dryer went quiet and Thornton spoke. "Never let a client think the job was too easy, so they must have overpaid," she said. "I've had clients complain about getting charges dismissed before trial, thinking they only get their money's worth if they roll the dice with a jury. I'll tell Cody we needed every penny, that he left us a real mess but we took care of it. He won't complain. You have no idea how terrified that man is of the people he'd meet in prison."

"I'll bring the fifty, minus expenses, after I eat."

"Cody's already said goodbye to that money. You say hello."

"All of it?" But Marcy had hung up.

When she saw her modeling career shriveling up, like the skin on an old lady who'd spent too much time in the sun, she worried if there would be any kind of life for her when it was done. Nothing new. No more excitement. No more adventure. No more money.

The hell was I thinking? She finished her chocolate and made herself a Beauty Bonanza Smoothie for breakfast.

TWENTY-EIGHT

IN HIS LIBRARY WALTER Fager was surrounded by words of the law, ghosts of people he once knew and trusted. Friends he'd used and abused. None were answering his call now that he needed them.

Hell, it had never been the words that mattered anyway. What mattered was what they triggered: his client stepping through the courthouse doors, going home to his own bed. Or swallowing hard as the bailiff led him back to his cell.

Geronimo's reaction to hearing "guilty," that's what mattered.

Fager had spent almost every hour since Geronimo was released searching for the right words, pouring them into motions and briefs Mascarenas could use—if he'd get off his ass. But the words slept on pages churned out of his printer, scattered on the floor of his office, bullets that would never be fired.

Fager straightened his tie. Local television and courthouse reporters were waiting in his conference room. He would announce his petition drive to bring to justice the man who had butchered his wife and was mocking the legal system every second he remained at liberty. Later this afternoon would be more words at Linda's memorial service. Words that did nothing, changed nothing, accomplished nothing.

What mattered was Linda, ashes in a pot.

And maybe real bullets in a gun pressed between Geronimo's eyes. Maybe Bronk was right.

Fager gathered the stack of petitions and went to face the media. He killed the lights in the library on his way out, thinking maybe it was time to convert the room to something else.

Bronkowski stood in the back of the conference room to watch Fager's performance. Robbie Weldon passed out copies of Fager's prepared statement. An enlarged photograph of Linda in a sun hat, smiling, surrounded by Santa Fe's historic plaza, rested on an easel next to the chair Fager would use.

Fager entered, haggard but hard and determined. He was dressed in a navy pinstripe with a brilliant white shirt and deep red tie. Bronkowski checked the shoes and saw ceiling lights reflected in polished leather.

Fager settled into a seat at the conference table, sipped water, and read his single-paragraph statement. As a rule, that should be the extent of a Walter Fager press conference. But he took questions and went off script. Bronkowski worried that Fager had dropped his guard.

The man inside the crisp suit was coming apart, a little at a time.

The small flicker of doubt in his mind faded when he saw reporters on the edge of their chairs. They were eating this up. A heck of a story. A criminal defense lawyer now feeling the same pain and helplessness he and his clients had for years inflicted on others.

"Do you now understand why so many people hate you?"

Bronkowski was startled by the reporter's directness. The calmness of Fager's answer suggested he had already asked himself the same question.

"I always understood why people hated me. What I never understood is why one woman loved me so much."

Bronkowski left while Fager was still going. He had an appointment with John Pitcairn about his overnight work on Estevan Gonzalez. On his way to his car he saw a VW van with young people in sandals and fleece jackets lounging inside on a mattress. The van was covered front and back with bumper stickers about wolves and whales, global warming, and keeping some place called Otero Mesa wild. These were the people Fager had hired to gather petition signatures. They were perfect for collecting names at coffee shops, St. John's College, and the farmer's market. Fager just might pull it off and force the DA to empanel a grand jury.

———

Pitcairn's research had turned up more on the instant millionaire.

A DWI bust six years ago showed Estevan Gonzalez living in a trailer park in Pinedale, Wyoming. The booking form described him as unemployed. A public defender handled the guilty plea. Estevan forfeited his 1989 pickup. Last year he registered two new Cadillac Escalades, no auto loan noted.

He had recently registered with the Wyoming Department of Motor Vehicles a Can-Am trike, a Pleasure Way motor home, and a classic 1962 Corvette. Again, no loans noted. Pitcairn's initial review had missed Vista Verde LLC, of which a Dolores Gonzalez was president. Her husband Estevan was VP and treasurer. The company owned a gas station and convenience store and the RV park in Pinedale where he had formerly resided. Just two blocks off the square in Jackson Hole, a Mexican restaurant called Sí Señor was also theirs.

This on top of the other businesses Pitcairn told him about last night.

"Still can't see where he's getting his money," Pitcairn said as he worked his ornate Italian espresso machine, steam curling around his head, fogging his glasses. He used a pencil from his pocket protector to stir in sugar. "He hasn't taken out mortgages or loans, just assumed existing debt when he bought a business. That mansion in Teton Village with its own movie theater? Cash purchase. You want an espresso? You can't get it like this at Starbucks."

"How many of those you drink a day?"

"And night? About twenty."

"I like my joe in something bigger than a thimble." Bronkowski turned back to the report. "I don't see the kind of cash flow he'd need for all this. It's gotta be the art business where he really gets his money."

"A gallery in Jackson Hole? I haven't found it. Maybe an investment through a holding company."

"He's holding an investment, all right, here in Santa Fe. By the balls."

———

Bronkowski could not prove it, but was sure Estevan Gonzalez was blackmailing Cody Geronimo. A trip to Jackson Hole to nail it down would be a waste of time. A guy who could cash in on his sister's murder was not going to talk just because a PI from Santa Fe rolled up his Teton Village driveway in a brown Camry. Maybe a tip to the IRS about his sudden and unexplained wealth would get something going. That would take years and there was no way to steer the tax man's questions to an old murder of a Mexican maid.

He drove from Pitcairn's place to the Berardinelli funeral home. The lot was full. He continued down the street until he found a space. Before he left the car he pulled a tie from the glove compartment and knotted it under his collar.

The service was underway when he entered the private chapel. Fager was up front, talking quietly. Far more people had turned out than Fager had anticipated. They were not here for the grieving husband. They were Linda's friends. Unlike Walter Fager, she had friends.

He was surprised to see Marcy Thornton near the back, in a black pants suit, wide-brimmed black hat with a short, lacy veil. Even black gloves pulled almost to her elbows. Her eyes locked on Fager and never once drifted to the closed casket or the images of Linda projected on a screen behind him.

Fager was talking about Linda saving his life when he was lost. This was the time period after Bronkowski had found him in a scummy hot springs in T or C, the rundown desert town so blazing hot he didn't understand why anyone wanted to sit in boiling water. Fager disappeared again. He went to living in the mountains and coming into town only for food and booze. Then he had seen a place on the map called Hell's Hole.

"Sounded like my kind of place." Fager making a weak try at brightening the mood. "Twenty-two miles from the blacktop inside the Gila Wilderness. Towering old trees with a river pouring into a deep chasm in the rocks. A tent was there. Clothes on the river bank. A woman, red hair and pale skin, breaking the surface of the water, laughing at the expression on my face. I felt myself coming up from the deep with her."

Bronkowski had heard how Walter met Linda. This was the first he'd ever heard Fager tell how it made him feel.

"I was messed up after getting out of the Army. FUBAR." A few men in the room nodded, probably other veterans. "Linda fixed me, gave me reason to live, talked me into law school, dragged me here to Santa Fe." Fager paused, blinked, cleared his throat. "Now it's up to me to … " He couldn't finish. "Thank you for coming. Linda would be touched to know so many people cared about her."

The funeral director started recorded music to cover Fager's faltering. Josh Groban singing "You Raise Me Up." Bronkowski's cell vibrated in his pocket. He stepped outside. It was Goff. He returned the call, learned Goff was passing along a message from Aragon for Fager. She wanted to meet him personally tomorrow. She had something too important to pass through his PI.

"And about that fire," Goff said. "Laura Pasco, seven months left on probation for meth possession. The guy with her, she's on the lease, supposed to be living alone, he's got a prior for heroin with intent. Nine homes destroyed, eight others can't be lived in 'cause of water and smoke. The fire marshall says they found precursors, hydrochloric acid, ether, phosphorus, in the ruins of the garage. Pasco said it was her boyfriend's workshop, where he built and fixed furniture."

"You can use that stuff in woodworking. I've heard of ether to age wood. Hydrochloric acid for cleaning tools. I don't know about phosphorus except it's in wood."

"No record the guy was paying gross receipts tax for anything that came out of his supposed home business. No city permit for commercial activity. Zoning's got complaints about odors. The fire started on the cement floor in the garage near the dog door, someone poured in gasoline. Could be someone didn't like Pasco's boyfriend cooking on their turf."

That was the end of Pasco as a witness. Her evidence meant nothing without the table and proof of Linda's blood where she saw Geronimo wipe his hand. Nobody would believe her about Lily Montclaire looking to buy a banged up bar table for tens of thousands of dollars.

Josh Groban was done singing when he returned to the chapel. Recorded organ music was being piped in. Fager stood at the door shaking hands, receiving hugs and pats on the shoulder from Linda's friends. Bronkowski had forgotten to sign his name in the book Fager would probably not look at. He scribbled his signature then worked his way close to Fager. Marcy Thornton came last in line, the veil lifted from her face, her black-gloved hand now on Fager's elbow.

"My condolences."

"Thanks for coming, Marcy."

"You know, I'd be a burned out public defender pulling a lousy forty-K a year, wearing the same clothes to court all week, living in a one-room apartment with rent-to-own furniture, if you hadn't inspired me."

Thornton nodded at Bronkowski.

"Hey, Bronk. Next time I'm in Malibu we'll have to do lunch."

She withdrew an envelope from her purse and handed it to Fager. She gave them her back and left the chapel.

Fager turned the envelope over in his hand. Bronkowski saw a return address for the Disciplinary Board.

"I don't think that's a sympathy card," he said as Fager opened the envelope.

"It's a disciplinary complaint, for communicating directly with Cody Geronimo knowing he was represented by counsel. It's about our visit to his gallery, you playing the dude from Malibu."

"Personally serving a disciplinary complaint at the funeral of a guy's wife. Walt, you taught her well."

TWENTY-NINE

LONG ARMS WERE KILLING her. She couldn't reach him and here it came again. A jab slipping past her hands to be stopped by her nose. Fuck that hurt. Her eyes watered but she could see the roundhouse right coming for her jaw. She slipped the punch, moved into him, pounded his floating rib, his kidney, the small of his back as he turned. He gave her a pink smile over his shoulder. Just as she thought he was breaking off, the back of his heel caught the side of her head.

She went down, lights exploding behind her eyes, legs disintegrating under her. He dove onto her chest, cocked his strongest hand for the kill. But he pulled his punch and rested his knuckles on the bridge of her nose, his hand so big she couldn't see much except the edges of another pink grin, his mouth guard smirking at her. He got up and toweled off, humming to himself.

Chelsea, the Krav Maga instructor, stepped onto the mat and handed Aragon a tissue. Aragon tore it in half and shoved a wad into her bleeding nose.

"Nothing you can do that's legal against someone with that much size. I know it sucks," Chelsea said.

Chelsea, five-two, same as Aragon, trained at Albuquerque's Jackson-Winkeljohn Gym. She claimed to have sparred with Holly Holm.

She kicked off her shoes and tugged at the big guy's elbow, pulling him back onto the mat. "This is what you can do on the street."

Chelsea circled him. He dropped into a fighting crouch. The bright pink smirk was gone. Aragon saw uncertainty, maybe fear in his eyes.

"Hit me," Chelsea said

He came with that roundhouse right and was met with a blur of feet attacking his groin, a heel strike to the back of his knee that brought him down, teetering on the bad leg until it gave out. Chelsea was on him from behind with her fingers inside the corners of his mouth rearing him back like a rider on a horse.

"You okay?" she asked. The pink mouth guard, wet with saliva, was on the mat. The big guy grunted and nodded. She released the reins and he curled into a ball.

"You've got the strength to really hurt a guy," Chelsea said as Aragon helped her up. "No matter how big. But you're dead unless you close fast and hit him where no amount of bone or muscle can protect him. I'm talking about more than breaking balls. You can gouge eyes. Eight, ten pounds of applied, lightning-quick pressure, you'll have an ear in your hand. Crush her to your chest, facing each other," she told Aragon's sparring partner, on the mat hugging knees to his chest. "C'mon, big guy." She tapped her toe on his hip and he crawled to his feet.

Aragon stood in close, wanting to learn, tasting blood in the back of her throat. He locked his hands across her back and lifted her off her feet in a bear hug. Her arms were pinned to her side. Her cheek was against his. He squeezed her hard and it hurt.

"What to do? That gun you trust is out of reach. You've got teeth, Denise. Use them."

Aragon opened her mouth and closed on the soft skin along the guy's jaw line.

He let go and stepped back with a hand to his face.

"Excellent. Now grab her from behind, she's facing away from you."

"I don't want to," the big guy said.

"C'mon, she's half your size."

"She bites," he said, but stepped in and wrapped his arms around Aragon, his face behind her head. Again he lifted her off her feet.

Aragon tried kicking his groin but couldn't connect.

"Where is the strongest guy weak no matter how he's covered in muscle?" Chelsea asked, enjoying this. "Not just his nuts. Think."

Aragon reached back for his eyes but he turned his head. She got his ear and pulled hard. He dropped her immediately.

"Great job," Chelsea said. "Eyes, groin, ears, throat, groin. When they're bent over protecting their crotch, kick them in the head as hard as you can. Neck up, that's you're killing field." She smiled, the fierceness gone. "You're growing a pair of shiners. I like a yellow-tinted concealer for dark bruises. Start heavy around the eyes, then cover your whole face lightly. You need a powdered foundation to match your skin tone. If that doesn't do the trick, there's always sunglasses." The hardness returned. "Forget that crap about raw steak and liver. Eat it, don't put it on your eyes."

Chelsea had invited her down to the gym in Albuquerque. Female cops in the bigger city had formed a Krav Maga class to learn skills against knives and fists. You could always shoot, but that meant automatic suspension, paperwork, Professional Standards in your face, lawsuits. Aragon was definitely interested. No matter how much iron she pumped, how many miles she ran, she would always be smaller than what she ran into on the street. She liked the idea of bringing down monsters with bare hands. Or teeth.

The water at her feet ran pink as she showered in the locker room. Before she toweled off she stuffed a dry plug of tissue in her nose. She tucked into Dillard's at Coronado Mall for the makeup Chelsea recommended. She purchased sunglasses in a less confrontational style than the mirrored pair she wore on duty. The clerk at the register couldn't stop staring at the bloody tissue in her nostril.

At home she tried the makeup. The face in the mirror made her glad she had sprung for shades.

———————

Rivera sat in the back of the Eldorado's bar nursing a Scotch on ice. He wore a silk purple shirt under a black, narrow-lapel jacket. Aragon knew she looked like hell. At least her nose had stopped bleeding. It would flow again, she knew, with the slightest touch. Like noses bumping during a kiss. Not that anyone would kiss the face she brought to Rivera's table.

"What happened to you?" He pulled out a chair.

"Five left jabs and a reverse spin kick. But it was fun."

She told him about her afternoon on the mats.

"What'll it be, a drink or shot of morphine?"

"Iced tea, please. Hold the tea."

"Just ice?"

"Roger."

He returned from the bar with a glass of ice, a proper iced tea and a goblet of white wine.

"I'm just guessing here," he said.

She wrapped the ice in a napkin and held it against her temple.

He handed her a folder that had been resting on an empty chair.

"You wanted photos of Fremont's boots, on her feet with laces tied were my instructions."

"Thanks. Up or down?"

"Up or? Oh, the direction of Fremont's wounds. A little light conversation over drinks." He drank the last of his Scotch. "Up. The cut started above her knee on the right thigh and continued for ten point three inches. Same pattern on the left, but that wound was only three inches long."

"Doesn't that bother you?"

"Bothers you. Why?"

"Think about it. Fremont's laying on the ground, you're the killer, leaning over her, kneeling, most likely over her legs. She'd had sex."

"Rough, maybe rape. Go on."

"She's on her back after you've ejaculated. You sit back, knife in hand." She raised her fist. "Probably holding it like this. You'd pull the knife towards you. Pushing it away is too awkward."

"What if the killer was kneeling at her side? Then he'd be pulling the knife up the thigh?"

"Any sign of restraints? Ligature bruising?"

"No. She was doped up pretty good. But not enough to not feel a knife slicing her thigh."

"So how did they hold her?"

"Maybe from behind. There was bruising on her collarbone and shoulders. A strong grip could do that. Remember, we have semen in her anus. Different DNA. You were right about the two people."

"That was Lewis. He saw it first." She paused. "God. Did they cut her while they raped her? The guy in her ass reaching around to slash her thighs?"

"All wounds were antemortem."

The couple at the next table got up and moved to another spot in the bar.

"Maybe we should take this somewhere else." Aragon tried the wine. "This is good. Surprising how much energy you burn having the shit beat out of you. I need dinner."

"Food's good here. My treat."

"I've got something better."

He didn't say anything about the pickup truck she was driving or the country music that blared when she turned the key in the ignition. They swung by a liquor store and he ran in for a bottle of wine. She took them to the nearest Blake's.

"I've seen these all over New Mexico, always wanted to try one," he said as they rolled to the drive-up window.

They ordered Lotaburger combos and asked for two empty cups. Instead of pulling ahead to the next window to wait for their food, Aragon parked in a corner of the lot. They stood outside leaning against the tailgate in the crisp night air. Rivera produced a corkscrew he had bought with the wine. He poured. They touched cups.

He started with how much he loved the high desert and mountains after years with the Bureau in sweltering D.C. Never married, a brother with Homeland Security, parents in a retirement community south of Tucson. He wanted them to move to Santa Fe to be closer to him and a little farther from the border.

He asked a few questions, eased her into talking about herself. He focused on her face while she talked, shutting down the trained cop habit of sweeping eyes back and forth so you knew everything going around you. He was focused on her. She liked that.

A girl leaned out of the drive-up window and yelled that their order was ready. Rivera placed his cup on the bumper and went for their burgers and fries.

She took his cup with her into the truck and cleared the console so they would have a makeshift table. He returned with red, white, and blue bags that filled the cab with smells of grilled meat and green chile.

He took a bite of his first Lotaburger.

"Paired perfectly with Sauvignon Blanc," he said with a full mouth.

"Anything on the prayer flags?" she asked, steering them back to Cynthia Fremont.

"Definitely not Tibetan. We ran photos over to a guy at the Smithsonian. He says the writing is something called Ogham, the language of Druid priests."

"Druid words on Tibetan prayer flags. Stonehenge meets Shangri-La. Strange even for The City Different."

"We've learned a little more about Cynthia Fremont." He poured more wine for both of them. "High school grad, dropped out of North Carolina-Wilmington her freshman year. We've learned this from social media. She was studying religion at some alternative kind of school outside Asheville, The Institute for Spiritual Awakening. Classes in yurts and teepees. The school's owner says Fremont stopped after a couple sessions of drumming and chanting."

He dropped a French fry in his mouth, followed it with a sip of wine.

"She liked ravens. Used one as her Facebook profile. She was blond in earlier photos, hair dyed black since then. Her page hasn't been updated in about eighteen months. No Twitter account. A couple Amazon reviews of books about spirituality, Celtic culture, Himalayan religions. One with a chapter on celestial burial. We're still trying to locate relatives. So far no luck finding parents."

"You'll find them."

They ate in silence, like old friends who didn't need to talk. She tried to remember if she and Miguel had ever come here. He'd been killed before he started driving. This place was too far from home for them to have walked.

"I need this," Rivera said. "Fremont lying on those rocks." He stared through the windshield, all of him following his gaze outside the truck. "What the birds did to her," pulling words from deep inside, "watching the cut at OMI, pretending I don't smell anything, I don't mind being there. I need to grab ahold of life." He was back inside, close, his eyes on hers, again all of him following his gaze. "I know that sounds like a beer commercial. But," his hand on her arm, "you know what I mean? This is nice."

She liked the honest, vulnerable tone in his voice. The crisp FBI-speak was gone. A man in pain was speaking. A good man. An attractive man.

She'd had the same feelings before the Krav Maga class. Darkness pushing in, blotting out the light, turning every color grey, bled out. Sparring had chased the shadows while she focused on the big guy's pink smile, the punches snapping her head back. Rivera was talking about another kind of human contact. That would be good, too.

"I'd kiss you," she said. "But my nose would bleed."

"Give me your hand."

He held her palm to his lips. His breath was warm and soft.

"Smells like onions." He kissed her hand and they returned to a comfortable silence.

"Does the FBI have jurisdiction over crimes on BLM lands?" she asked when she finished her burger.

He didn't answer right away. She heard him sigh. "This was about the job all along."

The light of the drive-in's neon showed hurt in his eyes. She had to look away, wondering what was wrong with her.

"What category of crime are we talking about?" Sounding again like the Special Agent, now glancing at cars pulling into the lot instead of focusing on her.

"You need to hear it from Walter Fager." She'd ruined the evening. She might as well keep going. "He'll call you no later than the day after tomorrow."

Rivera wiped ketchup from the corner of his mouth and folded an empty burger wrapper into a perfect rectangle. She balled hers up and refrained from chucking it out the window.

"He's all over the news," Rivera said. "Someone who's been a nightmare for our side now stumping for law and order. He's going to call me about a crime on BLM land? Should I ask how you know?"

"It's connected to his wife's case."

"Why can't I hear it from you?"

He brushed back his dark hair with the side of his thumb. Miguel had done that. Was that why she was pushing him away, afraid how much he reminded her of a dead boy she couldn't save? Did that scare her?

She felt even worse for having hurt him. She said, "Not because lying to a federal agent is a felony. Because I don't want to lie to you."

To herself she said, don't be afraid.

———

"Denise, where are we going?"

She'd sensed Rivera wondering where they were headed for the past several miles. The roadway had narrowed from four lanes to a narrow gravel road. Santa Fe and its darkened mountains were behind them. In front, sixty miles away, low clouds caught Albuquerque's glow.

"We're going here."

The gravel road curved down a hill to a pan of hard sand under ponderosa pines. The nearest lights were a mile distant.

She cut the ignition, turned off the headlights.

"There's room in the back," she said.

She watched his face in the residual light from the dashboard. Then it went dark in the cab. She felt his hand on her cheek. The dome light went on as he climbed out and got in the back through the supercab's rear door.

It was dark again. She lifted the steering column and pushed it away. Her pants zipper made the only sound. She hooked her thumbs at the top of her jeans and pushed them and her underwear to her feet and over her cross-trainers.

The console was big enough to crawl over. Her hands reached Rivera's knees, pants still on his legs.

"Hey, what's this?"

The sound of a belt buckle being undone, the pop of a metal snap, a zipper grating. She grabbed fabric and tugged, then walked her hands up his bare legs. Good muscles, warm skin. She pulled her body forward and sat on his thighs, crossing her legs behind his back.

He was ready for her. She gasped, air leaving her lungs like it had been displaced when he entered her.

"Man, you're strong," Rivera said. "You could break me in half."

She squeezed tighter.

"Easy," he said.

"Easy," she said and moved slowly, her head brushing the ceiling each time she rose then lowered herself.

When they were still he stroked the bristle on her scalp.

"I really like this. Lewis told me why you wear it so short. You're all in, aren't you?"

She brushed a lock of hair from his forehead. Rich, black hair. Soft and thick like a boy's.

Like Miguel's. And that was okay.

THIRTY

For the first time Thornton saw weakness in Walter Fager. She had never heard him talk from the heart about anything except the joy of kicking DA ass. But his words at the funeral service, his off-script comments at his press conference—he was showing himself to be human, and capable of being hurt like anyone else. She needed a minute of quiet to think how to use it.

What she didn't need was a hysterical client screaming at her.

Geronimo had gone straight to his ranch from the airport on his return from New York, or Paris, or wherever he had been. Someone had broken in, he was saying. Broken glass all over. Footprints marking his clean floor. The surveillance camera was gone. She could hear trucks roaring by. He was screaming at her from the shoulder of the interstate. She hung up, closed her office door, and thought about Fager.

Geronimo called two hours later. He was back in Santa Fe and still screaming. He had seen the news. Walter Fager on every station. A television crew was setting up outside his gallery, yelling questions from the sidewalk. He swore he saw the bald lady cop circling the block for the fourth time.

"I paid you. Now look here."

"No, you look," Thornton shot back. "It's wheel-spinning. They're frustrated. Your case is going nowhere. I've taken care of it."

"The police found my ranch. It was Aragon who broke in. I know it."

"We *don't* know that. It could have been anybody. And there's nothing there for them to find, right? You followed my instructions."

"Someone's at the door. They have cameras."

"Don't answer. I'll be over to handle the media," she said, seeing a chance to get her face on the news. "While I'm out in front keeping them busy, you leave by the back. Walk to the river, to the stone foot bridge. I'll meet you and take you home. Okay? Are we calm now?"

Geronimo mumbled something about turning a hose on the camera crews.

"Fine. Handle it by yourself. I've got other clients who follow the advice they pay for."

Geronimo screamed again, then said he would meet her at the bridge.

"I'm not charging enough," she told herself after hanging up.

Before his arrest, she had billed Geronimo hourly. With him facing charges she'd insisted on a flat fee, paid up front, plus costs such as copies, postage, supplies, expert fees and the mileage she would charge for being his chauffeur tonight. She also billed Montclaire's time and expenses as costs. Half of Lily's hourly rate was profit for her.

If the case came up during dinner or drinks, she applied the "Palace Bar Rule," Fager's terminology, after what had once been the hangout for Santa Fe lawyers and judges. Just mention the client and the tab became a litigation cost.

It was a great deal for her but she needed a new agreement. There was going to be a lot more work to do.

She phoned Montclaire.

"Lily. We need someone watching the grand-jury room. The ground's shifting." She heard male voices in the background and Montclaire shouting something away from the phone. She wondered how many men Lily had with her. "I want someone there every day. This could go on for a while. We'll talk tomorrow at nine. Have fun. Night."

She called Montclaire back as soon as the line went dead.

"It's me again. Listen, Walter mentioned something at the service about leaving the army all fucked up. FUBAR, he said. When I worked for him he'd stand at the door and ramble on with war stories. He talked about being in Bosnia with Bronkowski and how it was like Laos. I never understood what he meant. See what you can find." Male voices again in the background. Laughter, glass breaking. "Lily, how well do you know those guys with you? Right, you'll know them a whole lot better in a couple hours. Try not to draw blood. Bye."

She brushed her hair and threw a jacket over her shoulders. Nighttime. The casual relaxed look for the cameras.

But she was far from relaxed. Instead of facing down reporters in front of Geronimo's gallery, she needed empty time to let her mind run, see a strategy she could kick into gear. Aragon wasn't going away. She had never stopped working the case despite direct orders from the Deputy Chief and what turned out to be a meaningless suspension. It probably was Aragon who broke into Cody's ranch house. God knows what she found that Cody wasn't telling her about. She and Lily had been there once when they were setting up the white knight corporation to shield the asset from creditors. She knew then she would return on a criminal case. Cody was a busy boy and expected mommy to tidy up after him.

What if Tasha Gonzalez rose from that irrigation ditch pointing a bony finger in Cody's direction? Estevan Gonzalez had gotten rich bleeding Cody for hush money. He'd come back for more the minute law enforcement contacted him. Cody insisted he had never touched Tasha. She had always suspected Estevan killed his own sister to take her out of his deal with Cody. But Estevan had more to talk about than the disappearance of one Mexican woman.

The Judy Diaz barricade wouldn't hold if the DA really pushed. She could see the Supreme Court overturning Diaz's ruling and assigning the case to another judge. Judy had jumped the gun. It would have been better to let the case move through normal procedures before derailing it. The Supremes might bring in a judge from another district, one of the good-old boys from the oil patch who could give a shit about Santa Fe and its politics. Straight up rulings on the law, evidence you couldn't dodge, public fury over a brutal crime, no friendly softballs from the bench.

Hell, she needed to think like Walter Fager.

———————

At five minutes to one, Thornton gave up trying to sleep and rolled out of bed. She turned on a light and pulled a legal tablet from a drawer.

She started with evidence. Her favorite was Cody's book purchase. Someone buying an art book. *Ladies and Gentlemen of the jury, that's our murderer?*

She'd get a few snickers. But if Judy Diaz's ruling were overturned? That key under the body was a major problem. They'd be ordered to return the bones found in Cody's pocket. Luckily, they hadn't been photographed. Maybe risk turning over pigeon bones, better than claiming the bones had disappeared. Any judge, even Judy, would allow the prosecution to argue negative inference from the destruction of evidence.

So much she didn't know. Aragon had found something in the garbage behind the store. Someone might have seen Cody through the window. Laura Pasco could emerge as a hostile witness.

Walter and his grand jury dreams. Crazy.

Or not.

At 2:47 a.m., after rearranging furniture, checking investments, booking a facial and massage online at Ten Thousand Waves, and sorting out clothes she was tired of, she opened a bottle of merlot and the *Roads of New Mexico* atlas. She determined which county contained Geronimo's ranch and called her client. She didn't care what time it was.

"Tomorrow morning call the Valencia County Sheriff. Report a burglary at your place and theft of a surveillance camera. Yes, *the* camera. Tell them you had it aimed outside the back window, up the canyon. No, you're not really hoping to get it back, but don't say that."

She emptied her glass. Just one more thing to tell the Great Artist and her mind could rest.

She waited for a break in his tantrum: Those reporters outside his gallery. They trampled flowers in his garden. How could they show his work on television without his permission? What good were copyright laws? Nobody respected private property anymore.

"That metal table at your ranch, that sick antique," she said, out of patience, interrupting a whine about the way his gallery appeared on the news like some cheap pawnshop. Now he was acting surprised that she knew what was in his workroom on the ranch. "How do I know? The corporation you hired me to front paid for it. Shipping cost more than the thing itself. Either get rid of it or dress it up so the sheriff doesn't see it for what it is, if he comes out on your burglary complaint. Cody. Stop. Do it. Good night."

THIRTY-ONE

JOE DONNELLY KNEW SHE and Lewis would not give any statements to Professional Standards outside the presence of a union representative. Yet here he was at her door unannounced, dropping in like family, the low morning sun behind him making her shield her eyes.

What he said stopped Aragon from closing the door in his face.

"You did the right thing saving those paper towels. We've got Geronimo's DNA, and Linda Fager's blood."

Aragon tugged at her night shirt, her toes cold from the outside air. She said, "Skin cells. Love 'em," and forgot what she really wanted to say.

"If you had waited any longer, the evidence could have disappeared into a garbage truck."

"Why are you here?"

"To tell you good job, Denise. When was the last time you heard that? And what the hell happened to you?"

There it was. Using her first name, just as when he had come around to her side in his first internal affairs investigation of her work.

"Just made coffee," she said, and led the way to the kitchen area in her efficiency apartment. Donnelly did not scan her place like an investigator making the most of an opportunity. She handed him a cup that said, "NRA Whitington Center." Her cup said, "Girls Just Wanna Have Guns."

"Black," he said, and she poured. "Like those shiners. I hope the other person looks worse."

She swept newspapers off the sofa. She had gone to sleep without pulling it into a bed. Before Donnelly knocked on her door she had been reading the front-page story on Fager's crusade. The morning television news had his story again: The heroic fight for justice, one man against a heartless system. Never mind how he used that system when he had a paying client.

She sat and pulled a blanket over her legs. Donnelly remained standing, nowhere to sit except on the blanket next to her.

"First, I'm telling you, Judge Diaz's complaint to the mayor about you taping Geronimo talking to Thornton, it's going nowhere. I talked to a dozen law professors and ex-judges. Only Diaz's lefty teacher at UNM Law saw any problem with what you did. Mascarenas shared with us a brief Fager wrote for him. It's good. We stepped off the area where you recorded Geronimo. He had no reasonable expectation of privacy. Objectively reasonable being the test, I learned. It's Judge Diaz who's unreasonable and never objective."

"Worse when Marcy Thornton's on the case." Aragon let it go at that. She wasn't about to stick her neck out with accusations she couldn't corroborate.

"We both know the score on those two," he said, surprising her how easily he said it. "But that's a long-term project. We can't do anything on the state level. Forget the DA taking on the Chief Judge.

The AG lives by the rule that you don't prosecute members of your own party. We'd need friends at the federal level."

Aragon smiled. After what Rivera would hear from Fager, they would be making plenty of federal friends.

"And," Donnelly said, "I don't like hearing that Walter Fager deserves a taste of his own medicine. Linda Fager deserves no less from us because of who she married. The way she was killed, there's a good chance her killer will do it again."

"He's had plenty of practice."

Donnelly studied her over the rim of his cup.

"I know you haven't been observing your suspension. Your face tells me what your mouth won't." He held up a hand. "I don't want to know. Keep on doing what you're doing. I came to tell you I'm getting the forensics out of deep freeze. It's my own channel. Dewey Nobles won't know. Over the transom you'll get everything a lead detective on a homicide is entitled to."

"What's a transom?"

"You make me feel old. I want to talk about Omar Serrano."

"I don't."

"I received an audio file of him sexually harassing you. Calling you Butch."

Sneaking around with a hidden recorder taping fellow officers was not Lewis's style. Serrano's partner, Fenstermacher, had been present, standing back with a pissed-off look. He had caught her at the copy machine a day later and apologized. Maybe burning Serrano on a harassment charge was the only way he could get assigned to a better partner.

Cops nailing other cops over PC shit. A homicide detective getting over the transom, whatever that meant, what she needed to catch a killer—the SFPD had come to this.

"Don't know anything about it," she said.

"Has he engaged in sexually hostile comments, made you feel uncomfortable because of your gender or sexual identity?"

"He makes me uncomfortable because he's a lousy cop."

"Agreed. I want him riding a Segway at the train station, checking busker licenses, nowhere near real police work."

"You want real police work, stretch out the suspension. I need more time."

"First I heard of a cop wanting stiffer punishment. Listen to that audio file. Confirm it's Serrano and you'll get more time."

"Not an even trade. Pegging a murder investigation to a hazing beef. C'mon."

"Good women can move into Serrano's slot."

"The women on my mind are named Linda Fager, Cynthia Fremont, Tasha Gonzalez. They're not chasing a promotion."

That made Donnelly smile. "Okay, I'll tell Dewey I'm the one needs more time because you're such a hard case."

"Dewey. When does Professional Standards notice him? He makes Diaz and Thornton possible. When are you going to take him on so that the real police work you value so much can happen every day? So Professional Standards investigators and homicide detectives don't have to conspire to get the job done before the Deputy Chief wakes up?"

"Thanks for the coffee." Donnelly handed her his cup and let himself out.

Even if it was only manufactured homes welded together, Aragon liked Javier's monastery in the pines a lot more than this one. The Buddhist compound sat back from busy Airport Road, behind a dirt parking lot.

The entrance was at the end of a narrow alley, the monastery's high white walls on the right, a neighbor's dogs and chain-link fence topped with razor wire on the left. Approaching the monastery's main gate, Aragon felt she was walking the state pen's exercise yard.

Above the white wall, a tower with shining Asiatic eyes looked down on her. Gold leaf reflected sunlight. She saw a spot where gang graffiti had been covered over. The taggers had reached within six feet of the tower's decorations. She wondered how long the gold leaf would last.

At the end of the grim gauntlet she found a plaza of single-story wooden buildings. A retreat center had drawn people with license plates from all over the country. Roshi's white Audi roadster was there. Nobody was around except for a woman in a patterned dress sitting cross-legged on a porch, eyes closed, rocking slightly. Aragon looked for an office but found only a door through white walls to the temple grounds.

The meditating woman opened her eyes.

"Please enter," she said. "You are expected."

Aragon had not called ahead. Maybe they said that to everyone who appeared on their doorstep.

Inside the walls, a Scandinavian sort of man—long jaw, mop of blond hair, blue eyes, thin limbs—was raking leaves. All of three leaves. He told her the Roshi was praying and would be out in a minute. He spied a fourth leaf across the courtyard and picked it up by its stem to add to his tiny pile.

Just as she began to enjoy the stillness inside the walls, the thumping bass of a gangster war wagon passed on the street. The man tending leaves flinched at the assault on the courtyard's quiet. The sound receded as the priestess, today wearing a saffron robe, emerged from a curved doorway. The priestess shielded her eyes against the glare, then opened arms wide.

"Jeep."

"Buff Roshi. Can we talk?"

They moved to a bench at the edge of a rectangle of smooth river stones.

"What happened to your face?"

She was tired of the question and again explained the Krav Maga class.

"We have definitely traveled different paths," Buff Roshi said. "I hope we can catch up, do something together. Old times. What would be fun?"

"Any Holly Holm fight."

"Pass. How about Pitbull? He's coming to Albuquerque."

"The rapper?"

"He's great. My boyfriend loves him. But this will be our night."

"Can we take your car?"

"Sure. I should have asked. Is there anyone in your life?

"Yes. No." She didn't know how to answer about Rivera. Maybe she could talk to Buff, down the road, when they got to know each other again. "Do you go," Aragon looked at the robe, "like that?"

"Come on. Tight jeans and J Lo chiffon. But you're not here about a girl's night out."

"Buff, I need to know more about celestial burial. Did you see photos of the girl?"

"I didn't look very closely. I didn't want to."

"May I describe her wounds? It's important."

Buff Roshi nodded. She took a breath, preparing herself.

Aragon described the lacerations on the thighs. "Is that part of the ritual, or another anomaly, like the writing on the prayer flags?"

"The body is opened to ease its use by creatures of the air and speed transformation of the corporeal individual. In some ceremonies the viscera are exposed."

"The body is opened *after* death?"

"Of course. This is a burial ceremony."

"This girl was alive when she was cut."

"Perhaps you have a sacrifice, not a burial."

"The wrists almost suggest suicide. But with the legs, I can't buy it."

"The possibility of suicide makes me no happier." Buff Roshi tilted her head to the sky, sighed, came back. "Buddhist views are more complicated than you find in Christianity's blanket condemnation. Some Buddhists say saints would not kill themselves, though we have contrary accounts. Some hold the belief that the truly enlightened, those who have mastered themselves, may choose as they please in regards to the death of their mortal carcass. For the unenlightened, Buddhist ethics prohibit suicide. It is an irrational act of desperation and folly. In her next life she must again face that desperation and the evil fruit of seeking annihilation. Was this young woman perhaps suffering a terminal illness?"

"The autopsy found minor liver damage, maybe from substance abuse. Otherwise, an attractive, healthy young woman."

"And the writing on the flags?"

"Tentatively identified as Ogham, which I'm told was the language of Druid priests."

"I think you'll find your answer in the message of those flags." Buff Roshi folded her hands. "I must tell you I am very disturbed by this. I see a perversion of Buddhist beliefs and practices. Now I fear the same has been done to the faith of my Wiccan friends. Many of their ceremonies are conducted using the old Druids' language."

Another war wagon rolled by beyond the walls. Aragon waited for its clamor to pass before continuing.

"I have one more thing to ask. Our girl had sex shortly before she died. Does that fit at all with this transformation thing?"

"Transformation thing. I may use that in my lessons on nirvana."

"I didn't mean to ... "

"No, I like it." The Roshi smiled. "About sex. Buddhism does not see one's genitals as a pathway to enlightenment. But Wicca in its original form was a fertility religion." She held up two fingers of her right hand and closed her eyes. Aragon wondered if she was shutting out the world or searching her memory. She opened her eyes with a look of sadness. "A woman in Albuquerque a few years ago, Sylvia something—as in sylvan forests and woods—used sex in a self-shaped transformation ritual. She killed her partner when he was inside her. That is desecration in any faith tradition."

"I remember. A young Anglo woman picked up an older man, Hispanic, father of three. I think they met in a casino. Took him to the mountains, and killed him as he came under a full moon. The experience was supposed to change her, and it worked. Changed her from a young woman with a future to a lifer without parole."

"Let's change the subject," Buff Roshi said, and took Aragon's hand, an old friend again, not so much the religious official. "I really want to hear about your life, why you became a police officer, what that's like. Maybe you could join us for an introduction to meditation. A guided introduction. With the stress and horrors of your work, you might find it beneficial. Do you ever wonder why the people you pursue do what they do?"

Only if it helps me nail them. I could give a fuck what makes them tick.

That's what she'd say to another cop. To this gentle woman she said, "Thanks, Buff. I'll keep it in mind."

THIRTY-TWO

"MAYBE THIS IS THE start of something new for you, Fager. Like a reformed burglar advising businesses how to prevent break-ins. Finding weak locks, windows easy to open. You could be telling the district attorney how to spot the next sleazeball move coming from sleazeball lawyers. Hell, you should know."

"Shut up," Aragon said, and shot Goff a glance telling him he would be gone if he kept it up.

She sat across from Fager and Bronkowski, Lewis on her right. Juanita's Café again, between lunch and dinner traffic. Goff, on her left, had started with a bowl of menudo before the rest arrived. She pushed a map clipped with a business card at Fager.

"So far, the information's been one-way. I want that evened up." She tapped the map. "Geronimo's ranch. We can't go in without a warrant."

"And you being suspended and all," Bronkowski said.

She returned a sour smile. "But you two don't need a warrant. Even if you trespass, you can tell us what you learned, and no suppression motion will knock it off the table."

"The silver-spoon doctrine," Lewis said.

"Not quite," said Fager. "That doctrine was rejected by the Supreme Court years ago. It allowed federal agencies to use evidence illegally seized by state law enforcement. And just because evidence is found by a private citizen does not mean it is insulated from a suppression motion. The question is whether that individual was effectively a police agent. A citizen becomes a police agent if they act under the instruction of the police, or the police controlled how they conducted themselves. So," Fager looked straight at Aragon, "be very careful about your next words."

Aragon raised eyebrows at Lewis.

"He's the lawyer," Lewis said. "I only know what I found on the Internet."

"And it's the silver-platter doctrine," Fager said. "Not spoon."

She could see Fager waiting for her to frame her next words. She had planned on telling him where to go and what to look for, exactly how to document what he saw and report back.

Instead she said, "It's up to you, if you want to go to this place. Or not. Or that piece of land up the canyon from the house that may or may not be of interest because of what may be in the ground. You are free to throw this map away. Frankly, we don't care what you do. Have menudo with Goff, for all I care."

"We'll give it a look," Fager said, and passed the map to Bronkowski. "What piece of land up the canyon?"

She had found the right words to turn Fager loose.

"It's federal land. But unless you're a mountain goat you can't get there without crossing Geronimo's property."

Lewis took over. He produced blowups of still frames from Game and Fish overflights.

"What does that look like?"

Fager and Bronkowski studied the photos. Goff ate silently with one eye on them, watching for their reaction.

"A graveyard," Bronkowski said.

"Even a dumb Polack could see that," Goff said, and turned his eyes back to his food.

"Maybe after," Aragon said, "if you do go there, you might want to call that number on the card."

Bronkowski read aloud, "*FBI Special Agent Tomas Rivera.*"

"If we feel like it," Fager said. "We might call."

"Sure, if you feel like it," Aragon said. "Now, what have you been up to, Leon?"

Bronkowski looked to Fager. The lawyer nodded, then turned his attention to the aerial photo. Bronkowski gave them everything he had been doing since Linda's murder, including his conclusions about Estevan Gonzalez blackmailing Geronimo and the cause of the residential fire on the west side of town—Lily Montclaire getting ahead of them, nixing a key witness and critical evidence.

Aragon said, "We've operated on the assumption that Geronimo killed Tasha. Step back for a sec. What do we have? She worked for Mujeres Bravas. They cleaned Geronimo's gallery. There's that. But that's all we can confirm. It was Estevan Gonzalez, and only him, who said she had been getting cash to model for Geronimo. Yet Tasha was found nowhere near any place with a connection to Geronimo. I'm with you that Estevan's blackmailing him. But maybe he's blackmailing Geronimo with something else, like what's in that ground behind his ranch. Rick found an interesting pattern in Santa Fe's missing women."

"I went back twenty years," Lewis said. "Grouped missing women by age, weight, race, nationality. The largest number are Hispanic, age thirty-five to fifty-five, all dark hair, heavyset. Most were illegal immigrants. Some disappearances were reported immediately.

Others only much later, after the family stopped worrying about ICE. All the missing women in this category came from Hermosillo."

"Who else came from Hermosillo?" Aragon asked, but knew the answer. Lewis had called her from his van in his garage late last night.

Lewis said, "Estevan and Tasha Gonzalez. The women worked at least one day for Mujeres Bravas Cleaning Service. They reported to an Allsup's and were picked up, driven to the job by a guy named Steve. He paid cash."

"Back up," Goff said and put down his spoon. "Where you taking us? That Geronimo didn't do Tasha Gonzales?"

"She was not found any place connected to Geronimo," Aragon repeated, starting slow then gaining confidence as thoughts she'd been carrying found words. "Maybe Estevan had something to do with bringing women to Geronimo. Maybe Tasha was in on it. Estevan's a plotter. I think he's been squeezing Geronimo for a decade, but had the discipline to lay low until now. Maybe he wanted it all for himself. Or maybe Tasha did not want to profit off dead Mexican women and he got her out of the way."

Fager tapped the aerial photo.

"So the missing Mexican women might be here. Of course, no way you could know that, never having been there."

"Goff, I didn't see it in the file. Did you talk to Estevan?" Aragon asked as she avoided Fager's intent stare.

"Not the way I wanted," Goff answered. "He left behind a big panel truck. I always wondered about that truck."

"Maybe bringing people up from Hermosillo," Aragon said.

"And you let him fly into the wind," Bronkowski said to Goff. "A little by-the-book detective work and you would have learned he went north. Jackson Hole, Wyoming."

"Fuck you, Bronkowski. I had the rug pulled before I got going."

"I learned it with one phone call."

"Walt, you want to say something," Aragon said to steer the discussion from two guys bumping chests.

"I can't see Linda fitting any pattern with those women," Fager said. "The ones in the ground might be more like Linda, not Mexican at all."

"You might want to take plenty of water," Aragon said. "It's hot out there, even this time of year. What's there, you can't drink."

Fager lifted the map.

"But there's a river right here," he said, "Four witnesses just heard you say the water is undrinkable. Marcy Thornton will learn everything about this conversation we're having. She'll ask how you could know the water is undrinkable, unless you've already trespassed on Geronimo's land. What do you tell her without requiring all four of us to lie and conspire to bail you out?"

Lewis reached across and dropped a finger on the blue line.

"Rio Salado" he said. "Salt River. Anybody would guess the water's no good."

"That's right," Aragon said, and tapped Lewis's foot under the table.

Fager examined the map, then looked hard at her. He pushed himself away from the table, ready to rise.

"Yo, before you go," Goff said. "Not you, Bronkowski. I know your answer. Fager, that case you did, the DWI multiple homicide, the family coming home from church, that bullshit narcolepsy defense you concocted to blame the father. What were the names?"

"Silviano Mares," Fager said. "Not guilty. The jury returned in three hours."

"The drunk driver, your paying client," Goff said, eyes narrowing. "How about the family, the dead kids, remember them? The father who killed himself?"

"Actually, no I can't."

223

"What I thought."

"The Shelbys," Bronkowski told Fager.

"If you say so."

"I better go now," Goff said.

He stood up so fast he knocked his chair over. He slammed the chair back into place at the table, once, twice, like he wanted to drive its legs through the floor tiles.

Fager ignored him. He was staring at the aerial photos of the graveyard. Bronkowski said, "What the fuck?" Lewis scribbled "Shelby" on a napkin. Aragon's phone rang. It was Rivera. They had found the knife that cut Cynthia Fremont open.

———

Outside, after the meeting broke up, Fager and Bronkowski sat in the Mercedes talking it over. Bronkowski was eager to check out the ranch. He had been curious about the property since it turned up in his research into Geronimo's bankruptcies.

"We need something like that." He nodded at the Ford F-350 with Aragon at the wheel backing into the street.

Fager said, "She knows what we're going to find. She needs us to pass it to the FBI. Down the road, when Marcy's deposing you and me, or taking her shot when we're on the stand, we explain how we just happened to stumble across evidence no cops had been able to find."

"We're that good."

"We are."

"So you're okay being used like this?"

Fager activated the ignition, adjusted the mirror. "Does Hertz rent Jeeps?"

"Got it. That crap Goff pulled, I don't see why we need him in this."

"That was the last meeting I'm in with him at the table." Fager steered away from Juanita's onto Airport Road. "Shelby, huh? I remember his eyes, the father, when I was done with him. I came back to the table thinking I'd gone too far. I didn't know he killed himself."

"Out in California," Bronkowski said, wondering about the baby-blue BMW parked in the dirt lot next to the restaurant, a woman's head ducking down as they drove past. "I got Goff's treatment at our last meeting. Looked it up later. Daniel Shelby moved back where he lived before Santa Fe, where he got married. Did it there."

"How?"

"Shot himself."

"I remember Marcy's eyes, too. I turn around after I pass the witness, she's lit up. Behind me Shelby, Daniel, in pieces on the stand. I hurt him, worse than I knew, and Marcy's turned on. I suppose I showed her how to get away with doing that to people, judges holding them down while you break bones, this power we have as lawyers. She came away from that trial inspired."

"You don't need to be feeling guilty about Marcy," Bronkowski said. "You were doing your job. And she was just a lawyer in your shop, not your daughter."

"Right, I got enough to feel guilty about."

They waited six back from the light at Cerrillos. Bronkowski noticed the BMW again, two lanes over, out of place among pickups and chopped Civics.

"I don't get this," Bronkowski said, "lowrider Hondas."

A woman was driving the BMW. Long hair. Rings on the fingers holding the steering wheel. Too much glare on the windshield to see her face.

"I didn't mean that—that you need to feel guilty about anything."

"Maybe I do," Fager said, and pulled into the intersection when the light changed.

Bronkowski looked again for the BMW, but it had dropped behind them.

THIRTY-THREE

MARCY WANTED TO KNOW what Walter Fager was up to.

Montclaire followed him and Bronkowski to the Mexican dive on Airport Road. She got out of her car and walked by the cantina's front window. Fager was talking with detectives Lewis and Aragon, and a fat slob she didn't recognize. She called Marcy and was told to stick with Fager when the meeting ended.

His Mercedes turned onto Cerrillos toward downtown. When he pulled into his office lot, she continued into the alley where she could watch his car. Fager and Bronkowski were loading a video camera and a case of plastic water bottles into the trunk. They got back in the car. She caught him on Paseo de Peralta and followed him to the hills, where he had a house.

She couldn't stay close on empty residential streets. She swung around his block and came up on his house from the other direction. The Mercedes was in his gravel drive. She parked in the driveway of a neighbor who appeared to be away from home. Twenty minutes later Fager came out dressed, for the first time in her memory, in something other than pinstripes. He wore jeans, heavy boots, and a Carhartt jacket. Bronkowski appeared with two knapsacks. She ducked out of sight. She heard a noisy diesel engine, tires on gravel, then the quieter sound of a car on a paved road. She counted to ten then followed.

They drove through Santa Fe, south on Cerrillos, and pulled into a Hertz office. Parked in the lot of an adjacent business, she watched them at the counter. They came out and headed to the back of the lot. Soon, a Grand Cherokee rolled by with Bronkowski at the wheel and Fager riding shotgun.

She was glad she had nearly a full tank as the Grand Cherokee continued south onto the interstate. At Albuquerque she checked in with Thornton. Marcy sounded nervous and told her not to lose them. When they emerged on the south side of the city, the rugged pyramid of Ladron Peak came into view. She knew where they were heading and why.

She began to worry about keeping the tail without being seen as traffic thinned. She dropped back. At the Bernardo exit she saw light glinting off a vehicle on the dirt road leading to Ladron Peak. The road bent back on itself after it crossed a deep arroyo. The Grand Cherokee appeared at the head of a rooster tail of dust thrown up by its wheels. She left the interstate and hit the gas.

Montclaire drove a BMW 3 Series rear-wheel-drive coupe. She remembered the road to Geronimo's place. It got worse with every mile. Ruts jerked her car from side to side. A few miles later she got stuck in sand washed across the road.

She got out. Her spike heels sank. The tires were buried to their hubcaps. The plume of dust from the Grand Cherokee grew small in the distance. She had no water, no food. The wind cut through her shirt and she had only a thin leather jacket in the back seat.

The sound of a chugging motor approached. A 1960s flare-side Ford pickup rolled down the slope toward her. She saw the outline of a cowboy hat and a rifle rack through the windshield. The truck braked and a weathered Hispanic man got down.

"Two pretty ladies on my ranch in two days. This one has hair."

She was ready to throw that hair over her shoulder, cock a hip, and turn on the charm to get this old man to use the winch on the front of his truck to pull her out, or drive her into the nearest town, if that's what it took. His eyes were telling her she looked pretty damn good standing in tights next to her German car, the wind pushing her blouse between her breasts.

Instead she asked, "This woman without hair? Was she about this tall?" and held her hand at shoulder height.

———————

Montclaire raised her eyes to the rearview mirror and waved to the old man in the pickup on her rear bumper. He flashed his lights to say goodbye then fell back as he slowed to turn around. Her tires reached hardtop. The interstate was just ahead. She stopped at a cell tower and called Marcy.

"Get the biggest retainer Cody can pay."

Together they saw how the pieces fit. The meeting at the Mexican restaurant, Fager and Bronkowski heading straight for Cody's ranch, Aragon orchestrating it all, accomplishing more on suspension than she could have gotten done with Dewey Nobles in the way, where they could reach her.

Marcy told her to get her own Jeep and video camera, a sleeping bag, and enough food for a couple days. She was returning to Cody's place.

"I don't feel comfortable being out there alone."

"You won't be lonely," Marcy said. "Every cop in the state is headed your way."

THIRTY-FOUR

ARAGON DROPPED THE PHONE into her lap when she changed lanes. "I'm impressed, again," Rivera was saying when she got it back to her ear. She was on her way to return Javier's truck and retrieve her car. She and Rivera had been talking since she reached the interstate.

FBI pathologists had confirmed she and Lewis were right about the confused lividity at Cynthia Fremont's hairline. She had been carried for hours, postmortem, her head hanging face-down between her arms. They were also right about two people laying her out in the Volvo's trunk. Two sets of prints found on her boots, and thumb prints on her shoulders and upper arms matched latents lifted from the trunk lid. Those people had been in the car with Fremont driving, her prints on the steering wheel, theirs on windows and arm rests.

It was almost certain those people were men. Fremont had sex inside the tent by the lake only hours before her estimated time of death. Thanks to Aragon's instincts, they had found the tent in time to preserve traces of semen and lift prints from its plastic floor that matched friction ridges in latents from the car. DNA matched the semen in the tent to what had been found inside Fremont. The DNA so far had not matched any samples on record.

More good stuff because they found the campsite so quickly: Rivera's crew made casts of three sets of boot prints. One set matched the boots on Fremont's feet. Another belonged to a very large person. They were Redwing Irish Setter boots, size fifteen wide. The remaining set of boots, size nine, were made by a company called Oboz. It sounded exotic, but a few inquiries revealed they were sold all over the country in a variety of retail outlets.

"Nice work," Aragon said.

She was impressed. Again. It would have taken months to get those sorts of results from a New Mexico crime lab. And now Rivera had the knife, found by divers in the lake. He'd sent a photo to her phone.

She had never seen anything like it.

With its serpentine blade the knife could have been a stage prop. The long handle was black, made of stone, topped with a brass knob. Yet another Smithsonian expert was tasked to tell them more.

"On Linda Fager to get a prelim autopsy, Rick had to call in favors, then get chewed out for being too aggressive."

"Nice thing about working for the federal government," Rivera said. "It's called resources. The SAIC in South Carolina had two agents visit Fremont's parents today. They haven't talked to her in over a year and had no idea she was in New Mexico. They thought she had gone to India or Tibet. We know the coffee shop where she hung out, thanks to a cup sleeve recovered from the car. I've got my youngest agents dressed like hippie drifters talking to kids in parks. But still five of my people are on chairs fighting boredom." He paused. "I have to block out time to think how to deploy all the resources I'm expected to use. Hard to handle that kind of pressure."

"Nobody will be bored after Fager calls."

"I bet you can tell me exactly what he's going to say."

"Hey, I'm good, right?"

"Maybe too good for your current employer."

She left the interstate and headed into Pecos, where there was a gas station at the crossroads. She would return Javier's truck with a full tank.

"What are you saying?"

"You might consider changing teams. You've got the qualifications we need."

"I've got the demographics you need. Latina. Female. Those boxes get checked before anybody asks whether I know my job."

"You'd have your pick of the whole country."

"I've already picked. My war is here, Tomas. I know these trenches." The gas station was coming up. "You need mules, call me."

"That's some sharp turn in the conversation. What are you talking about?"

"Let me know when you hear from Fager. Adiós."

She lined up the pickup at a pump. The gas station was part of the village's only store. It stocked everything from groceries and band saws to salt blocks for livestock. After topping off the tank, she moved the truck closer to the door and went inside. She wanted to replace the six-pack she had passed along to Fermin Bustamante.

Beer was at the back, next to milk. She pulled out a six of Bud and returned to the front, to the single cash register. Two young men smelling of sweat and wood smoke were ahead of her. The cashier rang up cans of corn and beans, and a small pile of Clif bars. One man was wiry, about five-six, arms so caked with dirt they looked like sleeves. The other was twice his size, almost as big as Lewis and wearing a down vest that made him even bigger. He wore leather boots laced up his calves. As the cashier scanned each can, they dropped it into a bright red nylon bag with a circular logo that seemed familiar. Aragon got only a glimpse: black, red, blue, and white, wavy letters spelling out Big Agnes. She thought of a girl in a mummy bag, empty cans for corn and beans found at a campsite next to a mountain lake. A Clif bars box in the trunk of the Volvo.

Aragon kept her eyes on the young men as they exited the store. She gave the cashier a ten and left without change.

She found them under trees divvying up the cans, transferring them to backpacks.

"Guys." Their eyes went to the six-pack in her hands. She hadn't planned it that way, but the beer helped her get closer. They were relaxed, ready to hear what she had to say.

Aragon put the beer on the ground near their feet. She wanted her hands free. The big guy wore Redwing Irish Setters. Javier wore boots like that. So did one of the people who had been in Cynthia Fremont's camp.

"You have plans for that?" The wiry one put a foot on the Bud. He wore a light hiking shoe. She couldn't see the brand name. "We'll trade for a little weed." He smiled. "Or we can party and share."

She thought about her gun, locked in the glove box in the truck.

"Party of three," the big one said, and showed teeth separated by pink gums, reminding her of the pink plastic mouthpiece of the guy who had punished her in the Krav Maga class.

She pulled her badge case from her hip pocket and flipped it open.

"I want to ask you about a girl, Cynthia Fremont." She pointed with the badge case. "That bag you're carrying."

The bag came at her head—seven, eight cans inside—the wiry one swinging with both hands. She spun in the same direction and came around as the weight of the bag carried his arms and shoulders forward, giving her the side of his body. Somewhere in her spin she had dropped her badge case. She drove a fist his into his neck then kicked out a knee. The joint popped loud enough she heard it over his groans.

The big one had moved behind her as she took down his smaller friend. She felt herself lifted, huge arms locking across her chest. She couldn't reach his biceps with her teeth. They were too low on her rib cage, across her diaphragm, squeezing her in two. She tried kicking, her heels glancing off thick thighs, his arms forcing air out of her lungs. She threw back elbows, hoping for a jaw or the neck, but only hit his muscular shoulders. He tossed her up an inch while he adjusted his grip and started to carry her into the trees.

She reached behind with both hands, searching for an eye, wishing she had fingernails so she could scratch his face. She found ears. They fit into her hands like holds on a climbing wall. She banged her head backwards into his face, contracted abdominal muscles, hooked her feet inside his knees for leverage. And pulled, doubling up to put her whole body into it.

His arms released. She dropped to the ground, bringing him with her. His weight knocked the last air out of her chest. She heard screaming, then she could breathe. The big guy had rolled off her. He was grabbing his head, blood seeping through his fingers.

She sat up with an ear in each hand and the wiry guy staring at her with eyes bugging out of his face.

A woman at the gas pump covered her mouth with a hand. Aragon said, "Call 911. I'm a cop." She checked the two men, one holding his knee, the other with red hands cupping his head. They were in no shape to run. She sprang to her feet and into the store past a startled cashier. Down an aisle to the frozen food. She laid the ears between bags of frozen peas then rushed outside, prepared to chase the men down if she had misjudged their condition.

They had not moved. The woman at the gas pump was on her cell phone. Aragon found her badge on the ground and showed it. Then she took off her shirt and crouched by the man without ears.

She said, "Let me help," and lifted his hands away to wrap her shirt around his head.

The ambulance and sheriff's Suburban arrived from different directions. She had called on her own cell and told the sheriff what to expect, a nearly bald woman, an off-duty cop in a bra smeared with blood, and two guys doing a lot worse. A pair of deputies secured the backpacks the men had been carrying and the stuff sack loaded with cans. An EMT recovered the ears and transferred them to a small cooler. He said she did good to run past the blocks of ice in the freezer by the front door. Plastic bags of frozen peas were the way to go. No risk of frostbite.

She rode in the back of the ambulance with the wounded. She called Javier to let him know where to find his truck. He would meet her at the hospital with a clean shirt.

Next she called Rivera, told him she might have the guys he was looking for.

He said, "I'd like to see how much you get done when you're not on suspension and flying solo. Think how effective you'd be with our resources backing you up."

She said, "The FBI doesn't have mules, and don't forget to call me after Fager checks in."

An armful of tranquilizers quieted the big guy. The wiry one watched Aragon like a terrified cat. One of the EMTs held out a box of sterilized hand wipes so she could clean blood from her face and shoulders.

She put the wipes aside, leaving her face as it was and crawled close to the wiry guy.

"You're going to tell me what happened, or what I pull off they won't be able to sew back on. How did the girl die, the one left out for birds?"

"Raven."

"Yeah, ravens were eating her."

"*She* was Raven. That was her name."

THIRTY-FIVE

LEWIS FOUND IT ON the back of the *Santa Fe Reporter,* the city's alternative weekly. It ran in a column with ads for a paranormal investigator, Chinese massage, colonics, something called "human patterning," a medical-marijuana doc, and Diana's Sacred Fire Reiki. Lewis had been at Whole Foods, at checkout, and picked up the weekly for something to read while he waited.

He brought the paper with him to the Christus St. Vincent ER. Rivera had arrived ahead of him. Through Aragon they learned that the smaller man identified himself as Timothy Osborn, and his big friend as Scott Rutmann. After leaving Fremont's body in the Volvo's trunk, they had hiked east through the wilderness, avoiding trails and finding their way to the store in Pecos. Osborn said they met Fremont through the ad.

"She did interviews," Aragon said. "Osborn and Rutmann got the job."

"The sleeping bag," Lewis asked. "Did I have it right?"

"They carried her in the bag in case someone came along. They would sit on it, pretend they were resting. But there was no one else on the trail at night."

Lewis showed them the classified.

It had run for a month. He had called the publisher and learned the ad had been purchased with cash. It read: *Change me from am to BE. Needing two male apprentices. Must be worthy of my body and fit my soul. I am twenty-two in this life, ageless in others. Hurry, my wings must spread. I must fly.* The ad gave a telephone number for someone named Raven.

"They didn't think anyone would believe them," Aragon said. "They thought it was all about sex. Spreading wings, spreading legs. Nothing to do with what they saw under the prayer flags."

Rivera said, "The Ogham translation we got today contains the word raven. Doesn't make any of this more believable."

"We can prove they carried her off the mountain," Aragon said, "put her in the trunk. Had a three-way. That's where our direct evidence ends. Osborn says they didn't hurt her. They woke up. She was out of the tent. They boiled water for tea, got stoned. Ate corn cold out of the can. Then went to see why a cloud of dark birds was on the hilltop."

Lewis shook his head. "Bullshit. She did that to herself? Next it's some psycho in a cave wearing wolf skins slices her up, but they were too zonked to hear anything. That's how it was, officer. A wood troll. Honest."

"No latents on the knife," Aragon said. "Osborn says he threw it into the lake. Out of disgust. But why the lake unless he was trying to destroy evidence?" She turned to Rivera. "What kind of knife is it? Osborn said it creeped him."

"We're still waiting on that. But we've got this." Rivera cleared magazines off a table and laid out nine index cards. "One word on each flag. Each index card represents a flag. Unfortunately, when the site was dismantled, no one recorded the placement of flags in relation to each other."

One of the cards had Cynthia Fremont's assumed name, Raven.

"They say something about her." Aragon moved the cards into different orders, willing a meaning to emerge. "I wonder if there's anything to there being nine flags."

"I wondered, too," said Rivera. "There's a Nine Flags Christmas festival in Nacogdoches, Texas. It's the name of an album of Cuban music. A concept for a theme park that was never built. And the name of a race horse."

"I don't think that word *watch* is about a timepiece." Lewis tapped one of the cards. "I think she's telling us, whoever reads the flags, to watch her."

"You think Fremont had these flags made," Rivera said.

"When did they meet her?" Lewis asked. "How long before the trio went up the mountain?"

"Five days," Aragon answered. She tapped two other cards. "*Fly*, and *wings*. Two more words from the ad. Another reason to believe the flags were Fremont's."

Rivera said, "I'm going to have to talk to Osborn and Rutmann. I don't buy their story, that they went into the woods for sex and dope, and Fremont—Raven—freaked out on them."

Aragon said, "The birds eating her freaked them out. Osborn says that's why they carried her all the way down the mountain to the only secure place they could think of, the trunk of her car."

"You had that part right," Rivera said. "Are we going to believe that Raven/Fremont climbed to the celestial burial site while her semen donors were passed out, and mutilated herself? No way. I'm with Lewis."

"Wheel of Fortune," Lewis said, and they waited for him to explain.

"Vanna and Pat come on before *SpongeBob SquarePants*. I bet my kids and I can figure this out. For starters." He separated several cards from the others. "We have the pronoun *I* three times, the only pronoun here. So this is about whoever—I'm betting Fremont—had these flags made. Start matching up verbs with nouns, trial and error. We can do this. See." He arranged four cards to read, *I have raven wings.*

"But how do we know what's right?" Aragon asked. "What if we can use all the cards to say more than one thing? Which is it?"

Rivera jumped in. "We need to look more closely at the photos taken of the site before it was dismantled. Even if we only get some of them right, the rest will fall into place."

"The FBI probably has an entire department for word games," Aragon said. "Like shoelaces."

Rivera nodded. "Cryptologists. They're primarily counter-espionage, but are tasked to domestic crime as needed. They broke the Aryan Brotherhood's code. I'll send this over. And we'll try to find out who made these flags."

"Game on," Aragon said. "Super Dad and his girls versus the G-men codebreakers."

Rivera's cell rang and he stepped out of the waiting room. Aragon and Lewis played with the cards, stringing together phrases, rearranging the same cards to say different things, but never using all the cards in one statement.

When Rivera returned, Aragon could see he wasn't thinking about words on prayer flags.

"That was Fager. Now I know what you meant about needing mules."

THIRTY-SIX

THORNTON RESERVED A RENTAL Ford Expedition at the Albuquerque Sunport. Montclaire picked it up and was met by a courier with keys to Geronimo's ranch. She bought clothes, an inflatable mattress and pillow, fleece blankets, and hiking sandals at REI, food and bottled water at Whole Foods, and the most expensive camera at Best Buy, all on the client's tab. She spent the night at Hotel Andaluz, ordered room service for breakfast, and drove back to the house on the Rio Salado.

First thing she did after unloading the Expedition was walk up the valley. Marcy wanted to know what she had to deal with. When she could get a signal on her cell, Montclaire called to report Cody hadn't told them the half of it.

She set up on the flat roof. In the afternoon she saw the convoy approaching and felt like she was in an old Western, an Indian watching wagon trains crossing the desert, or cavalry charging to the rescue. But they were too late this time around.

Marcy said this day would come, Cody wouldn't always follow her advice. Clients never did, thank god. You didn't want brilliant, meticulous clients. You wanted careless, reckless clients with lots of money. That made Cody almost perfect. He had only two shortcomings. He thought he was brilliant and meticulous. And he whined.

Sunlight bounced off the windshield of the lead SUV, the others in a bank of dust stretching for half a mile. They stopped where Montclaire had parked her rented Ford Expedition to block the gate. Dust settled. Doors opened.

A Hispanic guy wearing mirrored sunglasses, looking good in his FBI windbreaker, got out of a white Suburban.

"You're trespassing," Montclaire shouted from the roof. "Get off this land."

He walked behind her rental and recorded its license. She aimed a camera at him, then swung it to the vehicles lined in the dirt road.

Men and women, most with FBI vests or jackets, piled out of SUVs. Aragon and Lewis got out of the lead vehicle and walked to a horse trailer towed by a supercab pickup last in line. A large man and a woman in camo unloaded six mules and cinched saddles around the animals. Aragon, Lewis, the handsome Hispanic guy, and three other men in FBI jackets mounted up and rode into the hills at the base of Ladron Peak. They dropped behind rocks then emerged upriver, beyond Geronimo's property line. They headed downhill to join tire tracks that crossed Geronimo's yard and moved up the canyon through a cut fence. Montclaire was sure Fager and Bronkowski had made those tracks and cut that fence.

Back at the front of the house a black motor home and cargo truck joined the SUVs. FBI personnel unloaded equipment, set out tables and chairs, and erected tarps over everything. Then more mules shuffled out of the trailer and more people rode around Geronimo's property line. A helicopter appeared overhead, probably government, no reason yet for a news chopper to fly sixty miles from Albuquerque.

She filmed while updating Marcy on her prepaid cell. Montclaire said she should have just torched Cody's place, got rid of whatever was in the house the way she got rid of the table from the bar. Marcy kidded her about becoming a pyro, then said it might have been a good idea. There was another table that had her worried, something Cody had her buy through a dummy corporation. It wasn't the kind you eat at. You'd never think of eating at that table once you realized what it was. For now it was safe. Whatever cops find up the canyon, they have to tie it to Geronimo and the house to give them probable cause to enter. That wouldn't be easy.

"I love the law," Marcy said. "It keeps us civilized."

A gunshot echoed off the cliffs. The man and woman in camos were rising from a crouch. The man held a rifle. The woman pointed. Montclaire picked up binoculars. A dead coyote lay a hundred yards out. Marcy rattled on about her love affair with the Fourth Amendment while the man and woman closed on the carcass. The woman knelt, unsheathed a long knife, and started cutting.

"There's people skinning a coyote."

"That's not whose hide they're after. Stay focused, Lily."

Montclaire saw it: Thornton in her office, shoes off, feet on her desk, sipping wine, while she was out here roasting on the roof, surrounded, under siege. Crazy people butchering coyotes. Up the canyon, police unearthing Cody's toys. Cops watching her through binoculars. Somebody with a telephoto lens now photographing her atop the house. She gave them a pose, hand behind her head, cupping her neck, face tilted to catch sunlight, lips pouted. Giving them the finger with her other hand.

I'm not out here for my health, she wanted to tell her boss. Not my idea of a good time.

She asked, "What are you doing?"

"Very important work." She heard Marcy swallow. Yup. She was doing the feet-on-the-desk, wine-in-hand routine. "I'm waiting for Cody's wire to come through. I took your advice. It's the biggest retainer he can afford." Another pause for another sip of wine. "Hang in there, kiddo. That fifty-K bonus you just got, it won't be the last."

She climbed down from the roof. Inside Geronimo's workroom she saw the table, a strange antique thing, porcelain and metal with a hole in the middle, some kind of drain, and an aluminum tub underneath. It seemed clean, but with all its cracks and joints, no way Cody could have washed it perfectly. She studied how it could be dismantled. She had room in the Expedition. Back it to the door, take the table out piece by piece under sheets to hide what she was carrying. On the trip back to Santa Fe, heave castors out of the window, the legs in irrigation ditches, the rest over fences at junkyards on the south side of Albuquerque. Scatter the thing across ninety miles of New Mexico, not enough in one place anyone could guess what they had found.

————————

When the second team of riders arrived, Aragon understood why Rivera had not packed shovels. They carried vapor probes, tubes smaller than straws that were shoved into the soil and detected ninhydrin-reactive nitrogen. More reliable than cadaver dogs, and you didn't have to feed them or bag their waste from a controlled crime scene. Rivera showed the technicians where to start, though the rectangular depressions could not be missed.

It took only minutes to announce the first body under three feet of soil. An hour later they had a total of fourteen. Rivera returned to the main gate and made calls. More black motor homes arrived. Javier found a direct route to the graves. He led technicians, two to a mule, in the river between towering rocks. The animals clambered out of the freezing water onto the bank next to the graves. The techs stepped into white suits and began excavating bodies.

Forensic anthropologists from the University of New Mexico. State police. Valencia County sheriff's deputies. BLM law enforcement. More FBI. The black motor home with antennas, a mobile crime lab. Another motor home, the mess hall. A camp grew at the main gate, a half mile from the graves, using Javier's route.

Aragon called Goff, told him to get word to Fager about what he had set in motion.

"I knew Tasha Gonzalez wasn't his first," Goff said. "I don't want to think how many we could have stopped if we'd brought him down then."

Aragon asked, "Why wasn't Tasha here?"

THIRTY-SEVEN

THE PHONE TREE WENT from Goff to Bronkowski to Fager. Fager knew discovery of the graves would blast Linda's case away from Judge Diaz into a federal investigation of a serial killer. Fourteen other women—he was sure those were women in the graves—plus Tasha Gonzalez and Linda. The news would help his petition drive, swing the media against Geronimo and anyone who stood with him. Now prosecuting Geronimo would benefit the DA's reelection. Thornton would be issuing on-the-fly no-comments before escaping in her Aston.

Fager thought about that number. Fourteen. He called Bronkowski back.

"Did you keep that folio from Geronimo's gallery? How many of those weird statues was he selling?"

Fager stood under the bleached skull of the monster elk and peered into the windows of the Secret Canyon Gallery. Hours after closing, the store, the street dark and quiet. Inside, pools of light on an empty floor. Only one statue, if you could call it that, stood in a spotlight's white circle.

"We reopen at ten tomorrow."

Cody Geronimo stood behind Fager in his silver-tipped boots, the ponytail over a shoulder, taller than he remembered. Right there, alone, no one else around, the man who had killed his wife.

No, he was here for information. How would Bronk get this guy talking?

"I was hoping to see those statues I read about in the paper. Something new for you. I'm a fan. I follow your work."

"You're hardly a fan, Mr. Fager." Geronimo stepped past him to unlock the door. "I recognize you from your first visit, trying to be inconspicuous, the only person in the room in a suit and tie. Your fat investigator playing with me. Please come in."

Nobody knew he was here. No witnesses on the street. He could have Geronimo behind closed doors. A chop to the artery on the side of his neck. A knee on his chest to hold him down.

"Mr. Fager, please. This may interest you."

Shoot him, Bronk had said.

Geronimo adjusted a dimmer. The pool of light around the single statue intensified. Fager stepped inside and reminded himself, again, he was here for information.

"No reason to lurk at the back of the crowd. No need for pretense. You have the privilege of a private showing. Does any particular piece speak to you?"

"There's only one." Fager rolled his shoulders, trying to relieve the tension locking his spine. Geronimo stepped closer and Fager found himself backing away. Bronk was right, this wasn't easy.

Geronimo smiled. "The other fourteen sold quickly. I put together, as your man put it, this one with material I was fortunate to have on hand. Here's your opportunity to be the first to see it, buy it. Make it yours."

Fager read the plaque mounted on the statue's base: "The Drum Within." Feathers, sticks, wire, stones, dried grass. A piece of coral. Frayed rope. A broken cinder block. No sign of anything like a drum.

"Does this particular work speak, call out to you in a familiar voice?"

He couldn't take it. How had Bronk been able to shake this guy's hand?

"You won't be wearing that smirk much longer."

Geronimo's smile grew wider.

"The drum is alive, with a heartbeat. I see that drum beating behind the eyes of every person. Sometimes, I can see the stick striking a stretched skin, the beat pulsing, the air dancing. That is a special moment."

They were circling the statue, their toes at the edge of the spotlight's circle.

"Airwaves," Geronimo said, "strike the eardrum. The hammer strikes the anvil. The beat vibrates the stirrup in the inner ear, then our nerves, our entire being. So the spirit of the drum lives within each of us."

"I see something ugly."

"Not ugly. Very beautiful. *Muy linda.* Certainly you know *linda* is Spanish for beautiful."

Fourteen statues for fourteen bodies. Now one for Linda. The missing bones from her inner ear. The drum within.

Geronimo was watching him work it out.

"Is this where you tell me I won't get away with it? I will be brought to justice, made to pay for my crimes?"

"This is where I get my gun and shoot you in the face."

———————

In his Mercedes, keys in the ignition but engine off, Fager wished he had his Beretta. He called Bronkowski to talk himself down. Bronk wasn't answering. But someone was calling him.

"Shoot him."

Marcy Thornton saying it. He checked the caller ID, not believing it was her voice.

"But you can't hire the best criminal defense lawyer in the state," she said. "I'll have a conflict as the first witness against you."

Geronimo watched him from his gallery's window.

Thornton went on, chirping, giddy.

"I got paid up front. Nobody's going to ask for a refund if my client suddenly stops breathing. I'd start a vacation, then rush back to pick up the business you lose after the Supremes yank your license."

"Why are you calling me, Marcy?" Trying to figure out what she was saying had calmed him down as good as talking to Bronkowski. It gave his mind something to work on, take him away from what he was feeling next to a statue holding pieces of his wife, three feet from her killer, now forty, Geronimo still in the gallery's window, watching.

"I can't remember if it's whiskey or bourbon."

"What are you talking about?"

"What you drink. You used to have a bottle in your desk. Pour two fingers when you kicked ass in court. You'd smoke cigars, buy dinner, steaks for everybody. We'd take dessert to the office and work until daybreak so you could do it over again the next day. I kept clean dresses in the closet for the all-nighters. I can't remember sleeping much, but I remember what you'd say when you lifted a glass: 'The law is what you make of it. So make the most you can.' I liked that."

"It's bourbon. Why'd you really call?"

"Then it's a case of Kentucky's finest as a way of saying thanks." He heard what sounded like a bottle being uncorked. "I've been sitting here, drinking too much wine, not seeing how I deal with what's coming Cody's way. Then you give it to me. Damn." He heard a glass break. Thornton's voice away from the phone, cursing, then she was back. "So I want to say thanks. It's not all there yet. But you pointed me in the right direction."

"Marcy, you're drunk."

"You had that black and white of Winston Churchill behind your desk. Growling, the way you'd stare at an ADA telling you the ship's leaving the dock so your client better get on board. You'd tell us about Churchill smacking down some stuck-up Parliament bitch telling him, *You, sir, are drunk.* And Churchill, coming back, *Madam, I may be drunk now, but in the morning I'll be sober and you'll still be ugly.* I liked that, too."

"Call it a night, Marcy."

"I may be drunk now, Walt. But in the morning you'll still be the man who killed your wife."

Fager's eyes went up to his rearview. The flashing lights of a police cruiser were behind him. Officers were getting out, approaching along both sides of his car.

"Are the cops there yet?" Thornton's voice, slurring words, spoke from the cell in his hand.

At the gallery's window, Cody Geronimo pulled a curtain across the glass.

THIRTY-EIGHT

BRONKOWSKI MET FAGER OUTSIDE the Santa Fe County Detention Center. He had stood there many times waiting for Fager's clients to walk out with shoes missing laces, their wallet, watch, phone, and loose change in a paper bag. Now it was Fager stepping outside at dawn, no tie, wingtips loose on his feet, and his suit marked by chalky dust. Bronkowski had seen similar smudges on clients who tried sleeping on benches in their cells. A guard told him it was roach powder.

Fager should have wanted a shower and a change of clothes.

He wanted to go to his office. No hello, good morning. No thanks for showing, Bronk, old pal, always there when I need you.

"I have to amend my replevin action."

"The lawsuit," Bronkowski said, "to make Geronimo give up pieces of Linda."

"He's got her in one of those statues. Joked about it. That's when I said I was going to shoot him."

"Finally, words I want to hear."

"Where's my car?"

"Impound. I'm parked across the street. We keep the windows down."

Driving through morning traffic, bumper to bumper with state workers heading to their desks, Fager said, "Marcy's enjoying this. Called me, shitfaced, to gloat. She's nervous she can't handle what's coming her way."

"What are your charges?" Bronkowski asked, but was thinking, Marcy nervous?

"Stalking. A misdemeanor. It's not going anywhere. Marcy won't provide discovery. No way she'll let me interview Geronimo."

"You? You warn people against being their own lawyer."

"I want them to hire me."

"I think Marcy kept you talking until the cops arrived. Not drunk. Not nervous. She made it a better case than if they caught you miles away. After business hours, you're right outside Geronimo's gallery. Explain that."

Fager silently watched the city roll by. Bronkowski could smell him, even with cold air from open windows rushing around them.

A guard checked them into the impound lot. They cruised aisles searching for a black Mercedes among vehicles seized from drivers on their second DWI and beyond. Fager talked about how he once represented a man with nineteen drunk-at-the-wheel busts. Thanks to a drinking buddy in a black robe, the case was repeatedly postponed until the arresting officer missed a trial date. The judge dismissed and tried to look better for the record by telling Fager the court never wanted to see his client again.

"And you assured the court," Bronkowski said—he'd heard the story as many times as Fager had represented the famous drunk— "that this will be the last time Mr. Hamlin stands before your Honor.

You were right. A week later Hamlin flattened his Kia on a semi hauling pipe."

He thought about Goff grilling them on the Shelby family and wondered what became of the client who had killed them. He wondered why that case gnawed at Goff. Fager was still on his war story, but sounding different, the boasting not there this time.

"That judge," Fager was saying, "I never told you who it was. Judy Diaz. We weren't drinking buddies. She was new on the bench, I gave lots of money to get her there. Now she's forgotten. I can't give what Marcy gives her."

"There's public financing for judges."

"Not then. You maxed-out reported donations. More went into envelopes. I don't know, twenty grand I gave her, maybe more. That was her street money. I put the judge on the bench who freed Linda's killer."

"You'll drive yourself nuts connecting dots like that."

"Eight hours in that cell, I began to see it. Listen, first time Marcy ran interference for Geronimo, she was fresh out of my office. She copied my pleadings. She used my playbook. If I hadn't written a good one, Linda would be alive."

"Walt, don't."

"Linda encouraged me to become a lawyer. How do I thank her? I help get her killed."

"Oh, bullshit." Bronkowski wanted to get Fager outside, slap him. He was glad to see a Mercedes at the end of an aisle up ahead. "There's your car," he said.

"Not just Diaz." Fager, still with the dots. "I got other judges elected because they'd be good for defendants. I didn't care if they were ignorant or dirty, as long as they did what I wanted. They're in for life. Retention elections are a joke."

"Think of the innocent people you helped."

"I only wanted to know what could get into evidence. I never once asked a client, 'Did you do it?'"

"I did. Didn't always like what they told me. What the hell?"

Bronkowski aimed his headlights at Fager's Mercedes. *Scumbag* had been keyed in the black paint.

"You're not driving that home. Your fans in the police department might have set you up. Stay here."

He got out and approached the Mercedes. He wondered how he could effectively search the car. Cops knew how to find stuff; they would know how to hide it. He couldn't strip quarter panels, disassemble doors, drain the gas tank to find drugs that may have been planted. He was probably being watched. Any of these cars and vans could hide surveillance.

He opened the driver's door. Just a crack and the stench of a dog run met him. The seat was covered.

"Fuck you very much," Bronkowski said. He pulled his cell to call for a tow truck and heard laughter in the shadows.

THIRTY-NINE

RIVERA LED THE WAY to Fat Sat's Bar and Grill, not far from Belen's Holiday Inn Express, thirty miles from the gravesites, but the closest motel to Ladron Peak. The FBI rented nearly half the place for the next week. Rivera provided rooms for Aragon and Lewis so they would not have to drive back to Santa Fe tonight. He was also buying drinks. Beer for the detectives, scotch for himself.

Six of Rivera's people remained behind to guard the graves, grabbing sleep and meals in the black motor home. The mobile crime lab was still out there, lights burning, anthropologists working on identification of fourteen skeletons. To Aragon's amazement, Rivera expected to know age, ancestry, and gender by morning. That resource thing again.

On the bar top she was pushing around the nine index cards with words from the flags at the Fremont scene.

Rivera said, "Our cryptologists think they've got it. Let me."

She backed off and as he arranged the cards.

I am raven. I give so I may fly.

"The G-men codebreakers beat Super Dad and his girls," he said. "Lucky photos of the prayer flags in place made it easy."

Lewis touched his phone and showed them a text message.

"My research team had it three hours ago. Without photographs."

"You're research team? Right, your daughters. Bravo." Rivera raised his glass. "And we now know the knife's an athame, a ritual blade in Wiccan ceremonies. That fact might shed light on your question, Denise, about any significance in there being nine flags."

"I was only brainstorming," she said.

"You might have hit something. The number is a potent Wiccan symbol. Three signifies the triple goddess, or triple moon. On the athame is a carving of a full moon between two quarter moons facing opposite directions, the symbol for the triple moon. Nine is three times three, making it that much more powerful."

"Your man in the Smithsonian," Lewis said, "he came up with this?"

"It was referred to an expert in Britain."

"All very fascinating," Aragon said. "Good stuff for a TV show. *CSI: The Witch's Blade*. But does it get us anywhere?"

She remembered Roshi Buff sensed some similarity between Fremont's case and another in Albuquerque involving Wiccan rituals. A woman sacrificing her lover under a full moon. Lewis had remarked on the moonlight the night they found Fremont in the trunk, so bright he read Fremont's registration without a flashlight.

Osborn and Rutmann, were they copying a ritual? Could men be witches?

"Closer, maybe," she answered herself, "to asking the right questions. Did your Dr. Shoelace come up with anything?"

"A left-handed person likely tied the laces," Rivera said. "Fremont, we learned from her parents, was right-handed. She pitched softball in junior high."

"I heard 'likely.' How can you be certain?"

"It's not definitive. But if either Osborn or Rutmann are lefties, with their prints on the boots we're closer to concluding they put them on her."

"Why?" Aragon asked. "To march her up the hill to be killed?"

"I thought I'd be able to sleep tonight," Lewis said. "Now thinking of Cynthia Fremont, a teenager playing softball, it starts me worrying how my girls can get mixed up no matter how much I love them. I don't want to think about those women we found today, Geronimo enjoying his millions, his sleazy lawyer, the idiot boss we have to face back in Santa Fe. I just want my brain to shut down so I don't think about anything for a while."

"Why God gave us scotch," Rivera said.

Aragon went outside for air. Ladron Peak spiked against the western horizon, pushing its darkness into the glowing Milky Way. The exhilaration of being right about what was buried out there was gone, replaced by sadness like an icy stone in her chest.

Javier had his monastery in the woods to escape a world he hated. Roshi Buff had her refuge of incense and meditation amid the razor wire and war wagons. Scotch would provide a hiding place tonight for Rivera, maybe Lewis, too. The drinking done, there would be the late-night knock, Rivera in the hallway, whispering her name through the door. In each other's arms they'd drive off skeletons rising from desert sands.

None of that worked for her.

She drove to Santa Fe, not waiting for morning to get back to work.

———

Montclaire couldn't sleep inside Geronimo's ranch house. She had seen the beds in his Santa Fe home, each about a quarter acre of mattress and down. One was done as a raft, the mattress moored across logs lashed with jute rope and totem poles for the corner posts. Here the only bed was the creaky steel thing, a relic from a bunkhouse, as creepy as the embalming table in his workshop. Camped on the roof, she smelled roasting meat from the FBI barbecue at the motor homes and SUVs at the gate. She thought of climbing down to join them, fit, handsome men and women. But they would be all business. They'd probably search the house while she was away.

She wondered what had happened to the coyote that had been shot. The couple in camos was down there in their own camp, close to the river, where the mules were hobbled for the night. They had something on a spit over a wood fire.

She was miserable until Thornton called, drunk, giggling about Fager. That reminded her about Thornton's interest in Fager's military service. She called John Pitcairn and explained what she needed. A pack of coyotes broke out in manic yelps. Pitcairn asked where she was calling from. She told him to put a rush on it.

A shot in the darkness startled her. The big guy in camos was moving through the sagebrush. She saw his shadow in the starlight. A flashlight with a red beam came on. He lifted a dead coyote by the tail.

Marcy had better be right about more bonuses on the way.

Lewis went outside when Aragon did not return to the bar. Her car was gone. His call reached her twenty miles into her drive home. He urged her to drive carefully, she didn't want to give Dewey Nobles the gift of a call from the state police.

He had one scotch, then left as Rivera was ordering another round. On the extra bed in his hotel room Lewis spread photos of Santa Fe's missing women. He organized them by physical attributes for a quicker response to whatever the anthropologists would tell them in the morning. He checked e-mails and saw a message from the crime lab. The soil sample Aragon had collected from the Rio Salado matched the mineral profile of the salt in Tasha Gonzalez's hair. That put her at Geronimo's place. But it did not answer why her body was dumped miles away in an irrigation ditch instead of buried among the other graves.

For the next hour he learned what he could discover online about the Mujeres Bravas Cleaning Service. He started with the Public Regulatory Commission and found nothing. Mujeres Bravas was not a New Mexico corporation or incorporated elsewhere and licensed to do business in the state. A Lexis search turned up a company using that name in Massachusetts. They were not house cleaners, but a dance troupe—strippers for bachelor parties.

The City of Santa Fe had no record of a business license. DMV had no vehicles registered to the company. The Department of Labor database held nothing. Archives of *The Santa Fe New Mexican* and *The Reporter* did not help. Possibly the newspapers had run Mujeres Bravas ads, but he did not know how to make that kind of search without skimming every edition.

He remembered how his wife checked out contractors and rug cleaners. He searched Yelp and Angie's List and found a phone number and address that Bing revealed to be a UPS store. Mujeres Bravas operated out of a rented mailbox. He would call the phone number in the morning.

He made a pot of motel-room coffee, then read customer reviews. Mujeres Bravas customers were generally satisfied except for complaints about high turnover within the crews and a lack of training displayed by their replacements. Several reviewers applauded the cash discounts. Others complained about the company's refusal to accept credit cards. One complaint was posted by a woman using the name Roberta, who said having to meet the team leader to hand over cash was inconvenient for an executive secretary to a busy lawyer.

Lewis opened her profile. She did not provide a photo. She had no online friends. But she had posted reviews of the Santa Fe locations of Staples, Lowe's, Office Depot, and several courier services, process servers, and an exterminator. "Roberta" rated two law firms. The Law Offices of Walter Fager and Associates got five stars on Yelp and an A on Angie's List. Marcy Thornton got trashed.

He knew many lawyers had secretaries doubling as notaries public. The Secretary of State's website listed all licensed notaries. He had to search by first names. After another cup of coffee he found Roberta Weldon. Her address was Fager's office on Paseo de Peralta.

Tasha Gonzalez worked for Mujeres Bravas, as did a number of the women in his missing-women file, middle-aged Mexicans who reported to work at an Allsup's, who were picked up and paid in cash by a guy named Steve, maybe short for Estevan. Goff had learned Mujeres Bravas cleaned Geronimo's gallery.

That Fager used the same cleaning service didn't prove anything, directly. But the questions it raised did the job of keeping him from thinking about a girl who might have fed herself to birds.

FORTY

Again Joe Donnelly was at her door in the morning. Aragon let him in and returned to the third cup of coffee she was forcing into herself. She was wearing only the tank top and boxers she'd slept in, and didn't care what he thought or saw.

Donnelly spoke to her back.

"How am I supposed to keep you off the radar when you're setting off fireworks?"

She didn't ask if he wanted coffee. She wanted the whole pot for herself.

"You catch the men who murdered Cynthia Fremont. Tearing off the guy's ears. We've got TV and newspapers screaming for your story. Dewey wants you in his office now."

"Since when were you his messenger boy?"

She drained her cup and poured another. She'd been up all night rereading everything, jotting notes, staring at maps, studying crime scenes from different angles. Staring at photos of Cynthia Fremont's boots.

"I came to give you this." Donnelly dropped a manila envelope on her dinette table. "Forensics on Linda Fager."

"Tell Dewey I'm enjoying my suspension."

"That's over. You're back on duty. Lewis, too."

"I don't know where he is," she said, a little too quickly. She didn't want Lewis pulled away from what he was doing. Donnelly caught it and cocked his head. She recovered fast. "I think he headed to the mountains for a personal time-out. With him it's always work, family, work. Never a moment for himself. Maybe he's fishing."

"So he'll show up sunburned like you?"

Aragon looked past Donnelly to the entryway mirror. Her bruised eyes were healing. She had turned a deep bronze from her time in the Ladron backcountry. Lewis would be cooked to a crisp, with his pale skin.

Donnelly probably knew exactly where they'd been.

"He fishes. I hunt," she tried, then changed her mind about continuing the stonewall. When she was done telling it, holding back only her breaking and entering into Geronimo's ranch, he asked to shake her hand.

"You remind me why I became a cop. Now let's go see Dewey and why he makes that hard to remember."

————————

They were admitted to the Deputy Chief's office by a female cadet with hips and a flip in her auburn hair. She stared hard at Aragon's buzzed scalp.

Noel Carpenter came running behind them before the door closed. He was PIO for the Santa Fe Police Department. A year ago he'd been the TV catastrophe reporter at gas-line explosions, flash floods, and sinkholes. He doubled his salary switching to government work. The cadet's face said she liked the thick curls and dimpled cheeks that made him a good one to stand in front of cameras.

Deputy Chief Nobles waited at his desk, centered against a window reflecting sun off the gravel roof outside. It was hard to see his face. Aragon smelled him before she could make out all his features. That spicy aftershave. The thick gel in hair he was so proud of.

She blinked in the glare, thinking of Nobles' constant squint from the skin tightened by surgery. He turned his head, giving them a profile, a reconstructed nose half the size it had been when he drove a patrol car. He pressed a remote that pulled blinds across the light.

"Detective Denise Aragon comes in from the cold. Sit down."

She followed Donnelly's cue and pulled a chair to a spot in front of the desk. Carpenter leaned against a file cabinet.

"Congratulations on the Fremont case. Your apprehension of the murderers, followed by your compassionate efforts to save that man's ears, have generated a ton of positive media for this department."

"Good stuff," Carpenter said. "The public was riveted by the story of a girl found in a trunk at a place so special to Santa Feans. In a matter of days you solved what might have been a hopeless homicide."

"I'm not sure it was murder," Aragon said. "I'm less sure than yesterday."

"We want you to join the Deputy Chief and the DA's press conference," Carpenter continued. "Mid-afternoon to catch the evening news. We're taking this case off the feds' hands. We want you to explain how you brought these murderers to justice."

"Did you hear me? I have questions."

"Let's not muddy the lede. The focus should be on solving the murder and your courageous action."

"Hello," Aragon said. "It might not be murder."

"Of course it was murder," Nobles said. "No other plausible explanation. Cynthia Fremont didn't fall and skin a knee. She was sliced open the way you open a package of hamburger. Those men assaulted you in the course of your duties."

"She left a message. It might be a suicide note."

"Not in the file."

"In flags for the celestial burial ceremony."

"A satanic ritual," Nobles said. "Those men used her for sex, then offered a sacrifice to the devil."

Where'd you get that shit? Instead she said, "I spoke with Osborn in the ambulance. He's not a killer."

"The file contains no interview of the suspect."

"I've been on suspension. Civilians don't enter reports in police files." She sensed the Deputy Chief's displeasure but leaned forward to press her point. "Sir, I ripped the ears off a young man who maybe did nothing wrong but put a dead girl in a trunk so animals couldn't eat her. I didn't look anything like a police officer when Rutmann grabbed me. He could say he was trying to protect his friend from a crazy woman who had just busted his knee. Osborn was between us, so I can't swear Rutmann saw my badge. We have a potential agg assault on Osborn, swinging at me with cans in a bag. But nothing on Rutmann that gets past reasonable doubt."

"Are you telling me you won't cooperate?"

"I'm telling you my investigation has not eliminated the possibility that Cynthia Fremont committed suicide."

"The DA sees it different," Nobles said, his hands flat on his desk. "I'm assigning Serrano and Fenstermacher. You will provide them everything before stepping aside. You will not enter into the file any statements from Osborn obtained while you were on suspension and operating without authority from this department. Your replacements will conduct their own interview. You will join us in the main conference room at two o'clock p.m."

"I'm not going to say anything."

"That's right. You just stand there. Where's Lewis?"

"Fishing," Donnelly said.

"You're making a bad move, Dewey," Aragon said. "You should be putting everything on Geronimo. Your little show to grab headlines is going to blow up on you."

"It's 'sir,' Detective Aragon. I ordered you off the Geronimo case. What have you been up to?"

"Hunting," Donnelly said, which earned a raised eyebrow from the Deputy Chief.

"Two o'clock, detective," Nobles said, and the meeting was over. Aragon and Donnelly rose and moved toward the door. "Wear your wig, the one you use for court. Pulling off a guy's ears, you're scary enough."

"We need to soften your image," Carpenter said. "A little make-up, too. Please."

On the way to their cars Aragon told Donnelly, "Dewey could make me appreciate criminal-defense lawyers."

"I hope those boys hire Walter Fager or Marcy Thornton."

"Thornton's going to be very busy. Fager, he's got his own problems."

FORTY-ONE

This time Marcy Thornton served her ethics complaints using her law office's runner. The envelope delivered to Fager's office contained a copy of a complaint with the Disciplinary Board about Fager trespassing on Geronimo's private property and causing criminal damage in the form of a cut lock on the front gate, a broken window, and a purloined security camera. She hit him with the catch-all rule, the cleanup batter at the end of the Code of Professional Conduct. Rule 16-804 was entitled, simply, "Misconduct." It could cover anything a lawyer could stretch words to fit.

Thornton's second ethics complaint walked the facts through several definitions of misconduct: paragraph (a), committing a criminal act that reflects adversely on the lawyer's honesty and trustworthiness; paragraph (b), engaging in conduct involving dishonesty, fraud, deceit, or misrepresentation; paragraph (c) engaging in conduct prejudicial to the conduct of law; and, if that didn't cover it, paragraph (d), engaging in any conduct that adversely reflects an attorney's fitness to practice law.

She wanted the Supreme Court to disbar Fager and prohibit him from ever again practicing law in the state of New Mexico.

She asked the Disciplinary Board to order Fager to replace the busted lock and window, at nineteen dollars and ninety-eight cents for the lock and one hundred fifty-seven dollars for a window she suspected was actually broken by Aragon days before Fager went out there.

When Bronkowski entered his office, Fager ranted about the window for a solid ten minutes before mentioning anything about maybe losing his law license.

What he noticed was the smell. Fager had not gone home, showered, or changed out of the clothes he wore in jail. He needed a shave. He was living on coffee and sugar.

Fager was falling apart.

Bronkowski stepped away to tell Roberta Weldon to get breakfast for their boss, then made Fager shut up about Marcy Thornton and the fucking window already.

"Good news from down south. The U.S. Attorney has an announcement this afternoon. Geronimo's their new most wanted."

"I want him in the state pen, max wing, not a federal country club."

"Walt, he could end up on the feds' death row, which we don't have any more."

"He'll live with hope that Congress will abolish capital punishment, or the president will commute his death sentence. I should have shot him when I had the chance."

Fager dragged his hands across his face, stretching his cheeks, making his bloodshot eyes bulge. He sighed and downed half a cup of cold coffee.

"I might need to go to Texas," Bronkowski said. "See a guy named Grady."

"Who's he?"

"Maybe somebody who'll let me take apart a Cody Geronimo original."

———

The night before, after he had seen Fager's Mercedes towed from the impound lot to a detailing shop, Bronkowski took a cab to Fager's to get his own car back. Then he swung past Geronimo's gallery. He parked two blocks away. He didn't want the car driven by Fager's investigator identified and added to the evidence in Walt's stalking case.

Walking back in the darkness he thought about Fager telling him Geronimo had Linda in one of those weird statues.

The gallery was completely dark. Peering through the windows he saw an empty floor. The statue Fager had seen had been moved out.

What was that crap Geronimo was feeding that lady dripping turquoise at the gallery opening, about a spirit within each of his statues? Her husband had smelled bullshit. But he still wrote the check. For the wife, insisting she sensed what the great Cody Geronimo sensed.

Fourteen graves. Fourteen statues.

Grady Fallon, oil man, enough money he'd burn three-hundred grand on something he'd just as soon throw out back with the trash. A guy like that should be easy to find.

He went home and searched the Internet for oil and gas producers in Texas and Oklahoma, throwing in the last state because he couldn't be sure about placing the oil man's accent. Good thing. Under the membership tab for the Oklahoma Independent Petroleum Association he found Grady Fallon, CEO of Tomahawk Pipe and Casing, Oklahoma City.

He'd made that drive across two panhandles plenty of times. He could do it in six hours. By the time he knocked on Grady Fallon's door, the whole country would have heard about bodies coming out of the ground next to the house in the desert.

FORTY-TWO

ARAGON STOOD UNDER HER black wig next to Omar Serrano, her head hot, wanting to scratch her scalp. She saw a room of empty chairs. One cameraman from an Albuquerque station. A reporter from the *Santa Fe New Mexican* so young he could be an intern. It was like the night with Cynthia Fremont in the trunk—the expected media mob somewhere else with a bigger story.

The cameraman shut down before Nobles finished talking. The young reporter asked for a spelling on a name, no other questions, clicked his pen, closed his notebook.

Aragon felt something brush her thigh. She looked down. Serrano's hand, fingertips against her dress. His palm had been there a second before.

"You look good with hair," he whispered, leaning in, now his tricep against her breast.

She stepped in front of him and scraped the stiff edge of her shoe down his shin bone, another move she had picked up in the Krav Maga class.

"Cunt," Serrano said, hopping backwards, lifting his knee to his hands.

Nobles and Carpenter looked across the room at Serrano standing on one leg. The reporter flipped open his notebook. The cameraman hesitated in snapping shut his equipment case.

She swept the wig off her head and pushed through swinging doors into the hallway. She called Lewis and got voicemail. A second later he texted back. He was in Albuquerque at the press conference being held by the U.S. Attorney. SRO. He'd call when it ended.

———

U.S. Attorney Reuben Ortiz had big plans for himself. Paper-sharp collars, gold-and-blue tie knotted perfectly. Onyx cufflinks above his wrists, a hundred-dollar haircut that emphasized his widow's peak. He was from Las Cruces, where he'd run the violent crimes unit in the DA's office. He was intensely partisan, opportunistic, and set on running for U.S. Senator when one of the white boys representing New Mexico stepped aside or stumbled.

Lewis could overlook all that. Here was a man who put bad guys in jail.

Tomas Rivera stood at his side. Two photogenic Hispanic men. Confident. Precise. What they had to say would open every broadcast and grab headlines in all the state's newspapers.

Ortiz opened with an overview, identifying the participating agencies, thanking the University of New Mexico for pitching in with grad students willing to pull an all-nighter to expedite the forensic work. At Lewis's request, any mention of himself and Aragon was avoided. Ortiz credited the find to Walter Fager and Leon Bronkowski, who were conducting a private investigation into Linda Fager's murder.

Ortiz said his office would sweep up her killing as part of a larger investigation into what clearly appeared to be the work of a serial killer.

Usually, law enforcement was reluctant to use those two words. But with so many bodies it was going to be in the stories anyway. Ortiz simply set the terms for how it would be discussed.

Ortiz passed it over to Rivera, who provided the finer details. The recovered skeletons were all female, all about middle age. Using 3D-ID technology, the anthropologists identified their ancestry as Hispanic-Mesoamerican. No clothing or jewelry was found in the graves. All skeletons bore marks of scouring and cutting from a sharp instrument. Manner of death could not be determined due to advanced decomposition.

Left out of the briefing were observations that each of the bodies was missing bones. Rivera also held back that the bodies were laid out with heads facing west, on their backs, arms at their sides, feet hip-width apart. An aerial view of the gravesite was provided, but unnecessary. News choppers had gathered their own images for tonight's broadcasts and B-roll for stories to follow over coming years.

Rivera said efforts were underway to identify the victims. Lewis had convinced him to focus on the missing Hispanic women he had culled from SFPD's records. Rivera did not mention that the FBI office in Cheyenne, Wyoming, had assigned two agents to start working on Estevan Gonzalez and his unexplained, sudden wealth.

A reporter asked if they knew who owned the building downstream from the gravesites. Ortiz stepped to the mike and said, "SCG, Ltd., a New Mexico corporation controlled by Santa Fe attorney Marcy Thornton. The property had previously been owned by Cody Geronimo, also of Santa Fe. We believe he still has unrestricted use of the property. He is a person of interest to our investigation."

As reporters shouted questions, a woman entered the back of the room and carried a single sheet of paper to Ortiz. He read it, then handed it to Rivera. From somewhere, a stack of papers made its way among the reporters, each taking one then passing it along. The last sheet made its way to Lewis.

Marcy Thornton would hold her own press conference at four o'clock this afternoon. What she had to say would greatly assist the federal government in its investigation of the bodies found on federal land near Cody Geronimo's ranch. She would also reveal new information solving the murder of Linda Fager.

FORTY-THREE

Joe Mascarenas wasn't in court or his office. He was in room 416 at the Heart and Vascular Center of Christus St. Vincent Regional Hospital. His feet were elevated, pale white and delicate above plump brown ankles and calves. Aragon averted her eyes to avoid seeing up his surgery gown. He had a tube in his arm, monitors above his head, and work papers piled on his chest. Three boxes of files on a handcart had been rolled to his bedside.

The tubing from an oxygen tank on the wall lifted from his cheek as he smiled at her.

She took his hand, which was oddly small, like his feet. "You're doomed, cuz."

He raised reading glasses from his nose. "It's a bad case. My co-counsel can't handle qualifying the kid to testify. The girl keeps going off into another personality when we get to the rough stuff."

"You're the bad case. What happened to diet and exercise?"

He lifted his shoulders inside his hospital gown and let them sag.

"I hear you've been enjoying your time off. Take a seat and tell me about your staycation."

"I need advice, Joe. I feel like I'm in a dead-end alley, walls falling on me from all sides. Are you up to talking?"

"I can use a break. Child-abuse cases," he exhaled, but didn't finish. "Sit. Tell me."

She started with discoveries at Geronimo's ranch.

"Are we okay with Fager being the source to trigger the search?" she asked.

"He'll testify he acted on his own, an independent agent. Walt won't open any doors he doesn't want opened."

"Fager." She frowned. "Was I wrong in getting him involved? Maybe I should have been more sensitive to what he was going through. You know, I'm not sure I hate him anymore."

"Both of us got him involved. And yeah, maybe we didn't see the grieving man underneath. He is a mess. That stalking charge is not going away, and he's making it easy to prove."

"Could he be convicted?"

"In a bench trial, for sure. None of our judges tolerate victims taking matters into their own hands. That's worse than the underlying crime, insinuating the system can't be trusted to work, that citizens should not simply swallow what gets dished out. I don't know any victim's family that accepts a not-guilty verdict, that agrees with the defendant that justice was done because the prosecution couldn't meet its burden of proof."

"Fager can demand a jury, not leave it to a judge."

"That's a trial I would avoid," Mascarenas said without hesitation. "Jurors aren't protecting their power and privilege. They'd see it Fager's way. He's going to face disciplinary action whether he's acquitted or the charges dropped. Easier standard of proof, and all the members of the Disciplinary Board are insiders, like judges, invested in the game the way it is."

His mouth was dry. She handed him a cup of water. He sipped and inhaled deeply, out of breath just from talking.

"What else?" he asked.

"I'm back on the clock."

"That's good."

"It's not." She filled him in on Nobles hijacking the Fremont case. "I can't be part of the team out to put two guys in jail for life when I'm not sure they're killers. I can't be part of that police department. Joe, you know if I was convinced those guys did kill Fremont..."

"You'd pull their ears off?"

"Funny."

"Give me the facts." He sank into his pillow and held his cup out. She poured water and walked him through everything she knew about how Cynthia Fremont came to be in the trunk of her Volvo.

"Is your report of the statement you got from Osborn in the file?"

"I've been told not to write it up."

"We'll come back to that. Thing is, this is a two-headed case. I hate them. Fager was a genius at it. When we had him nailed on facts, he would manufacture a completely different reality. He'd take what we had worked our asses off to put together and use it to build his own story. He turned into a prosecutor against an alternate defendant of his own creation. Took only one confused juror to make it work."

Mascarenas paused for air then continued.

"The evidence doesn't prove either theory, murder or suicide, conclusively. Every piece of evidence that might back those guys' claim they didn't kill Fremont can also be used to argue they did. Hanging over everything, could she mutilate herself like that? I say they go down. Unless the prosecution steps on dynamite."

"What dynamite?"

"Back to you. Being ordered not to enter a defendant's statement in the file. No matter what Osborn said, true or not, they gold-plated it by trying to keep it out of the case. The jury will hate them for it. A judge could drop the hammer, hard. Disbarment for the prosecutor, if he knew, and the end for Dewey. It could come to perjury if defense counsel asked the right questions."

"Yeah, but, dynamite explodes, there's nothing left nearby. That's what I'm telling you. I'm done as a cop. I can't be a traitor and I can't be a team player. Detective Denise Aragon, blown to bits, shreds hanging off trees."

"Let me think how to play this." But his eyes said he was already done thinking.

"What?"

"Plant your own land mine. Get Dewey to step on it. Soon. The longer the case goes, the harder it is to kill. Down the road it becomes all about defending the decision to prosecute rather than the truth of what happened."

"Land mine? Help me out here."

"I have these anxiety dreams, cases blowing up on me, things lying hidden that took my head off, cut me below the knees. I don't forget them when I wake up, sweaty, my heart going like crazy. Maybe I've been carrying those dreams in my head all these years for something like this."

FORTY-FOUR

ARAGON SAT NEXT TO Mascarenas's bed listening to his ideas on how to deal with Dewey Nobles. He would be glad to see a different Deputy Chief. The entire DA's office would celebrate. God forbid Dewey ever moved up.

She checked messages before going to her car and saw a text from Lewis. *Meet U No Where.*

Lewis was at Killer Park before her, in his minivan reading a file. Maybe he was getting charged from this place too, tapping into the boost she got coming here. Or seeing it as the truth always there behind Santa Fe's style and charm. You had to know where to find it, go out of your way a bit, take streets tourists only used if they were lost.

A good spot to put you in the right frame of mind for the work they did.

She parked nose-to-nose and got in next to him.

"We've got less than twenty minutes." He handed her a copy of Thornton's media alert.

"Nobles wants you. I told him you were fishing."

She brought Lewis up to speed, then it was his turn.

"Montclaire's back in Santa Fe. A van from Taj Security pulled up at Geronimo's ranch, two Sikhs, big white guys with heads wrapped in towels, relieved her. Rivera had a three-car team trailing her on I-25. She was throwing things out the window, castors, metal table legs. She pulled off at the Broadway exit, drove into a junkyard. They couldn't follow, but the owner showed them what she left. A galvanized washtub and the top to some kind of porcelain antique table, with a hole in the middle. They're putting the pieces back together, and should have it identified soon. Another Washington expert."

"It's the embalming table I saw at Geronimo's place. But they've got to figure it out themselves."

"There'll be plenty more experts. Fourteen bodies, we got bumped into the serial-killer category. The FBI still considers that a priority."

"Linda Fager?"

"Rivera's meeting with Nobles after we learn what card Thornton's going to play. But the U.S. Attorney is letting Santa Fe have Fremont. One girl doesn't justify pulling resources from their serial-killer case. What are we going to do about Fremont?"

"Am I crazy for thinking it may be suicide?"

"You've been thinking about it. I've been trying not to. Here's something you haven't seen." He reached for a briefcase on the middle seat, pulled out a document stapled in one corner, folded a few pages back and handed it to Aragon. "The full autopsy on Cynthia Fremont. We've been operating off briefings from Rivera's people. Read about the leg wounds."

As Rivera had told her, the incisions started above the knees and extended toward Fremont's groin. But there was much more detail here.

"Nothing like hard facts to get you thinking," Lewis said. "Same keen-edged instrument for all wound tracks. One of the guys could have been holding her while the other cut. Rutmann's big enough that Fremont wouldn't move if he sat on her. So maybe we can explain why no ligature marks from restraints. But look at the right thigh wound. Multiple passes of the blade going deeper. And a parallel superficial incision."

"We've seen this before. On teenagers who cut themselves."

"They test the knife against their skin. It doesn't hurt as much as they thought. They make another pass, pressing harder, see how much they can take. They leave trailing wounds where the blade comes out of each progressively deeper cut. Fremont's got trailing wounds."

"I need to be certain. I'm almost there. What about the superficial cuts on the left leg and across her abdomen?"

"You could argue more evidence of torture. I can see how the FBI saw it that way, before we knew the Raven backstory and what the flags said. I think she was experimenting, then got serious on her right leg. She was right handed. The shallow cut on her left leg is angled. Maybe she was reaching across her body. The deep channel on the right leg goes straight up the thigh. She would only have to pull her elbow back. Makes things more manageable when the pain takes over. Back to my question, what do we do?"

"Watch how I tie my boots."

Aragon didn't wait for Lewis to ask why. She went to her car and came back with her hiking boots and a photograph. She slipped off her cross trainers, then laced up her boots and dropped her heels on the console, her back pressed against the door, so Lewis could see.

"Notice how I skip some eyelets, lace the boots my own special way?" She put the photograph next to her boots. "Fremont did her own thing. Where the ankle starts she twists the laces together across the tongue, cinching the boots to hold her heel in, then finishes regularly."

"Somebody else wouldn't know." He thought a little more. "Osborn's and Rutmann's latents are on the boots only because they carried her. She put her boots on after stripping off her clothes, after the sex."

"How are the kids?"

"You have this habit of radically changing the topic of conversation."

"Too young to have a daddy without a job," she said. "I'm not going to do anything that can blow back on you. I'd rather pack my desk and forget I ever shined a flashlight on Cynthia Fremont. I'm not too old to join the army. Or be the village cop somewhere in the boonies, dealing with cattle on the road and people stealing firewood."

"So you're not going to tell me what you're thinking of doing?"

"Not yet. Sorry." She held his eyes then broke off.

He pursed his lips and nodded. She wasn't sure if he resented her keeping him in the dark. He could take it as a lack of trust, when what she meant was to protect him.

"The dreaded legs tomorrow, six a.m.," he said after a few moments, not giving her a clue how he felt. "We still on?"

"You hate squats."

"Not like you hate dead lifts."

"I'd miss working with you—if this doesn't go right."

He checked his watch. "Time to catch Thornton's show."

"Sit up front and make faces?"

"Burp and fart, pick our nose. Hiss when Thornton says she only wants truth and justice."

Aragon said, "So what are we doing here?" and knew it was still good between them.

FORTY-FIVE

"Lesson one I got from Walter in my first trial," Marcy Thornton said, facing the mirror. She picked a blond hair off the lapel of her black silk jacket. "When you look a jury in the face, they have to see you believe your own words. Helps to have a little truth in the mix, he'd say, like false movie buildings in westerns held up by a few solid timbers. He liked talking like that. We got these speeches after he'd win a case, a little bourbon in him, helping us baby lawyers along the path to being badass lawyers. He said something I really like, Walter at his most eloquent: With a single pillar of truth to lean on, you could build a city of lies. He was some builder, that Walter Fager."

"Pants are right for this," Montclaire said, on Thornton's office couch touching up chips on toenails with a toothpick dipped in polish. "You need them paying attention, not leering at your legs."

"Then you wear pants, too."

"Damn," Montclaire found another chip. "Sandals were all wrong for Cody's ranch. You have remover? This isn't working."

"In the bathroom, under the sink. Keep up with me on the visuals," Thornton said, and tugged her cuffs through the sleeves of her jacket. "I want my jurors knowing our facts before they're selected. We can't do this once Cody's arraigned."

Montclaire spoke from the bathroom off Thornton's office, her head in the cabinet under the sink.

"Pitcairn came through. He was inspired."

"His bill is inspired. But we've got Fager's military records."

Montclaire returned with a little bottle in her hand. "Forget it, this is taking too long. Closed toes."

"We both do pants."

"Both of us in black, we'll kill. Back in a sec. I haven't forgotten how to change in a flash."

"I can't believe I actually get paid to do this," Thornton said.

———

Lewis hung at the back of Thornton's conference room, where he could see everyone. Aragon sat up front with reporters. Nobody questioned her as she claimed a chair directly in front of the podium, set up with a microphone and single white rose and easel to the side. Behind that, a secretary was extending a projection screen along the length of a pole with a clip on top. In the aisle between chairs Aragon saw a PowerPoint projector.

Montclaire entered first, long legs under black pants, a little flare above her high heels, a folded leather bow over closed toes. She propped on the easel an enlarged photo of an aluminum ranch gate and a lock hanging by a snapped hasp. Then came Marcy Thornton.

Short, energetic steps carried her to the podium, the cut of her black suit making her seem taller. She looked out over a room full of reporters and cameramen. Her gaze settled on Aragon.

"Detective. Glad you're getting this first hand. My journalist friends don't always quote me accurately."

Aragon leaned back, crossed her legs and aimed her belt recorder at Thornton like a weapon.

Thornton addressed the room. "We provide these facts to assist the authorities in discovering the truth, and bringing the real murderer to justice."

Aragon leaned into the reporter next to her.

"Did she say something about truth?" She didn't whisper.

Thornton gave Aragon a bitter smile.

"This broken lock." Thornton pointed to the photo on the easel. "For years my client has observed signs that someone has been trespassing on his ranch land. He thought they were souvenir hunters, searching for arrowheads, bullets and such at the site up the river where Apaches fought the U.S. Calvary over a hundred years ago. So that he could substantiate a complaint to the appropriate agencies, he installed a surveillance camera. That camera was recently stolen and its theft reported to the county sheriff."

Never mind the camera was in Geronimo's workroom, aimed at the embalming table. Aragon kept that to herself.

"Before the camera was stolen, it recorded a middle-aged man driving across my client's property, clearly with a destination in mind. My client eventually identified that person as Walter Fager."

Aragon texted Lewis: *Film at ten. Not. Only G's word. Video card was wiped.*

"My client is understandably leery of the police, after he was wrongly accused some years ago of murdering a woman named Tasha Gonzalez. Then came his latest wrongful arrest at the hands of the same law-enforcement authority. But I digress. My client followed Mr. Fager's tire tracks. What he found disturbed him greatly. My client found a graveyard beyond his fence line. We believe Mr. Fager began visiting this site before my client bought the property, at a time when Mr. Fager wandered New Mexico in a drunken haze, having gone AWOL from the Army after the Balkan War. I will return to that."

The reporters leaned forward. Aragon checked that her recorder was working.

"Cody Geronimo noticed something else even more troubling." Thornton paused for effect. "Each time after fresh tire tracks crossed his land there would be news reports of police searching for another missing Santa Fe woman. Cody Geronimo uses a cleaning service called Mujeres Bravas. He got to know some of the women who cleaned his gallery. Some of them were among those reported missing. With that information in mind, he came to see me. As he was turning into the parking lot, the one you all used today, there outside Mr. Fager's office he saw a Mujeres Bravas station wagon. Mr. Fager uses the same cleaning service that employed the missing women."

Lewis texted Aragon: *True. Fager uses MB.*

"Cody Geronimo was scared. Of Mr. Fager. Of the police. He reached out to someone close to Mr. Fager, for more information and also to warn her. Linda Fager. He went to her store on the pretext of buying a book, but really to introduce himself and tell her he had very troubling information about her husband. She might be in danger. He said enough for her to get upset. Not angry at him making accusations against her husband. Upset that it had the ring of truth. She asked him to leave, but to return when she had time to compose herself. Cody Geronimo was seen in the bookstore talking with Linda Fager by two people, whose physical descriptions we will provide to the police."

And who we will never find, Aragon thought. A risk-free throwaway that makes you look like a good guy.

"Cody Geronimo was also upset, and had a beer to calm himself. What he found on his return was utterly horrible. I need not describe the details, but assure you Mrs. Fager was so brutalized it threw my client into shock. He mindlessly dropped his car keys. He was terrified the killer might still be in the store and ran outside. He wandered, trying to stop hyperventilating. When he returned to his vehicle, the police were there. He was about to tell them what he knew and what he had seen. But they rushed him. Due to his prior bad experience with Santa Fe police, and unsettled by the horror he had seen up close, he panicked and fled, and was wrongly arrested shortly afterwards."

Aragon threw a question at Thornton. It might be her only chance. The way it worked from here on out was lawyers asked questions of cops.

"All the women found behind your client's ranch were Hispanic. Linda Fager was Anglo and fair skinned. Can you explain that inconsistency?"

"Not an inconsistency at all. Mr. Fager killed his wife because of what she had learned from Cody Geronimo." Pencils scratching, flashes exploding, reporters mumbling to themselves as they wrote furiously. "Mr. Fager entered the store after my client informed her about the man she was married to. She confronted him. He butchered her and had the audacity to make the 911 call. The police should have seized his shoes and clothing, bagged his hands, and taken him into custody instead of the innocent man they profiled because he is Native American."

The reporter next to Aragon dialed his cell phone. "Mr. Fager," she heard him say. "This is Hank Thomas of *The New Mexican* ... "

"Please take your conversation outside," Thornton said, and the reporter moved to the hallway. "Yes, we are saying that Walter Fager is the murderer, of those poor women in the desert and his own wife. He is now trying to cast his guilt upon Mr. Geronimo. He is exploiting a police error to portray my client as the prime suspect. All of it, his pathetic petition, his silly lawsuit, his statements to the media—all of it is designed to divert attention away from himself."

"What's this about his time in the military?" a female television reporter asked. Montclaire was at the PowerPoint projector. A black-and-white image appeared on the screen beyond the podium. A tall, lean American standing with darker men, some in turbans, some with scarves over faces, old rifles slung over shoulders. The setting was wild and mountainous. The American was armed with an M-16, a grenade clipped on his chest and a K-bar knife on his thigh.

"This photograph hangs in the office of Walter Fager. I saw it when I worked for him. That man with the rifle is a much younger Walter Fager."

Aragon detected glare in the photo, as though it had been shot through a window.

"Mr. Fager insists he served in Bosnia before the U.S. military officially entered that nation."

Montclaire advanced the slide. A map of the Balkans appeared with a red arrow marking a small town whose name Aragon could not read.

"Just recently Mr. Fager revealed that upon leaving the military he was, in his words, 'fucked up pretty good.' We have learned the reason for his being fucked up pretty good."

The next slide showed a pile of bodies inside a farmhouse.

"Batke, Bosnia. This photograph was taken by a young man from the village before he fled. According to records of the International Criminal Tribunal for the former Yugoslavia, Muslim women were slaughtered here by Croatian militia. A Muslim charity has made contradictory claims."

A commotion at the back of the room silenced Thornton. Walter Fager stood in the doorway, jaw set, staring at the screen.

Thornton squared her shoulders and continued.

"Walter Fager has told everyone who ever worked for him that photograph of him as a young soldier was taken in Batke, Bosnia. The Muslim elders of that community alleged it was an American who killed their wives and daughters. The allegation was dismissed as an effort by Muslim extremists connected to Al Qaeda to incite anti-American hatred. The Pentagon insisted Americans had never reached Batke. The war crimes investigators did not know about that photograph in Walter Fager's office."

Another photograph lit the screen. An aerial shot of a cleared plot in rugged mountains, distinct depressions in neat rows marking the ground.

"The Red Crescent found this field outside Batke."

The screen shifted to show an aerial view of the graveyard beyond Geronimo's ranch house. Neat rows, distinct depressions in the ground.

"And this is where the FBI discovered those poor women. Do you see any similarities? Draw your own conclusions."

Walter Fager charged Marcy Thornton.

Aragon came out of her chair as quickly as a male reporter two seats away. Fager reached Thornton before they could intercept him. He lifted her off her feet by the front of her shirt and threw her against the wall. His hands went for her throat.

Aragon grabbed Fager's right hand, put him in a wrist lock and bent back two fingers. He was on the ground in less than a second. The male reporter straddled him and bent back his other arm.

"Hey," Aragon said. He was hurting Fager.

"FBI. Rivera sent me."

The television crews removed cameras from tripods and moved in, competing with reporters snapping photos on cell phones and news photographers with digital zooms. A mix of fascination and pathos spread through the room. The man writhing on the floor, now sobbing, now spouting curses, was not the Walter Fager who had dominated Santa Fe's courtrooms and terrorized assistant district attorneys for decades.

Aragon said, "His office. Next door."

She released her wrist lock. Lewis helped the FBI agent lift Fager to his feet. Fager went quietly as they pushed their way through the media throng. Reporters trailed, shouting questions. Cameramen ran ahead for what was going to appear on the evening news like a perp walk.

The agent said his name was Tucker and helped get Fager to his office. The photo of Fager in Bosnia was there behind the desk, next to a photo of a scowling Winston Churchill. They asked if he had firearms in the office. He shook his head, said his gun was at home. A distraught secretary, paralyzed in her chair at the desk outside the door, confirmed that information. They checked Fager's desk anyway and found no weapon.

Aragon got Rivera on the phone. They agreed Fager would not be at liberty long. A motion to revoke his release would likely be filed, with a hearing first thing tomorrow. She said Thornton had done a better job than they had tying Linda Fager to the other murders. Rivera wanted time to consider Thornton's play and would call back later.

Next Aragon called Bronkowski. He said he was on the road, heading to Oklahoma.

"If you want to help your friend, I need to know what guns he keeps at home."

FORTY-SIX

EVERYTHING FROM ALBUQUERQUE TO Oklahoma City was brown. Six and a half hours of endless sky, straight road, and a horizon that never got closer, until a silver-skinned spire above downtown threw spears of reflected light across the prairie.

Bronkowski had stopped once for gas. He was eating and drinking out of the cooler on the seat next to him. No need to stop to tap a kidney. That's what Coke bottles were for.

He pulled over when Aragon called. He told her he had last seen the Beretta in the dining room, but Fager may have returned it to the desk in his home office.

She asked what he was doing in Oklahoma. He explained about chasing down the oilman who had purchased a Cody Geronimo statue. He would turn around immediately. Fager needed him. She said he would do more good completing his mission than rushing back to be with his friend. If his hunch was right, none of Thornton's misdirection would matter.

When the call ended, Bronkowski sat on the interstate's shoulder with semis shaking his Camry. After a few minutes he put the car into gear and continued into Oklahoma City.

He had done his research. Grady Fallon had been a broke cowboy delivering irrigation pipes to ranches when he got the bright idea of selling scrap pipe to wildcatters. Now he was pulling up pipe three miles long from the North Sea and reselling it on the other side of the globe to Russians punching holes in the ocean bottom north of Japan. Tomahawk Pipe and Casing today had more office space in Asia than in Oklahoma.

He had reached Fallon at his office in one of those towers looming over the prairie. Fallon said he'd be glad to talk about the statue he brought back from Santa Fe in his motor home. Maybe Bronkowski could figure out why he couldn't get it in the house. Nothing to do with size; it made the dogs go crazy. Bronkowski remembered Fallon's wife saying the statue had spoken to her. Now it was speaking to the guy's dogs.

He took the bypass around downtown and I-35 north, following Fallon's directions to Edmond. He exited at a Walmart by the highway, then headed east into rolling green hills, where he was told to find a lake. A private road bordered by white pipe fence (no doubt excess inventory of Tomahawk Pipe and Casing) led him around a tree-lined shore to a plantation-style mansion. A black motor home fit for a touring rock band sat in a circular drive, where it peeled off to a six-car garage.

The man Bronkowski had seen in Secret Canyon Gallery was washing sidewalls with a hose in one hand and a beer in the other. Fallon could probably buy every truck wash in the state and here he was cleaning his own tires. As Bronkowski got closer he saw a full wet bar, with stainless-steel refrigerator and sinks, projecting from the motor home's flank.

291

Fallon was dressed in blue jeans, with the belt buckle hidden under his belly. He tilted the bottle to his lips as Bronkowski got out of his car and came over.

"In the gallery you're a guy from Malibu with money to burn. On the phone you're a PI working for a friend whose wife was murdered."

"I was working then, too. That guy in the suit with me, that's my friend."

"You're the third person today who's called about that thing." Fallon cracked another beer for himself and offered one to Bronkowski, who accepted. "That news about bodies at Geronimo's place. I've already been offered thirty percent more than I paid last week. I expect to double my money when he's arrested. Damn," he drank beer and swallowed, "I thought the oil racket was ugly."

"I'm not here to buy. I'm here to tell you what you've bought."

"I can see what I bought. Glued-together garbage."

"Somewhere in that glued-together garbage," Bronkowski said, putting down his untouched beer. This wasn't news you delivered with a Bud in your hand. "Are pieces of women Cody Geronimo killed."

Fallon let out a whoop.

"That explains it. C'mon inside. I gotta tell Ginger."

Ginger was dressed in pink and jumping up and down to an exercise video on the biggest screen he had seen outside a football stadium. A two-story window framed the lake outside the house.

"You need to hear what this fellow has to say," Fallon said as he picked up a remote and paused the video, leaving the instructor suspended on the screen in mid-leap.

Fallon insisted she sit for the news. Her eyes went wide in horror before Bronkowski had finished.

Two dogs entered the cavernous room. One was a fluffy Bichon Frise, the other a black Labrador with the white whiskers of age around its muzzle.

"That's the one goes nuts over the statue," Fallon said, leaning down to scratch the old Lab's ears.

"He's our boy's dog," Ginger said. "Bobby's in Arabia."

"Bahrain," Fallon said. "The Lab's name is Uncas—you know, *Last of the Mohicans*. Bobby raised him from a pup in Alberta when Tomahawk was going and blowing strong in the Rockies. Bobby did search and rescue. Uncas was a star. Found three skiers buried in an avalanche."

"And he goes crazy around that statue?" Bronkowski asked.

"Whines and moans, then gets to growling. That upsets Little Bijou. She runs in circles and snaps," Ginger said. "It's because Uncas smells someone inside that statue, isn't it?"

Fallon opened a china cabinet. It was a faux beer cooler. He pulled one for himself, and offered another for Bronkowski, who waved him off this time.

"You want me to give that statue to the police," Fallon said after he took a long drink. "They'll take it apart. I'm out three-hundred grand. All because an old dog is trying to tell us something."

"I don't want that thing on this property." Ginger had her hands on her hips.

"But it spoke to you, hon."

"I'll hear it in nightmares. Get rid of it."

Fallon opened the hidden beer cooler again and took the remainder of the six-pack.

"You can't fit that big ol' thing in your rice burner," Fallon said. "Let's take it apart until Uncas shows us what's in there he don't like."

Ginger pressed play on the remote. The instructor returned to earth and spread her feet wide. Ginger rushed to catch up.

"She keeps trying to get me to do pilots," Fallon said as he headed out with dogs at his heels.

"*Pilates!*" Ginger shouted over her shoulder as she did some kind of jumping jacks. "Thinks he's being clever, showing his ignorance."

"Nice meeting you," Bronkowski said, and turned to follow Fallon.

"Mister B," Ginger called out as she dropped her head between her knees and looked back through her legs, hair sweeping the floor, breasts on her jaw. "I'm sorry I can't say your name. If he breaks out the Early Time and fires up that diesel, you get yourself and those babies right back here."

The vanity plate on the front of the motor home said Black Castle. Inside was a fireplace and tile floor. An ivory steering wheel at a driver's seat as big as a La-Z Boy. Chandeliers. Teak paneling, a full sofa, two recliners, a smaller version of the exterior wet bar, and televisions everywhere. The Geronimo statue called "Spirit Wing" stood in the middle of the floor, just up the steps from the driveway. The Lab had its lips curled back, black gums and worn canines showing. A sorrowful whine escaped its chest.

"Toolbox behind the driver's seat," Fallon said, as he held the old dog by its collar.

Fallon was ready to disassemble a piece of art that cost more than Bronkowski's house. It was Bronkowski who hesitated. Even if they found a bone or skin or whatever human was in there, he saw Marcy Thornton turning it around: He worked for Fager, the damning evidence was never in the statue, Bronkowski had planted it at his boss's order to falsely throw guilt on Geronimo, part of Fager's scheme to divert attention from himself. And where did it really come from? From the women Fager murdered and buried at Geronimo's ranch.

"I need a video camera. We have to document taking it apart, finding what we find."

"Right there." Fallon pointed to the big screen. "I let Ginger take the wheel while I talk to my people all over the world. I see them, they see me, so they know I really exist. I need to remember how to make it record. Runs through a computer somewhere in the belly of this rig."

Fallon used a phone built into the dashboard to call his wife inside the house. Bronkowski heard Ginger's voice saying, "Are you crazy?" when Fallon asked if she would come out to give them a hand. She told him how to work the camera while Uncas whined and paced and scratched the front door to get out. The Bijon Frise raced across the floor, its nails scrabbling tiles, snapping at Uncas when he came near, taking his turn scratching to get out.

Fallon locked the dogs in the back room, where Bronkowski saw a king-size bed under a chandelier and another gargantuan TV.

They were able to disassemble the statue, one scrap of leather, feather, stick, reed, and stone at a time. Below the surface they found bones connected by wires and screws. They dismantled the strange skeleton and arranged the bones on the tile floor. Fallon brought out Uncas, but forced the other dog back into the bedroom. Uncas alerted immediately on the largest bone. Bronkowski didn't need a dog to tell him he was looking at a human shoulder blade.

"Spirit Wing. Jesus."

FORTY-SEVEN

RIVERA GATHERED THEM IN his war room to discuss Fager's meltdown. He had ordered take-out. The sight of red, white, and blue Lotaburger bags made Aragon smile.

Tucker, the agent who had posed as a reporter, was there. Lewis had wrangled time away from the kids for the late-night meeting. Goff wanted to come, but Aragon kept him away.

"He really hates Fager. Foaming at the mouth," she told Lewis on their way to the FBI's office. "Ready to kill him for making Thornton look believable. He'll feel better when Fager's in jail. The motion to revoke his conditions of release is Judge Diaz's first hearing tomorrow. She assigned it to herself, saving us the trouble of guessing the outcome."

She told Goff to make himself useful. Park outside Fager's office. Let her know if he went home, where he kept a loaded Beretta. Aragon was prepared to use the conditions of Fager's bail to stop and frisk him as soon as he stepped out the door.

Gathered around Rivera's conference table, they dug into the food, ate quietly, all hungry after a long day of work.

"Feels great to deliver good news," she said. The men had to wait for her to swallow the last bite of her burger to explain. She wiped her lips, took a sip of Coke. "Bronkowski's on his way back with a human scapula from inside one of Geronimo's statues."

"A huge break," Rivera said. "We can see if it matches any of the bodies at the ranch."

Lewis said, "We get a match, it gives us PC to go after the other statues and see what's inside them. We can get into his house, his gallery, that modern wing at his ranch." He caught Aragon's eye. "Lord knows what's in there."

"Right. Who can imagine what we might find?" she said.

She liked the energy. For the first time she could remember, she had complete confidence in every law enforcement officer she saw.

"We have to include Geronimo's sales records in the first warrant." She added a serious tone to her voice. "Find out who bought the other statutes. Collectors are not going to be happy having us dismantle artwork that's soaring in value as news of this case spreads. Bronkowski lucked out. He found probably the only person ready to turn a Geronimo masterpiece back into worthless trash."

Rivera said, "We'll get sued."

"DOJ has a million lawyers. They can figure it out. We've got another problem." She laid her hand on Rivera's arm. "We need your help staying with this. Tomorrow we go back on rotation."

"What if the FBI formally requests the participation of detectives Aragon and Lewis in a joint task force?" he asked. "Linda Fager will be an integral part of that investigation. I'll insist you carry that case for the task force, since you were the first detectives on scene. We'll also request you reopen the Tasha Gonzalez inquiry. I can have the U.S. Attorney make the pitch. He knows we owe this show to you."

"Dewey won't buck DOJ. Hell, he'll take credit for getting Santa Fe PD included," said Lewis. "You'll have to put up with him at the table."

"He'll be pulling out chairs for your boss," Aragon said.

"We'll give him a spot to stand for every media event. In the background, with the potted plants."

"So what's next?" She hunted loose fries in the bottom of her bag.

"The skeletons are en route to Quantico. Those bones will tell a story." Rivera handed her the last of his fries when she came up empty. "Rick, I can give you five people to canvas relatives of the missing women on your list. You tell them what to do."

"An army," she said with food in her mouth.

"Also on its way to Quantico is that table Montclaire ditched. Cost us twenty bucks to buy it from the junkyard. Maybe the best investment the agency ever made. We find hair or blood, we get another match to the skeletons. Since the table came from inside Geronimo's ranch—we've got Montclaire on video trying to sneak it into her Expedition, you can tell what's under the sheets—we'll get any warrant we want."

"We'll get Geronimo's gallery with what Bronkowski's bringing," she said. "And if that table has any DNA match, we've got Montclaire on felony obstruction. She wasn't destroying evidence without Thornton telling her what to do. Maybe Montclaire would roll on Thornton." She thought a little more. "Shit, and then maybe Thornton rolls on Judge Judy."

"We'd have to prove Montclaire knew there was evidence of homicides on that table to get to Thornton," Lewis said.

"Why else would she be scattering pieces along the interstate? She knew it was evidence that would hurt Geronimo. And there's the fire Bronkowski thinks she started to destroy the bar table where Geronimo sat after killing Linda Fager."

"We can't prove that bar table had Linda Fager's blood on it." Lewis and her kicking a case back and forth, the way they'd do it at Killer Park. The FBI agents sat back and watched. "It's all ashes," Lewis continued. "So much for a second obstruction charge."

"I'm more interested in arson, a second-degree felony. How do we wrap that around Montclaire? I bet I can break her. I don't think there's much steel behind that pretty face."

"We won't get to talk to her without Thornton at her side. We won't get two words out of Montclaire."

"We'll get two: 'Fuck you.' We need to split them up. But how do you peel a client away from her lawyer who's also her boss?"

"All good. Lots of work for everyone. Lots to think about," Rivera said, reclaiming control of the meeting. "Now for news you may not like. I have to open a file on Fager."

Nobody seemed surprised.

Rivera explained anyway. "DOJ's war crimes people have to consider Thornton's allegations about Bosnia. It's a huge distraction. But if we don't investigate Fager as thoroughly as Geronimo, maybe more so, we pay for it at trial."

"We not only have to prove Geronimo did it," Lewis said, "we have to prove Fager couldn't, didn't, and wouldn't."

"Absolutely. And we have to tackle the fact that Linda Fager didn't fit with the other women. We don't know exactly why Geronimo killed Linda Fager. It's troubling out behavioral analysts."

"She looked at him. That's all it took," Aragon said. "We got it on tape."

"We must get that tape in evidence," Rivera said. "I'm confident we'll succeed in federal court. You wouldn't have retained a copy?

One you missed in complying with Judge Rivera's ridiculous order, one you left in a tape player perhaps?"

"I don't know everybody in this room well enough to answer that," she said. She looked across the table at Agent Tucker. "We just met today, no offense."

He nodded, showing he understood what she was saying under the words.

"Or," Rivera said, "we sever Linda Fager from the others, separate trials, and don't give Thornton an invitation to confuse the jury."

"That's an invitation for her to confuse two juries," Lewis said.

That's why Goff's rabid, Aragon thought to herself. *He sees Fager letting Geronimo off the hook, again. It doesn't matter why he fell into Thornton's trap, or how much he's suffering. It just makes Goff hate him more.*

"Can't blame him," she said.

"What?" Rivera and Lewis asked at the same time.

"Nothing."

They divided tasks. Lewis would contact families of the missing women with Tucker assisting. Rivera was going to be occupied obtaining authorization and funding for the joint task force. Aragon would run down a current Mujeres Bravas crew. Their blue and green station wagons were easy to spot. She would ask how the women found work, who they considered their boss, who paid them, and show photos of the missing women.

Aragon left feeling confident, though the Fager thing was a loose end. Thornton was going to get run over, her client crushed under her. Too much physical evidence was coming at Geronimo from too many directions. Even the sort of jurors who made it into the box in a Santa Fe courtroom would not be fooled.

She headed to her apartment and collapsed on the sofa in time for the night's last news broadcast. There was Fager throwing Thornton around like a rag doll. It was worse on camera. She watched herself putting Fager on the ground and Agent Tucker holding him there. The contorted, unshaved face under Tucker's knee was hard to recognize.

Her phone rang. Joe Mascarenas was watching the same news from his hospital room. She was prepared to tell him everything was under control. But the cameras caught something she had not noticed in the chaos: Thornton's satisfied smile as Fager's hands closed on her throat.

"You see that?" Mascarenas said. "Defense exhibit one."

Linda Fager's killer had strangled her, crushed her windpipe. Thornton could show the video, with blown-up stills on corkboard in front of the jury box. Have them out through trial, she forgot to take them off the easel by her table, apologizing to the judge but doing it again and again. And every time, needing no words at all to tell the jury Walter Fager was the one who should be on trial.

FORTY-EIGHT

Adrenaline got Bronkowski almost across the Texas panhandle before he had to pull into a DOT rest stop. The place was fortified against tornadoes, a concrete bunker where drivers could huddle while the prairie was being chewed up and cars and trucks hurled into the sky. He napped for two hours, then got moving again, forcing himself through Amarillo by morning so that damned song didn't get in his head and drive him nuts.

The day grew around him as the outline of the Sangre de Cristo mountains rose from the desert. He forked north off I-40 at Clines Corners and took U.S. 285 toward Santa Fe. Only forty-nine miles to go. He called Fager, again. He had called him before leaving Fallon's place. Again after Oklahoma City, and a couple times on the long, empty stretches to keep himself awake. Fager had answered none of his calls.

In Santa Fe he went straight to Fager's house. No lights inside. No answer at the door. The Mercedes was not in the yard or garage. Bronkowski drove to the office building. A car was parked in front with a man slumped over the wheel, probably a drunk passed out before wkilling someone and not needing the services of Walter Fager and Associates. But as he pulled past, Bronkowski recognized Sam Goff and started to worry. He parked and let himself in the back. The security system had been activated and Bronkowski punched the code. He tripped over books at the entrance to Fager's office. Inside, empty coffee cups everywhere and paper spilling from desk to floor. The printer was open, with the toner cartridge pulled out. He left the way he entered, armed the system, then walked down the sidewalk to Goff's car.

He rapped on the driver's window and Goff's head shot up from its pillow on the wheel.

Goff rubbed his eyes and rolled the window.

"Where is he?" Bronkowski asked.

Goff looked at Fager's building, then back at Bronkowski.

"He was there all night. A light in his office."

A thought occurred to Bronkowski and he went rigid.

"How long you been out? When was the last you checked the clock?"

"I don't know. Damn. I didn't mean to close my eyes. Maybe he went home to sleep."

Bronkowski hurried back to his car.

———————

Goff waited until Bronkowski was out of sight, then drove in the opposite direction, into the winding roads where big houses stood above Santa Fe's old Spanish buildings.

He pulled into Fager's drive and crunched gravel as he approached the front door. Clearly no one was home, but he pushed the doorbell. He gave it three tries, with plenty of time between rings. He turned his back to the house and faced Fager's yard, the sun above the mountains, a hawk coasting in a blue sky. Someone was walking a dog along the street. Goff yelled out, asking if they had seen Walter Fager this morning. They called back that they didn't know anyone by that name.

Goff pulled his cell and dialed Aragon. He got her on the way to work.

"That motherfucker's gone. Fager. I was on his office all night. Maybe I nodded off, just a little. I'm at the house. He's not here, either. Bronkowski's looking, too."

"Hold," Aragon said as the voice of the police dispatcher crackled in the background. He waited. She came back on. "Sam, you really fucked up." He heard a car horn blast. She swore at cars to get out of the way.

"What's going on?" he asked.

"Shots fired at Geronimo's gallery," she said, and the line went dead.

————————

One officer guarded the gate at the sidewalk. Another stood at the front door under the elk antlers. A third officer was talking to two women across the street. A fourth emerged from the Secret Canyon Gallery and took a deep breath.

Aragon clipped her badge on her collar and pulled her crime-scene bag from the trunk. She snapped on two sets of blue latex gloves, thinking back to the night she and Lewis almost ran out of supplies, bouncing from the Fremont scene to the bloody bathroom at the back of Fager's Finds. She grabbed her last pair of plastic booties from her bag and turned to face Santa Fe's latest murder.

The officer at the gate said there was one dead inside. The two women across the street had called it in. They saw the shooter.

She entered the front yard. Terra cotta statues had been blown apart. Amid the fragments, one pot stood intact, suffering only a through-and-through. She saw a bullet hole in the wooden post supporting the portal. She stretched the plastic booties over her cross trainers and stepped inside.

A brass casing caught light from the front door. Silver-tipped cowboy boots pointed to the ceiling. Cody Geronimo had repaired his Tres Outlaws. He had tips again on both boots. But he was down to one eye. A hole had replaced his left.

His ponytail was wet rope in the blood pooling behind his head.

She scanned the room. A clear shoeprint by his body. A handprint in blood on the doorframe, another on the wall at the front entrance.

Fresh air cooled her face. The window behind Geronimo was shattered, just a few shards remaining in the frame.

The officer she had seen talking to the women across the street was waiting for her outside. More police arrived, and an EMT crew that would not be needed. Her cell chirped. It was Lewis. He was on his way from home. She told him to bring gloves and booties, she was out. She saw Goff pull up behind the ambulance. He got as far as the cop at the gate.

She noticed another shoe print on the painted concrete floor just inside the door. It had been made by a large man. She was pleased the first officers on the scene had stepped around it.

"Baca," she said to the cop who had been talking to the women across the street. She knew him. He had worked patrol for six years and was good at it. "What did they see?"

"They were watering their garden in the yard of their gallery. They live around back. They heard shouting, and a man was standing here looking at them. They didn't notice the gun in his hand until he shot a ceramic bear. That must have been it." He nodded at pink rubble containing one recognizable bear paw. "They couldn't say how many shots he fired, but a lot. When he was done, he stood still, facing them, giving them a good look. He drove off in a light brown Camry. New Mexico plates. The bright yellow kind, not the new blue plates. They couldn't see the number. I put that out right away."

"Good job. Description of the shooter."

Baca checked his notes. "Six-three, three hundred pounds. Curly black hair. Jeans. Plaid shirt. Thick belt, big buckle."

"What did he have on his feet?"

"They couldn't see. And he was wearing a black leather vest."

She was expecting a description of Fager. This was Bronkowski. She walked over to Goff at the gate.

"Do you know Bronkowski's concealed carry?" she asked.

"He wears a snubby in the back of his pants."

"This guy fired more than five shots. There's nine-millimeter casings on the floor."

"We know Fager has a Beretta nine. Who was it said they were going to shoot Geronimo in the face?"

"The shooter was Bronkowski. Two witnesses saw him."

"Bronkowski didn't trust automatics. Never carried one." Goff thought for a second. "That's why he rushed off. Came here. Saw what Fager did. Put it on himself."

"I don't get it."

"I could never figure why he was Fager's poodle. I talked to some cops who go to meetings at the VA where Bronkowski opens up. Fager saved his life when they were in Bosnia."

"He'd take a murder rap for his friend?"

Police and emergency vehicles now blocked the street. The medical investigator's wagon was here. She made a mental note to tell them about the slug in the wooden post. But there was something she didn't want them to see.

"This is bullshit," Goff said. "Fager's the guy. Maybe they were in on it together, and Bronkowski's part was to confuse the evidence. You arrest the wrong guy. He walks at trial. They've got something cooked up."

"We've got handprints," she said, but Goff had her wondering. The prints were too perfect, almost staged so they could not be missed.

"Whose prints are on the casings? I bet Fager," Goff said.

"What was Bronkowski driving?"

"Piece of shit Camry. Beige or tan."

"How about light brown?"

"There a difference?"

She needed a moment alone before the technicians and police photographers got here. "Sam, you better split. I don't want you in the reports."

He slipped into the crowd that had gathered across the street. Cops were busy setting up a perimeter. OMI's people were checking equipment or slipping into clean suits. She eased around the side of the gallery and found the storyteller figurine she had planted on the wall between buildings. The surveillance camera from Geronimo's ranch was still inside. The broken window was at her back as she tucked the camera in a jacket pocket.

Lewis was now at the gate talking with the officer. He came into the yard and they met by the ruins of the pink bear. Her mind was on what the camera may have recorded. It might show Goff was right, Fager at the studio, in and out before Bronkowski arrived. It might also show nothing but the window's reflection.

She said, "We have Bronkowski ID'd as the shooter. He's in his car."

"I don't know about his car. But I think I know where Bronkowski is. A motorcycle crashed into the overpass by the National Cemetery. Harley. Big guy in a leather vest. A Beretta in the wreckage. The bike was destroyed. The guy riding it is in worse shape."

FORTY-NINE

WHITE CROSSES MARCHED IN neat rows up a grassy slope. At the top an American flag flew above veterans' graves. The highway in front of the cemetery was empty, traffic diverted through downtown while crews swept the road of debris and an accident reconstructionist diagrammed the scene.

The track of Bronkowski's Harley showed he left the blacktop forty feet before the overpass. A single furrow down the middle of the dirt and grass median, back tire in direct line with the front, aiming straight for tons of reinforced concrete.

Pieces of the Harley were crushed on the abutment and scattered beyond. The Beretta was found in a saddlebag snagged on a piece of exposed rebar. Ten yards away, a photograph of Linda Fager had been caught on the thorns of a cholla cactus.

Bronkowski was on life support. Walter Fager was still missing. His black Mercedes had not been sighted. The state police had taken the BOLO statewide.

A crowd of onlookers had clustered on slopes on either side of the highway. People placing flowers on veterans' graves paused to watch. The news crews were content to get their film from a hundred feet away. Only one person pushed closer. Goff. Lewis went to where two uniformed officers had blocked him with their chests. He returned with a message.

"He's got a point. No sign Bronkowski was trying to brake. A motorcycle would have fishtailed if he slammed on the brakes."

Aragon spoke her thoughts. "He doesn't use his own gun to kill Geronimo. He goes home to get his Harley, then tries to kill himself. Why here?"

She looked uphill at the crosses. Men, a few women, who had served in the nation's wars were buried here. Many of those graves held New Mexicans who had survived the Bataan Death March, then died one by one as later generations fought in Korea, Vietnam, Iraq, Afghanistan. And in an undeclared war in a little country now called Bosnia-Herzegovina.

Aragon answered herself. "To die among other soldiers."

"Goff's still insisting Fager did it and Bronkowski's paying a debt."

She asked a member of the accident team for the Linda Fager photo. It was enclosed in a plastic sleeve. A drop of blood smeared the plastic. The upper left corner of the photo had been torn off.

Was Bronkowski in love with Linda Fager? Maybe this had nothing to do with Bosnia.

Lewis answered a call while she stared at white crosses.

"Fager's house has been secured. And Bronkowski's. The Camry's there," he reported.

"We need that bone."

A beige Camry was parked at Bronkowski's address on a residential street south of the Capitol building. One uniformed policewoman stood by the car, another at the door of the modest frame stucco house. Aragon put a hand to the driver's side window to shield the glare. Inside, a cardboard Budweiser case, closed with duct tape, strapped into the passenger seat.

Lewis said they should get a warrant, and she agreed. The car wasn't going anywhere. No reason to create legal issues. She would write it up. Lewis would shop judges.

They moved on to Fager's house. A patrol car blocked the drive. An officer dozed in the sun on the front step, but came alert at steps on the gravel drive. Again they concurred on the wisdom of a warrant before entering the house.

But no warrant was needed for the garbage cans at the curb. Aragon kicked one over. A busted portrait frame spilled out, followed by a few stuffed, white plastic bags. The frame was made of oak. Its back had been ripped off, a triangle of photograph caught in the corner. She suspected it was the missing piece of the bloodstained Linda Fager portrait found in the debris of Bronkowski's crash.

Her nails were cut too short to ease it out. Lewis freed it with tweezers on his Leatherman.

"Did we have this upside down?" she asked her partner. "Is Fager missing because he's dead? Maybe that blood on this photo is his. Maybe Bronkowski killed him because he killed the woman Bronkowski loved, and Geronimo because…"

She didn't know how to finish.

Lewis sealed the piece of photograph in a plastic baggie. "This gives Marcy Thornton a whole new box of ammo to shoot up our case against Geronimo. I wonder if Tasha Gonzalez ever cleaned Fager's office."

"Just when we saw things winding down, they blow up again." Aragon kicked over another trash can. Only sealed, white plastic bags spilled out. Cadets would search them later. They returned the bags to the cans and Lewis sealed lids with yellow tape.

"I've got something I need to check," she said. "It might be nothing. But it might answer a lot of questions."

First, she needed to speak with Mascarenas. She went off by herself behind Fager's house and called her cousin. He was in a hospital lab having blood drawn, keeping his cell close for work. She told him about planting the surveillance camera on the property of Secret Canyon Gallery. Mascarenas asked his phlebotomist for a minute alone. Then he told her that what she had done was absolutely illegal.

"But you might as well take a look."

Lewis was loading the garbage cans in his minivan when she returned to the front of the house.

"I need to get to my apartment to use my laptop. Can you take me to my car?"

They drove for three blocks before Lewis spoke.

"Whatever happened to that camera that caught you breaking into Geronimo's ranch? That's what you called Mascarenas about." He kept his eyes on the road. "I never said a thing. Identified the camera for you. Explained how it worked. Then nothing." Lewis lowered his chin. "I might as well have been breaking that window with you. How much worse can it get?"

"Working the grill at Blake's for the rest of our lives."

"Do you think my wife and I haven't had this conversation? Have you heard me saying anything about wanting another partner so I don't get hit with your blowback?"

She pulled the camera from her jacket.

"We need a laptop. With an SD reader."

"On the floor behind the seat."

He pulled to the curb. Trees gave them shade to view the screen. She removed the SD card and fed it into the slot on the side of his computer.

There was a separate video file for each instance the camera's motion detector was activated. The first images confused them. A shapeless, shimmering ocean surface. Then it went dark. The next file was the same, and two more after that. Not until the fifth file did they see something recognizable.

"That's a squirrel's tail." Lewis pointed. The full animal came into view. A black squirrel moved across the bottom of the screen, raised its tail and was gone.

"We've been seeing reflections of light and clouds in a window," he said. "I don't think the camera can see through glass, or be triggered by motion on the other side. Go to the last file. The one right before the shooting."

"Probably more of the same. This wasn't worth the risk."

The last file was recorded earlier that day, at 3:11 a.m.

"Can they see in the dark?" she asked.

"What good's a surveillance camera that doesn't work when bad guys come out?"

"This isn't the shooting. The call came in after seven."

She clicked on the file and they saw something very different from the other clips. Light and colors rushed at them too fast, except for the final startling image. Lewis reached over and showed her how to replay the file at very slow speed. Now they could discern a square of light with a round hole almost dead center in the frame. The square began to fall apart, a sheet of ice cracking. Big pieces fell away until there was a jagged edge of glass in a window frame.

Now a view of a beamed ceiling, walls hung with paintings, the back of a man's head, the scalp ripped open, a gaping hole, a ponytail dropping out of view to reveal the face of another man looking straight at the hidden camera. His extended arm held a semi-automatic handgun, the shadow inside its barrel lined up almost with the center of the screen. He reached inside his jacket and withdrew a stiff sheet of paper and let it fall. Then he turned and walked off camera.

"What are we seeing?" she asked. "I think I know, but I want to hear it from you."

"It starts with the window, light coming from inside the gallery instead of being reflected on the outside. That round hole. The bullet that exited Geronimo's head continued through the glass and triggered the camera's motion activation. The window shatters and we're looking into the gallery. We're seeing Geronimo from behind, the instant after he's been shot. He falls and we see the shooter." Lewis drummed the steering wheel. "Can you make any sense of this?"

She turned away to think. They were outside a brewpub that had not yet opened. The sidewalk was littered with cigarettes from last night's drinkers. An advertisement plastered to the light pole offered rides for people worried about driving with more than a point-eight in their system. "You Drink, You Drive, You Lose," it said across the bottom.

"What was that name you wrote on the napkin?" she asked. "The last time at Juanita's with Fager. Sherman? Sheldon?"

"Shelby."

FIFTY

"KILL THAT WORD AND tell it again."

"Sir?"

"You say 'routine' in the same sentence with 'Detective Denise Aragon,'" Joe Donnelly said, scowling at Lewis. "You're full of shit."

Aragon watched her partner trying to put the right words in the right order so the Professional Standards investigator would come on board. She saw herself a couple days back giving Fager the words he needed, and holding back ones that would have driven him away. Fager knew what was going on, underneath the words. So did Donnelly. He just needed to hear Lewis say it right.

"And after observing that the projectile had passed through the victim's skull and out a window, destroying the window, detective Aragon, pursuant to standard procedures..."

"Back up," Donnelly said. "Start at 'destroying the window' and don't give me a 'standard procedures' whitewash. Tell me what the hell she did."

"Yes, sir." Lewis took a breath. "Seeing that the projectile had continued on through a window, destroying the window, Detective Aragon went outside to determine the course of the bullet to ascertain if it could be recovered. She observed on a wall between the gallery and the next building what appeared to be a recording device concealed inside a figurine, a clay Navajo storyteller variety. From the figurine she recovered a surveillance camera aimed at said window. The camera was manufactured by SleuthCon, model number..."

"I don't need that."

"Partial latents from the camera match Geronimo's right index finger and thumb."

"That I need. Prints on the SD card inside?"

"None."

Donnelly stroked his chin. "I suppose he could have handled the card by its edges." His hand came away from his face, the index finger pointing to the ceiling. "Or the process of slipping the card into place wiped it."

"Yes, sir. Highly possible."

"Works for me."

"Furthermore," Lewis continued, not catching Aragon's look telling him he had said enough, "the shooter doesn't have standing to challenge a search of Geronimo's gallery. He has no legal interest in that property, thus no reasonable expectation of privacy entitled to Fourth Amendment protection."

"Now you're a lawyer."

"No, sir. Channeling ADA Joseph Mascarenas."

"That must hurt."

"What about our other question?" she asked, stepping in now that Donnelly had signaled he was ready to move forward. "About getting a civilian involved in a homicide investigation."

"Get me the manual."

She dug a copy of the department's code of conduct from her desk and passed it to Donnelly.

"It's not biased-based policing," he said, turning pages he probably knew by heart. "No allegations of sexual harassment or gender-identity discrimination. Can't have a hostile workplace for someone not an employee." He paged some more. "Well lookie here. Under the department's statement of key values in achieving its mission, it says we uphold community participation through sharing and understanding. Community participation. Sharing. That's what you did. Can't fault you for honoring our statement of values."

Donnelly left their office to listen from an interrogation room across the hall. Lewis arranged two chairs to face the computer screen on his desk. He remained on his feet. He would stand against the wall as Aragon ran the show.

She heard Sam Goff coming down the hall, shouting hellos to cops he once worked with. He entered the little office and looked around at a room he had called his for over a decade.

"That's still up there." Goff nodded at a framed copy of *The Albuquerque Journal,* the headline about the UNM Lobos upsetting the number one college basketball team.

She put a cup of coffee on the desk by the computer and kicked out a chair.

"Something you need to see."

"Where's Fager?"

"Still missing. But this will answer a lot of questions. Sit down, Sam."

Goff took the chair and tried the coffee.

"My old desk. I remember making that cigarette burn. We could smoke in here. Tells you how long ago that was. Coffee's still lousy."

Donnelly came in quietly and stood with Lewis. She tapped the keyboard. The still image of light shining from inside a window held the screen until she pressed "play." The video ran in slow motion. When it was done, she froze the final image.

Sam Goff, Beretta in hand. Fager's Beretta.

Goff pushed back his chair and started to rise. Lewis needed only lay his hand on his shoulder to keep him in his seat.

"So we know how," she said.

Goff would not look at his face on the computer screen. He dropped his eyes to the cigarette burn in the desk, maybe thinking back to a time when he ran shows like this.

"We left you to watch Fager. You knew his gun was at his house. You got in through the back door. We found scratches on the lock. Thanks to Bronkowski being helpful, you knew exactly where to go. And you took a photo of Linda Fager. It had been in its frame so long, a corner stuck and was ripped off. Then you went to Geronimo's. You walked in, gloves on, and shot him. In the face. How Fager said he would do it. You were damn quick to remind me."

"Where'd you get that?" Goff pointed a bent finger at the screen. His voice was distant and defeated.

"Geronimo had it set up," Lewis said. "We found it searching the scene."

"A routine search," Donnelly said, "following standard procedure."

Aragon continued. "You dropped the Linda Fager photo next to Geronimo. It fell into his blood. DNA confirms it. No blowback on the gun. Maybe Geronimo was backing away, wondering what the ex-cop who investigated him for Tasha Gonzalez was doing, showing up in his gallery late at night."

Donnelly moved so he and Lewis bracketed Goff, ready for when Aragon finished.

"You returned to Fager's office. He was gone. You were supposed to call so we could catch him with his gun and hit him with a bail violation. You needed a cover story to explain how you could have missed him if you had been watching all night. So you pretended to have been sleeping. Maybe you even slept some until Bronkowski woke you. Then you returned to Fager's, called me from there, still playing the part. You yelled to a neighbor walking a dog to make sure you were seen. After the news of Fager missing, they were good enough to call us."

"Where was the camera? I checked. He had lousy security. Just motion detectors."

Three detectives met eyes. They had heard the beginning of a confession.

"Checked when, Sam?"

"Fuck. Before I shot the piece of shit. Alright?"

"You insisted Bronkowski was not the shooter." She felt her confidence growing, seeing it hold together. "You were right to make us question why Bronkowski had not used his own gun. I'm guessing that after Bronkowski left Fager's office he went to his house. Didn't find him there. So he rushed to Geronimo's. He was worried about Fager doing something stupid. What he saw confirmed his fears. He cleaned up, thinking Fager had done it. He took the photo and the gun. But he did more. He put down arrows pointing to himself. He intentionally stepped in the blood. No shooter would have left a bloody palm print. It wasn't a stabbing. He gave that little show outside, shooting up the statues, to make sure he was seen."

Goff still would not look at her.

"Now you're going to tell me why," he said.

"Because Fager saved Bronkowski's life in Bosnia. He was paying it back."

"Not Bronkowski. Me."

"Why you did it? We've got that, too. You went after Fager at every one of our meetings. I thought it was about him ending your career. I wasn't paying attention when you kept bringing up another case. The Shelbys." She raised her gaze to Lewis.

Donnelly added his hand to Goff's other shoulder while Lewis spoke.

"Mascarenas remembers you in court for the trial. Figured you were caught up in the sad story with the rest of the city. A whole family wiped out by a repeat drunk driver. The surviving father destroyed emotionally when defense counsel convinces jurors he killed them by falling asleep at the wheel. The killer walks. The distraught father takes his own life. People forgot. Not you."

"They were my kids."

Lewis chewed his lip. Aragon could see this was hard for him, a father imagining what another father could feel.

"Shirley divorced you," Lewis continued, "right when you came to Santa Fe, before you joined the force. That's why nobody ever met her. She married Daniel Shelby, changed her name and the kids'. You hated Fager, but not because of what he did to you."

"I did plant the gun on Gallardo," Goff said. "*I* deserved what I got. My children, they … " He didn't finish.

"You saw Fager getting another killer off," Aragon said. "This time unintentionally, but that didn't matter. That's when you saw a way to get your revenge on Fager and at the same time keep Geronimo from ever hurting another woman. Maybe you felt guilty about not stopping him the first time you had a chance, despite blaming it on everybody else getting in your way. You would take out Geronimo and pin it on Fager. Sam, look at me."

He lifted his chin.

319

"We had Geronimo. No matter what Thornton threw into the fan, how much Fager was falling apart. We had him. Bronkowski brought back a bone from one of Geronimo's statues. It's going to match one of the women in those graves. We would have found all the statues, and the one with pieces of Linda Fager inside. We've got his DNA on paper towels with her blood. He'd go down for the women buried on federal land and the DA would refile state charges on Linda Fager. We don't even need my recording of him talking to Thornton."

"They all get away," Goff said. "Somehow."

"Not all of them," Donnelly said and reached under Goff's arm. "Stand up."

FIFTY-ONE

"It's a fee until it's paid. Then it's our money in the bank," Marcy Thornton said. "The estate could try to get it back to cover debts. Since I'm Cody's executor, that's not going to happen." She winked and pushed an envelope across her desk to Lily Montclaire. "A hazard bonus, the balance of the expense retainer. For having to stay at that scary ranch all by your lonesome. Cody would have approved, but I don't care if he wouldn't."

Montclaire opened the flap on a wad of hundred dollar bills.

"I think I'll go to Paris. Can I have a week?" She riffed the bills, remembering posing at the tip of the island that held Notre Dame, modeling black-on-black suits coming into fashion then. Before color was rediscovered. Before lines at the corners of her eyes ended her career.

"Take two. Take three. No need to build up Walter as a decoy anymore. The feds won't worry about him if I don't make them. And since my client has no further need of my services…" Thornton winked again. Montclaire hoped that wasn't becoming a habit. "I'll take some time myself."

"What about Fager's state charges?"

"The stalking charge died with Cody. I could insist Walt be prosecuted for assaulting me. But, no. You don't get paid for time spent playing the victim, wasting hours waiting to testify. I'll settle for getting him disbarred. He is competition, after all."

"So Fager's running for no reason?"

"Is he running? Maybe he's just gone. Like when he disappeared after the Army."

Thornton leaned back in her big chair. She kicked off her shoes and rested her feet on her desk.

"We should celebrate."

"Celebrate Cody's murder?"

"Celebrate that I still haven't lost a case at trial."

"Maybe I'll go to Helsinki. Great party scene. What else can you do but get drunk and screw when it's always dark?"

"I'd go to a warm, sunny beach."

"Too much sand. You get to hate sand doing three-day shoots on the beach, getting rubbed down with oil then rolling around so it sticks on your skin, or leaning back on your elbows, legs open out to sea, waves washing sand up every crack. A week later you're still finding it."

"Something just occurred to me." Thornton sat up straight, energized. "Would you hold off on your vacation? I think I see how Geronimo's estate can sue. Goff's got no money, just a lousy cop pension. But I have the feeling he was working behind the scenes with Aragon. You run that down. We allege he was acting as an agent of the Santa Fe PD and reach those deep pockets. She was negligent. She knew his history as a rogue cop."

"He used Fager's gun."

"We sue him, too. And Bronkowski, acting as his employee, *respondeat superior*, trying to dispose of the gun that killed Cody.

Bronk crashed before he could finish the job. He won't be available to testify otherwise. Goff will take the Fifth. We draw every inference we want from his silence. This is a civil suit, no prohibition against adverse comment on a defendant's refusal to testify. And who's going to believe Walter didn't want Geronimo dead? He stays gone, he defaults and we execute on his property. You could have his office. We'll hire assistants to handle the drudge work, the subpoenas, research. You concentrate on what turns cases around. You're becoming very good at getting rid of big problems."

Thornton's mind was turning fast. Montclaire saw the excitement in her tight little body. "As executor of Cody's estate, fifty percent plus costs sounds fair for this hardworking, brilliant lawyer. After the litigation, the estate will be paying me to manage settlement funds. The gift named Cody Geronimo lives on."

Montclaire sighed. "Before we got distracted by Cody's drama, we were having a bitching time with a cute boy with a sunburst tattoo around his sexy outie."

"It was an innie."

"You can't bite an innie."

"Anthony."

"It was Andrew. My compensation for hanging around is we pick up where we left off. No interruptions. We party like we're twenty and perfect again."

"*This* is the party." Thornton threw open her arms. "Aren't we having fun?"

FIFTY-TWO

ARAGON AND LEWIS OPENED a separate file on Goff. The first and last entries came easily. The crime scene, Geronimo on the floor of his gallery, then fast forward to Goff's arrest. Filling everything in between had them cross-referencing reports in the Linda Fager and Ladron bodies files they had not yet written. They owed Rivera updates on the Fremont case. The Tasha Gonzalez file needed to be updated with results of testing on the Rio Salado soil samples and information about her brother's financial miracle.

Lewis was having an easier time with his share of the paperwork. He was diligent about entering notes into his laptop at day's end. Aragon scribbled on scraps of paper and empty Lotaburger bags. Some notes made their way into a spiral ring notebook that fit into the back pocket of her jeans.

Getting ready to start writing, she came across the name Sylvia Bukar.

It took her a minute to remember Roshi Buff talking about the ritual Wiccan murder in Albuquerque. She'd spent a few minutes looking into the case. Bukar had used the promise of sex to lure a middle-aged man to the foothills of the Sandia Mountains and drove a knife through his heart while she straddled him. Aragon had jotted the information in her notebook and forgot about it.

Timothy Osborn referred to Fremont as a witch. Albuquerque cops had said the same thing about Bukar.

Her notes contained the name of the Albuquerque detective who worked the case. Enrique Brito. She called his office and learned he was at the Bernalillo County courthouse in a drive-by shooting trial. She called the mobile number she was given.

"Was wondering if you would ever call back. I'm on break. We've got five minutes."

"You called me?" She heard a match striking and him sucking air, firing a cigarette.

"Left a message with a Detective Serrano. Asked for you but got him."

Aragon's kick drove an open drawer into her desk.

"I saw the news about that girl in the sleeping bag," he said. "The part about the ceremony in the woods made me think of my witch."

Traffic sounds and him breathing heavier. She guessed he was climbing stairs on the side of the courthouse to find a quieter spot to talk.

Brito continued. "I understand you're off the case."

"I've still got a finger in it."

"You want to look at her cell phone real hard."

After Osborn and Rutmann were arrested, the FBI had gone through Fremont's cell-phone records to verify and date calls between her and the two men. The first call fit the time frame of the ad she ran to attract them. A series of calls back and forth ended on what turned out to be the day they all drove to the ski basin parking lot and hiked into the woods. That was as far as their analysis had gone before Santa Fe took the case. Now Serrano had Fremont's cell with the other evidence.

"Bukar gave us this story," Brito said. "The guy picking her up at a bar, forcing her to the mountains and raping her. She stuck him to defend herself. But her cell had his number in her directory. Get this. His name was Juan Valdez, like the coffee guy. She had his number under 'Sacrifice.'"

"The two with Fremont, her cell had their real names."

"What I was getting at is you should see when Fremont and Bukar talked."

She leaned forward as though Brito were sitting across the desk instead of standing outside a courthouse in another county.

"How do you know they talked?"

"Bukar's out in Grants, but I keep an eye on my witch." Grants was the New Mexico Women's Correctional Facility west of Albuquerque. "I want to know who visits her. Intelligence if more guys turn up dead inside circles drawn in the dirt. The Wiccans were pissed she was claiming her ritual was part of their spring celebration. She used a Wiccan knife, did it under some special phase of the moon. But theirs is a religion of peace. Where have we heard that before?"

Aragon wanted to hear about Bukar and Fremont. "Get to it."

"Mostly family visitors making the drive. No one of the Wiccan persuasion. No witches, warlocks, or wizards dropping by. Every week women from this Christian thing Bukar's into now. And Cynthia Fremont."

"When?"

"About three times. My notes are in my desk. I'm pretty sure all this year."

"Will Bukar talk to me?"

"Take a Bible. She won't shut up."

"This knife, I'd like to see it."

"We never found it. Bukar claims she threw it away in disgust," Brito said. "Look. I've got to get going. I'm up next for an ADA in diapers. Had to tell her how to get in my expert opinion on street lingo. A 'cap' is not something you wear on your head. 'Send it' has nothing to do with texting."

"You said it was Wiccan. The knife."

"Bukar bought it on eBay. I'll send you a photo."

He e-mailed the photo after court was done for the day. The knife Bukar used for a human sacrifice was the same black-handled serpentine knife that killed Cynthia Fremont.

FIFTY-THREE

THE NEW MEXICO WOMEN'S Correctional Facility sat on old Route 66, now a frontage road to the interstate, a three-hour drive from Santa Fe. Same concertina wire, heavy metal doors, thick Plexiglas as a men's prison. Same smells and sounds. Same grim gray everywhere, in the paint, the concrete, the bars, the crushed-gravel exercise area inside grey fencing. But here and there, on the metal scanner, the back of a computer terminal, a locked door: decals of pink ribbons showing staff support for breast cancer research.

Aragon displayed her badge and a guard called for Sylvia Bukar to be brought to a windowless room separate from the visiting area. The woman who entered stood about six feet tall. Dark hair, sunken cheeks. The orange jumpsuit hung off a bony frame. She carried a Bible. Around her neck she wore a wooden cross likely made in the prison's work shop, glued together, no nails or staples.

"I don't know you," Bukar said.

Aragon again showed her badge. Bukar took her time to read the ID card under plastic.

"I like Santa Fe," Bukar finally said. "There's a church there, like Notre Dame, but small. They never finished it."

"The Basilica of St. Francis." She pointed to Bukar's open collar where a blue Virgin Mary was drawn in her skin. "You get that in here?"

"One of the Catholic girls did it. I'm into the Virgin. I didn't grow up knowing about holy women."

"I'd like to talk about Cynthia Fremont."

"She wanted to be a holy woman." Bukar had a worn and distant prison look. A wave of sadness passed over her face. "That girl needed to let God just reach down and find her. She was such a Lone Ranger."

"She came to see you."

"Couple times." Bukar fingered her wooden cross. "She always had questions."

"About?"

"Why it didn't work."

Bukar's dead prison eyes returned.

"She wanted to know about your ritual."

"It *was* mine. I made it up. God, I was crazy back then."

"You want to tell me about it?"

"I tell it in Bible study. Some of these girls were way crazier than me. It was supposed to change me, give me power, make me strong, lift me off the ground. Look what it did for me." She tugged at her orange shirt. "And I stopped a man from being loved and giving love. He had three children."

"What did Cynthia Fremont want?"

"Same thing. To be something better, stronger, something so different she wouldn't recognize herself. She was trying to learn from my mistakes."

"She killed herself, you know," Aragon said. "Didn't kill anyone else."

"I had it wrong, she told me last time she was here. It didn't work for me because I was taking instead of giving. She used some Chinese or something for the bad energy I turned loose by hurting another person. Said it had to be energy of profound generosity. Those were her words. Profound generosity. Something I read really clicked for her."

Bukar opened her Bible. Aragon checked her watch. She was not going to sit for a lesson on Biblical genealogy, fifteen minutes of begats, or the hidden code in unrelated passages strung together by a woman who once thought human sacrifice was the path to personal improvement.

"No man has any greater gift to give than his life for his brother," Bukar said without looking to the page she opened.

"Friend."

"Who?"

"At the memorial for officers killed in the line of duty at the Academy, it says that. The Wall of Honor. But 'friend' instead of 'brother.' Greater love hath no man than to give his life for his friend."

"Cynthia liked that a lot. Especially when she changed man to person and brother to mother."

"No person has any greater gift to give than his life for his mother? I don't get it."

"Mother Earth. Cynthia decided that by giving her life to Mother Earth she would be transformed. She wouldn't really die. She'd live as something different. She asked me once what I want to be. *Girl?* Out of here, I told her."

Aragon thought about the site of Fremont's personal ceremony deep in an untamed wilderness, the offering of her body to birds, leaving what was left for other animals. Even the sex beforehand with two men, another act of giving.

Bukar's information did not come any closer to making sense of what Cynthia Fremont did to herself.

"I've been praying for forgiveness," Bukar said. "But God tells me he has nothing to forgive. That girl was going to kill herself no matter what I gave her. Or what I said or didn't say when I had the chance. She left happy last time. Like she had figured something out. Maybe she's better off now, not in pain anymore."

That sounded like a throwaway line, but Aragon sensed Bukar meant it. "What pain?"

"That girl was eating aspirin like candy. I never asked, but I figured something was hurting her bad."

The autopsy showed Fremont had no health issues except minor liver damage possibly due to substance abuse. A detail she had forgotten from the very beginning of the case came back to Aragon. The tox screen showed elevated levels of acetylsalicylate in Fremont's blood stream. Aspirin. A cheap blood thinner. Fremont had anticipated the blood clotting that made wrist slashing a poor choice for suicide.

"Just now you said she would kill herself no matter what you gave her. You gave her your knife. Sylvia, that's what she used."

Bukar wrapped her arms around her Bible and squeezed it to her chest.

"I told her where to find it. That was when I was still crazy, before God reached down for me. I'll ask the girls to pray for her tonight. And me."

Back in her car, she reread the tox screen. There it was, an extraordinary amount of aspirin in her system. Also a high blood-alcohol content. Alcohol acted as a blood thinner, something you learned as a beat cop. Street drunks could bleed like crazy.

And high levels of acetaminophen, working in tandem with the other neurodepressants. Fremont had dosed herself to make it easier to take the pain.

The sun was setting on the mountains above Santa Fe on her long drive back. The fading light turned them deep red. The Sangre de Cristo mountains. Blood of Christ. She wondered if Fremont had seen this and decided that was the place to let her own blood flow. Adding something from Christianity to her cocktail of Buddhism and Wicca and whatever else she threw into the mix.

Covering the bases, throwing it all against the wall, hoping something would stick. One lucky number or a winning combination—whatever worked—on a lotto ticket looking like those "co-exist" bumper stickers with symbols from all the world's religions smashed together.

Or maybe Fremont was just an unhappy, sad, screwed-up kid leaving others to deal with the mess she left behind, thinking nothing of the two young men she'd tricked into helping her.

She should feel sorry for a girl who killed herself. She wasn't feeling it.

The planning and determination it took, the will power to fight through the pain—Fremont *wanted* this. And would have had it except the two guys she selected were so horrified they didn't let the birds finish. Instead of a raven—*Hurry, my wings must spread. I must fly*—Cynthia Fremont became a body found in a trunk, not the first, not the last.

She caught herself doing what she told Roshi Buff she never did, meditating on the why behind the violence and ugliness she faced in her job. But she let her thoughts run loose as the road took her home.

FIFTY-FOUR

MASCARENAS CALLED ON HER way back from interviewing Bukar. He was still in the hospital. She should stop by. Somebody was there who wanted to talk with her.

Walter Fager stood up from the chair by the bed when Aragon entered her cousin's room. His pin-striped suit was a mess, pants caked with mud, a tear in the knee.

"Where the hell have you been?" She looked him up and down, ruined wingtips to stubbled cheeks and greasy hair. "Do you know about Bronkowski?"

"Bronk. If I'd listened, he wouldn't be in a coma." Fager blew air through his lips then set his jaw. "I'm going to take care of him. If he makes it out of the hospital, a nurse will be living with us."

Mascarenas said, "Tell her where you went."

"I took Linda back to where we met, when she saved my life."

"In the Gila Wilderness," Mascarenas said. "Rangers noticed his Mercedes at a campground. Kind of out of place."

"I poured her ashes in the water where we swam together."

"There's a warrant," Aragon said, "for failing to appear at your bond hearing. I heard Judge Diaz had a smile when she signed it. Kept the rest of her cases on hold while her secretary made copies."

"Thornton dropped charges but the FTA's still in the system," Mascarenas said. "We'll get it cleared. Bigger news is Walt's coming to work for us. The docs won't release me and the judge won't delay opening arguments again. Walt will second-chair my young prosecutor."

"Long time since I filled out a W-4," Fager said.

"Don't you have something hanging over your head?" Aragon asked. "A little issue about your law license?"

"If Marcy's disciplinary complaints get me suspended, I'll stay on as a paralegal."

"Walt wants to start a new career, as an underpaid, overworked, unappreciated, bruised and battered good guy," Mascarenas said.

Fager's suit was something Italian, maybe Armani. His shirt a mess, probably beyond being cleaned, maybe it cost as much as her monthly car payment. She'd never noticed his belt. You don't stare at a defense lawyer's stomach when you're on the stand. You go eye to eye, not seeing anything below his chest. Maybe his backside when he finishes with you and returns to his table.

Fager's belt buckle looked like a gold scales of justice set in hammered silver.

Sticking out of those Italian sleeves, French cuffs. Man wears gold and onyx cufflinks for his sojourn thing in the wilderness. Steps out of the woods a different person because he ripped his pants. Drives to Santa Fe—four, five hours in his Mercedes—thinking what to do next with his life. Bingo! Show the good guys what they've been doing wrong. That's the ticket.

"Bullshit," she said, and it was her turn to show her back.

She made a show of it, too, the way she spun around, pushed through the door, letting it swing back into the room, banging against the waste can on the floor.

"Talk to her," Mascarenas said. "While she's still loco."

Fager caught up with Aragon in the hallway, just past the nurse's station.

"Listen."

She stopped, looked back over her shoulder, the rest of her still heading away.

"I'm serious. I want to switch sides. Look what I've been through. My wife, my best friend."

"You feel responsible."

"Yes."

"Don't let me stop you. Talk about people who didn't mean anything to you, how you're responsible for what happened to them, too. That I'd like to hear."

He forgot how short she was. She carried so much strength in her arms and shoulders, had a way about her that made you think she stood taller. Maybe he'd forgotten because she'd always been sitting, on the stand, more recently across a table at Juanita's.

"You're not talking, Fager."

From this angle he saw the scar in her scalp. He'd never noticed that before.

"I've watched you for years," she said, "wondering how you can do what you do. For some of the suits, it's the money. Cash up front, no results guaranteed. Others, they have this problem. They'd like to be one of the outlaws, but don't have the balls. So they get close enough for a thrill, rub elbows with stone-cold killers. Some are just twisted. You, you're angry at the world. Maybe lately you decided you maybe hate yourself a little. Maybe a lot. You need more than that for what we do. More than that to feel responsible."

"Let's step in here." Fager nodded toward an area away from open doors to patient rooms.

He waited for her to move first, not sure she'd follow him. She shook her head and walked to where molded plastic chairs were bolted to the wall under a television playing without sound. He didn't recognize what was on the screen, some cartoon with a square yellow character and marine life.

"Shit," Aragon said. "SpongeBob. Talk. My cousin believes you. Sell me."

"There's not likely anything I can say to convince you. Joe believes he can use me. Judge me on what I do for him."

"His child-abuse case."

"For starters. I hope Goff's next."

"Then you go back to your side of the line."

"No."

"You feed your anger. Get a lot of attention sitting at the DA's table. I see the interviews, the big stories. Advertising you can't buy. Walter Fager, he can do it all. Let him do it all for you. Don't let those bastards hang a bum rap around your neck. Call now."

"No."

"You can't change the pinstripes on a shark," she said. "Show me a reason to trust you with the kind of calls we have to make when we're fighting scumbags like you."

"I've got Joe on my side. I don't need this."

"You can't do Joe's job unless you've got me and every other cop who's gonna make or break your case."

"So what do you want?"

"Help me take down a dirty judge."

"Judy Diaz."

"Roger. Then there's no going back. Old friends won't trust you, the way I don't right now. You're in on busting the Chief Judge, I don't see bad guys thinking you've got an inside track at the courthouse. They're taking their business down the street."

Fager took one of the molded plastic chairs. When he sat, the tear across his knee showed pale skin. Above his head, SpongeBob danced with a starfish.

He said, "You forget I may not have a law license much longer."

"Means nothing to me. I don't believe that would shut you down. That lawyer in Taos, the one for the planning department. Shaking down developers. He lost his license but opened an office next to the county building. Realized he didn't need a law license to walk developers around, introduce them to old friends, arrange lunch with his cousin, the county commissioner. He took a hit, but never jumped ship. Doors stayed open. Be on the team that takes the robes off Diaz, takes the gavel out of her hand, all those familiar doors will be locked tight."

"No more hustling for clients, no more referrals. No co-counsel gigs."

"Our side has a different business model."

Sitting next to her on the molded plastic chairs, he was taller again, but not by much.

"Something you said back in Joe's room," Aragon said. "If you'd listened, Bronk wouldn't be in a coma. What did you mean?"

"No harm telling you now. Bronk wanted to shoot Geronimo, not wait for you to play it out, then trust the courts to put him away."

"He'd done that, we wouldn't have found the bodies. I would have been hunting him."

"It would have been me."

"I'd get you."

"And I wouldn't be able to hire the best criminal defense attorney in Santa Fe. That's what Marcy told me. She'd be the first witness against me."

"You don't talk like that again, ever, if you cross over. Not even joking around. But speaking of Thornton."

Fager waited for her to finish her thought.

"Find a way to tie her to Diaz, one that sticks, I might start to forget you're Walter Fager."

"You know about them?"

"There's know, and there's prove. Something else I want to run by you. Keep your defense lawyer hat on a little longer."

———————

Mascarenas looked up from reading a brief as the door opened. Aragon entered first, nodded, telling him it was all okay and took the only chair. Fager came next. He stood in the center of the floor, nowhere to sit. The rookie reporting for duty.

"We'll need a background check," Mascarenas said. "Fingerprints, all that. That thing from the Army, it can't be hanging over your head."

"I've got an AWOL on my record," Fager said, "that's all. I traded silence for an honorable discharge. You won't find anything else. Except Marcy's pending complaints."

"I can put you on special prosecutor status. After that, you have to go through orientation. DA boot camp. Get your mind right."

"What about Goff? I want to be on the team that puts him away."

"Not going to happen." Mascarenas pointed a pudgy finger. "You're a witness. From now on you play by the rules. You don't go near that trial except when you're on the stand. You can submit a victim impact statement, watch when he's sentenced."

Aragon reached for her cousin's hand. It seemed smaller. He'd been losing weight on a hospital diet, but had a long way to go.

"I have an idea how to handle Dewey Nobles."

Mascarenas squeezed her hand, surprising her with his strength.

"You figured how to plant that land mine, didn't you?"

———————

The Criminal Investigations floor was empty. Lewis was in a meeting about Goff at the DA's office. Serrano and Fenstermacher were at OMI prepping the pathologist for the Fremont grand jury. A shooting at the old Villa Linda Mal—she never used its new name—had drawn out the rest of the detectives. Two carloads of kids chasing each other through the parking lot, bullet holes left behind in McDonald's and Staples. Shoppers wounded. One of the shooters dead in a Honda Civic abandoned behind the mall. The West Side Lokos were pushing east.

She would never find a better time than now.

She walked from her little office to the coffee station that served this end of the building. Her path took her past Nobles' door. He was at his desk on his computer. She knocked and stuck in her head.

"Sir?"

"What is it?"

"I would like to request travel funds to cover myself and Lewis going to Jackson Hole, Wyoming. The Tasha Gonzalez case. We need to re-interview her brother, and talk to his wife. He could be our murderer."

"It was Geronimo. Sixteen cases closed in one fell swoop. The fourteen women at the ranch. Linda Fager. Tasha Gonzalez. Request denied."

"I thought you might say that."

He looked up, directly at her, a furrow deepening across his forehead.

"Then why ask?"

"I needed to know where you stood. One more thing." She idly rotated the doorknob while he glared at her, making it clear he wanted her gone. "On Fremont, you're committed to moving forward with a murder-one prosecution against both men? You won't consider evidence of suicide?"

"We've been over this."

"Yes, sir. I'm getting coffee. Would you like some?"

He didn't respond and she left his doorway.

She continued toward the odor of scorched coffee. The pot had been on the burner for hours. She turned off the heat and sat the glass carafe in the sink. She intentionally made a lot of noise preparing the next pot. She wanted Nobles very much aware of her in the building with him.

With a cup of coffee in hand, she returned to her office, again pausing at his door.

"It's fresh if you want."

He ignored her. But he would know she was headed back to her office.

She moved quickly. She wrote up her interviews with Brito and Bukar and pasted it into an e-mail to Nobles. She hit send. Then she pressed the speed dial on her cell for Rivera and put him on speaker. It was ringing when she put her cell down and opened a newspaper.

"Denise," Rivera's voice spoke from the surface of her desk.

Down the hall she heard a door open and heavy footsteps approach.

"Free for dinner tonight?" she asked. "I was thinking Lotaburgers and white wine. That was a really nice time we had."

Salt-and-pepper hair stiff with gel appeared in her doorway. Cinnamon and cloves in the stagnant office air.

"Hold a second. My boss is here. He's not happy."

She laid the newspaper over the cell phone.

"Aragon, what kind of crap you trying to pull?"

"Deputy Chief Nobles."

"I got your e-mail. One, you're supposed to be off the Fremont case. Two, I told you not to put anything else in the file."

"You said not to put my interview of Timothy Osborn in the file."

"Don't split hairs."

"Sir, I didn't put anything in the file. I sent you an e-mail with my interviews of APD detective Enrique Brito and convicted killer Sylvia Bukar. I thought you should have them so you could make the decision about how they impacted murder charges in the Fremont case. Bukar makes it clear it was suicide, but I didn't want to make that call. Especially since it's not my case anymore."

"Did you copy anyone else?"

"No, sir. Your eyes only."

"I deleted your e-mail. That's my decision. Insane rambling from an insane woman. One day Bukar's a witch, the next a Bible thumper. Tomorrow she'll be a Martian. We're not going to complicate a clear case with meaningless distractions. I want you to delete it from your e-mail records."

"I don't feel comfortable doing that."

"Are you disrespecting my authority? Do you think I'm someone you can ignore?"

"Sir. I showed what I think of you by sending my report directly to you and no one else."

"I don't have time for a test of wills. Move aside."

She let Nobles have her chair. He touched a key and the screen awakened, still on the message she had just sent him. He deleted it.

"Aragon, this conflict between us cannot continue."

"Yes, sir. I agree. It won't. Things are going to change. In a very big way, sir."

"Well." Her meekness caught him off guard. "Good." He stood to his full height and looked down on her, the furrow between his eyebrows back in place. "You may be the girl hero today. That glow will fade soon enough."

Heavy footsteps carried him back to his office.

She lifted the newspaper and picked up the phone.

"Tomas, you still there?"

"Did I just hear your boss instructing you to destroy evidence?"

"No comment."

"That's why I don't have the Osborn interview. He told you to hold it back."

"No comment."

"The Bureau has not closed our file, though DOJ is signaling a pass. Your boss is obstructing an ongoing federal investigation."

"I'm not saying anything. Call him yourself. Ask if Timothy Osborn ever talked to anyone from SFPD. Ask if there's any evidence Fremont was contemplating suicide. Ask if she consulted a former witch named Sylvia Bukar. Ask where she got that Wiccan knife. Ask Detective Brito if he has a photo."

"I doubt Nobles will tell me the truth."

"Lying to a federal law-enforcement officer. I read somewhere that's a felony."

"I have to write this up. I can't ignore what I just heard. And yeah, I'm going to call the guy. He lies to me, I'll take it across the hall to the U.S. Attorney."

342

"If you put something in writing, is that discoverable in a state case?"

"If we're subpoenaed. A smart defense lawyer will knock on our door. We were there at the beginning. He'll be curious why we didn't file federally."

"I would think so."

"Denise, were you really calling me to ask me out?"

"I was. But there's no telling what kind of crazy shit happens in a day."

"Can we get the pickup again? It felt like we were in a country-western song."

They arranged a time and said goodbye as Lewis entered the room with a stack of files under his arm.

"That bone Bronkowski brought back," he said. "Came from the woman in grave number six, Dolores Atencio, immigrated here from Hermosillo, got her green card right before she disappeared. That one was easy."

"The other thirteen?"

"Collecting DNA from families we can find. We'll get it done."

"We always have things to do, don't we?"

Lewis took his seat and stacked files on his desk. "You'll love what we're hearing from the Pueblos."

"They don't want Geronimo being Indian now that he's a serial killer."

"Sitting here at your desk, seeing beyond the walls. You need to teach me that trick."

"Maybe the FBI's army of experts can tell us what he really was, make the tribes feel better."

"The big news is Goff's laying down. Full confession. He gets twenty-five to life. He'll come up for parole before he's using a walker, sooner with good time. I'm okay with that. You?"

"I hope he makes it," she said. "Those years will be harder as an ex-cop."

But her mind was on how Fager really knew his stuff. At the hospital, he had fleshed out her sketchy outline of a plan. Not only would his improvements keep two young men from conviction for a murder they didn't do, they solved her Dewey problem. And none of it would come back on her. She had not gone outside the department to burn a fellow officer. She had not played snitch for internal affairs. It was going to be the FBI's initiative and a defense lawyer's diligence that took Dewey down.

It would stick.

Fager and Mascarenas, off the top of their heads, impressing the hell out of her, had hashed out the legal issues of letting Rivera hear Nobles through her cell phone. New Mexico law allowed eavesdropping on a conversation as long as one party consented, even if others had no idea anyone else was listening. If some judge pulled a Judy Diaz, it wouldn't stop Joe Donnelly. There was no motion to suppress in internal disciplinary hearings.

Dewey thought he had deleted her e-mail. A defense lawyer could easily get a court order to have it resurrected from the hard drive. The FBI could retrieve it in half an hour.

She was thinking what a hell of a team Fager and Mascarenas were going to make when she realized Lewis was talking to her.

"What have you heard on Fremont? Hotdog and Sauerkraut are acting like they've already notched their gun barrels, murder one for each defendant. Dewey's authorized all the overtime they want. Omar's back to talking about a new boat."

"Maybe he'll take you fishing."

"They're doing another press conference tomorrow. He's throwing in more people than we ever got on Geronimo. He sees Fremont paving his way to the chief's office."

"You're asking what I hear?"

"Yeah. What are you hearing? What's going to happen?"

A land mine inside her computer, Dewey's foot on the pressure plate, no way to step off.

She propped elbows on her desk and slowly spread her fingers wide.

"Boom."

FIFTY-FIVE

Memorandum
From: Walter Fager
To: Joseph P. Mascarenas, Dep. Dist. Atty., Violent Crimes Unit
Re: Prosecution of Lilith Aimee Montclaire

Joe,

It has been six months since I made my offer. I understand you must wait upon results of my disciplinary hearing before determining how I may serve your office. My hearing begins tomorrow and will command my attention for two weeks. I wanted to get this memo to you today so it comes from an attorney licensed to practice law in this state. Two weeks from now, that may not be the case.

A prosecution of Ms. Montclaire should be a coordinated state and federal effort to pry open bigger doors in the ongoing investigation of Estevan Gonzalez and Marcy Thornton. To that end, I would recommend "front loading" the case to achieve Montclaire's cooperation at the earliest stage. Rather than hold back the most damaging evidence for trial, I recommend putting it all before her at once, combined with an offer of leniency conditioned upon an acceptable proffer of the assistance she can provide.

OBSTRUCTION/TAMPERING

Laura Pasco says Montclaire offered to pay an inexplicable amount of money for a damaged bar table. That evidence, standing alone, seems incredible. Fortunately, her boyfriend, Peter Ney, had removed a table leg when he attempted to effect repairs on site at the Howling Coyote, thus permitting it to escape the fire set by Montclaire (discussed below). Linda Fager's blood has been found on that table leg. With DNA results from the embalming table Montclaire attempted to destroy matching that of five women buried at Geronimo's ranch, the government has a powerful case on these third-degree felony-obstruction charges, the sentences for which can run consecutively as they are discrete in time and place. Attachment A provides a more detailed analysis.

AGGRAVATED ARSON

The search of Montclaire's garbage cans uncovered receipts for approximately one gallon of gasoline, two thermos bottles, and a stainless steel bucket, all purchased separately within an hour at different locations across Santa Fe. My compliments on completing the search before our Supreme Court ruled the state constitution provides citizens an expectation of privacy in the trash they put out for collection. As an employee of the DA's office, I will do my best to attack that absurd ruling.

I suspect Montclaire obtained these receipts with the intent of charging them against Geronimo's account (something I require of my investigators). She threw them out when there was no longer a client who might request an expense accounting.

Please note that Montclaire's BMW requires the highest octane level of gasoline. She purchased but one gallon of the lowest octane level. Clearly, the fuel was intended for a purpose other than powering her automobile.

The red-light camera that caught Montclaire speeding through an intersection near Pasco's home within minutes of the fire is helpful, as is video showing her filling thermoses at a gas pump, obviously trying to hide from the security camera in the store but ignorant of the camera in the ATM behind her.

Victim impact statements from twenty-three families and firemen injured in battling the conflagration will impress any judge. This is a second-degree felony, with a likely sentence near the maximum of nine years incarceration, which should run consecutively to the obstruction sentences. Restitution will be staggering. See Attachment B.

————

The memo continued for another five pages, with as many lengthy attachments.

Aragon watched Thornton across the table in the windowless police interview room, scanning Fager's memo while Montclaire tried to appear disinterested. She caught Montclaire's eyes drifting to the pages in Thornton's hands. Montclaire sensed her watching and met her eyes.

"Do you have something to say, Lily?"

"Fuck you," Montclaire said, but there was nothing behind the words.

Aragon punched Lewis's shoulder. He dug his wallet from his back pocket.

Thornton stopped reading to watch Lewis sliding a ten-dollar bill into Aragon's hands.

"I bet we'd get two words out of your client, and what they'd be," Aragon said. "I won."

"I don't have time for games." Thornton waved the pages in her hand. "Walter wrote this before he lost his hearing. Now it's a disbarred lawyer's rantings and bitter resentments. Do you have something more credible to say to me?"

"Nothing to you. To Lily."

"I am her attorney. You speak through me."

Aragon opened her own copy of Fager's memo.

"You didn't read far enough. The last page. A lawyer has a duty of utmost loyalty to a client. They must protect a client zealously, not disclose anything told them in the course of representation. Those obligations don't run the other way."

"We are through here. I echo Lily's words of wisdom: fuck you."

"This is your copy." Aragon pushed the memo to Montclaire.

Thornton intercepted it.

"I'll take that."

Lewis handed Aragon another copy, which she again extended across the table to Montclaire.

"Lily, you want to read this for yourself. Your lawyer cannot put her interests above yours. But nothing prohibits a client from giving up their lawyer if that is in their best interest. We want what you know about Estevan Gonzales, how Ms. Thornton was buying his silence to cover for Cody Geronimo, what she was doing to enable Geronimo to continue killing, to conceal his crimes, how she was ripping him off."

Thornton rose from her chair.

"Come on, Lily. They're playing with your head."

Aragon nudged the memo closer to Montclaire.

"You're looking at three stacked sentences. The feds may take a run at you when we're done. Your face, that body, may have helped you in this world. Where you're going, you don't want to be the prettiest thing in the shower."

"I've heard this pitch a million times. If they had something, they'd have filed charges." Thornton put her hand on Montclaire's shoulder, two fingers stroking her neck, making her look up. "You're not just a pretty face." She winked. "You're smart enough to see what they're doing."

Montclaire took the memo.

"Okay. I'll read this. What if I have questions?"

"You want to talk to someone, there's a number on the last page. Walter Fager won't charge a dime."

"He's got a conflict of interest," Thornton said, her voice rising. "And he's prohibited from communicating with a person he knows to be represented by counsel. That's part of what got him disbarred."

"He said you might say that. Since he is disbarred, none of those rules apply to him anymore. Funny how that worked out."

"Marcy, take your hand off me."

"Lily, don't do this. You're out of your league."

"The more I help you," Montclaire said as she lifted Thornton's hand from her shoulder, keeping her eyes on Aragon, "the more you help me. That's how it works, right?"

Under the table, Aragon and Lewis tapped fists.

Aragon said, "Counselor, you're no longer needed here."

"You can't dismiss me."

"But I can," Montclaire said. "Goodbye, Marcy."

Thornton opened her briefcase to slip the copies of Fager's memo inside. Pages missed and drifted to the floor. Nobody spoke while she bent to pick them up, jam them into the briefcase, and snap it shut.

She went through the door, leaving it open, her heels clacking down the hallway's hard floor.

Lewis got up and closed the door. Aragon placed a tape recorder on the table, pressed record and said, "The time is 10:49 a.m. With me is Lilith A. Montclaire and Detective Rick Lewis. Ms. Montclaire is not under arrest and has just dismissed her attorney, indicating she is willing to proceed without counsel. Is that correct?"

"Yes."

"Let me explain how this works. When you're ready to talk, we will expect what's called a proffer. The best way to explain that ... "

"Her name is Andrea, the one Marcy gave the judge," Montclaire said. "Before I forget again. Now, you were saying?"

ACKNOWLEDGMENTS

Patricia Anaya, the wife of New Mexico's great novelist Rudolfo Anaya, took time to read a very early draft of this book and encouraged me to keep going. She saw in Cody Geronimo the kind of very bad guy who could emerge from New Mexico's strange mix of beauty and charm, corruption, and darkness.

The wonderful folks of the SouthWest Writers Workshop and the Jackson Hole Writers Conference, whether they know it or not, kept me going. Matt Kennicott introduced me to Krav Maga in Santa Fe. His class, led by a fierce, diminutive woman, gave me tons of ideas for Denise Aragon's character.

Along the way, investigators previously with the New Mexico Attorney General's Special Investigations Division answered many law enforcement questions. Vern Beachy, who, as a reporter with Albuquerque radio station KKOB AM770, exposed the crimes of Taos artist R. C. Gorman, helped me flesh out my villains, including those in the power structure who profit from (and perhaps enjoy) shielding evil from justice. Wow—radio stations with fearless investigative reporters. We need those days again.

Thank you, Elizabeth Kracht, my agent with Kimberley Cameron and Associates, for believing in me and making the storytelling better. And also thanks to Terri Bischoff, my editor at Midnight Ink, for taking me on board and steering my first book in the Denise Aragon series to publication. And much gratitude also for Kathy Schneider, the Midnight Ink production coordinator, who added the final, important touches. And a big thanks to Barbara Ann Yoder, an old friend and great editor and writing coach, who helped polish the manuscript that landed me an agent.

My wife, Kara Kellogg, has been my most committed and unwavering supporter. When I doubted myself, she urged me forward. She donned her very clear editor glasses and gave my work its most important, first critical read. She put up with me when I emerged from writing still in the character of one of the people in my book, instead of the man she married and wanted to share her life with. More than once—many times more—she suffered through my drifting off as I worked out a plot twist, ignoring everything and everyone around me until my head cleared.

And still she loves me.

Last, I want to acknowledge four remarkable, brave, powerful women. This is most definitely a work of fiction, but the accounts of the female law enforcement officers killed in the line of duty and remembered on the Wall of Honor at the New Mexico Law Enforcement Academy in chapter 17 are absolutely true. It is my sincere wish that the character of Denise Aragon always honors them.

ABOUT THE AUTHOR

James R. Scarantino (Port Townsend, WA) is a prosecutor, defense attorney, investigative reporter, and award-winning author. His novel *Cooney County* was named best mystery/crime novel in the SouthWest Writers Workshop International Writing Competition.